Piers Anthony was born i family to Spain in 1939 an father was expelled from became a citizen of the US in 1958, and before devoting himself to full-time writing, worked as a technical writer for a communications company and taught English. He started publishing short stories with *Possible to Rue* for *Fantastic* in 1963, and published in SF magazines for the next decade. He has, however, concentrated more and more on writing novels.

Author of the brilliant, widely acclaimed *Cluster* series, and the superb *Split Infinity* trilogy, he has made a name for himself as a writer of original, inventive stories whose imaginative, mind-twisting style is full of extraordinary, often poetic images and flights of cosmic fancy.

By the same author

PIERS ANTHONY

Book Two:
Incarnations of Immortality

Bearing an Hourglass

PANTHER
Granada Publishing

Panther Books
Granada Publishing Ltd
8 Grafton Street, London W1X 3LA

Published by Panther Books 1985

Copyright © Piers Anthony Jacob 1984

ISBN 0-586-06273-4

Printed and bound in Great Britain by
Collins, Glasgow

Set in Ehrhardt

Contents

1

Ghost Marriage

Norton threw down his knapsack and scooped up a double handful of water. He drank, delighting in the chill that struck his teeth and stiffened his palate. It was easy to forget that this was an artificial spring, magically cooled; it seemed natural.

He had hiked twenty miles through the cultivated wilderness of the city park and was ready to camp for the night. He had food for one more meal; in the morning he would have to restock. That could be awkward, for he was out of credit. Well, he would worry about that tomorrow.

He gathered dry sticks and leaves, careful not to disturb any living plants, and structured his collection for a small fire in a dirt hollow. He found some desiccated moss and set it within his pyramid. Then he muttered an incendiary-spell, and the flame burst into existence.

He fetched three rocks, set them against the expanding fire, and unfolded his little fry-pan. He unpacked his Spanish rice mix and poured it in the pan, shaking the mix to keep the rice turning as the heat increased. When it browned, he added handfuls of water, evoking a strenuous protest of steam, until satisfied. Then he rested the pan on the stones and left it to sizzle nicely alone.

'Can you spare a bite?'

Norton looked up, surprised. Ordinarily he was alert for other creatures, especially people, even when concentrating on his cooking, for he was attuned to the sounds of nature. But this one seemed to have appeared from nowhere. 'This is what I have,' he replied. 'I'll share it.' Actually, that meant he would be hungry on a half-ration, but he never liked saying no.

The man stepped closer, his feet making no noise. He was

7

evidently in his mid-to-late twenties, about a decade younger than Norton, and in unusually fit condition. He was well dressed in upper-class city style, but had the calloused palms of a highly physical man. Wealthy, but no effete recluse. 'You're an independent sort,' he remarked.

It took one to know one! 'Wanderlust, mostly,' Norton clarified. 'Somehow I always want to see the other side of the mountain. Any mountain.'

'Even when you know the mountain is artificial?' The man's eyes flicked meaningfully about the landscape.

Norton laughed easily. 'I'm just that kind of a fool!'

The man pursed his lips. 'Fool? I don't think so.' He shrugged. 'Ever think about settling down with a good woman?'

This fellow got right down to basics! 'All the time. But seldom for more than a week or two.'

'Maybe you never encountered one who was good enough for a year or two.'

'Maybe,' Norton agreed without embarrassment. 'I prefer to think of it as a distinction of philosophy. I am a travelling man; most women are stay-at-homes. If I ever found one who wanted to share my travels – ' He paused, struck by a new thought. 'In that sense, they are leaving me as much as I am leaving them. They prefer their location to my company, much as cats do. I move, they remain – but we know each other's natures at the start. So no expectations are violated.'

'Man does, woman is,' the man agreed.

Norton sniffed his rice. 'This is about done; it's spelled for quick cooking. Have you a dish? I can make one of wood – ' He touched his sturdy hunting knife.

'I won't need one.' The man smiled as Norton glanced askance. 'I don't eat, actually. I was just verifying your hospitality. You were ready to go hungry to share.'

'No man can live long without eating, and I can see you're no ascetic. I'll carve you a dish – '

'My name is Gawain. I'm a ghost.'

'Norton, here,' Norton said, noticing how the man accented the first syllable: GOW-an. 'I'm a jack of any trade, expert at none, except maybe taletelling.' Then he did a double take. 'Pardon?'

'A ghost,' Gawain repeated. 'Here, I'll demonstrate.' He extended his strong hand.

Norton clasped it, expecting a crunching grip – and encountered air. He brought his hand back and touched Gawain's arm. There was nothing; his hand passed through suit and arm without resistance, disappearing into the man's body. 'You certainly are!' he agreed ruefully. 'No wonder I didn't hear you approaching! You look so solid – '

'Do I?' Gawain asked, becoming translucent.

'I never met a real, live – uh – '

Gawain laughed. 'Real, at any rate.' He firmed up to solid semblance again, having made his point. 'Norton, I like you. You're independent, self-sufficient, unconceited, generous, and open. I know I'd have enjoyed your company when I was alive. I think I have a favour to ask of you.'

'I'll do any man a favour – any woman, too! – but I don't think there's very much I can do for a ghost. I presume you're not much interested in physical things.'

'Interested, but not able,' the ghost said. 'Sit down, eat your supper. And listen, if you will, to my story. Then the nature of the favour will be apparent.'

'Always glad for company, real or imaginary,' Norton said, sitting down on a conveniently placed rock.

'I'm no hallucination,' the ghost assured him. 'I'm a genuine person who happens to be dead.'

And while Norton ate, the spectre made his presentation. 'I was born into a wealthy and noble family,' Gawain said. 'I was named after Sir Gawain of the ancient Round Table of King Arthur's Court; Sir Gawain is a distant ancestor, and great things were expected of me from the outset. Before I could walk I could handle a knife; I shredded my mattress and crawled out to stalk the household puk – '

'Puck?'

'Puk – a small household dragon. Ours was only half a yard long. I gave it an awful scare; it had been napping in a sunbeam. My folks had to put me in a steel playpen after that. At age two I fashioned a rope out of my blanket and scaled the summit of the playpen wall and went after the cat. I vivisected her after she scratched me for cutting off her tail. So they brought in a werecat who changed into the most forbidding old shrew when I bothered her. She certainly had my number; when I toasted her feline tail with a hotfoot, she wered human and toasted *my* tail with a belt. I developed quite an aggravation for magical animals.'

'I can imagine,' Norton said politely. He himself was always kind to animals, especially wild ones, though he would defend himself if attacked. There were things about Gawain he was not fully comfortable with.

'I was sent to gladiator school,' the ghost continued. 'I wanted to go, and for some reason my family preferred to have me out of the house. I graduated second in my class. I would have been first, but the leading student had enchanted armour, even at night, so I couldn't dispatch him. Canny character! After that, I bought a fine outfit of my own, proof against any blade or bullet or magic bolt. Then I set out to make my fortune.

'There are not many dragons around, compared to mundane animals, and most of them are protected species. Actually, I respect dragons; they are a phenomenal challenge. It's too bad that it took so long for man really to master magic; only in the last fifty years or so has it become a formidable force. I suppose it was suppressed by the Renaissance, when people felt there had to be rational explanations for everything. As a result of that ignorance, dragons and other fantastic creatures had a much harder time of it than they had during the medieval age in Europe. Some masqueraded as mundane animals – unicorns cutting off their horns to pass for horses, griffins shearing their wings and donning lionhead masks, that sort of thing – and some were kept hidden on private estates by conservationists who cared more for nature than for logic. A number developed protective illusion so they looked a good deal more mundane than they were, and Satan salvaged a few, though most of His creatures are demonic. But now at last the supernatural is back in fashion, and fantastic creatures are becoming unextinct.

'But some creatures do get obstreperous. Most bleeding-heart liberal, modern governments have bent the other way so far they've gone off the deep end and outlawed poisoning or shooting or using magic to kill these monsters. So the bad dragons have to be dispatched the old-fashioned way, by sword.'

'Why not just move the bad ones to reservations?' Norton asked, appalled at the notion of slaying dragons. He was one of the bleeding hearts the ghost described; he knew dragons were ornery and dangerous, but so were alligators and tigers. All of them had their right to exist as species, and the loss of any species was an incalculable loss to the world. Many highly significant aspects of magic had been derived from once-suppressed creatures, such as potency-spells from unicorn horns and invulnerable scale armour from dragon hides. But he realized it would be pointless to argue such cases with this fortune-hunting warrior.

Gawain snorted. 'Mister, you can't *move* a dragon! They're worse than cats! Once a drag stakes out his territory, he defends it. Enchant the monster and move it to a reservation, it just breaks out and returns, twice as ornery as before, killing innocent people along the way. No, I respect dragons as opponents, but the only really good dragon is a dead one.'

Norton sighed inwardly. Perhaps it was a good thing for the world that Gawain was now a ghost.

'That was my speciality,' Gawain continued. 'The hand-slaying of dragons. It was dangerous work, to be sure – but the rewards were considerable. Because it was quasi-legal, fees were high. I estimated that five or six years of dragon slaying

11

would make me independently wealthy. That was the point: to prove that I wasn't simply inheriting wealth, but could produce it on my own. I knew my family would be pleased; every man in it increased the fortune, if he lived long enough.'

Gawain meditated for a moment, and Norton did not interrupt him. What would be the point? Norton had on occasion spotted the traces of dragons in the parks and had always given the monsters a wide berth. He might be an environmentalist, but he was no fool. It was said that some dragons in parks were halfway tame and would not attack a person if he gave them food or jewellery, but Norton had never trusted such folklore. The best way to deal with a dragon was to stay clear of it, unless a person had a really competent pacification-spell.

'I know what you're thinking,' Gawain said. 'Obviously I met one dragon too many! But in my defence, I do want to say that I was successful for five years and had almost amassed my target level in bonus money. I would be alive today if that last dragon I faced had been genuine. But you see, it wasn't; it had been mislabelled. Oh, I don't blame the natives – not much, anyway; they were a fairly primitive tribe in South America and they spoke a mixture of Amerind and Spanish, while I spoke the language of champions, English. Normally language is not much of a barrier; my armour and sword bespoke my profession, with the dragon design on my shield; and as for the women – a man never needs a language of the tongue to speak his use for them, especially when he's a warrior. These things are fairly standard, anyway; the conquering hero always gets his pick of the local virgins. After all, it's better for them than getting chomped by the dragon!'

He paused a moment, his lips twitching. 'Funny that some of those girls don't seem to see it that way.'

He shrugged and returned to the main theme. 'But I think they were honestly ignorant of the nature of their monster. Of course, I should have checked it out in the Dragon Registry – but I had travelled a long way, and the nearest civilized outpost was a half day's trek distant – couldn't use a standard flying carpet for this, of course, since those things are coded into the tour computers, and that would have given away my business – it would have delayed me a day just to do that, and maybe alerted the Dragon Patrol. So I tackled that dragon blind, as it were. I'll never do that again! I was cocky and foolish, I know – but I was familiar with the specs on just about every type of dragon in the world; I figured I was okay this one time.

'So there I was, afoot and armed with sword and shield, as is proper for such encounters, and I boldly braved the lair of the monster. And monster it was! I could see claw marks on the big trees some ten feet up. A real challenge! I marched up to its cave and bellowed out my challenge, and the monster came charging out, no fire, just growling – and then I realized my mistake. That was no dragon – it was a dinosaur! A largely bipedal carnivorous reptile – allosaurus, to be specific; I looked it up after it was too late. It was supposed to be extinct; I think Satan revived it, just to take me down a peg.'

Now Norton spoke. 'Isn't a dinosaur much like a dragon?'

'Yes and no,' Gawain said seriously. This was his field of expertise. 'It should be as easy to slay one as the other, as they are of similar nature. Dragons have fire and better armour, and some are unbecomingly smart, while the ancient carnosaurs – well, they have to do it all by tooth and claw and power, so they're both more singleminded and desperate. I was geared and trained for dragons; I knew their typical foibles. A dragon, for example, will always try to scorch you with its fire or steam first; dodge that jet, and you can often get in a lethal stroke while it's recovering its breath. It's blast-oriented, you see, not thinking about what comes next. But the allosaurus – that monster didn't even pause to see how it scored, because it had no attack heat. It simply charged, catching me off guard. I had been ready to dodge to the side, and that was no good this time. I stabbed it in the neck with my sword, but it didn't seem to notice. That's

13

another difference – a dragon will roar with pain and rage when injured – they are inordinately proud of their roars – and whip about to snap at the wound. I've seen a dragon get stabbed with a knife and reach about and bite that knife right out of its body, along with a few pounds of its own flesh, and toast the wound afterwards to cauterize it. This carnosaur just kept going for me. Its system was more primitive. You know how a snake's tail will keep twitching after you cut it off? True reptiles are slow to die, even when hacked to pieces. So again I misjudged it – and again I paid. The brute knocked me down and took a chomp of my body, armour and all. I didn't even try to scramble free; I knew a body-chomp would only dent the monster's teeth.

'That was my third error. Apparently enchantment has a sizable psychological component; people believe in its power, so it has power. A dragon would have known the armour was impermeable, since the smell of the spell was on it, and protected its teeth by easing up. The crunch would have been more show than serious; just testing, as it were. But this allosaurus dated from before the time of true magic and it gave a full-hard chomp, the kind that crunches bones.'

'But magic isn't all psychological!' Norton protested. 'When I lighted this fire, the wood didn't need to believe in magic; it was ignited anyway.'

'True. My armour was impervious to the teeth of the monster,' Gawain agreed. 'But the mail was flexible, so I could wear it with comfort and not be restricted when fighting. That reptile had very powerful jaws. When it crunched, no tooth penetrated – but I was squished to death. A dragon never would have done that, for fear of hurting its teeth against the magical hardness of the armour – but that stupid reptile did. It broke a number of its teeth and put itself in dire straits – but it wiped me out in the process.' The ghost sounded disgusted.

'Now I understand,' Norton said. 'I regret meeting you in

such circumstance.' That was polite; Norton might have regretted meeting Gawain alive, too.

'No fault of yours,' Gawain said. 'You are a courteous listener. Many people fear ghosts or ignore them.'

'Many people are more settled than I am,' Norton said. 'Perhaps that applies to their minds as well as their bodies. Since you profess no anger towards me, I accept you as a well-meaning companion and hope I may in some way help you.' For, ironic as it seemed, he found himself liking the ghost. Gawain alive stood for nothing Norton stood for, but as a ghost, he was an interesting companion. Maybe that was because his evil was safely behind him.

'I like your manners,' Gawain said. 'I can see we don't see eye-to-eye on everything and I think it's because you're a gentler man than I was. Be assured I offer recompense for the favour I ask. Would you like to learn how to slay dragons?'

'Oh, I do not require pay for any favour!' Norton protested.

'Then it wouldn't be a favour.'

'This is not really a minor matter. I would prefer to pay. The favour is in merely agreeing to do it.'

'Why, then, I should be happy to learn how to slay dragons, though I hope never to have to use such knowledge.' That was an understatement; he would never knowingly go near a wild dragon without defensive magic – and with that magic he would not have to slay it. 'But what is this favour?'

Gawain frowned. 'I prefer to provide more background first, lest you be unable to accept the request.'

Norton was growing quite curious about this. The ghost was a tough, direct sort, with quite alien values, but he was also a gentleman by his own reckoning. Why was he being so circumspect about this? 'By all means, sir.'

'When I died, I had amassed a fair fortune, in addition to my inheritance,' the ghost continued. 'Actually, the inheritance has not yet come down to me, as my father lives, but I am the only heir. It is important that the estate remain in the family. Therefore, my surviving family arranged for a ghost

15

marriage. That is, they married me to an excellent and healthy young woman of proper lineage who – '

'Pardon,' Norton said. 'Forgive the interruption, but you have lost me. How can a ghost marry?'

Gawain smiled. 'Yes, I thought that would throw you. It threw *me*, first blush. It is a device used when a noble family wishes to preserve its line – when the heir is defunct. They marry the ghost to a suitable girl – one he would have approved of in life – who then bears his heir.'

'But – '

'But a ghost can't impregnate a living woman. That is indeed a problem.'

'Yes. I really don't see how – '

'I'm coming to that. My wife may associate with any man she chooses – but she *is* my wife, by the ghost marriage, and her child is mine. He will inherit my estate and carry on my line.'

'But then she's being unfaithful to you!' Norton protested.

'I had trouble with that concept too, at first. But I came to terms with it. She knows she must provide the heir and that I can not do it personally. But I am involved, for I am choosing the man. With her consent, of course; marriage is a partnership. She has refused several good prospects.'

'Are you sure she really wants to – ?'

'Oh, I'm sure,' Gawain said confidently. 'She is a good and honest woman. She is not trying to renege. She merely wants to do it exactly properly. She has this magic talent: she can tell by looking at a man how good a consort he would make. That's one reason my family selected her. They didn't want the heir sired by some ne'er-do-well bum with poor heredity. She really is special. If I had met her in life, I surely would have loved her, though I wouldn't have had much patience with her views about dragons. She can't bear to hurt any living creature. So if I bring her a man she deems good enough to – '

Realization struck Norton. 'This favour – '

The ghost nodded. 'Precisely. I want you to meet my wife, and if she likes you – '

'Wait!' Norton spluttered. 'I take my women where I find them, when they are amenable, but never a married one! That wouldn't be right.'

'I like you, Norton. You have the right instincts. I was afraid out here in the park I'd find only wishy-washy sentimentalists, but you've got style. I think my wife would like you, when she didn't like the warrior types I sent before. Look at it this way: I have no physical body and I need an heir. I'm asking you to substitute for me in this one respect. After that you can go your way, with no further commitment. It's like repairing my house for me, and I'll pay you for the service – '

'Some service!'

'Literally.' The ghost chuckled. 'I realize this is hard for you to accept right away and I like that in you. But at least come to meet Orlene. Maybe she'll reject you.'

From the way the ghost spoke, Norton had no certainty of that. Gawain thought this girl, Orlene, would like him. If he went, expecting to be rejected, and then . . . 'I don't know – '

'Please, Norton! You're a good man – and I must have that heir.'

'I understand that part. But to cuckold you – that's against my philosophy.'

'I am, after all, a ghost. You can consider her a widow. If it helps, you can remember that you will have no rights over her at all. You cannot marry her, and your part will be forever unrecognized. Legally there is no adultery here. So this is the ultimate chance to sow wild oats – '

'Complete irresponsibility! That's not what I – '

'Well, then, think of it as artificial insemination, and you're the donor. Hell, man, that's done all the time, in life, when the living husband is infertile.'

This was haywire, but the concept helped. The ghost did have a case. 'All right – I'll meet her,' Norton said guardedly.

'And I'll teach you how to slay dragons!'

17

'Oh, you don't really need to – '

'Yes, I do. I insist on paying for it!'

Norton realized that what a man paid for belonged to him. Gawain had to have his personal, private claim on the heir. 'Yes. But first we had better find out whether she's even interested. This may all be for nothing.' He wondered what this fine girl who had sold her body in such fashion for security actually looked like. Quality and lineage could normally net a girl a good husband, unless she was ugly or had a vile temper. That latter kind might be the sort who would settle for a ghost.

'We can go right now,' Gawain said eagerly. 'There's an elevator not far from here.'

Norton thought to protest, but remembered that he was broke, so would not be able to camp out much longer anyway. A stay with a good woman, even an ugly one, was at least worth considering. He really could not claim to have anything better to do.

He doused the fire and cleaned up the area so that future hikers would not be annoyed. Wilderness hiking and camping were privileges, not rights, and were strictly licensed. He was always careful not to mistreat the cultivated wilds. He burned only deadwood, left the animals alone, and tried not to harm even caterpillars and worms. He never littered. It was not that anyone was watching; it was that Norton had genuine respect for the heritage of nature and for the parks that sought to emulate it.

They walked a quarter mile to a giant blazed oak tree. Norton touched the lowest branch and stepped inside the chamber that opened in the trunk. The elevator descended to the residential level, where they stepped out and took a conveyor belt to the ghost's address. Gawain, of course, could simply have popped across directly, but he preferred to honour the living conventions among the living.

This was an affluent section of the city, as befitted the ghost's description of his family's status. Poor people did not worry much about preservation of their estates.

They stepped off the belt, took a smaller side-passage belt, and moved into the really refined region of the Who's-Who lineages. A uniformed guard barred the way as they stepped off. 'Identity?' he asked Norton sternly.

'It's all right, Trescott,' Gawain said. 'He's with me.'

Trescott eyed Norton's somewhat sweaty and worn hiking outfit disapprovingly. 'Very good, sir,' he muttered.

'The guards don't always let themselves see me,' Gawain explained. 'Unless I take pains to manifest to them. Ghosts are not much in fashion here; the management worries about property values.'

'Or about scruffy-looking characters like me,' Norton said. 'I feel out of place here.'

'Um, there's a point,' Gawain agreed. 'We really ought to spruce you up a bit to make a good impression.'

'I am what I am,' Norton said. 'If she has the power to judge a man's true worth at a glance, what difference does clothing or polish make?'

'There is that. Very well, we'll try it this way. But if she accepts you, you'll have to dress the part.'

'First things first,' Norton said, not totally pleased.

They arrived at the door. 'Now I can't go in,' Gawain said. 'Rules of the cosmos. Everyone can see a ghost like me except the one most concerned. You'll introduce yourself.'

'What, smile toothily and say, "Hi, girl, I'm here to – "?'

'Tell her Gawain sent you. She'll understand.'

'Sure,' Norton said glumly. How had he gotten into this? He felt like a travelling salesman about to approach the farmer's daughter.

'Good luck,' Gawain said.

Norton wasn't sure whether 'good luck' would mean acceptance or rejection. He nerved himself and touched the door's call button.

2

Verification

A panel became translucent after a moment. 'Yes?' a soft-voiced woman inquired. He could not quite make out her features; the glass was, of course, designed to pass a clear image only one way.

'Uh, Gawain sent me.' Idiocy!

The door slid aside, and she stood framed within. She had hair the hue of honey and eyes the same. Her figure was adorably proportioned, and her face was cute. She was the loveliest creature he had met.

Orlene studied Norton. Her eyes seemed to shine. 'Oh, I was afraid this would happen someday,' she said.

'This wasn't exactly my idea,' Norton said. 'I'll go.'

'No,' she said quickly. 'No fault in you! I just was not prepared.'

'Since I'm unsuitable, I won't bother you further.' He felt quite awkward, sorry he had come here, yet also deeply regretful. He had been braced to meet a different sort of woman; for one like this, he would do almost anything.

'No, wait,' she said quickly. 'I didn't mean to – please, sit down, have some tea.'

'That's not necessary, thank you. I'm intruding. This whole business – ' He turned away – and paused. Gawain was right there behind him, spreading his arms to block his retreat. He did not want to walk through the ghost.

Orlene came up and took his arm. Her touch was light and gentle and utterly right; he had a momentary mental picture of a porcelain statuette, a work of art, inconceivably delicate, precious, and cool. 'Please,' she repeated.

'He set it up,' Norton said, indicating Gawain.

'You don't have to say that,' Orlene said, sounding just a bit nettled. 'You don't have to justify yourself.'

'Yes, I do! He's your husband! I can't simply – even if I were satisfactory, I mean, it would still be wrong.'

'My husband is dead,' she said.

'I know. That's why – ' Norton shrugged, confused about his own emotions, wishing he were back in the forest. 'How can you face him like this and – ?'

'Me?' she flared. She was one of those few women who really did seem as pretty angry as happy. 'How can you men exchange stories, and use a great warrior's death to try to – to – !'

'But he *told* me!' Norton said. 'Gawain brought me here! Ask him! He'll tell you!'

She looked into Norton's face, then turned away, hurt. He felt like a monster who had just pulled the wings off a dozen beautiful butterflies.

'She can't see me,' Gawain said. 'She can't hear me. I told you that. She doesn't really believe in me.'

Norton was shocked. 'You mean she thinks this is just a scheme to – to hit on – ?'

'I told you you'd have to handle the introduction yourself,' the ghost reminded him. 'She's ready to accept you; don't mess it up.'

Norton turned to Orlene again. 'You really can't see or hear – Gawain?'

'Of course I can't,' she said, her face still hurt. 'Only his picture.' She gestured to a framed painting on the wall inside.

Norton turned around to get a better view. It was Gawain, garbed in his armour, with a dragon painted on his shield and X'd out. The bold killer of dragons.

Norton shook his head. 'This is all wrong. I think I have insulted you, Orlene. I misunderstood – the situation. I apologize and I'll leave.'

'Oh, you mustn't leave!' she protested. 'I don't care what brought you here, really. You glow so brightly! I never expected to see – '

21

'I glow?'

'Her magic power,' Gawain said from outside. 'The right man glows. You're it, all right.'

'It's hard to explain,' Orlene said. 'It doesn't mean I like a man, or want to. It just means that, objectively, he is – ' She spread her hands helplessly.

'I think I understand,' Norton said. He had thought he would be rejected, once he saw how lovely she was; now he was unable to turn down what was offered, though he remained disturbed by the situation. 'Perhaps I will accept your tea after all.' He stepped back into the apartment.

Orlene closed the door behind him, shutting out the ghost. That was a small relief. Norton sat in a comfortable chair while she bustled in her kitchenette, dialling the tea.

The problem was that she was too pretty, too obviously nice. Norton felt subjectively as if his touch would despoil her. This was no one-night-stand woman, and it would be a crime to treat her that way. Especially since she herself was not aware of the ghost's active participation. She would think that he, Norton, was simply a man taking advantage of a widow. Well, not exactly a widow. But it bothered him.

Except for one thing – she saw him glow. She had no need to accept him; she could tell him to go and he would go. Why should she claim he was right for the purpose? Was her magic real, or was it a pretext to pick and choose? Was she in fact any better than she took him to be? She seemed like the ideal woman, but appearances could be deceptive. Especially when a ghost was involved.

Orlene brought the tea in an old-fashioned pot and poured cups for them both. This wasn't tea time, but time was not of the essence here. What was required was something to occupy their hands and eyes and nominal attention – a pretext to be somewhat at ease together. That was, Norton suspected, the true basis of tea; it was a social amenity.

But it wasn't enough. There was only so long a person could nurse along a cup of beverage, and it was necessary to

22

make small talk meanwhile. How long could they postpone getting down to the subject?

Norton's desperately wandering eyes spotted a large, pretty, parlour-style book, the kind with phenomenal illustrations and very little text, as befitted the fashionable, wealthy nonreaders of the day. He reached for it.

'Oh, that's the picture-puzzle guide,' Orlene said quickly. 'Magic technology art. I haven't gotten into the puzzle, though I've been meaning to. I understand it's very difficult.'

'I like puzzles.' Norton opened the book. The first picture was of a section of the city park, with its tall trees seeming almost alive. Almost? Now he saw their leaves fluttering in the wind. It was a moving picture and it was three-dimensional; his eyes shifted focus as he peered into its background. He had heard of books like this, with holographic illustrations, but never handled one before.

Experimentally he poked his forefinger at the picture, for his eyes had lost track of the surface of the page. His finger penetrated beyond that surface, finding no resistance. Startled, he drew back.

'It's a window to the park,' she explained. 'You could climb through it, if you could fit.'

Impressive magic! Intrigued, Norton turned the page. The next was of the nether transport centre, with the escalator belts leading down to the matter transmitters. People were stepping off the belts, inserting their talismans in the MT slots, and moving through to their destinations. A big clock on the wall showed the present time and date; this was live! He wondered whether, if he should somehow squeeze into that picture, he would then be able to take a matter-mit window to another city or planet. No – he lacked the necessary token and lacked credit to buy one. Too bad; he really loved to explore, and if he had ever been able to afford interplanetary travel –

He turned another page. This picture-window showed another planet directly: the blazing sunside surface of Mercury, so bright that the heat seemed to radiate out from the

23

sheet. He touched his finger to the nearest baked rock – and drew it back quickly. That *was* hot!

'You say this one is merely a puzzle guide?' he asked, perplexed.

Orlene rose gracefully and went to a cupboard. Her dress rustled, and for the first time he became aware of what she was wearing: a kind of golden-tan wraparound affair, obviously intended for convenience rather than for presentation, but it fitted her marvellously. He suspected she would look wonderful in anything, however.

She brought down a box. 'To the jigsaw puzzle,' she explained. 'Of course, it's been decades since they actually cut them out with saws, but the name sticks.' She cleared away the pot and cups and set the box down.

Norton opened it. It was filled with bright, curly, flat fragments, indeed very much like the pieces of a jig-sawed puzzle. But these glittered with animation. Moving images here?

He picked one up and squinted at it. Sure enough, it showed several leaves of a tree, and they did indeed flutter in whatever wind there was. It was a section of the first illustration in the book.

'But there are a number of scenes in the book,' he said.

Orlene touched a button on the side of the box. Abruptly the image on the piece Norton held changed. Now it appeared to be part of the wall of the subterranean transport station. He looked at the other pieces in the box and saw one that displayed part of the face of the station clock. Its minute hand showed exactly the minute that Norton's own watch did. It was now only a fragment, but it kept accurate time.

'All the scenes are available,' Orlene said. 'You just set it for the one you want to do – or change it in the middle. There's another button to change the shapes of the pieces so they don't get too familiar. I understand it's a lot of fun, especially since the completed puzzle is large enough for a person to step through and enter the scene.'

'Science and magic are merging faster than I knew!' Norton exclaimed, impressed.

'Well, they always were pretty much the same thing,' she pointed out. 'Once the Unified Field Theorem merged the five basic forces, including magic – '

'I think I've been spending too much time in the wilderness!'

'The wilderness is nice too,' she said. 'We mustn't sacrifice the old values for the new.'

He glanced at her with fresh appreciation. 'You like the wilderness?' He remembered Gawain's remark about her affinity for animals.

'Oh yes! The estate has a section of the park; I go there often. Somehow it seems less lonely than the city.'

What a delight she was! But still he wasn't sure. He was not able to view people with a magic glow. 'Let's do this puzzle,' he suggested. 'The park picture.'

Orlene smiled with glad acquiescence. 'Let's!'

And that finessed the main issue nicely. She did want him to stay, for otherwise she would not have agreed to get into a project like this that could take days. And – he did want to stay. Not necessarily to honour the ghost's request, but to explore the possibility. The notion of helping Gawain in this fashion no longer seemed so unreasonable.

They laboured on the puzzle, first sorting the colours of the park scene, then aligning the straight-edge pieces, getting the border done. Norton was an old hand at this sort of thing, except that his experience had been with the old-fashioned kind of jigsaw. This magic-picture variety was new, but the fundamental principles of strategy and matching remained. A picture was like a story, with rules of structure that were vulnerable to exploitation in a case like this.

Orlene turned out to have a good eye for colour and shape and was able to locate pieces he needed. She was assisted by her magic, she said; the particular piece she looked for tended to glow. He saw no such effect, but her accuracy in drawing pieces from the great mixed pile lent credence to the claim. The two of them were working well together.

Norton glanced at the clock and discovered that three hours had flown by. They had completed the border and much of the forest path and were working on two trees, but there was a long way to go. Edges and paths filled in deceptively rapidly; the solid masses of single-colour regions would be much slower. 'Maybe we'd better let it rest for the night,' he said.

'Yes. Let me get you some pyjamas.' They both understood that he would be staying here indefinitely. The agreement had formed, unvoiced, as the outline of the puzzle took form. Like the puzzle, the details remained inchoate.

Norton did not ordinarily use pyjamas, but he didn't argue. He was a guest of this estate, and it was no place to flop in his clothes. Except – 'Pyjamas? Do you have male clothing here?'

'They were Gawain's,' she said delicately. 'You're close enough to his size, and I'm sure he would have wanted them to be used.'

Surely so. Norton squelched his misgivings and accepted the pyjamas. Orlene showed him to a well-appointed room, separate from hers; their relationship had not progressed to the critical stage. As he had known from the moment he first saw her, she was no one-night-stand girl. And he, abruptly, was no love-'em-and-leave-'em guy. He was committed for the full route, whatever it might be.

He discovered that he was quite tired; it had indeed been a long day. He undressed, stepped into the sonic cleaner, stepped out dry and tingly clean, then got into Gawain's pyjamas, reluctantly accepting their symbolism. They hung on him somewhat baggily.

He got into bed and realized that this was not the ordinary flop-house bunk he was used to. It was an oilsponge couch. His weight caused the sponge oil to give way and shift, but not instantly; it was more like sinking into thick mud. The truth was, mud was excellent stuff, as children instinctively knew,

26

despite the bad press provided by their mothers. It offered enough support to prevent drowning, while being malleable enough for freedom of action. It was also fascinating stuff in itself, suitable for splashing or mudballs and body-paintings. Of course this bed was not mud and would not splash or separate, but the *feel* was similar. Norton let himself descend into its enfoldment with sheer bliss.

'How did it work out?' a voice asked.

Norton opened his eyes, annoyed. Gawain the Ghost was there, standing expectantly beside the bed. 'I had almost forgotten you,' he said.

'I certainly hadn't forgotten *you*!' the ghost replied. 'Three hours – did you beget my offspring?'

'What the hell are you doing here?' Norton demanded. 'I thought you couldn't enter this apartment.'

'You misunderstood. I can't enter the room in which my wife stays, and she can't directly perceive me regardless of where we are. But I can enter my own residence when she's absent. I do it all the time.'

'She's absent? I thought she was in her bedroom.'

'She is. She's absent from this room,' Gawain clarified. 'If she entered it, I'd have to vanish. I'd just step through the wall until she was gone.'

Norton thought of something else. 'I understood it was death to see a ghost. That's why people don't like it! Does this mean I am going to die?'

Gawain laughed. 'Yes, in a manner of thinking. You will die – in due course. Maybe fifty years hence. Every living person will. But seeing me won't hasten your demise one whit, unless you should happen to die of fright.' He put his forefingers in the corners of his mouth and pulled his lips open in a grotesque face. Because he was insubstantial, he was able to stretch his mouth entirely beyond the borders of his face. 'I'm not that kind of ghost. You're thinking of Molly Malone of Kilvarough. She's a nice and lovely ghost indeed; if I weren't already married – ' He left it unfinished.

'Well, to answer your question,' Norton said shortly, 'I did not have any intimate relation with Orlene. She's not that kind of woman, any more than you're that kind of ghost. And I can't guarantee that I *will* have that kind of relation, or when.'

'Now look, sport,' Gawain said indignantly. 'You're here accepting the hospitality of my estate. You owe it to me to deliver!'

'To cuckold you?' Norton demanded, again expressing his inner irresolution. 'To seduce your pristine, faithful wife?'

'It's not like that, and you know it. You're here to perform a service.'

'I thought I was here to do you a favour.'

'Same thing. Once you do it, you can leave. Except I still have to teach you how to slay dragons.'

'Well, Orlene is no dragon! The fact is, she is really a nice person, not a gold digger at all. If she decides not to – to want the favour, I'm not going to force it on her.'

'What do you think *she's* here for?' Gawain demanded. 'She's a guest of my estate too!'

'She's your *wife*!' Norton shouted. 'She has a perfect right to be here!'

'Not if she doesn't produce! Listen, Norton, I'm locked in this state until I have a proper heir. She owes it to me to generate him promptly.'

'Well, then, why didn't you marry some slut who spreads her legs for any man who looks at her? Why inflict this on a nice girl?'

'I *told* you,' the ghost responded hotly. 'There are standards to maintain. Our family is of noble lineage.'

'Well, I have standards to maintain, too – and so does she.'

'Anyway, I didn't select her; my family did. They – '

The ghost vanished in mid-sentence. Norton looked about, startled – and saw Orlene at the doorway.

'Are you all right, Norton?' she asked worriedly. 'I heard you shouting – '

And she couldn't hear the ghost! He'd have to watch that.

What had she heard? He felt a slow flush nudging up his neck and cheeks as he considered that. 'I – I don't suppose you would believe I was talking to the ghost?'

'I really wish you wouldn't – '

'Call it a bad dream, then. I'm sorry I disturbed you.'

She looked doubtful. 'You're such a good man. Do you really suffer from – '

Norton laughed, somewhat too heartily. 'How can you know I'm a good man? I'm an ordinary man, perhaps less than ordinary, since I have never had much success in life. Not like you.'

'Oh, no! I am nothing!' she protested. 'You glow!'

Norton studied her. She was in a pinkish-white peignoir, and her honey-golden hair hung loose about her shoulders. There was something enormously appealing about her, and it was not mere beauty or sensuality. But he resisted that appeal, choosing instead to challenge her. 'You refuse to believe I can see a ghost, but you expect me to believe you see a glow? When the ghost and the glow say the same thing?'

She smiled wanly. 'I suppose it is inconsistent. But so many men have come with stories about the ghost of my husband, I know it's a crude male game. I would like to believe you are different.'

Somehow Norton felt rather small. 'I did see the ghost – but I don't necessarily agree with what he said.'

'I do see the glow,' she said. 'But I don't – ' She smiled. 'Good night, Norton.'

'Good night, Orlene.'

She retreated and closed the door.

Gawain reappeared. 'I see the problem,' he said. 'Neither of you is a dragon slayer; you don't like to go at it directly. But if she says you glow, she'll accept you. It's just a matter of time. All you need to do is stay here and – '

'And be supported by a woman,' Norton finished. 'I find that hard to accept.'

'It's my estate, damn it!' Gawain swore. 'She doesn't have a

29

thing of her own. It's all mine. She won't inherit; only the son she bears will. She knows that.'

'Suppose it's a daughter?'

The ghost looked blank. 'A what?'

Norton was beginning to appreciate the fact that Gawain's purpose did not align perfectly with Orlene's purpose. He wanted to preserve the estate; she wanted a proper personal situation. He wanted a son to inherit and carry on the line; the personality of that son was not a concern. She surely wanted a fine child who would be a joy to her and to Gawain's family and to the world and a credit to the estate. He was concerned about money and power, she about quality and love. She would prefer to have an attractive, intelligent, and sweet girl – like herself – while he would be outraged by anything less than a strapping, bold boy – like himself. Norton's sympathy was sliding towards the woman's view.

But he was here at the ghost's behest, and there was merit in Gawain's position. 'I'll try to accomplish your purpose. But I won't rush it. It's not that I want to sponge off your estate, it's that I think you have a better wife than you appreciate, and I want it to be right.'

'I want it to be right, too,' Gawain said, sounding aggrieved. 'I want my son to have the best of everything.'

Norton didn't comment. As he came to understand the forces operating here, he did not feel more at ease. But there seemed to be no better way through this than to remain here, get to know Orlene, and do what the ghost wanted when the occasion was propitious. Then move on quickly, lest he become too much attached. How much easier this would have been if the girl had been a gold digger or a slut!

He closed his eyes, and Gawain did not speak again. Soon Norton was asleep, drowned in the comfort of the mudbath bed.

He dreamed he was back at the puzzle-window, trying to place a piece. As he stared at it, assessing its contours, those contours changed, coming to resemble the outline of a nude

30

woman – and the woman had hair like honey, and breasts the same. He tried to avert his eyes from that ineffable sweetness, embarrassed. It was not that he had any aversion to such a body; it was that he felt he was violating Orlene's modesty.

But the shape expanded to life size, showing more detail, becoming the living, breathing woman, naked and appallingly desirable. He tried to set her down – for his hand was still on the piece, grasping it where he had no right to grasp – but found himself drawn in towards her. In a moment he would fall through the piece, into the world of the puzzle – and where would he be then? Desperately he pushed her away – and she fell to the floor and broke into a thousand puzzle fragments, and he knew these could never be reassembled, no matter how hard he tried to fit every bit together.

He woke – and Orlene was there, her arm about his shoulders as she sat on the bed. Her warm breast pressed against his upper arm, soft through the material of her apparel and his. 'Wake, wake, Norton, it's all right!' she soothed.

If she had a baby and it screamed in the night, even so would she comfort it – and what baby could be better off?

'I'm awake,' he said. 'You don't need to – you shouldn't be here.'

'I couldn't let you suffer,' she said. 'Was it the ghost again?'

'No, not this time. Just a bad dream. I'm afraid I'm not very good company.'

'You were glowing so brightly!'

He coughed. 'That's a false glow! I dreamed of you – that I destroyed you, without meaning to.'

'No, the glow isn't wrong,' she insisted. 'I know you are right for me. In fact, if I weren't already married – ' She broke off, out of sorts. 'Oh, I shouldn't have said that!'

'I think I shouldn't stay here any longer,' Norton said. 'You are so nice – I would never want to be the instrument of – of any problem for you.'

'You won't be,' she said confidently. 'I know.'

She believed in her glow. But his dream had been compelling. In past times supposedly sensible men had disparaged dreams as mere visions of internal events, but recent research had verified their magical properties. He could not be sure this dream was prophetic, but he didn't want to take the chance. 'All the same, I think it would be better if I left.'

'Oh, please, Norton, don't do that!' she exclaimed. 'It's so difficult to be alone all the time! You're the first who's right. I'll do anything you want – '

'Orlene, I'm not trying to coerce you! I'm trying to protect you. From me, maybe. And I think I can do that best by leaving you.'

'It's morning,' she said abruptly. 'I'll fix us breakfast.'

'Thank you. Then I'll go.'

She disengaged, stood, and hurried out. Norton got up, used the various facilities of the bathroom – and discovered that his clothes were gone. Orlene had evidently taken them for cleaning. The perfect housewife! 'What do I do now?' he asked himself rhetorically.

'You use my clothing,' Gawain replied. 'It will fit you well enough. I had more muscle, but our frames are similar.'

Norton realized he had no choice. Assisted by the ghost, he donned trousers, shirt, slippers, and an elegant robe. All of the clothing was of fine material and well made, and little golden dragons were embroidered on each item. 'You *are* rich, aren't you!' he muttered.

'Definitely,' Gawain agreed. 'I'm not in the Five Hundred, but I was a candidate. If I had lived long enough – ' The ghost broke off, looking momentarily pensive. 'My son will never lack for material things. He'll be able to buy himself a Senatorial seat, if he wants to. I understand politics is more lucrative than dragon slaying.'

'Good for your child,' Norton said shortly. 'I'm not sure I'm going to sire it.'

'Orlene won't let you go,' the ghost warned. 'She knows you're the one.'

'How can she stop me from leaving?'

32

Gawain pursed his lips. 'You've got something to learn about the wiles of women!'

Norton brushed on out to rejoin Orlene, in no fit temper.

She had breakfast ready: bright green pancakes fresh from the Venusian fungus farm, and what appeared to be genuine beehive honey. That figured. He had to smile, and his mood abated. He joined her at the cozy dinette table.

Suddenly it seemed very domestic. He had never been the domestic type, but it was nice enough now. Orlene was very fetching in a green housecoat, her hair tied back with a scarlet ribbon. Green coat, honey hair, matching the pancakes and honey; did she do that unconsciously? But the ribbon –

Scarlet? 'You know, there's an old song about scarlet ribbons – '

'Yes,' she agreed. 'I'll play it for you after breakfast.'

'You have it on tape?'

She smiled obscurely. 'No.'

After breakfast she showed him to another room. There was a baby grand piano there. She sat down before it and played beautifully.

'How did you come by talent like that?' he asked, impressed, as she finished the piece.

'It's not talent. I've been practising since I was six years old and more since I've been married. It helps to wile away the time; I don't feel so much alone when I'm playing. Anyway, musical skill is the fashion for debutantes.'

'You were a debutante? How did you get into – this?'

'The ghost marriage? My family arranged it, but I didn't object. Gawain's family is very well connected, and I want the best for my children too. This was the best marriage I could make.'

'But to a dead man!'

'Well, a ghost doesn't make many demands on a girl. I think of it as like being widowed early, except there's no grief. I never knew him in life.'

'But to – you have to – '

'I always did want a family. That would be the same if he were alive.'

'If he were alive, you would have known what you were getting. This way – '

'I do know,' she said. 'This way I have a choice. The best possible father for my children, regardless of the accidents of lineage or wealth.'

'The glow? Frankly, I doubt – '

She grimaced prettily. 'You prove the ghost exists, and I'll prove the glow does.'

Actually, he believed she saw the glow; he had noticed it at work on the puzzle. But he also remembered his nightmare. The two might cancel out, her positive vision and his negative one, leaving the future in serious doubt. 'Why don't you just give me back my own clothes so I can leave? Then neither of us will have to prove anything.'

'Do you really want to leave?'

'No. That's why I'd better.'

'And they talk about female logic!'

He had to smile. 'I'm trying to do the right thing, as I see it, though I admit I'm not seeing it very well right now. It would be too easy to like you too well. I don't think that's what I'm here for.'

'Like me too well for what?'

'To love you and leave you.'

She was silent a moment, looking at him, and he feared he had spoken too directly. She had married a ghost; what could she know of the intimate way of man and woman? 'Do you have to leave?'

'Of course I have to! I'm only here for a – '

'But it will take some time to know that the job is – done.'

He hadn't thought of that. 'You would want me to stay – after?'

'I think so.'

'You're that sure of me? When you hardly know me?'

'Yes. The glow doesn't lie.'

'Then I guess we'd better exchange our proofs.' He had no doubt that both ghost and glow would be verified to the other party's satisfaction; this was really an excuse to change his mind. Orlene had conquered him without using wiles.

'I really don't want the proof,' she said. 'Too many other people have claimed to see the ghost. I was only making a point.'

Norton sighed. 'I'm afraid I do need proof. To justify myself. The ghost of Gawain asked me to come here, and I want you to believe that. That has become important to me – that I'm not an imposter or opportunist. I don't care how much I glow; it's my motive I'm establishing.'

'But how can you prove a ghost that only you can see?'

'For one thing, others can see him too. We have only to ask them.'

'No, I know they all tell the same story, to tease me. Women are supposed to be so credulous!'

Norton considered. 'Very well. Since this is Gawain's estate, he should be conversant with every detail of it. He should be able to tell me things I would have no other way of knowing. Ask me questions only he could answer.'

She frowned. 'Do you really insist on this, Norton?'

'I really do. I must prove to you what brought me here. I don't want you to take my word.'

She considered, cocking her head to one side so that her tresses fell partway across her face. That was, he thought, a fetching effect, making a partial mystery of her features that enhanced their appeal. 'I haven't been into everything here yet and I'm sure you haven't. Suppose he calls off the items in – ' She glanced about. 'In that storage chest?' She indicated an ornate chest beside the piano.

'I'll ask him,' Norton agreed. 'I'll have to go to another room, though, to talk to him, because Gawain says he can't be in the same room with you.'

'I doubt he's in the same world with me!'

35

'Maybe I can stand in the doorway and talk to you both. Will that be all right?'

'Whatever you wish.' She obviously expected nothing to come of this.

Norton went to the doorway between the two rooms. Orlene remained at the piano.

'Hey, Gawain!' Norton called. 'Will you appear?' He was afraid the ghost would embarrass him by avoiding this test.

Gawain popped into sight. 'Good notion, Norton! I'll be happy to prove my existence to her!'

'Good enough. Orlene, he's here. Ask a question.'

'You can see him?' she asked, rising and approaching the doorway.

'Yes. But don't go into the other room; he'll vanish.'

She stopped at the doorway. 'I don't see him.'

'But he can see you,' Norton said.

'Even when you're not looking?'

'Certainly,' Gawain said.

'He says yes,' Norton reported.

'Very well. Let's try this: you close your eyes and face away from me, and let him tell you what I'm doing.'

'All right.' Norton faced the ghost and closed his eyes.

'She's holding her right hand above her head,' Gawain said.

'He says you're holding your right hand over your head.'

'Now she's writing in the air, script – I can't read it, it's backwards.'

Norton relayed that.

'Oh,' Orlene said, startled.

'Okay, she's turned around,' the ghost said. 'Now I can read over her shoulder. T H I S pause I S pause R I D I C U L O U S.'

'This is ridiculous,' Norton repeated.

She was silent, but he heard rustling.

'Say!' Gawain exclaimed. 'She's stripping!'

'She is?' Norton asked, startled in his turn.

'Great galumphing dragons!' the ghost said. 'I'm sorry I'm not alive! I had no idea she had architecture like that!'

'He says you're – undressing.' Norton said. 'He says you have an excellent figure.'

'Oops, that did it,' Gawain said regretfully. 'She covered up in a hurry. Man, I wish I was in your shoes!'

'He says – '

'I can guess!' Orlene snapped.

'Well, he *is* your husband,' Norton said. 'And since he can't share a room with you, he has not before had an opportunity to see – '

'Unladylike remark,' she said. 'What's in that chest by the piano?'

Norton lowered his hands; he had unconsciously brought them up to cover his closed eyes. 'Gawain, will you tell us – '

The ghost shrugged. 'The truth is, I don't remember. I was mostly out slaying dragons. A housekeeper took care of the apartment.'

'He says he doesn't remember,' Norton reported.

'I thought as much!'

'But I could check,' Gawain said. 'Let her leave that room, and I'll tally the contents now.'

'He says he'll check now,' Norton said, 'if you'll just step into the other room.'

Orlene passed him and entered the other room. As she did so, the ghost vanished – and reappeared in the room she had vacated. Gawain walked to the chest and plunged his hand in through the polished wood. 'What do you know,' he remarked brightly. 'My old trophies! Best dragon kill of the year – that sort of thing. These should be up on the mantel on full display!'

Norton relayed that. 'Oh?' Orlene asked. 'Let me see.' She walked back into the room, switching places with the ghost, and tried to lift the lid. It didn't budge. 'It's locked.'

'The key's in my bedroom,' Gawain said. 'In the left dresser drawer, if the fool maid hasn't moved it.'

Norton told Orlene, who went and fetched the key, then unlocked the chest. Inside were trophies, exactly as described. 'It's true!' she said. 'You couldn't have known, Norton! *I* didn't know! Unless you got the key last night and – but no, the chest is undisturbed.'

'Ask anything else,' Norton suggested. 'I'm sure we can satisfy you.'

'I'll try one other thing,' she decided. 'What's Gawain's sister's name?'

'I have no sister,' Gawain said.

'He says he has no – '

'What's his mother's maiden name?'

'Thrimbly.'

'Thrimbly,' Norton said.

'When did she get married?'

'June fourteenth,' Gawain said. 'Three thirty in the afternoon, in a private ceremony. The minister was the Reverend Q. Lombard. The wedding cake had a dragon rampant on it, breathing a column of firewater. All the guests got tanked on that water, including my father; he passed out, and my mother didn't speak to him for the first week of the honeymoon. I was lucky to get conceived!'

Norton repeated the continuing details. Orlene raised her hands in surrender. 'You see the ghost! I've got to concede that! Now it's my turn to prove the glow.'

'Just what is the glow?' Norton asked. 'Do I light the shadows?'

'No, not like that. It's – well, have you heard of the animal-spell people? The ones who can shake hands, and the hand of the one they meet feels like the appendage of the animal he most closely resembles? A wolf's paw, a barracuda's fin, or a snake's scale? Actually, that's figurative; animals aren't like that, not with the bad qualities. But with this magic, the person can tell if another is vicious, greedy, sneaky, or

38

whatever. Well, with me it's vision. I can tell who is the perfect companion, for me or for someone else. I see the aura illuminate. I have to set my mind to tune in to one person, then view the others through his situation, if you see what I mean.'

Norton shook his head. 'I'm afraid I don't. I know I'm not special; there have to be many better marriage prospects than I.'

'But you aren't a marriage prospect. You're a – '

'Never mind what I am! I begin to see your point. You actually do need a love-'em-and-leave-'em guy.'

'A nonmarrying guy. And most of those aren't worth much as persons. You are. Of course, if I weren't married, and wanted a husband, my situation would be different. I would want not only a good lover but also a good provider. You might not glow so strongly then.'

'I'm sure I wouldn't! I'm broke!'

'So it does require some tuning in. When I first saw you, you glowed so brightly I knew you were the one – and I wasn't ready. I thought I might have tuned in inaccurately. I mean, I knew what I had to do, but it was so sudden. I knew my life had changed and that the time to conceive the heir had come. Now I'm getting used to it; I think those hours on the puzzle helped, and soon – '

'Why don't we take a walk outside, and you can show me how your glow works on others,' Norton suggested.

'All right. Let me get into street clothes.' She hurried to her bedroom.

Gawain reappeared. 'Now you're making progress!' the ghost said with satisfaction. 'I was able to listen through the wall this time; I can't always do that.'

'Damn it, *must* you see it as just that one thing?'

'Certainly. That's what you're both here for, isn't it? To beget my heir?'

'I don't know. If I go through with this, I'm afraid I'll leave more than my seed behind.'

39

'Oh, don't get maudlin about it,' Gawain said. 'You've probably had almost as many women as I have! Think of it as one more dragon to be slain.'

'She's no dragon!'

'Oh, I don't know. Women and dragons – I'd call them two of a kind.'

'You don't love her?'

'Of course not! I'm dead!'

'*I* could love her. I don't want to hurt her.'

'Then *don't* hurt her! Give her what she needs – a son.'

'I had a dream that I destroyed her. I worry about that.'

'You can't hurt her if you leave her after it's done.'

'Some people are hurt worse by being left,' Norton muttered.

'Don't worry. She'll have the very best care money can buy, courtesy of my estate.'

'I wasn't thinking of physical hurt, necessarily. She's a young, vibrant girl. I don't think she can give herself to a man without giving all of herself. She – '

He paused, for Gawain had vanished. Orlene stood in the doorway. She was dressed in a modest green street skirt with matching jacket and hat and shoes, and now looked very businesslike. Her fair hair was pinned back with green barrettes. Somehow all that green reminded him of the breakfast pancakes, of the park scene in the puzzle, and of the lovely wilderness itself. 'The ghost again?' she asked.

Embarrassed, Norton nodded. 'He has only one thing on his mind.'

She cocked her head at him again. 'And you don't?'

'I have a care for the damage I may do to others.'

'I think that's why you glow so brightly.'

He shrugged. 'Maybe. But maybe I want more than I have a right to want.'

She touched his hand. 'I told you before, Norton. You don't have to go after it's done.'

'I think I do. You are a married woman.'

She looked at him so intently that he became nervous. 'What are you doing?' he asked.

'I'm visualizing you as a prospective husband, to compare the glow.'

'Don't do that! I'm not your – can never be your – '

'That's odd,' she said. 'That hasn't happened before.'

'*What* hasn't happened?'

'The glow seems to have split. Part of it is extremely intense, but part of it is dim. As if you would be both a very good husband and a not-very-good-husband.'

'How can that be?'

'I'm not sure. You see, the glow doesn't figure character *per se*. It includes the total person, the total situation. How good a person is, how loyal, how effective a provider, how lucky or unlucky – the perfect man might be downgraded because an unfortunate accident will cripple him in five years, making him worse through no fault of his own.'

Norton felt a chill. 'I might have an accident?'

'No. I don't think it's that. Maybe it's that you could be the perfect husband, but you won't be, because I can't marry you. You're too good for the job – overqualified. So you suffer.'

'Overqualified!' Norton exclaimed incredulously.

'I don't know,' she said quickly. 'That's just a conjecture. I don't understand all the aspects of the glow. I just see its brightness.'

'Well, stop considering me as – as the impossible. It's time to go out.'

'Of course.' She took his arm, and they went out.

Travel on the fast belts took them to this floor's nearest mall, where shoppers thronged in the fashion they had done so for millennia at such centres. This could be a market at Babylon or in a medieval city. The stores had changed somewhat in detail in the ensuing interval, however. Today they were holographic images, each in its alcove, the goods being displayed with lifelike realism, each tagged with its price. The shopper had only to touch the image of the item he wanted; it would be shipped directly from the warehouse to his home, and his account as identified by his fingerprint patterns would be debited accordingly. Of course, these were mostly standard items whose details were generally known; the more individual ones required a different type of shopping. Marked containers of food in set units did not need to be physically verified, while specially fitted clothing did. There were booths for fitting via holo imaging, but that still required undressing.

They stopped at an ice cream stall, where the holograph of a chef stood by a chart of a thousand different flavours and types. Orlene touched the panels for their choices – honey flavour, of course – and the cones snapped into the adjacent holders, to be taken physically. The account of Gawain would be debited. Norton, of course, couldn't order; he had no account. In the vernacular of the day, he was of no account.

Orlene also saw a popular book that looked interesting, so she touched its holo too; in a moment it was printed for her on the machine's supply of paper. It was a historical novel, set in the fascinating time when people believed in neither magic nor science, so had wretched lives. She put the book in her purse.

They sat on a bench, licking their cones in nominal fashion, and watched the people passing by. Orlene called out the brightnesses of each one. The problem, she explained, was that any person's suitability as a partner varied greatly, depending on whom he was partnered with. Thus she could get several readings with different match-ups.

Norton was intrigued, but remained uncertain whether the glows she perceived were really magic or only imagination. He wanted to verify some cases, but did not feel right about walking up to strangers and asking how their interpersonal relations were. Orlene surely perceived the glows – but just how accurate were they?

Then the proof came, abruptly. Orlene called out an older couple, walking hand in hand, evidently still much attached to each other. They were well dressed and handsome for their age. Yet Orlene called out a striking difference in their glows. The woman's glow was strong; she was almost perfect for the man. But his glow was absent. In fact, it was negative: a dark shadow. 'He's completely wrong for her!' Orlene whispered.

'I can't believe that,' Norton protested. 'Look how well they relate to each other! Even if he has a mistress on the side, he's got to be good for this woman. She's well cared for and contented.'

'The glow is absent,' Orlene insisted. 'He's *bad* for her!'

'That just doesn't make sense!'

Then they had to be quiet, for the couple was approaching. In fact, they sat down nearby on the bench. Norton wrestled with himself, trying to decide whether to speak to them, to try to resolve the discrepancy.

'Just a little tired,' the man was saying.

'Yes, of course,' the woman agreed.

Then the man fell off the bench.

Norton jumped up to help him, for he knew something about emergency aid. But he realized as he saw the man's staring face that he was dead. 'Resuscitation unit!' Norton snapped, and a machine burst out of the nearest wall and rolled over to attend to the man.

It took the machine only a moment to confirm Norton's diagnosis. 'Unit failure – beyond repair,' it clicked.

The ambulance unit came and loaded the body aboard, taking also the shocked widow. It was all accomplished so swiftly and neatly that many shoppers never realized anything had happened – which was, of course, the point. People did not like shopping where death occurred, with good reason; sometimes vengeful ghosts remained.

'Oh, that's so horrible!' Orlene said shudderingly. 'Must we stay here?'

'Of course not.' They walked to the moving belt.

But as they were carried back towards the apartment, Norton realized that the glow had been confirmed. The man

43

had been a poor partner for the woman, not because of any failure of resources or personality or loyalty, but because he was not going to be with her very long and, in fact, had been about to bring her crushing grief. Thus the glow, instead of being absent, was black. The glow had known – before the fact.

He had to accept the glow; it was legitimate magic. That meant he had to accept its verdict on him: he was right for Orlene. But what, then, of his dream? That suggested he was wrong for her – perhaps in the fashion of the man they had just seen die. Which was he to believe?

'Your glow is wavering,' Orlene muttered. 'Are you thinking of leaving me?'

Norton started guiltily. 'I don't know what is right.'

She held his arm tightly. 'Oh, please, Norton! I couldn't spend a night alone after seeing – that.'

He realized that she had never been exposed to violence or death, so was not equipped to handle it. Of course she would be severely shaken. This would be the worst time to leave her.

They arrived at the apartment. As the door closed, Orlene turned to him, flung her arms about him, buried her head in his shoulder, and sobbed. She had been fairly well controlled in public, but now she was letting down. He held her; there was nothing else to do. Norton had always liked to help people and he could not refuse her his companionship and support now. Or was he, he had to ask himself, rationalizing?

After a time she relaxed. She disengaged and went to the bathroom to put herself in order. 'I'll never eat ice cream again,' she said as she disappeared.

Ice cream. Guilt by association. She had eaten it just before the tragedy. An illogical connection, but valid emotionally. He did not feel much appetite for ice cream now himself. Or for shopping malls.

'You fighting with her?' Gawain demanded, popping into sight. 'I heard her crying.'

'Couldn't you see?' Norton demanded irritably.

44

'No. You weren't visible from the other room. I can walk through walls, but I can't see through them. All I could do was listen to the muffled sounds.'

'We weren't fighting.'

'What, then?'

'What business is it of yours?'

'Listen, mortal, it *is* my business!' Gawain retorted. 'This is my estate, and she's my wife.'

'A wife you never knew in life and don't love now.'

'Well, I'm a ghost! What use to love her?'

The ghost had a point. Perversely, that made it easier for Norton. Whatever he did with Orlene would not be treading on Gawain's sensibilities. 'We saw a man die. That shook her.'

Gawain snorted. 'I've seen many men die. I'm dead myself.'

In more than one sense. 'I think I see now why she had so much trouble believing in you. She doesn't like death and doesn't want it near her.'

'She should have thought of that before she married me!'

'It wasn't entirely her choice, any more than it was yours. Men usually marry for sex appeal, but women marry for security. It's the nature of the human species, or of our economy. If women were the prime money earners, they might marry for other reasons, and if men had no better way to gain security than through women, so would they. I'm sure she would have married a living man if that had been feasible.'

'Well, she didn't! And now she has a job to do – and so do you. I don't want to wait in limbo forever. Tell her you won't stay unless she puts out now, today. She'll move it along for sure, since she doesn't want to be alone.'

'I'll do nothing of the kind!' Norton responded angrily. 'She's no piece of meat!'

'She's the breeder for my heir! She's not here to pussyfoot around. She's vulnerable now; you can make her perform in the next hour, if you – '

'Listen, Gawain, I never pressured a woman in my life! And I would never take advantage of a situation like this!'

'No, you'd just sit around interminably, sponging off my estate!'

'To Hell with your estate!' Norton shouted. 'You asked me for a favour! I never had any intention of taking anything of yours!'

'Then do what you came to do and get gone!' the ghost shouted back.

'I'll get gone right now, if that makes you happier! You can find another man to do your favour!'

The ghost backed off, literally and figuratively. 'I told you, she's choosy. It's got to be you.'

'I am not at all certain of that. In any event, it will be of her choosing, not yours or mine.'

But Gawain was gone again. Orlene stood in the doorway, in a grey housecoat. 'Gawain again?'

Norton nodded. 'I shouldn't let him provoke me.'

'I suppose he has a case. He wants his heir.'

'Yes. But he neglects the social aspect.'

She glided to him. 'Norton, at first, I confess, I was suspicious, despite the glow. You glowed, but you weren't committed, and the ghost – ' She shrugged. 'But since then I've watched you glow as you talk with him. It flickers as you react. It is not a lie detector, but the glow is not under your control, so it suggests to me how you really feel. When you spoke just now of leaving, it damped right down. You weren't bluffing.'

'I'm not a bluffer,' Norton agreed ruefully. 'He wants me to perform like a hired stud and get out. I thought I could, before I met you, but now I can't.'

'I know,' she said softly. 'You really want to do the right thing.'

'Yes. And that may be to move out right now.'

'No!' she cried. 'Please, Norton, no! I told you I couldn't stand to be – '

'But you'd be alone tomorrow if I did it his way.'

'Gawain's an idiot,' she snapped. 'He doesn't know the first thing about siring an heir. I couldn't get pregnant today if they inseminated me artificially. It's not that time of the month. And if it were, there's no guarantee that one time would do it. The only way to be sure is to remain until a test establishes the pregnancy – and that could take several months.'

Norton spread his hands. 'You're right, of course. I'm as foolish as he.'

'You tell him that now,' she said. 'His efforts are only delaying things. I'll give you two minutes.'

'But that means I would have to stay for – '

'Months,' she said. 'Do you object?'

'No!' he said, his feeling surprising him.

'Then tell him. Then he won't nag you about that any more, and we can be in peace.' She turned and left.

Gawain reappeared. 'I heard,' he said. 'The vixen is right. Okay already, I'll take a tour around the world. You stay here until you're sure.'

'What about all my sponging off your estate?'

'I said that in anger. I apologize. I want you to stay. Will you?'

Norton sighed. 'Yes.'

'But first I'll teach you how to slay dragons.'

'That was to be my payment,' Norton said. 'But we didn't realize how long it would take me to deliver. Let's consider the room and board as payment instead.'

Gawain smiled, waved, and disappeared.

Orlene returned. 'All right?'

'Yes. He agrees. He's gone.'

'You're sure?'

'Well, I can't be *sure*. But he said he was going on a tour of the world. I think he realized that his purpose will be fulfilled better if he butts out for a while.'

'Yes. I never liked the idea of his watching. After all – '

'He can't share a room with you and he can't see through walls. So if you close things up – '

'That's a relief,' she said. 'I – that is, I'm not good at saying this – do you want to do it now?'

That was all the invitation Norton needed. He surprised himself by declining. 'There's no point. Wrong time of the – '

'You don't want to – to do it just for the fun?'

Norton hesitated. 'With any other woman – who looked like you – I would be glad to. I have – before. But this is not for fun. It's business. I can't justify it any other way.'

'Why not?'

Norton stared at the floor. 'I can never marry you.'

'You want too much.'

'Yes, I suppose I do. I never did before, but now – '

She walked around the room. 'I think that's what turned me off the other men who came. Oh, it's true their glows were low – but if one of them had had a high glow, I wouldn't have liked it, because all any of them wanted was free sex. I'm not a prostitute, and if I were I wouldn't give it away free. I can't really be with a man unless he cares.'

'But a man who cares – wouldn't want to have it this way.'

'Look,' she said abruptly. 'Lots of men have mistresses who last through several wives. Because the mistresses are true love interests. What is legal is not always actual. Why would you have to leave – ever?'

'I'm a wanderer. I have never stayed long in one place.'

'But if a woman were willing to travel with you?'

'None has been, so far. And you are bound to the estate.'

'No. I am bound to produce an heir to the estate. Then I can travel with whom I want to.'

What joy! 'We've known each other less than a day.'

'Oh, of course it might not work out,' she said quickly. 'I am merely making the point that you can love me if you want to. I know I can love you.'

'May the Lord have mercy on me,' he said slowly. 'I think I want to.'

She held something out to him. 'Let me give you this, as a token of our illicit potential love.'

48

He looked. It was a ring in the form of a small green snake. The head was slightly raised, serving in lieu of a precious stone. The eyes shone; perhaps they were gems.

'But I have nothing to give you in return!'

'Yes, you do. Give me yourself.'

It made a certain sense. She, as a married woman, could not truly give herself to him. But he could give himself to her, as companion or whatever. She had a dead husband; now she wanted a living man. One who cared.

He accepted her ring and put it on his left middle finger. It fitted perfectly and comfortably, as if made just for him.

'Now – ' Orlene said.

'This has very little logic,' he warned her.

'I know. Do what you will with me.'

He laughed. He picked her up and carried her into the sitting room. He kissed her and set her down by the puzzle. 'I want a piece, woman!'

She smiled. 'Yes, sir!'

They got to work on the puzzle.

3

Thanatos

What followed was very much like a honeymoon. They made love often at first, then settled down to a pleasant routine. They finished the puzzle and started on another. They toured the estate, which was vast and rich, with apartments on several levels of the city, a marked section of penthouse park, and a private matter transmitter in the basement level. There was even a section of a posh sports club; Gawain owned an enclosed tennis court and a table in the restaurant. Gawain had never played tennis; it was only an investment to him, handled by the anonymous experts who ran his financial affairs. But Norton knew tennis, and so did Orlene. Neither of them was professional level, but both were adequate, and they enjoyed playing each other. Norton was a healthy man, and Orlene was a fine figure of a woman, especially when exerting herself physically.

There was no discernible point of demarcation, but it was not long at all before Norton knew he was thoroughly in love. Orlene never said she actually loved him, but he understood that; she was loyal to her technical marriage to the ghost. In every other respect she was Norton's. She fixed his meals like a housewife; she hiked with him in the park, being thrilled when she caught a new bird on camera; and she shared his sleeping bag at night. If he had found a woman like her before, he certainly would have married her. They even had quarrels – but never, now, was there any mention of his leaving. They were wedded in all but name.

The ring she had given him turned out to be no minor trinket. It was magic. She refused to tell him *how* it was magic. 'A woman needs some secrets,' she said teasingly. 'Since my body has none remaining for you, the mysteries of the ring will have to do.'

That intrigued him mightily – but several things prevented him from cracking that riddle promptly. First, Orlene kept him busy with a whirlwind of joint activities. They viewed the latest top-grade holoflicks together, went null-gravity swimming, and visited the estate's outlet on the planet Venus – no wonder Orlene was able to get delicious, fresh, Venusian fungus for meals! – which was less impressive than he had expected, because the Venus apartment was merely another chamber with a single thick-lensed viewport opening on to the perpetually murky storm of the surface. It would have been hard to tell it was another planet if it hadn't been for the changed gravity. When nothing else offered, Orlene would teasingly display portions of her perfect body, and duty as well as inclination compelled him to pursue it. But there came a moment when she slept and he was awake, and he remembered the ring. Now was his chance!

He took hold of the ring with thumb and forefinger to pull it off – and discovered the second problem. It would not budge. It was not tight on his finger; in fact, it was so comfortable that he was never aware of it unless he focused on it – but it seemed to constrict itself when he drew on it. The harder he pulled the tighter it was. It was also invulnerable to twisting. He went to the bathroom and soaped his finger – the bars of soap were an affectation, since the sonic shower made them unnecessary, but affectations had a long shelf life – yet his efforts made no difference. He tried to pull the skin of the finger tight so it couldn't bunch up under the ring, but that, too, was ineffective. 'This thing must have an adhesive-spell!'

'No, it doesn't,' Orlene said behind him. He jumped guiltily; he hadn't been aware of her waking. Spying his discomfort, she laughed merrily and proffered a kiss; it was three more days before he thought of the ring again.

This time she was visiting the estate doctor for her routine weekly checkup. Part of the condition of her marriage to the ghost was that she remain healthy so she could bear a healthy heir. She was fastidious about all her duties. Thus Norton had a little time to himself in the doctor's lounge.

He contemplated the ring. The tiny gem eyes of the metallic serpent seemed to look back at him. 'So you stay with your owner,' he remarked. 'Is that the extent of your magic?'

Then he almost leaped out of his chair. The ring had pulsed twice, gently squeezing his finger!

Norton was alone, but was aware that doctors' premises had ways to observe their occupants. Therefore, he acted as if he were in public and subdued his reaction. Perhaps, anyway, he had imagined those pulses.

'Did you do that, ring?' he asked it in a low voice.

There was a single squeeze, firm but not painful.

He was on to something here! 'You understand me?'

One squeeze, constriction and release, brief but definite.

'And you respond to questions by squeezing?'

One squeeze.

'One squeeze for yes, two for no?'

Squeeze.

'Do you ever do three squeezes?'

Squeeze.

'When?'

This time there were three squeezes.

'That doesn't answer my question!' he whispered. 'What does it mean when you do three?'

Squeeze, squeeze, squeeze.

Norton pondered. 'Let's see – you answer yes or no. Would three squeezes mean you can't answer yes or no?'

Squeeze.

'So three means either you don't know the answer or you can't phrase it as a yes or no?'

Squeeze.

'When I ask you a non-yes-no question, the answer has to be three squeezes?'

Squeeze, squeeze.

Two? What did that mean? It was 'No', but was it for the answer to a non-yes-no question having to be three squeezes? Norton pondered, then saw what he had missed. 'When I ask you a question whose answer is a number, then your squeezes indicate the number?'

Squeeze.

'Such as: what is the product of three times seven?'

Squeeze.

Oops. 'I meant, please give me the answer to that question.'

There was a pause, then three squeezes.

'That's not the answer, ring! What happened?'

Squeeze, squeeze, squeeze.

'Oh – you mean you aren't good at maths?'

SQUEEZE!

Norton smiled. 'We all have our weaknesses. No shame in that! But you can count?'

Squeeze.

'How many fingers do I have?'

There were ten squeezes.

Norton smiled again. 'Ring, I think I understand you now! Have you other properties?'

Squeeze.

'But you can't tell me outright what they are?'

Squeeze.

'But if I guess, you'll tell me?'

Squeeze.

'Very good!' Norton pondered again. Twenty Questions had never been his best game, but he was sure he could get the information he wanted, given unlimited questions. This was exciting!

Then Orlene reappeared, and he had to stop.

'Well, I'm not pregnant yet,' she said. 'Despite your efforts. I don't know whether to be disappointed or relieved. The doctor will see you next.'

'Me?' he asked, startled.

53

Squeeze.

That startled him again. Apparently, now that he had evoked the ring, it answered any questions it heard.

'To make sure you're fertile,' Orlene said.

'Oh.' Of course that would be a requirement of the ghost-bride's consort. Suppose he were infertile? That might be the end of their relationship.

'Go on in,' she said. 'She's waiting for you.'

'*She?*'

Squeeze.

Orlene smiled. 'You don't think I'd trust this to a male doctor, do you?'

'But I'd rather see a male!'

'Too bad,' she said wickedly. She leaned forward and kissed him briefly on the lips. 'Enjoy yourself.'

'Yeah, sure,' he agreed, disgruntled.

The doctor was a stern, middle-aged woman. 'Strip, son.'

'Look, I – '

She cracked a cold smile. 'Would you prefer to have a male orderly present to safeguard your virtue?'

'Oh, no, thanks. But – '

'This is routine. Believe me, young man, I've seen it before.'

Surely true! Norton did not consider himself, in his latening thirties, as young, but didn't care to make an issue of that at the moment. He bowed to necessity and stripped to his trunks.

She ran him through the normal paces, checking his temperature, blood pressure, ears, eyes, tongue, muscle tone, and whatever else her instruments were set for. Then came the awkward part. 'Now the trunks, please.'

He clenched his teeth and obeyed. After all, women had to suffer examination by male doctors; this could be considered turnabout. She hooked a finger into his crotch. 'Cough.'

He coughed, and repeated it for the other side.

Then she donned a plastic glove. 'Bend over, son. Put your hands against the support.'

'Don't you have some more modern way to – ?'

'It's much more fun this way,' she assured him.

He obeyed instructions again, and she greased her glove and did what doctors always did to men, physically. 'Hey!'

'Hold still. I'm securing the specimen.'

Evidently so. In a moment she took a glass smear off to her lab, and he was permitted to clean off the grease and redress. All this indignity just to verify –

'Ring,' he asked, suffering a belated inspiration, 'am I fertile?'

Squeeze.

To think of the awkwardness he could have spared himself! But the doctor probably wouldn't have believed the ring.

As it turned out, the ring was correct; he was fertile. Then he wondered how the ring had known. The fact that it could respond to a person's questions did not guarantee that it was omniscient. Magic came in many forms and degrees.

He rejoined Orlene, who was suppressing a smirk. 'You knew I was fertile!' he accused her.

'Of course. Otherwise you wouldn't have glowed.'

'Then why did you send me in to the doctor?'

She tried valiantly to contain it, but her giggle managed to escape. Why, indeed! Even nice girls liked to turn the tables on men on occasion. He would find a way to get even.

They returned to the whirl of activities, including more efforts to complete the ghost's mission. It was another week before Norton had a moment to question the ring again. By then he had figured out how to make his questions count. Orlene was taking an old-fashioned bubble bath. The estate had sonic showers for each bedroom, but there was something about bubbles and bathing that delighted women. Actually, he wouldn't have minded taking one himself, but his masculine image forbade it.

Norton was theoretically watching a news programme on holo, but he tuned that out mentally and talked to the ring instead.

'Parliamentary procedure,' the holo announcer was saying,

his head appearing to be right in the room, talking directly to Norton. 'The Satanic forces admit they don't have the votes to override the expected veto this time, but they hope to show substantial strength. Any break in the ranks of – '

'Ring, what shall I call you?' Norton asked. 'Do you have a name?'

Squeeze, squeeze.

'Would you like one?'

Squeeze.

'Then suppose I make up a name? You are my Snake Ring; I'll call you Sning, for SNake rING. How's that?'

SQUEEZE! Evidently the ring was enthusiastic.

'Good enough, Sning. Are you of Evil Magic?'

Squeeze, squeeze.

'Good Magic?'

Squeeze.

The ring could be lying, for Evil lied, but he didn't think so. Orlene would never have sought an evil artifact. That meant he could trust it.

It? 'Um, Sning, are you male or female?'

Squeeze, squeeze, squeeze.

'Sorry. I'll rephrase that. Male?'

Squeeze.

'Okay, you're a he. Now, I believe you said you have other abilities?'

Squeeze.

He zeroed in on the answer. 'What else you have – is it something you do or something you are? Do?' Squeeze. 'Are?' Squeeze. 'So it's both?' Squeeze. This sounded good! 'Are you animate or inanimate?' Again he got yes to both. 'You can change?' Squeeze. 'When I ask you to?' Squeeze. 'In fact,' he concluded triumphantly, 'you can be a live snake!' Squeeze.

Now he had to figure out what advantage this might be to the owner of the ring. In due course he established that Sning could come alive, slither off his finger – all he had ever had to do was ask Sning to come off, and removal would have been easy; he had stupidly tried force instead – scout the local territory, return, and report via squeezes what was going on.

Norton pondered only momentarily before grinning wickedly. 'Go scout Orlene,' he ordered. 'Very closely.'

The ring turned a brighter green, slid off his finger, dropped to the floor, and slithered rapidly towards the bathroom. Sning, extended, was only five or six inches long, but lively enough.

A minute passed. Then there was a scream. A few seconds later Sning zipped back, trailing some bubble froth. Norton put down his hand, and the tiny snake wrapped around his finger and went metallic.

'She saw you?'

A wet squeeze.

'Close?'

Squeeze.

'She screamed?'

Squeeze.

'And threw bubbles at you?'

Squeeze.

'Anything else to report?'

At this point Orlene appeared, half-clothed in bubbles. 'Don't you dare!' she snapped at the ring.

Norton laughed, his revenge complete – until she pounced on him, glistening wet and slippery, and doused his hair with bubbles. 'So you found out how to use the ring!' she exclaimed severely. 'I gave you too much time to yourself!' She jammed bubbles in his eyes, but they were the non sting kind. 'Send him after me again, and I'll drown you both in bubbles!' She stalked off, leaving a trail of dying bubbles.

'I only wish it could have been that female doctor,' Norton muttered rebelliously.

One other thing he learned about Sning: he was poisonous. His fangs were tiny, of course, but his venom was potent. A single bite could not kill a creature the size of a man, but could make him very sick for several hours, so that he might think he was dying. Sning would bite on order, but then would require a day to restock his poison.

'That's all right,' Norton said. 'I have no enemies; you don't need to bite anyone for me.' But it was perhaps just as well that he had not known about Sning's poison when encountering the doctor.

Later, after Orlene had calmed down – her annoyance had been mostly because he had unravelled the secrets of the ring so quickly – he asked her where she had got it. It turned out to have been in the family for generations, passed from parent to child or from spouse to spouse.

'But then it should go to your child!' he said. 'I'm not technically your spouse.'

'It's not a technical thing,' she said. 'I – care for you, Norton. I want you to have it.'

'Then I'm glad to have it.' He kissed her.

The following month she was verified pregnant. Then she changed; her interest in entertainments diminished, and she oriented increasingly on the family-to-be. 'But don't go away, Norton,' she cautioned him. 'I need you more than ever now.'

Norton wasn't sure of that, but certainly he needed her. He hoped that after the baby was born and the estate heir established, he and Orlene could travel again. But if not, then not. He was bound to her regardless. The baby would never legally be his, but the blood was his. However unconnected officially, he still cared. He had never figured himself to be a family man before, but it seemed he was. Orlene made it clear that she continued to need his presence and support, and he was glad to comply. He was a kept man – but, like many a kept woman, he had no interest in breaking free.

Time passed, and Orlene's girth grew. Norton started handling some of the household chores, simple as they were. It was surprising how readily he had been domesticated – but it seemed the glow had spoken truly. He was good at this. And she did need him – not for the routine, but for his continuing emotional and physical support.

The ghost stayed away, to Norton's relief. His other association with magic, Sning, was entertaining for a time, but he really had no reason to spy on anyone and had no questions in pressing need of answers, so he didn't use the snake ring for much except decoration. As Orlene's condition advanced, his romantic activity with her diminished and finally ceased; she wanted nothing to interfere in any way with the developing baby. He would have liked to resume his hikes in the park, but she could no longer come along, and he didn't care to leave her alone for any extended period.

As a result, he took to viewing historical holographs. He had grown tired of contemporary entertainment programmes, but the historicals enabled him to indulge his urge to explore in time as well as space. His wanderlust was balked by his commitment to Orlene, but this was a fair sublimation. He also took holo courses in a number of subjects, improving his array of background skills. He learned the geography of the world in greater detail, and of Mars, Venus, and Mercury; he studied that of the Milky Way Galaxy itself, though, of course, most of it was well out of reach. Oh, to explore those farthest stars . . . !

In due time the baby arrived. Orlene was radiant. She had done her job; she had produced the heir. He was a robust boy who seemed to resemble Gawain more than Norton and was named Gawain II. Norton was glad for her, but felt somewhat out of sorts. His own service had now been performed, but he couldn't bring himself to leave, and Orlene didn't want him to. 'We'll start doing things again,' she promised him. 'As soon as Gaw-Two is ready for baby-sitting.'

But she didn't use any baby-sitters, human, robot, or golem. She was too attentive a mother for that. That was, of course, one reason she had been selected for the ghost marriage. She paid attention to Norton in a dutiful manner, and very sweet attention it was, but she paid more attention to the baby. She insisted on personally breastfeeding Gaw, because that was nature's way, and on washing his soiled diapers by hand, because she didn't want to risk the chemicals of mechanized washing. She wouldn't put him in the sonic shower, concerned that the sonics could injure his undeveloped nervous system. She supervised every aspect of his little life with loving concern, because that was what she deemed a good mother was for.

Norton could hardly quarrel with this; he believed in nature. Yet aspects of it bothered him. For he was largely excluded from the process; officially he had nothing to do with the baby. The comprehensive equipment of the estate went mostly unused, and he was part of the equipment. Orlene also took Gaw to visit his legal grandparents, who, she reported, exclaimed in pleased wonder at his resemblance to his ghost-father. Norton, of course, was not invited on that trip.

He sank into a pointless depression. He was glad for Orlene's success and he had known the nature of his position from the outset. But still he found it difficult to accept. He had somehow supposed that the arrival of the baby would free Orlene to be with him, Norton, as she had been before the conception; now it was apparent that the baby had pre-empted whatever attention she might have been ready to bestow on him. He wished that somehow all this could have been his to share, estate, baby, and Orlene. He had become accustomed to the luxurious lifestyle of Gawain's means and to the constant attentions of a lovely young woman. In fact, he realized, he had been spoiled. He wanted, as Orlene had said at the outset, too much.

In the midst of one such reverie, the ghost reappeared. Norton was almost glad to see him. 'Well, sport, you've had a year,' Gawain said. 'How's it going?'

'Successfully,' Norton said. 'You now have your heir.'

'Ah, yes!' Gawain was so delighted he sailed into the air. 'I can finally go to Heaven!'

Gawain was going to Heaven? Norton shrugged. 'Only you can decide that. Take a look at your son. He's sleeping in the crib in the bedroom.'

'But I can't go near Orlene.'

'She's in the kitchen now, I believe, taste testing new baby food. She wants Gaw's first solid food to be just right.'

The ghost popped out. In a few minutes he popped back, looking worried. 'He resembles me too much.'

'You object to that?'

Gawain paced the floor. 'Something I should tell you, Norton. On my travels this past year I met some interesting people.'

'Why not? I certainly have no objection, and if I did, it wouldn't matter. I like to travel myself.'

'I met some of the Incarnations.'

'The whats?'

'The Incarnations. Two of them, anyway. War and Nature.'

'I'm not sure I follow you, Gawain.'

'They are personifications of fundamental concepts or forces. There are a lot of them, but only a few major ones. They sort of supervise their functions – Well, my point is, I talked with Nature, the Green Mother Gaea, and she promised to put my essence in my heir.'

Norton wasn't sure how serious or relevant this was. 'There can't be a literal blood connection – '

'Yes, there can be – if Nature so decrees. I saw some of her power – I tell you, I wouldn't want to cross that creature! – and as a favour to me, she – '

'You mean there is a literal Incarnation of Nature, who can change – ?'

'That's exactly what I mean.'

'So Gaw-Two really is of your bloodline – by magic?'

'I think so. I didn't stick around to watch; I just took Gaea's word. She scared me some; I mean, I'm a ghost, but the things she can do, that *any* of them can do – it's a completely different kind of power.' Gawain wiped his brow, looking pale. 'But there's one aspect I forgot.'

'The baby certainly resembles you! I thought it was coincidence.'

'No. Gaea did it. I think she's the strongest of the earthly Incarnations, but I wouldn't want to cross any of them.'

Norton didn't quite believe this, but did have respect for nature. A literal Incarnation of Nature should indeed be formidable. 'So why are you worried? She delivered, didn't she?'

The ghost paced faster. Had he been solid, he would have stirred up dust from the aseptic rug. 'There's a family malady, one of those recessive things, that tends to skitter sideways across generations. My older brother died of it; that's why the estate devolved to me. It usually takes them out young – before age ten, sometimes sooner. And it's getting worse.'

'But you were taken out by a dragon!'

'An allosaur.'

'Whatever. You didn't die of the malady.'

'No. But I carry it in my genes.'

Norton began to get an ugly suspicion. 'You don't mean – ?'

'Yes. I think the baby shows the stigma.'

'But Gaw-Two is healthy! Orlene had that checked out thoroughly!'

'This malady doesn't show at birth. It's a semipsychic thing that starts as a corruption of the soul and spreads to the physical body. The victim is literally damned – to a short life and a long hereafter in Hell. A doctor wouldn't be equipped to recognize it; even in this modern age, they tend to be sceptical of the supernatural. They think they know everything and that what doesn't show on their charts doesn't exist. But – ' He shrugged wearily. Evidently he knew, or supposed he knew, the signs.

'You say it kills the victims young or not at all?' Norton asked, dismayed despite his uncertainty. 'So if you're wrong about the stigma, then Gaw will make it through without getting it later?'

'Young yes. Always. Once the stigma becomes evident to a doctor, it's way too late. It's probably too late when the baby is born; it's an incurable, nonreversible progression, like a tree rotting at the core. The victim just wastes away and dies.'

'Surely modern science or magic can – '

Gawain shook his head. 'No. They tried everything to save my brother, but he died at age seven. I was only four at the time, but I remember – ' He shook his head. 'Oh, I should have kept my finger out of the pie! I've ruined it! There will be no heir! Oh, woe, woe!' He tore his insubstantial hair.

This looked serious. But Norton had an idea. 'Maybe Sning knows.'

'Sning?'

'A friend of mine.' Norton touched the ring, to wake it, though he wasn't sure the little snake ever slept. 'Sning, go check Gaw-Two. I want to know if he's got the fateful malady that runs in Gawain's family.'

Sning came to life, slithered off his finger, and zipped across the floor. Gawain stared. 'Where did you get that? That's not part of my estate!'

'Your wife gave it to me. In return for your baby.'

The ghost shrugged. 'Oh, well. I'm nervous about reptiles now, since one killed me. Will it hurt the baby?'

'No. Sning will just check.'

In a moment Sning came back. Norton put his hand down and the snake curled back into ring form. 'Does Gaw have the malady?' Norton asked.

Squeeze.

Norton felt cold. 'You're sure?'

Squeeze.

'How long will he live?' How many years?'

Squeeze.

'Only one year?' Norton asked, appalled.

Squeeze.

'It says only one year?' Gawain demanded tightly.

'That's what he says,' Norton agreed heavily. 'Of course, Sning could be wrong. He's not good at maths.'

'No, it's not wrong. I saw the stigma. It doesn't matter whether it's one year or seven; it's inevitable.' The ghost paced in another ragged circle. 'That Green Mother! She must have known! No wonder she granted me that "favour" so readily!'

'These Incarnations you describe – are they evil creatures?'

'Well, Satan is the Incarnation of Evil. But God is the Incarnation of Good. Most are neutral, though I think they favour God, or at least the existing order. But Nature – Gaea, the Earth-Mother – if you cross her, she's real trouble, and you don't always know when you cross her. She can be nice, real nice, but she can be real mean too. Oh, she's cost me everything!'

Norton didn't comment. It seemed to him that even if a personified Nature existed, it would be hard for her to keep track of every detail of the heredity of every baby born on Earth. It had probably been an oversight. But Gawain did not seem to be in any mood at the moment to concede that.

'We should have this verified medically,' Norton said after a pause. 'Even though this may be beyond medical competence. There are always breakthroughs, so that what is terminal in one generation becomes curable in the next. Can you direct the estate doctor to investigate your brother's history and compare symptoms?'

'I'd better,' Gawain agreed glumly. 'But you'll have to tell Orlene.'

'The doctor can do that.'

'Sure – his way. Look, Norton, I may be crude, but even I can see that's no good. Some of those doctors get their kicks needling people. Better it be done your way.'

Norton thought of the doctor who had tested him for fertility. He sighed. 'Yes.'

The ghost vanished. With dread in his soul, Norton went to tell Orlene.

First she refused to believe it. But when the estate doctor conducted his investigation, using as thorough a programme of scientific and magical tests as existed, guided by the case histories of others in the family, and verified the condition, Orlene had to believe. Then she was angry – at Gawain, Nature, Norton, herself – everything. She concocted desperate schemes to undo the damage, to bargain for her baby's life, to arrange somehow divine intervention to save Gaw-Two. But, of course, all this came to nothing, and she sank into a terrible depression. Nothing could console her.

Norton was helpless, as the baby's health declined. Gawain had been right; the malady had become worse in recent generations, and its course was savage. He could not comfort Orlene, for now it was apparent that her love for Norton was definitely secondary to her love for the baby. He could only accept her as she was, the perfect mother rather than the perfect partner. Gawain the Ghost disappeared.

The end came with seeming suddenness, though most of a year had passed since the baby's birth. Orlene was sitting, garbed in black, by the crib where the failing infant lay. She was only a shadow of her former self, looking almost as wasted as Gaw-Two. Both science and magic had failed; all they could do was leave the baby alone. It was a death watch.

Death came, personified. He was a hooded figure garbed in black. Orlene saw him first, issued a stifled scream, and flung her emaciated arms protectively about her baby. The dark intruder paused – and now Norton was able to perceive him more clearly. At first Death had been no more than a shadow, but now he was solid.

'Must you do this?' Norton demanded of the figure. 'Who are you, that you bring such grief?'

The figure turned to face him. Under his hood was a skull, bare of hair or skin or flesh. His eyes were hollow squares. 'I regret the necessity,' he said, his voice oddly soft. 'I am Thanatos, and it is my duty to collect the souls of those who expire in balance.'

'You are – the Incarnation of Death?'

'I am.'

'And you get your kicks from stealing innocent babies?'

Thanatos' dark hood turned towards Orlene, then towards the crib, and finally back to face Norton. He drew back one sleeve to expose a heavy black watch. One skeletal finger touched that timepiece. 'Come with me a few minutes, mortal, and we shall talk.'

Norton experienced a chilling awe of this sombre figure. He had not believed in the so-called Incarnations, despite the ghost's assurances, except possibly as mock presentations. Now conviction was growing. Thanatos was no joke; neither was he callous or indifferent.

They walked out of the room. Orlene did not move. She stood by the crib, her thin arms extended in a futile gesture of protection. Her face was drawn, her hair dull, with only her eyes still large and beautiful. She did not even breathe. Time seemed to have halted.

Outside the apartment, in the hall, a gallant pale horse stood. Somehow this did not seem surprising. Norton got up behind Thanatos on the horse. Then the horse leaped.

They passed through the levels of the city as if these were holograph images. Halls, apartments, service areas – all shot past like so many segments of a cutaway dollshouse as the horse sailed up. In a moment they reached the park at the surface. The animal's gleaming hooves landed without jarring, and now they were riding through the forest.

They came to a glade where the sun angled warmly down, and the horse halted and the two riders dismounted. The horse fell to grazing while Thanatos and Norton sat on a fallen log and talked. Somehow it no longer seemed strange to be talking with a skeleton in a cloak.

'I wish to explain about the baby,' Thanatos said. 'He is not innocent, odd as that may appear to you. He is in balance. Do you comprehend the term?'

'Balance? Not the way you must intend it. Do you weigh him?'

Perhaps the skull-face smiled; it was hard to tell, through the fleshless grin it always had. 'In my fashion. I have devices with which to measure souls, determining whether the accumulated evil over-balances the good. If the balance favours good, that soul is sent to Heaven; if evil, Hell. A person really does determine the nature of his afterlife by the nature of his life, by exercizing his free will. But some souls are in perfect balance between good and evil at the time of the client's demise, and these must remain in Purgatory.'

'You mean there really are places called Heaven, Hell, and Purgatory? I thought they were mere constructs of human imagination.'

'That too,' Thanatos agreed. 'They are not precisely places so much as states of being. They exist for our culture, as do the several Incarnations, for here there is sufficient belief in them. In other cultures, other frameworks exist. I have very few clients in those cultures where other beliefs obtain.'

'But *I* never believed in Heaven, Hell, or Incarnations!' Norton said.

'Not consciously, perhaps. Do you believe in Good, Evil, and personal choice?'

Telling point! 'The baby – how can there be evil on his soul? He has not harmed anyone. In fact, he's a victim of circumstances manipulated by others.'

'True. Gaea is very sorry about that; she had not been paying full attention, so her gift to Gawain was flawed. By the time she discovered that, it was too late for her to correct it. Ge must obey Ge's laws, too.'

'Gaea – Ge – you mean Mother Nature?'

'The Green Earth-Mother, yes. She is extremely powerful, but also extremely busy. She thought it a simple favour to one who was trying to do better in death than he had done in life, and she did not look deeply. Even Incarnations make errors – and such errors can be worse than those of mortals.'

'This error destroyed a man's line!' Norton cried.

'Gawain will be given a second chance,' Thanatos said. 'Gaea has interceded with Clotho for that. This is her manner of apology.'

'The baby will be cured?'

'No. That case is lost. Gawain will have the opportunity to remarry, more successfully.'

Norton felt another chill. 'Remarry? He's going to divorce Orlene?'

'No.'

'She'll bear another baby for him? But why, then, should he remarry?'

'Orlene will have no other baby. This is the major portion of this first baby's accumulation of evil – responsibility for his mother's untimely demise.'

'His mother's demise!' Norton repeated, shocked.

'I regret to inform you of this. But it will be easier for you if you understand. You bear no share of the guilt for this disaster. The blame is the baby's.'

'But the baby has done nothing!'

'The baby is about to die. That destroys the mother.'

'But the baby didn't choose to die!'

'In this case, I regret, the sin of the father is visited on the son. Had Gaea not interfered, the baby would have been healthy. You are of excellent genetic stock.'

'Oh, certainly,' Norton agreed. 'My family has always been healthy. But still – this transferral of guilt – *I* was the one who sired the baby! I had a dream – had I not – '

'I do not profess to agree with every aspect of the system,' Thanatos said gently. 'I only assure you that it is so. You are blameless, in the case of the son and the case of the mother. You must understand that, while the fate of the baby is in doubt, that of the mother is not; she will proceed directly to Heaven. She is a good woman, as pure in her distress as she was in her happiness, and insufficient evil attaches to her for the manner of her demise to deny her her destiny. I will not be present for her; you will be. I hope your knowledge of the full situation will abate your discomfort. You are a good man and can have a good life, if you can pass this crisis without being corrupted.'

'The concern of Death for my welfare is touching,' Norton

said bitterly. 'You tell me my – Gawain's baby must die, and the woman I love must die, but I should ignore all that and enjoy myself? Why do you bother?'

'Because I dislike unnecessary pain,' Thanatos replied seriously. 'Death is a necessary thing and it comes to all living creatures in its proper time; it is right that this be so, for a proper death is the greatest gift to follow a proper life, but the manner of its occurrence differs. I prefer that the transition be accomplished with as little unpleasantness as possible and that no extraordinary measures be taken either to extend the agony of demise or to shorten the natural term decreed by Atropos.'

'Atropos?'

'An aspect of Fate, who is another Incarnation. Atropos cuts the threads of life. When a person dies, the primary burden always falls on the living; therefore much of my own concern is with the living, as it is with you. I feel compassion for mortals, for their lot is often difficult.'

'Compassion!' Norton exclaimed.

'I realize this is difficult for you to understand or accept, but it is so.'

Norton stared into the hooded skull-face and discovered that he believed. This Death-spectre, Thanatos, really did care. Thanatos was trying to help Norton bear what it seemed had to be borne. 'That's all? You use your valuable time just to ease my concern?'

'No time is passing,' Thanatos said. He lifted his arm, showing the solid black watch. 'I used the Deathwatch to suspend time so that I could converse with you at ease.'

'Thank you,' Norton said, finding it simplest to accept this additional incredibility. He remembered how Orlene had frozen in place and he saw now that nothing in the forest moved, except themselves and the horse. Even the clouds were frozen in the sky, and the shadows had not budged. Truly, a supernatural power was in operation! 'Must be nice, having a device like that. To control time itself, at need.'

'You have a similar artifact,' Thanatos said. 'That may be the other reason I paused for you.'

'Other reason? What is the *first* reason?'

'The fact that you were able to perceive me. Few people not directly involved with death can sense my presence.'

'I love Orlene!' Norton said. 'Anything that affects her welfare affects mine!'

'Demonstrably true. And so you saw me – and I saw your ring.'

Norton glanced at his left hand. 'Oh, Sning. Orlene gave him to me.'

'Excellent magic can be incorporated in small things,' Thanatos said. 'Sning, as you call him, is of demonic origin, and almost as old as Eternity.'

'But he's not evil! How can he be a demon?'

'Demons, like people, differ. He is good – as long as he remains bound to the service of Good. You are fortunate to command his loyalty.'

This turn of conversation was so surprising that it distracted Norton from the horror of the main topic. 'Sning,' he asked the ring, 'is Thanatos genuine?'

Squeeze, squeeze, squeeze.

'How can you verify this? Do you need to touch him?'

Squeeze.

'You object?' he asked the spectre.

Thanatos shook his skull, no.

'Do it, then, Sning.'

Sning slithered off Norton's finger, into his palm, and towards the hooded figure. Thanatos pulled at the bone fingers of his left hand, and they slid off – in the form of a glove. Beneath it was a human hand, fully fleshed, complete with a smidgeon of dirt under the nails. He extended this hand, and Sning touched it with his tongue. Then the little snake curled back around Norton's finger, while Thanatos donned his glove and the hand became bone again. When in place, the glove did not show at all; the hand seemed to be genuinely fleshless, and Norton was sure it would feel that way.

'He's genuine?' Norton asked Sning again.

Squeeze.

'And all that he tells me is true?'

Squeeze.

'You are a good demon?'

Squeeze.

It was enough. 'You have amazed me,' Norton said to Thanatos. 'I did not believe in you, but now I do. I appreciate your courtesy – but I'm going to try to save Orlene.'

'Naturally. It is your way. The world is better for your concern.' Thanatos stood and gravely extended his hand.

Bemused, Norton stood also, accepting the hand. It did indeed feel like bare bones.

'Mortis!' Thanatos called. The magnificent stallion trotted back, and they mounted. Then the animal ran a short distance and plunged down through the ground and the occupied levels of the city. This time Norton could see that all the people there were as still as statues. One, in a rec-room, was caught in mid-leap, hovering half a foot above the floor. Time was indeed frozen.

All by the mere touch of a bone finger on a Deathwatch! What dreadful power this Incarnation possessed, to be thus casually employed for the sake of a private interview. If this was an adjunct to Death, what power did the Incarnation of Time possess? Norton's imagination failed.

They landed on the floor of Gawain's level, dismounted, and re-entered the apartment. Orlene remained frozen by the baby. Thanatos reached again for his watch.

'Uh, thanks,' Norton said, somewhat awkwardly. He was not resigned to what was happening, but he no longer blamed Thanatos.

The sombre figure nodded. Then time resumed.

Thanatos stepped to the crib and reached for the baby. Orlene stared at him and screamed: 'No! No! Go away, Death! You shall not have him!'

71

Thanatos paused. 'He is in pain. I will relieve him of that.'

'No! We have medicine!' She shoved at Thanatos, but her hands passed through him without resistance, as if he were a ghost. He had been solid for Norton, but not for her.

'There is a time to die, and his time has come,' Thanatos said sadly. 'You would not want him to suffer longer.' He reached down and drew out the baby's soul, like translucent tissue. Gaw-Two's laboured breathing stopped and he relaxed, looking strangely comfortable in death. His travail was over.

Orlene sank to the floor in a faint.

Thanatos faced Norton again. 'I regret,' he repeated. 'Yet it is a necessary thing I do.' He folded the soul and put it in a black bag he had brought forth. He walked out.

Norton felt numb. He went to Orlene and lifted her to the couch. She felt horribly light; she had lost even more weight than he had thought. This ordeal was destroying her!

Then he used the phone. 'There has been a natural death,' he told the face that came on the screen. 'Please send appropriate service to this unit.'

The girl nodded. This was routine to her; she did not feel the horror of it. He held the connection long enough for her to get a fix on the address, then disconnected. He went to attend to Orlene.

Now, he knew, came the hard part. He was numb, but not insensitive. What would he do when she woke?

She woke, and he did it. He told her the baby was gone. This was not the occasion for euphemism.

'I know it, Norton,' she said. 'Please excuse me. I have some things to attend to.' She went to the bedroom.

Was that all? He could hardly believe it!

She was that way for several days, calmly going about her business. Norton did not know what to make of it. She had been so desperate and, now that the worst had happened, was so composed. Had Thanatos misjudged her? Perhaps, after a suitable period, the two of them could enjoy each other's

72

company again and generate another baby, a healthy one, for the estate. Slowly, Norton's hope strengthened.

Then, ten days after the death of the baby, when Orlene had set all her affairs in proper order, including careful instructions for the disposition of her few individual belongings and her body so that there would be no awkwardness, she took poison. Norton found her slumped at the piano and knew as he saw her that it was too late, that her last note had been played. She had, of course, arranged it that way. She had not even said good-bye – and in that she had not been cruel but sensible, knowing he never would have let her do it, had he known.

4

Chronos

Orlene had not truly loved him, Norton now knew. She had not been free to, so she had transferred it all to the baby. She had loved Gaw-Two – nothing else. Norton had been a means to the end of the accomplishment of her contract and good company along the way. Perhaps she had thought she loved him, but now the truth was shown. Had she loved him, she would not have left him like this.

It was ironic, he thought, how she had used her magic perception, the glow, to determine the best prospect for a consort – and then been defeated by a problem in another area. The liability had not been in her consort, but in her husband, who had interfered with the process and subverted it, with the best of intentions. And perhaps the liability had also been in Orlene herself, for she had proved unable to survive the first great disappointment. Another woman would have cried and suffered, then gone on to conceive another baby, one who would redeem the effort and restore love and happiness.

Norton himself had been an almost coincidental figure, as intended by the ghost – and now was in love with a dead woman. What recourse did he have?

He doused his fire and retreated to the lean-to he had made from branches and leaves. He lay and looked out into the dusk. He was back in his preferred lifestyle, hiking and camping alone, but now it lacked the joy it had offered before. He had no immediate financial problem, thanks to the behest Orlene had made. She had indeed been meticulous, taking care of everything, before she died. Her note had recognized the service Norton had performed, pointed out that the loss of the heir had been no fault of his, and requested that he be

74

given limited credit in the account of the estate for life. Gawain the Ghost had authenticated the bequest, and the credit had been granted. Though Norton used it sparingly, he did find it helpful. It was handy to replenish supplies for hiking, as Orlene had intended – if she had not loved him, she had certainly been very fond of him – and when he drew on the account, this gave him a poignant awareness of her. How could he turn down her little gift, her tangible token of affection?

A figure appeared before him. 'At last I have found you!' Gawain said. 'I knew if I searched the parks long enough, I'd succeed.'

'Go away.' Norton muttered, shutting his eyes.

'Of course, the credit account helped,' the ghost continued blithely. 'That gave me the latest update on your whereabouts. But there are an awful lot of trees to check through! It would have helped if you'd left a trail – but you're too good a woodsman for that. You don't litter, you don't pollute, you don't waste – I'm lucky I caught the cloud of steam from your doused fire, or I would have passed you by again.'

'Be my guest,' Norton mumbled, trying to block his ears. 'Pass me by again.'

'You see, I've got another proposition for you,' the ghost went on, refusing to be annoyed. 'I liked the way you performed on the last.'

Norton's eyes snapped open. 'Damn it, I dreamed I would destroy her – and I did! My vision was correct. I planted the baby whose death shattered her life! Don't thank me for that!'

'You know that's not so,' Gawain said reasonably. 'You did your job. My interference was responsible. I've learned my lesson; I'll keep my finger out of the next pie.'

'How can you?' Norton demanded, annoyed by the metaphor. Pie, indeed! 'She's dead! You may not have loved her, but I did, and now she's gone.'

'Well, you see, her death has freed me to marry again,' Gawain said. 'Now I can find another woman, or my folks will, and she can bear my heir. I don't know who she'll be, but I can guarantee she'll be attractive, talented, and intelligent – your kind of woman, Norton! – and will do what my folks tell her to. So I want you to return to the estate and wait for her, and to – '

Norton was appalled. 'To service another woman? Don't you understand? I *loved* Orlene! I never want any woman but her!'

'Well, sure, and I appreciate your loyalty,' the ghost said, disconcerted. 'But it might be good therapy for you to – '

'No!'

'I know you're a good man. That's why I want you for this. I know you'll produce a good baby and not try to despoil the estate.'

Norton shut his eyes again. 'Go away. Find some other sucker.'

'You know what the real problem was? I wanted to be sure the baby was male. That's why I sought Gaea. Okay, I said I'd learned my lesson. You can sire a female, that's okay, I won't interfere – I'll just wait for the next and you can keep the girl if you want her. It's the boy I must have. I absolutely guarantee not to mess the pudding this time!'

'GET OUT OF HERE!'

The ghost sighed. 'I'll go, but I'll be back.'

When Norton opened his eyes, Gawain was gone. But it took Norton a long time to get to sleep. His heart still hurt, though it had been two months since Orlene's death.

After another two months, Gawain came to him again, catching him in another forest park. All the major cities were parked on top in the twenty-first century; it was one of man's necessary compromises with nature. Some cities featured natural wildernesses; others had magic gardens or alien landscapes. Many stocked exotic creatures in special habitats. From space, it was hard to tell the planet Earth was still inhabited by man – and that, Norton felt, was the way it should be.

The ghost fell in beside him as he walked. 'I've got her, Norton,' Gawain said without preamble. 'Lovely beyond belief! Sexy as a woman can be without driving every nearby man to madness. Name's Lila. Just come see her, and you'll – '

'Go away,' Norton said. 'I told you before, I'm not interested in any other woman.'

'But you can't go on moping forever! It's been four months, and you're a healthy, living man. You have natural urges. And Lila is ready for you; she's seen your picture. She likes you, Norton! In her arms you'll forget – '

Norton swung his fist furiously through Gawain's body. 'Can't you understand? I don't *want* to forget Orlene! I love her! I always will!'

'This isn't healthy, Norton,' the ghost remonstrated. 'Your body's fine, but your mind is in an unreasonable depression. I know how it is; I would be in a funk for days after I let a dragon escape. It would really be better if – '

'Never!' Norton cried. 'Go find another stud! I'm out of this!'

Gawain shook his head. 'You don't know what you're missing. Lila, when she walks – '

'Away! Begone, foul spirit!'

Daunted at last, the ghost vanished.

But every month or so, Gawain returned, insisting on pestering Norton with reports. Another man had been found – Lila had accepted him – she had not been given a choice – the two were going at it like professionals – Lila was pregnant – the man had skipped town, good riddance! – the fetus seemed to be developing normally – the heir seemed assured.

Meanwhile, Gawain insisted on giving Norton the lessons in dragon fighting he had originally promised. Norton finally relented to that extent. It was evident that the ghost was trying diligently to stay away from his second wife and incipient baby, observing but not interfering in any way, but still lacked confidence to depart this world entirely. Thus he used

Norton as a companion to keep himself out of mischief. Too many fingers spoiled the pie. So Norton studied dragon slaying, though he never expected to make use of this skill.

'First you have to have a good sword,' Gawain said. 'Preferably an enchanted-one, but it's best to learn on a mundane one, to be sure you have the basic skill. My old sword will be excellent, and I'm sure the estate will release it to you.'

'I don't want a sword!' Norton protested. But in the end he had to concede it necessary for this training and he accepted Gawain's sword, which was shipped to the park for him. The weapon was enchanted, but they pretended it wasn't, and he made progress in handling it and developing stamina.

The months passed, and Norton's depression eased without entirely dissipating, like a mountain slowly weathering down. There was indeed pleasure in companionship, even that of a ghost, and in activity, even practice in swordplay. And at one point the sword was useful: two anti-wilderness thugs, enraged by Norton's stern challenge to their despoilment of the park – they had not only littered, they had cut a live sapling down – attacked him with their knives and were brought up short when Norton calmly drew his sword and demonstrated his growing proficiency with it. He cut a lock of hair off each, using swings that somehow seemed to be heading for their necks, and they fled, fearing that an ear or a nose would be next. Norton was not generally a violent man, but he did indeed feel like a hero in that instance. If there was one thing that really set him off, it was abuse of the wilderness; there was so little of it remaining, and what there was, was so carefully cultivated. He deposited the locks of hair in the police box; the authorities would analyse it and have the identities of the culprits in an hour. Unless this happened to be a first offence, which was doubtful considering their attitude, they would be arrested and penalized before the day was out. A wilderness-phobia-spell or litter-eating-enchantment was just the punishment that type needed!

Gawain, indulging in her periodic checks on the status of his heir, reported in due course that Lila had birthed a fine, healthy daughter. Not as good as a son, of course, but at least it was proof that this pie had been finger-free. 'And the next should be a boy, who shall inherit the estate. Primogenitor, you know – the first-born male.'

Norton shrugged. This really wasn't his business.

'There's no man on the estate now,' Gawain said as if just thinking of it. 'You could still go and – you know.'

'No,' Norton said, but without the force of his prior refusals. After all, over a year had passed, and there was only so much wilderness to discover. The pleasures of a comfortable apartment and a voluptuous woman . . .

Gawain pounced on his hesitation with the practised expertise of a warrior. 'At least come see her! I swear, you never saw architecture like hers! And she's a passionate creature, too. She gets bored, you know, alone on the estate.'

'But there are surely other men – '

'Ah, but none as good as you, Norton! I really would prefer to have my son sired by you! He may grow up to protect the wilderness . . .'

Norton wavered and lost. 'All right.'

They took the nearest elevator to the basement, then matter-mitted to the city of Gawain's estate. Matter-mission was not cheap transport, but the estate was paying for it. Then they took the belts to the address. Soon they were there. It was just as Norton remembered it; the mere sight of the door was a shock to his system. Here he had first seen Orlene . . .

'Oh,' Gawain said apologetically. 'I can't – '

'I remember. You can't share a room with her. She can't see or hear you, and may doubt you exist.' Norton wondered what power determined the ghost's imperceptibility. Could the woman have seen him before she married him? Would he have vanished the moment she said, 'I do'? What was the point in this loss of awareness? The supernatural did not seem to make a great deal of sense at times.

He knocked on the door, feeling like a teenage suitor, though he was now nearing forty. In a moment its viewer scanned him; then it opened. Lila stood there. 'Oh, you're Norton!' she exclaimed breathily. 'I know you from your picture!'

Norton looked at her. Voluptuous she was indeed. Too much so; she had evidently put on weight during her pregnancy and not bothered to take it off after. Now she reminded him somewhat of a cow. Orlene had always been trim, even during her gravid period; she had not deposited flab on her thighs or chin. Lila had. She was still voluptuous rather than fat, but before long that distinction would become academic.

But it was more than that. Lila, in his eyes, was an impostor here. He knew she was legitimate; she had done the job she was supposed to do. She had succeeded where Orlene had failed, delivering a fully healthy baby, and she deserved credit. But his emotion refused to concede that. He could not touch this woman without feeling unfaithful to Orlene.

Sick at heart, he turned away. He knew he would never return here.

He was on Mars when Gawain caught up to him again. He was trekking across the cold, red sands, wearing a planet-suit and respirator. The ghost fell in beside him, as he had done in the park on Earth. Gawain, of course, needed no respirator; he was in shirt sleeves. At times Norton wondered about that, too. Surely Gawain had been killed in armour; why wasn't he still wearing that? Did ghosts have phantom wardrobes? Could they change clothing at will? Evidently so.

'There's really not much to see here,' Gawain said. 'Just sand, sand, and more sand. Why are you here?'

'Because it's far from Earth,' Norton replied crossly. 'I like to see new things.'

'And it makes it harder for me to find you?'

'That, too.'

'I bet you thought I wouldn't be able to get here, since magic is not an interplanetary force.'

'True.'

'But you forgot I have access to the estate matter-mitter. It was science, not magic, that brought me here.'

'Live and learn.'

'And now I have found you again.'

'So I noticed. Now go away.'

'Not quite yet.'

'Gawain, you have your baby! If there's no male heir, a female qualifies. Why don't you retire to Heaven now?'

'Well, actually, Heaven is not quite assured.'

'Wherever. It can't be worse than impotence on Earth, can it?'

Gawain shrugged. 'Maybe, maybe not. But I'm not going yet, because my business on Earth isn't quite finished. I need a male heir. This is not a legal matter, it's personal.'

'Then don't waste your energy with me! Go find another bull for your cow.'

'Oh, I have, I have! But these things take time.'

'You mean I'm stuck with you for another nine months?'

'Not exactly. But I do feel responsible for you.'

'You – for me?'

'Yes, me for you. After all, I got you into this. I brought you to Orlene and I messed with the heir's bloodline. So I set you up and pulled you down. I can't blame you for being upset.'

'That's over now,' Norton said grimly. 'You meant no harm.'

'Still, it's a burden on my soul.'

'How can a ghost have a burden on his soul? I thought a ghost *was* a soul.'

'Yes. So the burden has strong leverage. I feel the weight of it, pulling me down towards Hell.'

'But you were destined for Heaven!'

'Yes, I was, at the time of my death,' Gawain agreed. 'But the balance was close. You know the bit; it's as easy for a rope to pass through the eye of a needle as for a rich man to go to Heaven. Because I was a man of honour, even though my employment was not the kind you approve, I was more good than evil – barely. Then when I messed up your life, my balance shifted to negative.'

'I thought a person's earthly account was fixed at the moment of death. After all, if damned souls could change their status after death, they'd all be scrambling to tilt themselves back towards Heaven, after sinning freely in life.'

'You're right; it's fixed at death,' Gawain agreed. 'Or at least the initial setting is fixed; those who go to Hell will eventually win their way to Heaven, but they have a few centuries or millennia of misery before they expiate their sins sufficiently. A dead man has only a millionth of the leverage a live man has; that's why it's so much better to set your course correctly in life. But ghosts are borderline cases, as are the Incarnations. They aren't yet completely committed to Heaven or Hell, you see. If they interfere with the affairs of the living, they must answer for it, and the charge goes on their account. That was the risk I took, trying to arrange for my heir. Most people won't risk it, which is why there are so few real ghosts around, but I'm a fool for lineage. So now I'd better undo the damage I've done to your life, or it's Hell for me, literally.'

At last Norton grasped the nature of the ghost's concern. 'I'm sorry if you are doomed to Hell, but the damage is done. If I could rejoin Orlene – I mean, if I could get to know her before any of this happened, I surely would. But that's impossible.'

'No, no, it's not!' Gawain said eagerly. 'There is a way! I knew you'd be interested. I talked to Clotho about it, and she agreed to arrange it – if you wanted.'

'Arrange what?'

Now the ghost was diffident. 'Well, I assumed you'd like to travel back to see Orlene, before I married her. Of course, there is a small complication – '

'I don't trust your small complications!'

'But it's an opportunity that comes only once in a lifetime! What future on Earth have you got, anyway?'

'Not much,' Norton admitted. 'That's why I'm touring Mars.'

'I mean, as a living man?'

Norton halted abruptly, stirring up a swirl of red dust. It settled about his boots more slowly than he was used to, because of the reduced Martian gravity. That dust could really be something in the storm season! 'My life will end?'

'Well, not exactly,' Gawain said, shuffling his feet without raising any dust.

'Maybe you'd better tell me just precisely exactly what the hell you have in mind, to save your soul from Hell.'

'Nice phrasing, that,' the ghost said uncomfortably. 'You see, I discovered there is one person, one entity, who can travel back in time, and he's just about to vacate his office. So if you get there before then, you can assume it. You're a good man; Clotho says you qualify and she should know.'

'Who is this Clotho you keep mentioning?'

'Oh, didn't I tell you? She's another aspect of Fate. There are three, you see; she's the spinner. So if you take that job, you'll have the power to travel in time and you can do anything you want, *any time* you want. You can go meet Orlene when she's a child or when she's seventeen. Maybe you can sparc her the whole problem that caused her death and live with her the rest of her life. It's all right with me; I've got Lila now and a son in the making.'

'You're talking paradox! It's impossible to change the past!'

'Not for this office. This is the one person who is immune from paradox, because he controls time.'

'What's this about an office?'

'The office of Chronos. The Incarnation of Time.'

'The Incarnation of – you mean, like Thanatos?'

'Exactly. In fact, Thanatos was the one who suggested it. He talked with you, remember. He likes you. He recommended you for the position, and the Green Mother endorsed it – I tell you, Norton, it's yours if you want it. You can be the new Chronos!'

Norton was stunned. 'What – what happened to the old Chronos?'

'Nothing bad. He's getting born, or maybe conceived – I'm not sure when it counts – so he has to step down. He'll go to Heaven; his account is in good order.'

'Getting born? But his whole life should be ahead of him!'

'No, it's behind him.'

'I don't – '

'Well, that's the complication. You see, Chronos lives backwards. He has to, to know when everything has happened – I mean, when it will happen. That's his job – to time things. So when you assume the office, you'll proceed backwards in time, until the date of your birth or whatever; then you'll have to step down, because you won't exist any more. But since you're close to forty, you have about as much life behind you as ahead of you; you'll come out even that way. Time is no office for a young man! And you'll be able to be with Orlene again! Just think of that!'

'My head is spinning! There are so many questions – '

'Well, come and take a look! If you change your mind, you don't have to take the Hourglass.'

'The Hourglass?'

'The symbol of Chronos' power. When you take that, you assume the office, till birth do you part. But we must hurry; we have a long way to go, and I promised Clotho you'd be there today.'

'Today! But I need time to think! A decision like this – I never even heard of the office of Chronos before! I – '

'You can think on the way. Come on – summon a dune-scooter; it will take too long by foot.'

Bemused, Norton obeyed. He spoke into his suit radio, and in a moment the scooter was on the way to his coordinates.

While they waited for it, Norton pondered his decision. To

live backwards – to see Orlene again, alive and happy – yet he knew it would be impossible to interact with her, for that would change history. If he went to her before she married Gawain, so that she never became the ghost-bride, then Gawain would not summon Norton to sire the heir, so Norton would never meet her and love her – paradox. It just made no sense! It was impossible. Obviously he would not be able to interact with her, but only to watch her invisibly, the way Gawain had; Norton would be no more than a ghost to her. And yet even that was tempting, as the only way he could see her at all.

They reached the nearest transport station, then matter-mitted to Mars City and from there to Earth. Gawain faded into invisibility during this part of the journey, because not everyone understood about ghosts, especially customs inspectors. But he faded back in when they were alone, continuing to direct Norton to the correct address. This, as it turned out, was in a rundown section of a declining city. There were no pleasant levels here, no wilderness park topping; just a single level of decrepit pavement and foam-concrete apartment buildings. It was the kind of place a stranger was apt to get mugged.

Sure enough, a group of young toughs spotted him and spread out to cut him off. Norton was weaponless; he had, after all, been exploring Mars until recently, and it would have been pointless to carry Gawain's enchanted sword there.

'Don't worry about it,' Gawain said. 'I'll see you through safely.'

'But you can't touch anyone!' Norton muttered.

Gawain smiled. Suddenly he was in the uniform of a riot cop, cattleprod at the ready. 'Set me up,' he murmured.

Norton caught on. 'Hey, sir,' he said loudly to his companion. 'This ain't a bust; we're just checking for draft dodgers.'

Gawain waved the prod. 'Anybody I catch is a dodger. I guarantee it. I never missed a quota yet. A few pricks on max with this and he'll confess. 'Specially if I ram it up the – here, I'll prove it! Wanna make book on whether I can net one within one minute?' He veered to head towards the biggest of the approaching toughs. 'Hey, you – c'mere! Got something to show you.' He gestured with the prod, smirking.

The tough slipped between two buildings and vanished. The others faded back warily.

Gawain brought a phantom radio to his face. 'Hey, Snorkel – spread the net; we've got some live meat here!'

Suddenly the street was empty. Norton smiled; the ghost did have his uses.

They came to a halt in a rubble-strewn vacant lot. Norton was surprised, because space was precious. Gawain looked at his watch, and that, too, surprised Norton; how could a ghost have a functioning timepiece? 'Fifteen minutes to spare; he'll be along soon.'

'Chronos?'

'Sure. He has chosen this treasured spot to pass on the Hourglass.'

'You mean this is where he was born, so this is where – ?'

'Oh, no, of course he wasn't born here! That address is far away.'

'But you said he lived backwards, so – '

'He does – and you will too. But it's not a literal retracing of his life. That would be pointless.'

'I think it's impossible! The paradox involved – '

'I told you – Incarnations are exempt from paradox. His life proceeds forward, for him; it just seems backwards to us.'

'I'm not sure I like this at all! It doesn't make sense!'

Gawain's mien became serious. 'Believe me, it does make sense; you just have to learn to appreciate the *manner* it makes sense. Now Fate has gone to some trouble to set up this excellent deal for you. Note that no one else is here to take the Hourglass. The chance of a lifetime is being handed to you on a platter – all because the Incarnations are sorry about that little mistake with the baby. They help one another out in cases like that, you see. You would be ungracious indeed to turn it down at this late hour.'

'But I never asked for it!' Norton protested. 'I'm not sure I could handle it! I know nothing about time! All this is so – I mean, why *here*?'

'Because this is where they erected a fine monument to Chronos, saviour of the world, or something like that. It's a very significant spot for him. For the office.'

Norton looked around. '*What* monument, *where*? I think we have the wrong address.'

'In the future, of course,' Gawain explained patiently. 'He comes from the future, remember. This whole region will be renovated and formed into a splendid park, dominated by the monument. People will throng to visit it. Naturally he feels close to this spot.'

Norton was becoming increasingly nervous. 'Why isn't he here, then? There can't be more than ten minutes left.'

'He's approaching from the other direction. You'll see him only at the moment of the transfer of the Hourglass.'

'From the future?' Norton asked, his brain seeming to heat with the effort of digesting this concept.

'All you have to do is take the Hourglass when you see it,' Gawain said. 'It will appear right here.' He showed where someone had marked a crude X on the packed ground. 'You'll have to handle it yourself after that, because we'll be going in different directions.'

'Different directions,' Norton felt like an idiot, unable to organize his thoughts, let alone his attitude.

'I'll continue forward,' the ghost explained. 'You'll be going back. You'll be doing your own thing. Actually, I'll probably just relax and go to Heaven, catching it while I qualify so I don't have the chance to mess up again. It doesn't make any difference; you won't see me.'

The ghost's balance would be shifted to positive by this good deed, Norton remembered. Assuming it *was* a good deed. Well, if it wasn't, Gawain would pay the price! The ghost would not have another chance, for Norton would be committed.

Assuming he took the Hourglass. He hadn't decided yet whether to do that. He didn't like to be jammed into something like this, especially when there were so many imponderables.

'Oh, but you have to,' Gawain said, guessing his thoughts. 'Believe me, Norton this is the job for you! Gaea says you're perfect for it, and Clotho says they need a man like you to – ' He broke off.

'To what?' Norton asked with abrupt suspicion.

'Look out – it's time!' Gawain was peering at the region above the X. 'I guess this is farewell, friend. May your past be happy!'

Norton looked. There was nothing over the X. 'It's not time. There's a minute to go.'

'Your watch could be off.'

'Quit avoiding the subject. Why do the Incarnations want me as Chronos?'

'Well, I'm not really in a position to know, being only a ghost – '

Norton turned and started to walk away.

'Okay, I'll tell you!' Gawain screamed. 'It's Satan, the Incarnation of Evil! He's up to something – '

'I'll go to Hell?'

'No, not you! He can't touch you without your permission – or your acquiescence, anyway. He'll send all humanity to Hell, somehow, if he isn't stopped.'

'How can *I* stop Satan? I'm only one man – '

'There it is!' Gawain cried.

This time he was correct. A tall, white-caped figure had appeared at the marked spot, bearing a bright Hourglass. So it was true! Chronos had arrived from the future. And his office was there for the taking.

The Hourglass shone like the Grail, its brightness inherent and marvellous. A thin thread of silvery sand fell from its upper segment to its lower. The upper chamber was virtually empty; in fact, in a few seconds the flow would stop, the measure completed. That process had a mesmerizing effect; there was a transcendent significance to the termination of that flow.

Norton's mind was a whirl of speculations and doubts – but though he had come to no decision, his body acted. He stepped forward, reached up, and grasped the shining Hourglass.

The figure of Chronos faded out in the fashion it had faded in. The white robe seemed to detach itself from that fading figure and cross over to Norton as he took the Hourglass. He found himself standing on the X spot, the robe coalescing about him, sinking into his body, permeating him and giving him an odd sensation of timelessness and power. Now he held the symbol of his new office – but he did not know what to do. The universe seemed frozen.

A faint whisper came to him: 'Over . . . over!'

Without thinking it out, Norton turned over the Hourglass, just as the last sand passed through the central aperture.

The new upper chamber, almost full of sand, began to spill into the nether one. The first sand touched the bottom –

And the universe changed.

5
Lachesis

It took Norton a moment to figure out the nature of the change, for it was subtle, but he did know it was horrendously significant. He remained in the vacant lot, and the other two figures remained also, and the wind still blew the flag at the top of a nearby building. All ordinary things.

Yet the two figures did not seem to be looking at him, but rather through him. He glanced down at himself and found himself solid, though surrounded by the diaphanous white robe, which seemed to be more mist than material. What was the matter with those people?

Then he realized one aspect of what bothered him: one figure was Gawain the Ghost – but who was the other? A man in a Martian hiking costume –

Himself! Standing and watching – what?

'Hi!' he said, somewhat tremulously, but the figures did not respond.

It was coming clear. This was himself – as he had been a minute ago, waiting for Chronos to appear. Himself – moving backwards in time. Evidently the former Norton, oriented towards the future, could not perceive the present Norton, oriented towards the past.

And that flag on the building – Norton could feel the wind and knew in which direction it was blowing. But the flag was extending in the opposite direction. Either the wind at the top of the building differed from the wind below – or the flag was blowing *into* the wind.

Norton fished in his pocket for a fragment of paper. He held it up to the wind. It tugged directly into the wind – the opposite of what it should have done. He let it go – and

90

it fluttered windward like a salmon forging upstream. Strange!

He stretched his arm so that his wrist slid out from the sleeve of his new white cloak and he looked at his watch. It was running backwards.

So it was true! Chronos lived backwards. The course of his life was opposite to that of the rest of the universe. The flag tugged into the wind because he was perceiving it backwards. He felt the wind going back towards its source – but that did not change its actual effect.

He could not communicate with his former self, because he was now in a different frame. People were geared to perceive things of their own frame; they simply could not relate to something outside it. He himself had not seen what there was there to see, standing on the spot marked X: himself as Chronos. So now he knew how it was. In fact, he reminded himself, that was no stranger out there; it was Norton-normal. He had followed normal time until he took the Hourglass and turned it over to start the sand of his term of office. Now he followed the new time. He could relate to the rest of the world, perceiving it clearly, because he understood it. His new life continued forwards – in reverse.

But what was he supposed to do now? Surely there was more to this job than merely existing!

His eye fell on the ring Orlene had given him. Maybe this could help. 'Sning, are you still functioning?'

Squeeze.

'That's a relief! Do you know anything about this time-reversal effect?'

Squeeze.

Excellent. Now all he needed to do was figure out the right questions. Sning's presence was an enormous comfort to him at the moment! 'Is it true that I am living backwards, so am seeing the world like a holoshow played in reverse?'

Squeeze.

'But how can I relate to normal people, then?'

Squeeze, squeeze, squeeze.

Of course, he had phrased his question improperly. '*Can* I relate to normals?'

Squeeze.

'Is there something I can do to effect this interaction? So they can relate to me, too? So they can see me?'

Squeeze.

'Does it have anything to do with the Hourglass?'

SQUEEZE!

So the Hourglass was important; that was hardly a surprise! Norton contemplated the instrument. The thin line of sand was still gently glowing, off-white in colour, a steady thread connecting top and bottom.

Very well. This flow measured time, and it was evident that, though the instrument was called an Hourglass, it actually measured his full career. He had about thirty-nine years ahead of him – behind him – until the date of his birth, when presumably the sand would run out and he would have to pass the thing on to someone who had lived before him. That much he understood and accepted now, albeit grudgingly.

But obviously there was more to this office than merely living backwards. Surely Chronos had a job to do – and surely, then, Chronos had to relate to the real world. The Hourglass enabled him to do that – if he only could figure out how.

He studied the instrument. There were no visible controls on it. He turned it over – and suffered an abrupt wrenching of his being. Hastily he turned it back, and normality was restored. What had happened?

In a moment he worked it out; if the Hourglass measured his life, reversing the instrument would reverse his life. He would be undoing what he had just been doing; he would be returning to the moment of his assumption of the office, a few minutes hence. The wrenching was because living backwards biologically was not normal; his blood would be reversing its flow, and his digestion – just so. He would lose his free will, unravelling the just-made skein – and to what point? To renege on the commitment he had made when he took the Hourglass? That was not his way! So he would not do that again! He could continue his natural course, though that was now opposite to that of the rest of the universe. He would see this office through – whatever that might mean.

'Sning, are there other ways to affect my status?' he asked the ring.

Squeeze.

'Even though there are no physical controls on the Hourglass?'

Squeeze.

Whatever would he have done without the little snake! Orlene had given him a greater gift than he had realized at the time – and there, of course, had been the earliest true indication of her love. She would always be with him while Sning was with him – and he had no intention of parting with the ring, ever.

But back to business! 'But *how*? Do I just *will* it to do what I want?'

Squeeze.

Oh. Well, he would find out. *Let me travel swiftly in time!* he thought grandly.

The sand in the Hourglass turned bright blue. The world outside became a grey void. He was travelling – somewhere. Swiftly.

Stop! he thought, alarmed.

Abruptly the scene was stationary. The sand in the Hourglass was now black.

He stood in a dusky glade. Before him was something like a large cabbage-palm, and monstrous ferns were everywhere. There were bottle-brush things, but no grass. This was definitely not familiar territory!

He walked, examining the scenery. The only really familiar thing he spied was a distant fir tree. He saw no animal life – though of course any animals would hide from a strange creature like himself, so that was not in itself abnormal. He listened, but heard no buzzing of insects. Where was he? Had he moved in space rather than in time?

'Sning, did the Hourglass malfunction?'

Squeeze, squeeze.

'It moved me in time?'

Squeeze.

'Which direction? Forward?'

Squeeze, squeeze, squeeze.

Hmm, a problem there. Had his question been imprecise? Perhaps so. Which direction was 'forward'? The way he lived, or the way the world went?

'Did it move me into the world's future?' That worried him, because it was evident that human life had been eliminated, or at least greatly restricted here, and perhaps all mammalian life too. War or other disaster?

But Sning reassured him: squeeze, squeeze.

'Into *my* future – the world's past?'

Squeeze.

Back on track! He had it now. Forward, to the Hourglass, had to be *his* forward. Since he hadn't specified direction in his thought command, the Hourglass had simply accelerated him in the direction he had been going. Instead of moving backwards at the rate of one minute per minute, or one year per year, he had moved much faster and farther. Obviously years, for the city was gone; it had not yet been built. How long had this spot been inhabited by man? Decades, surely! In fact, it could be centuries, for even the local vegetation had changed radically.

'How many years into Earth's past have I gone?'

Squeeze, squeeze, squeeze.

'That's not three years, is it?'

Squeeze.

Norton smiled. That meant yes – that it was not three years. The three squeezes had been the signal of Sning's inability to answer.

'Is the answer better expressed in centuries?'

Squeeze – squeeze, squeeze, squeeze.

That was a new one! Four squeezes, for a yes-no answer. But there had been a pause after the first. That translated to yes – cannot answer.

'Centuries are better than years – but still not enough?'

Squeeze.

He was getting better at this! 'How about millennia?'

Four squeezes, with the pause after the first.

This was getting serious. 'Units of a million years?'

Four squeezes.

Serious indeed! 'Units of a billion years?'

Squeeze, squeeze.

'So it's not a billion years back – but a lot of millions?'

Squeeze.

'How many hundred million – to the nearest unit?'

Squeeze, squeeze.

'What do you mean, "No"? That was a numbers question!'

Squeeze.

Oh. 'Two hundred million, approximately?'

Squeeze.

'The time of the dinosaurs?'

Squeeze.

'Then how come I don't see any dinosaurs? No, cancel that; like most naturalists, I have a passing interest in paleontology. This is obviously along about the Triassic period; I should have recognized it before. No grasses, no flowering plants, but plenty of palms and pines and cycads. I'll rephrase my question: are there dinosaurs here – or rather, the pre-dinosaurs, the developing lines?'

Squeeze.

'But not right at this spot. I'd see some if I walked around enough, or waited here long enough, if my appearance or smell or noise didn't keep them away?'

Squeeze.

Now Norton noticed that there was no wind, no movement

of fern or frond, not even when he brushed against them. In fact, he had no contact with them; his hand passed right through them. 'Ah, I get it – time is frozen! The way Thanatos froze it – I'm Chronos now, so I can do that trick too! I ordered the Hourglass to stop, so it stopped me – absolutely, right where I was at the moment.' He contemplated the black sand in the Hourglass. It still flowed from upper to lower chamber, measuring out his life with its silken thread of motion; *he* was not frozen, just the world. 'So black is the colour of absolute stasis – of everything except me.'

Squeeze . . . squeeze, squeeze, squeeze.

Another qualified yes. He had better run it down; Sning did not squeeze just for the fun of it. 'The world *is* in stasis?'

Four squeezes.

'The world *seems* in stasis?'

Squeeze.

Fair enough. He was way out of his own time; he couldn't go around stopping the clock of the universe incidentally. Probably Thanatos hadn't really stopped the world, either – but the appearance was as useful as the reality. Perhaps Norton was in a special state of acceleration, so that the world seemed still by comparison. He stretched out his arm to view his watch – and saw that it had stopped.

Now, wait! *He* had not stopped, and he was wearing his watch. Was it broken? He brought it close to his eyes – and found it was moving, after all, forward.

He stretched out his arm again – and the watch stopped. Experimenting, he discovered that when the watch was more than a foot out from his torso, it reflected the world's time; when it was closer, it kept his own personal time. That was a worthwhile discovery! His ambience was limited, so that he himself could reach out of it. And of course that had to be; otherwise he would be carrying chunks of the world backwards with him, and that wouldn't do. He verified by further experiment that his time frame stopped at the level of the soles of his feet and the top of his head, and spread out like an aura between; actually, the white cloak pretty well defined it.

Then he remembered that his watch had been running backwards when he had checked it before. But he had been holding it out from his body then, so that was the world's time. *His* time was forward.

'So black sand means stasis – that can affect me also, if I so choose,' he said aloud. 'Partially, anyway; my blood flow does not reverse in my hand when I reach out, but my watch does change. So it's a kind of compromise state.'

Squeeze.

'Thank you for alerting me about this, Sning. I'm awfully glad to have your advice.'

The little snake did not squeeze, but turned a darker shade of green, evidently with pleasure.

Norton reviewed another aspect. 'And when the sand is blue – that's the colour of accelerated motion in time?'

Squeeze.

'So I can tell what's going on by the colour-coding of the sand. But how can I be here at all? This is far outside my timeline! No, don't give me three squeezes; I'll figure it out in a moment. I'm here – but not solidly. I'm like a ghost here. I can't touch anything, and probably no creature can touch me or even perceive me. So it's like looking at a holo – the world is a holograph, less real for me than it seems, and it is not aware of me at all.'

He paced along the paleontological terrain. 'I can travel anywhere in time, probably, forward and back. But I can't *do* anything; it's just a visit, a sightseeing tour. Only in my own time span – the span of my living life – can I actually affect the world. Once I figure out how.'

Squeeze.

'Good enough. Let's go home now.' He concentrated. *Back to starting point – but not as fast.*

The Hourglass glowed a little more brightly. The black sand changed colour, becoming pink. The world moved.

The sun travelled across the sky, picking up speed as the sand darkened. Night came – and passed in a minute. Day and night, of course! He saw an animal, in the day, but it was gone so quickly he had only a fleeting impression of something reptilian. The creature might have taken half an hour to pass, but that would have been mere seconds to Norton. Rain came, making the herbiage sparkle momentarily.

The pace picked up. Now it was like an old-fashioned motion picture, the frames flickering; he was able to tune out the dark intervals and see the land as a continuing thing, the plants growing and aging and disappearing. The seasons passed, but there seemed to be no winter here, just a browning of some plants; this was before the day of deciduous trees. Overall, there was very little change.

Faster, he thought. The sand became a brighter red, and the world buzzed through its paces at accelerated velocity. A fir tree sprouted near him, grew in seconds to a rubust specimen, stabilized – and was abruptly gone. A bolt of lightning? Root rot? Life ended so suddenly for plants! But, of course, a century or more had passed.

A hundred million years, he discovered, was a long time, even at the rate of a century a minute; he would have to watch, at this rate, for a couple of years, his time. *Full speed*, he directed, and the greyness of impossible temporal velocity returned.

Then he remembered: he had changed his position! He had walked away from his starting point, looking at vegetation. He would land a similar distance away – perhaps in the middle of a building. In the middle of a wall!

Before he could correct his error, the world firmed. He stood in the vacant lot, on the X. The two figures remained nearby.

'But I moved!' he protested, relieved.

Squeeze, squeeze, squeeze.

Again he worked it out. He had moved – but he had been outside his bailiwick, unable to affect that world. So apparently he had not affected himself, either. It might have been a different story, had he travelled only a year or two and walked about. He would have to be very careful in future. Past. Or whatever. This time the nature of the system had saved him from his own folly, but that might not always be so.

'Well, at least I'm learning how to use this thing!'

Squeeze.

'But I still don't know my job or how to relate to people here. Do you know?'

Squeeze, squeeze, squeeze.

'That's what I thought. You know a lot, but you've had no experience with the Hourglass itself. Well, I'll figure it out.' He smiled. 'In time.' Actually, this challenge appealed to his wanderlust; what better form of travel could there be than through time? The horizons were unlimited!

He studied the Hourglass again. The sand was now dull white. He had learned what white, blue, and black meant – and red. Red meant travelling backwards, or opposite his normal route. It was like the red shift in astronomy. Now, if he could just find the other colours and understand what they signified –

The two figures began to move. They retreated from the X spot, walking backwards. Surprised, Norton watched them until they were out of sight. Now he was alone.

Of course – Norton-normal and Gawain the Ghost had arrived about fifteen minutes before the rendezvous. That time had now expired, backwards. His jaunt to the distant past had taken several minutes, his time, which might have passed here, too; he wasn't sure yet how that worked. But what was he to do, now that he was alone?

He found it awkward carrying the Hourglass constantly, so he set it on the ground. Then he locked his hands behind him and paced in a circle, much the way Gawain had done. Did he really want to take on the immense complexities of this office? He had agreed to it almost casually, but he saw now that it was a most unusual commitment. The chance of a lifetime, as the ghost had said – but also the challenge of a lifetime. It was not too late to reverse the Hourglass and travel back to the time of acquisition; presumably someone else would turn up to take the office if he bounced it. Did he want that?

He turned to look back at the parked Hourglass – and found it right behind him, exactly in the position he had left it – except that it was within easy reach, not several paces behind. Had he paced in a full circle and returned to it? He didn't think so.

He walked straight away from the Hourglass and turned again. There it was, right in reach.

He paced backwards next, watching the Hourglass. It slid along with him, not rolling or jumping, just remaining exactly in position relative to him.

'You mean I can't leave it behind?' he asked aloud.

Squeeze.

The question had been rhetorical, but Sning had answered.

Norton picked up the Hourglass, held it a foot above the ground, and let it go. It hung there in the air. When he stepped away, it followed him. When he stepped into it, it retreated. Only when he moved it directly with his hand did it change its position with respect to himself. It was like a satellite, except it did not rotate.

Suddenly frustrated and rebellious, he grasped it and hurled it violently from him. But the moment it left his hand, it stopped, remaining in the air at shoulder height. It had no inertia, no momentum.

He could not, literally, lose it.

'But I don't want the thing following me all the time like a hatchling,' he remarked aloud. 'People will stare.'

Sning squeezed three times, not having any suggestions.

Then a new figure appeared. It was a middle-aged woman. She was walking forwards, towards him, from the opposite direction in which the other two figures had departed. She carried a roll of paper.

Forward? Could she be in his time frame?

She waved to him. She saw him! Excited, Norton waved back – but there was no reaction from the woman. Why was that?

'Hello,' Norton said cautiously.

The woman came to stand a few feet from him. She unrolled her scroll. There were words printed on it. HELLO, CHRONOS.

'Hello,' he said again. 'Can't we talk verbally?'

She passed her arm across the scroll, and it went blank. Then new words appeared. WE CAN INTERACT – BUT YOU MUST LEARN HOW.

'I'm trying to!' he exclaimed. 'But no one perceives me!'

She changed her sign again. I AM LACHESIS – AN ASPECT OF FATE.

Fate! Gawain had mentioned her. This was an important contact! 'How can I talk to you?' he asked. 'Can you understand me?'

Her new sign explained. I AM DOING THIS BACKWARDS. FOLLOW MY INSTRUCTIONS, AND WE SHALL RELATE.

'I'll follow them!' Norton agreed. He realized now that she was only partially aware of him, perhaps could not see him at all, but knew he was there. So she was following a routine to help him, trusting that he was responding. Once they managed to establish a genuine interaction, he would find out why Fate, in whatever aspect, was doing this. For now, he was grateful for her help.

YOU ARE LIVING BACKWARDS. I AM LIVING FORWARDS. WE ARE BOTH INCARNATIONS, BUT WE DO DIFFER IN THIS AND OTHER RESPECTS. WE MUST ALIGN.

'I agree!' he said uselessly.

THE HOURGLASS IS THE TOOL. YOU CONTROL IT WITH YOUR WILL.

'I realize that,' he said as she changed the page.

IT IS VERY STRONG MAGIC. MISJUDGMENT CAN WREAK HAVOC.

'So I discovered! I've been to the Age of Dinosaurs!'

THE COLOUR OF THE SAND IS THE KEY.

'That, too, I have already ascertained.'

WILL IT TO BE BLUE FOR AN INSTANT, THEN GREEN.

'Okay,' he agreed. He concentrated. *Blue briefly, then green.* It hadn't occurred to him before to control the Hourglass by orienting directly on the sand colour.

The greyness closed as the sand changed colour, but altered almost immediately. Now the sand was green.

'Congratulations, Chronos,' Lachesis said.

'Hey, this time I hear you!' he exclaimed.

She smiled. She was perhaps in her forties, her hair nondescript brown and bound in a bun, her face developing lines. She was somewhat heavy-set and generally unimpressive, but her eyes had a timeless, colourless quality that made him know that this was indeed a creature of incalculable power and subtlety. 'And I hear you, Chronos, and see you clearly at last. We are now in phase.'

'Because the sand is green?'

'Come with me, Chronos, and I'll explain.' She stepped forward and took his arm. 'It's the least I can do, after what we've been to each other.'

He suffered himself to be drawn along with her. 'We have?'

She laughed. 'Of course you don't remember! It's in your future. My past. I envy you! But I mustn't hold you in phase too long this time; no sense wasting your magic. Ah, here we are.' She paused at a piece of string dangling by a building. 'Take my hand, Chronos.'

He obeyed. She tugged on the string – and suddenly they were in a comfortable room, with elegant scenic murals on the walls that looked almost real enough to step into. He remembered Orlene's puzzle pictures with sharp nostalgia. This was the kind of apartment he would have liked for himself. 'Nice place you have, Lachesis.'

'Oh, it isn't my place,' she said quickly. 'It's yours.'

'Mine?'

'This is your mansion in Purgatory. Here in this edifice

time travels your way always; no need to strain the Hourglass. Let it go normal again.'

'Normal?' But as he looked at it, the falling sand turned from green to white.

'When you turned the sand blue for a moment, you jumped backwards, in real-world terms, a couple of days.' She glanced at him alertly. 'You did do that? It will be two days before the office changes hands, and I have every intention of being there with my signs to get you started, but that's in my future.'

'You were there, and I did it,' he agreed.

'Good. And when you turned the sand green, you aligned yourself with universal time. You normally live backwards, compared to the rest of us, but green turns you about so that your forward matches ours. It is a temporary state for you, requiring magical energy, so you don't do it unless you need to interact with a normal person. In this case, the need existed. But it isn't wise to do it too long, because of a possible three-person-limit complication.'

'A what?'

'We'll go into that technical matter at another time; I don't want to confuse you at the outset.'

'I'm already confused! Why did you have me turn the sand blue for an instant? Couldn't I have green-phased at the outset?'

'You could have, Chronos. But that would have carried you on beyond your term of office, since you were so close to its edge. I preferred to give you a couple of days' leeway to avoid that risk. You see, you can't travel physically beyond your term; you become insubstantial, unable to interact with us.'

'So I have discovered,' he agreed ruefully.

'Had you turned the sand green then, I would have been leading you here – and you would have vanished from my ken before arriving. You see, to you this is the beginning, but to the rest of us it is the end. To us, your term will expire and that of your successor will commence. Suddenly we will have a vastly experienced Chronos replacing the old novice. He'll have us all stepping smartly! He will know all our futures in a way none of us can.' She fixed him with her disconcerting gaze again. 'Time is power, Norton. You will learn to do things Satan Himself cannot handle. No one can touch Chronos in his area of expertise. You will be able to change reality itself. See that you do not abuse that power.'

Norton did not feel powerful at all. He noticed that now she called him by his given name; obviously she did know him from her past, his new future. 'I will try to handle the office properly,' he said. 'Uh, about Purgatory – '

'Purgatory is not part of the physical world,' she explained. 'When you want an extended interaction with a person, bring that person here, and there will be no problem.'

'I don't quite understand.'

'Of course you don't! You have just stepped into one of the most complex offices of the firmament; it will take you years to get the full hang of it. Fortunately you have time – literally. You *are* Time.'

'I think you'd better explain the whole thing,' he said. 'I'm pretty much baffled.'

'That's what I'm here for – this time.' She glanced at him slyly, as if making an off-colour allusion. 'And I will; I owe it to you, as I said. Only first I'd better introduce myself completely.'

Norton nodded agreement, somewhat in awe of this unpre-possessing figure with the knowing attitude and hypnotic eyes. Lachesis walked to the centre of the room. She shimmered – and in her place was an old woman. Her hair was grey and curly, her dress conservative – a long dark skirt, antique feminine boots, a frilly but unsuggestive blouse, and a small archaic hat. 'Atropos,' she announced, accenting it on the first syllable. 'I cut the Thread of Life.'

'I thought Death did that,' Norton said, startled by more than one thing.

'Thanatos collects the souls. I determine when those souls will become available.'

Norton nodded. He was not yet certain of the distinction, but did not feel ready to question it more closely. He had encountered Thanatos in the performance of his office and developed an abiding respect for that entity. In fact, it was really the example of Thanatos that had moved him to accept this perhaps-similar office of Chronos; Thanatos had shown that human concern and caring did not disappear, even in so awful a chore as taking the life of a baby. Death had stopped being a spectre to Norton with that encounter.

Atropos whirled – and became Lachesis again, in her dowdy, middle-aged outfit, her suit helping mask her somewhat portly figure. Her hair was now free of the bun, longer than Atropos', with less curl and more colour. 'I am Lachesis,' she announced, pronouncing it with a hard C, accented on the first syllable – LAK-e-sis. 'I measure the length of the Threads of Life.'

'I thought Chronos was supposed to – '

'Chronos controls time, not life,' she corrected him.

Again this distinction was not fully clear to Norton; again he kept his mouth shut.

Lachesis made a little leap – and landed as a voluptuous, bouncy young woman whose hair was long, loose, and midnight black with stars sparkling in it. Her gown was low-cut in front and high-cut below, showing breast and thigh to advantage. She wore an intoxicating perfume. 'And Clotho,' she concluded, again accenting the first syllable. 'Who spins the Thread of Human Life.' She stretched a fine thread between her delicate hands.

Norton hoped his eyes hadn't popped too obviously when this creature appeared. 'I thought maybe Nature – '

'Gaea determines the way things are,' she said. 'Not the courses of individual lives. But all the Incarnations interact to some extent.' She gave him a sultry smile, aware of her impact on him. Had Gawain's second wife looked like this at the time he saw her, what might have happened?

'Are you really three people?' he asked. 'You look quite different in each – '

'You may have heard it said,' she said gravely, 'that a woman is a young man's mistress – ' She twirled so that her skirt flared, showing her thighs to a naughty height. ' – a middle-aged man's companion – ' She ceased her motion, and she was Lachesis again, sedate. ' – and an old man's nurse.' She shimmered into Atropos, who now wore a nurse's uniform and looked formidable. 'It seems I am all three. Which are you?'

Norton was startled again. 'Uh – middle, I suppose. At the moment.'

Lachesis reappeared. 'So I suspected. Now I am your companion, though I have been other to you in the past.'

'I – you mean Clotho – in my future?' he asked awkwardly.

'Yes indeedy! You have not yet experienced what I remember.' She grinned. 'Naughty boy!'

Norton blushed to think of what he might be fated to do with Clotho that Lachesis already remembered so intimately. 'I haven't yet got the hang of living backwards,' he confessed. 'It seems quite awkward, especially when people, normal people, apparently don't see me at all.'

'You can change that at will,' she assured him. 'The Hourglass is your emblem and your tool, and an excellent one it is.'

'By willing the sand green?'

'That's it. That phases you in to the normal course. Didn't I tell you about that – or am I about to? You do that when you want to talk to a normal person or an Incarnation.'

'So I can move to the beginning of my original life, almost forty years ago, turn the sand green, and live a normal term as an Incarnation?'

She smiled tolerantly. 'Hardly, Chronos, for several reasons. First, that would fatigue the magic, and you'd lose cohesion in a few days; green mode is a short-term thing for you, as I understand it. Second, you have a job to do, and you can do it effectively only by living your normal course. Third, you aren't going to do that, even if you could; I ought to know.' For an instant, sultry Clotho glanced at him from beneath lowered lashes.

Norton found that unnerving. If Clotho was also the old Atropos, which one of Fate's three minds was analysing him as he performed what he supposed was private? All three of them had those disturbing eyes. A man who played games of any kind with one of these woman was apt to become the object rather than the subject.

'No, you can't remember, can you!' she teased him. 'Oh, I am enjoying this! After what you did to me in the halcyon bloom of my innocence – oh, yes!'

'My job,' he said doggedly. 'You said you'd tell me what I am supposed to do and how to do it.'

She sighed with mock resignation. 'Yes, you always were somewhat single-minded about that, and on the whole I believe you have done a decent job. Very well, I will start you off. You work most closely with me anyway.' She paused as if organizing her thoughts. 'It is the business of Chronos to establish the chronology of every event in the human section of the universe. Effect must always follow cause, age must follow youth, action must usually follow thought. Evidently your backward existence facilitates such timings. Without Time, all would be without form and void.'

'But I thought that was automatic!' Norton protested. 'A function of the universe, the way things are!'

'Now you know better, Chronos. Nothing in the universe is happenstance; everything is determined by the sum of the fundamental forces. Your art is to fit it all together so neatly that it *seems* automatic. Timing is critical, and Chronos is responsible.'

'But I'm only one person! I can't possibly keep track of every event in – in the human section of the universe!'

'You have a competent staff, of course. Your office personnel here in Purgatory handles the routine. Naturally, you don't do it all *personally*. This is the twenty-first century, after all! You make the major decisions, and your staff implements them immediately. A significant number of people remain in the annexe here at the mansion, matching your time flow, so as to provide continuity. I'm sure your predecessor left you highly skilled and dedicated personnel, knowing the office would pretty much have to run itself while you got broken in. But you do have the authority now; if you choose to do something foolish like reversing the course of time for the whole world, your staff will dutifully arrange to put effect before cause and keep the rest consistent.'

'I can do that? Reverse time for everyone?'

She nodded. 'This is no minor office you hold, Chronos, as I have hinted. Your power is unique. But don't let that go to your head.'

'I hope not!' He shook his head, trying to clear it, as if some of that power had already messed it up. 'What, specifically, should I be doing now?'

'First, perhaps you should put away your Hourglass when you're not actively using it. That will free your hands.'

'Yes. But I don't want the thing trailing me in space, either.'

'I suppose it would do that, if you let it. The Hourglass is the symbol and essence of your office; it can never leave your presence. Not until you pass it along to the next or prior Chronos. But meanwhile, all you have to do is squeeze it down to size and put it in your pocket.'

'I can do that?'

'Try it.'

He tried it. He put his hands on the top and bottom of the Hourglass and squeezed; it compressed smoothly, becoming a smaller replica of itself, then collapsed into a mere disc. 'It's not broken?'

'It is eternal. Impossible to break.'

'But how can the sand – '

'As I understand it, the Hourglass has not actually changed its form, merely its presentation. Just as folding a paper does not change its real dimensions or the nature of the writing on it, the Hourglass retains all its properties. To it, your world has squeezed down to two dimensions. All is relative.'

Norton shrugged, not trying to grasp that, and put the disc in his pocket. 'Will it still work in that shape? I mean, if I will the sand to change colour – ?'

'It should. Your contact with it can never be severed, as I said, so it should respond to your directive.'

'Anything else I should do?'

'I do have a few glitches to correct. I spin my threads carefully, but nothing in this cosmos is perfect, and sometimes they unravel. If you are ready to assume the harness, we can tackle them now.'

'Just tell me what to do.'

She conjured a tiny notebook from the air and riffled through the pages. 'This one will do. Two threads got crossed, so that each person will experience the fate of the other. Since one is scheduled to suffer a grievous accident soon, that is an error of consequence.' She closed the notebook and it vanished. Then she put her two hands together, fingers extended and splayed, and drew them apart. Several scintillating threads stretched between them. 'Take me back to where they cross,' she said.

'Wait! You said one person must suffer a grievous accident! Why allow that to happen? Why not make both threads smooth, both lives pleasant?'

She shook her head. 'That is not the way the cosmos operates, Norton. We do not live in a simple or peaceful universe. The eddy currents of violence swirl constantly, and consequence follows consequence. If I attempted to simplify this particular life – which I could indeed accomplish – it would only lead to a great mischief for other lives. God and Satan are at war – have been since time began – and the fallout from their strife is with us always. It is not for me to dictate on whom that fallout shall fall; it is only for me to mesh it properly. I am the servant, not the master – and so are you.

We both must do what we must do, implementing the rules that exist.'

Norton did not agree with that at all, but realized that he lacked a basis from which to argue. So he dropped it for the time being.

He peered at the threads she held between her spread fingers. Most went from finger to finger, but two were crossed. 'How – ?'

'This is analogy, of course,' she said. 'Or a convenient facsimile thereof. If I had the real crossing in my hands, I could unsnarl it here. You must take me to the actual space-time site.'

'Yes, but – '

'Oh, I keep forgetting! You've never done this before. Very well – I will talk you through it, step by step. First orient your Glass.'

'This?' Norton brought out the Hourglass and drew it back into shape. It remained functioning perfectly; the sand was still falling, and more of it had accumulated in the nether chamber.

'Yes, that. Expand its ambience to include me. You can tell by the brightness.'

Confused, Norton willed the Hourglass: *Expand ambience.*

The glow intensified. Lachesis brightened, literally; she glowed like the Glass. 'That's enough, Chronos. Ease off a little; you don't want to take your entire mansion with you.'

He diminished his thought and the glow faded slightly.

'That's good. Hold it there. Now turn the sand blue – but only slightly, only briefly. We're going back just a little way.'

He concentrated, and the sand shifted colour, turning faintly blue.

'Now travel along the threads till we come to the crossing.'

'How – ?'

'Oops! Too far. Back up a bit.'

He turned the sand ever so faintly pink. Suddenly he saw the threads between her fingers expand, perhaps in his mind's

110

eye, until they were veritable cables. The Hourglass seemed to have become a cablecar, cruising along the cables, carrying Norton and Lachesis with it. In the distance Norton could see other cables, extending from horizon to horizon. Then another cable closed with the first, and the two touched.

He concentrated, fading the pink almost to white, and the Hourglass coasted to a halt just at the crossing.

'Excellent,' Lachesis said. 'You're developing the touch already! Soon you'll be the expert I remember.' She stepped forward, put her two hands on the cables, and lifted them apart. Norton was amazed by two things: first, her ability to separate such monstrous and solid cables so readily; and second, the fact that he knew these cables were mere threads stretched between her fingers. How could she do any of this?

'That's it,' she said, returning. 'You may revert us to normal now.'

Norton relaxed – and abruptly the cables were gone and the two of them were back in the mansion in Purgatory. 'That was it?' he asked dazedly.

'Yes. You did very well.' She glanced at him appraisingly. 'But I think this is enough for you now. Relax, explore your mansion, get acquainted with your household staff. I will return tomorrow, your time, so that we can wrap up the other snarls; none of them are as critical as this one was.'

His tomorrow – her yesterday! 'But I don't – '

'You'll find out.' She changed form again, becoming a large spider. The spider shrank to normal spider size, ascended a thread, and disappeared. He realized that this was the type of thread he had taken to be a string when she brought him here from the empty lot. She travelled by threads.

Norton was alone again. He still had only the faintest notion of what he was supposed to do.

6
Satan

As it turned out, he had no trouble. The household staff was well trained and polite and ready for the changeover. Indeed, they acted as if they had been working for Norton himself for a long time. Lachesis had said time flowed backwards here, which meant these people should be from the world's future, but now he wasn't so sure.

As soon as Norton stirred, the head butler made an appearance, ready to handle any emergency discreetly. Norton was treated to an excellent meal served by a pretty maid and shown the complete premises. Much more quickly than he expected, he felt at home. It was somewhat like staying at a good hotel, and somewhat like living at Gawain's estate.

Gawain's estate – where Orlene had been with him. Suddenly this was less enjoyable.

He learned that all these personnel were souls in Purgatory, here because they had been in perfect balance when they died. It was not a bad afterlife for them and not a good one. By definition, it was in between. Eventually, if they served well, they would graduate to Heaven – but it took much longer to accomplish this in Purgatory than it would have in life. Life was intense and leveraged, he remembered; the Afterlife was diffuse and relatively calm. At least this was the case in Purgatory; Norton could glean no information on what went on in Heaven or Hell. All he knew was that every soul wanted to go to the former, and no soul to the latter.

He was relaxing in the afternoon – day and night seemed to follow the normal course here, though he suspected this was artificially arranged – watching the holo unit – which was filled with news about the changeover in the office of Chronos – when he had a visitor.

112

'Who?' he asked the butler, not believing the announcement.

'Satan, sir,' the man repeated calmly.

'I have no business with the Devil!'

'Shall I inform him you are indisposed, sir?'

But already curiosity was mixing with awe and horror. 'I – can he do anything to me here?'

'No, sir. One Incarnation cannot interfere with another without the other's consent, here or anywhere. Incarnations are inviolate, especially when in uniform.'

'Uniform?'

'Your cloak, sir. It is a barrier of time, acting automatically against any physical threat.'

Norton sighed. 'Then I suppose I'd better find out what he wants. Show him in.' One day ago he would have scoffed at the notion of meeting the Incarnation of Evil!

Satan was ushered in. 'The Prince of Evil, Father of Lies, my Lord Satan,' the butler announced formally without a trace of disrespect. These were the Devil's legitimate titles.

Norton had been braced for a demon creature with horns and a forked tail. He was disappointed. Satan was a perfectly ordinary-looking middle-aged man in a conservative, dark red business suit. His hair was reddish-brown, neatly trimmed and combed. He was clean-shaven. There was no trace of fire in his complexion. His gaze was bland, and he had a faint atmosphere of some masculine fragrance.

Satan stepped briskly forward and extended his hand. Norton saw no convenient way to avoid it, so he shook hands. Satan's fingers were firm and warm, but by no means hot. There was nothing to indicate any infernal association.

'Uh, to what do I owe the, uh, honour of this visit?'

'Oh, this is merely a social call,' Satan said with a winning smile. His teeth were white and even. 'You are new to this office, so I thought I'd be neighbourly and offer any assistance you may require.'

Norton frowned as they sat down. 'I am new here, true.

113

Perhaps I misunderstood. I thought you would not be interested in – in helping anyone else.'

Satan laughed. The sound was wholesome and warm. 'My dear Chronos – I am an Incarnation, like yourself! Each of us has his duty, and it behooves us to cooperate with one another. We have a common interest in order.'

'I thought – I do not mean to be offensive – that you opposed order.' Norton remembered the nefarious reputation of the Prince of Evil, the origin of all mischief.

Satan made a gesture of bafflement. 'Me? Oppose order? By no means! I support order; in fact, I would prefer to have more of it.' He smiled again, magnetically. 'Perhaps I differ slightly with God as to which one of Us should govern; but apart from that detail, Our designs are similar.'

Against his will and better judgement, Norton found himself warming to this affable entity. 'Well, in fairness I have to say that I do not side with you.'

'And why should you, Chronos? No one in his right mind wants to go to Hell! I would go to Heaven Myself, were it feasible.'

Norton had to smile. Satan's humour was infectious. 'You don't like Hell? Why do you stay there, then?'

'Because I have a job to do, sir! Who else would assume My office, if I were to desert My post?'

Who, indeed! 'Is it a necessary office? Why not just let Good predominate?'

Satan shook his head sadly. 'Alas the human condition does not permit. There is both good and evil in every person, and so there have to be final repositories for those aspects in the Afterlife. Without good and evil, free will would be meaningless and life would be pointless. Each person must choose his fate by how he lives, thereby defining his fundamental nature. Naturally the average person hates and fears the consequence of the evil in himself. If he did not, he would never make progress into good. But the flesh is fallible, and each person is also sorely tempted by the immediate benefits of the exercise of evil. Only in the course of life can his true direction be determined. Every person professes to love good and hate evil, but in his actions his real preference emerges. It is a most interesting study.' He shrugged. 'But I did not come here to bore you with shop talk, Chronos. How may I help you?'

'I'm not sure there is any need,' Norton said, impressed by Satan's discussion without trusting his motive. 'Lachesis has been helping me.'

'Of course she would,' Satan agreed readily. 'She is absolutely dependent on your service. I am sure she will make you most welcome, in one aspect or another.' He made a small gesture with his two hands that might have suggested the Hourglass, but surely did not.

Norton remained uncomfortable with his visitor. He was sure Satan had an ulterior motive. But there was no point in antagonizing so powerful an entity. So he continued to make conversation, wishing Satan would either get to the point or leave.

'We must all do the best we can in our offices,' Satan continued blithely. His capitals and noncapitals could actually be heard; he did not use them for Incarnations as a class, even when he was included in their number. 'We are all, in fact, artists, shaping our duties into monuments of accomplishment. I am always pleased when I am successful in extirpating the evil from a soul that would otherwise have been lost. That is, of course, what we do in Hell; we travel the avenues of last resort in dealing with the intransigent cases.'

'Uh, no doubt,' Norton agreed uncomfortably. He was aware that Satan was proselytizing; what bothered him was the fact that the arguments seemed to make sense.

'I understand you lost a loved one,' Satan said sympathetically.

'She's in Heaven now,' Norton said. He didn't want to discuss Orlene with Satan, either. He felt that Satan's attention would somehow sully her memory.

'I trust you are aware you do not have to be alone,' Satan

115

remarked. 'Here in Purgatory there are many souls, male and female, and all are eager to improve their balance by serving the Incarnations. Allow Me to demonstrate the possibilities.'

'No need,' Norton said quickly.

'No problem, sir. Just let Me summon your downstairs maid – ' Satan snapped his fingers, and suddenly the maid was there, dustcloth in hand, her hair bound in a kerchief. She looked startled. 'No, no, that outfit will never do,' Satan said in the manner of a kindly uncle. Abruptly her clothing changed, and she was garbed in a fetching evening gown. She was considerably more shapely than Norton had realized. 'Oh, yes, the hair,' Satan said, and the kerchief was replaced by a tiara studded with flashing diamonds. 'Maid, would you like to serve your master in a more personal capacity?'

The girl looked down at her lovely outfit and touched her shining hair. 'Anything my master wishes,' she agreed.

'Look, I have no desire for – ' Norton protested, though he was privately intrigued by this exploration.

'Oh, my, I nearly forgot,' Satan said. 'Of course you don't want the aspect of a stranger, for you are not a promiscuous man these days.' And the maid changed form and became the precise likeness of Orlene in her most vibrant health.

Startled, Norton stared. Orlene had never looked better!

'We can tailor her personality, too,' Satan said. 'I like My art to be thorough. She can be, in every material and social respect, the object of your interest.'

'But – but she's not the one I know!'

Satan squinted at him. 'In what manner have you known her, other than appearance and personality?'

'I – I just know this one is different!'

'Does it matter? She will serve you equally well. Perhaps better, for she has Eternity to gain by a successful performance.'

Disconcerted by the perfect likeness and the plausibility of Satan's argument, Norton could only stammer: 'But she isn't – the one I – it's just not the same!'

'Isn't it?' Satan frowned benignly. 'It has been said that man does, woman is. Yours is the performance that matters; she needs only to be its object. Try her, Chronos; I'm sure you will be pleased.'

'Try her?'

'I am sure you would not wish Me to assault your ears or hers with the vernacular description, especially since the same interaction can be described more precisely in polite language. I am, as I mentioned, at heart an artist; I appreciate the qualities of language. I have little sympathy with prudishness *per se*, but much with beauty. She can assume another form if you prefer. There is no deception here, only an effort to alleviate discomfort.'

'Any form she assumed – *I* assume would represent damnation for me,' Norton said uneasily.

Again Satan flashed his winning smile. 'I see you remain cautious. I assure you that damnation is not so readily come by, my dear associate. You will neither rise to Heaven nor sink to Hell until your term in office is done. As an Incarnation, you are largely immune to changes in your status, and what you do or do not do with any willing woman is irrelevant.'

'But with a soul in Purgatory, a mere spirit – ?'

'All are tangible to one another and to Incarnations here. This is not Earth, where spirits cannot freely go.'

Norton shook his head. 'This is not the type of pleasure I care for.'

'Ah, you will get over that soon enough. Ultimately, every living person is dedicated to his own pleasure.'

'You're right,' Norton said. 'I do remain suspicious of your motive. You are seeking to corrupt me, and I'm not sure I can afford to believe anything you say.'

'Well, I am rightly called the Father of Lies,' Satan said equably. 'I do take a certain modest pride in the quality of My artifices, and many mortals find them sufficient.'

The scoundrel was proud of it! Norton was disgusted. 'Well, if that concludes your business here – '

'Almost,' Satan said, not rising. He made a trifling gesture, and the maid resumed her own form and scurried from the room.

'So it wasn't just a social visit?'

'There is one minor favour –'

'Why should I do you any favour?'

'Well, it is a very small one, and I am prepared to pay rather well.'

Payment for a favour! He had been through that with Gawain! 'What can you offer another Incarnation, aside from temptation to mischief?'

Satan studied him, and now his eyes had the same disturbing intensity Norton had noted in the eyes of Fate. 'I understand you like to travel, Chronos.'

'Yes. I suppose that was the main reason I took this office, so I could travel in time. Once I learn to do it precisely, I'll –' He broke off, not wanting to say too much to the Prince of Evil.

'To see your woman again in life,' Satan finished smoothly.

So he couldn't hide this from Satan! Did that mean it was an evil notion? Chilling thought! 'What is this favour?'

'Merely to conduct one of My minions on a brief tour.'

'Why can't he travel himself? I hardly know my way around Purgatory yet.'

'A tour in time. Only you can arrange that.'

That was right – he was now the Master of Time. He did not want to do any business with Satan, but he was curious. 'To where in time?'

'Just a few years, for a few minutes. He won't do any harm; he'll just talk with a man.'

'Just talk? To threaten him?'

Satan shook his head. 'My dear Chronos, I do not threaten people! That is counterproductive. This is actually, though I blush to confess it, a good deed.'

'A good deed – by the Prince of Evil? How can you expect me to believe that?'

'You can verify it for yourself. There is no secret here; all is open. This man stands to lose the chance of his lifetime. My minion will merely put him on the right track.'

The chance of a lifetime – that was what Gawain had told Norton himself, when broaching the matter of the office of Time. But what chance would Satan offer anyone? 'Why should you do a good turn for any mortal?'

'As I mentioned sir, I do believe in order. My office cannot function without order. This mortal man's good fortune will contribute to a lifetime of order in that aspect of reality.'

Norton shook his head. 'You will have to do better than that, Satan! You must have a dozen other ways to promote order on Earth, without travelling in time to help any one person. Why do a favour for a mortal?'

'Well, Chronos, you are in a position to verify it directly. I will give you the coordinates so you can go there alone and see that this man will suffer no ill, only good, as a result of My minion's intercession. Only when you are completely satisfied on that score need you actually conduct My minion there. That is fair enough, isn't it?'

Grudgingly, Norton nodded. 'But I don't know how to travel precisely in time yet. I mean, to a particular point in human events. Lachesis took me on one trip, but we had her threads for guidance.'

'I will be glad to assist you in this,' Satan said. 'I have only the friendliest possible intent. You have merely to select on the calendar the specific date and hour and to will your Hourglass blue, with a preset stop at that spot. That is a fine supernatural instrument; it will obey you implicitly. Once there in time, you must negotiate the geographical distance.'

'By walking? That will limit my effectiveness.'

'Chronos, you are the Incarnation of Time. That means you have a certain practical control of space, too, for time and space are linked. You can travel anywhere on Earth you wish and to the colonized planets, too.'

Norton shook his head. 'I don't see how, unless you mean by using conventional transport facilities.'

'I am here to show you how. Simply take the Hourglass – '

'No. I don't want to travel with you.'

Satan took no offence. 'No need, my dear associate. I will explain the technique to you so you can practise yourself. First I must clarify the underlying theory.'

'That would be appreciated,' Norton said grudgingly. He wanted to be away from Satan, but he did need this information.

'Motion, like evil, is everywhere,' Satan said in a somewhat didactic manner. 'The Earth spins about her axis with a surface velocity of close to a thousand miles an hour at the equator, which translates to about sixteen miles per minute or a quarter mile per second. That might seem to be a fairly formidable velocity.'

'Faster than I can run,' Norton agreed. 'I am aware that this rotation causes day and night. But what – '

'Yet it is dwarfed by other aspects of motion. The Earth also revolves around the sun at a velocity of approximately eighteen and a half miles per second.'

'Causing the seasons and the year,' Norton said. 'But how does this relate – ?'

'But our sun, too, is moving, for our Milky Way Galaxy is rotating, and so the sun is carried around that galactic axis at the rate of about a hundred and fifty miles per second. Just as Earth's motion about the sun is about seventy-five times as rapid as the motion of a spot on Earth's surface about Earth's own axis, the velocity of galactic rotation is about eight times as great as that. Yet even this is relatively insignificant. The known universe is expanding, so all matter is in motion with respect to Galactic Rest. In that sense, we are travelling at approximately half the speed of light, or ninety thousand miles per second. Impressive, isn't it?'

'Yes,' Norton agreed. 'But I still fail to see the relevance to my situation.'

'Peace, comrade; I am coming to that. The point is that, though you and I appear to be at rest at the moment, we are in fact subject to numerous and potent vectors of motion. It is a complex scheme we exist in! And since motion is a function of time as well as of space – '

'Hey!' Norton interrupted. 'If I move in time without moving in space, I'll drift right off the face of the Earth! If I travel into the past a single hour, the Earth, as part of the moving galaxy in the expanding universe, will have moved ninety thousand miles every second, or – '

'Half a light-hour, or three hundred and twenty-four million miles, or the distance from Earth to Jupiter,' Satan finished heartily. 'Yes, indeed, Chronos, you would be lost in a moment, literally.'

'But since I live backwards, I should be totally out of phase! Because I'm going back to a time when Earth was far elsewhere from where it is now, but I'm the only one going back there, not the Earth itself! And when I jump to another time – '

'Relax, Chronos,' Satan said. 'Your very existence is safeguarded by the formidable magic of the Hourglass. It counters all the motions of the universe and maintains you in exactly the same location with respect to Earth's surface, regardless of how you use it. Without that protection, it is true, you would perish the instant you travelled in time, for you would in effect be flung deep into the core of the planet or out into the vacuum of space. That Hourglass remains with you and protects you from all mischief, its ambience forming your cloak.' He smiled engagingly. 'It even protects you from My mischief.'

'Can that be true?' Norton asked, dazed.

'Naturally anything I tell you is suspect. But I seldom concern Myself with trivial or obvious lies; they are neither artistic nor productive, and so are not worth My effort. Ask your serpent ring. That is not one of My demons.'

So Satan knew about Sning! 'Does the Hourglass really protect me from evil?' Norton asked the little snake.

Squeeze.

He liked the Hourglass better! 'And it can help move me in space as well as in time?'

Squeeze.

'Indubitably, Chronos,' Satan said smoothly. 'All you have to do is use it to void certain aspects of the motion-alignment spell. Then you will move – or rather, fail to move, while the universe moves past you. With a little practice, you will be able to travel anywhere on Earth at the rate of many miles per second. But do try it cautiously; the Hourglass can protect you from any exterior malaise, but only to a limited extent from your own folly.'

'Folly?'

'When you void part of its magic, you reduce its power to protect you. You could indeed get lost.'

Excellent warning! Norton had already experienced one careless jaunt into the distant past. Couple that with a voiding of its protection – could he have got himself eaten by a dinosaur? No, for he had never been solid, outside his allotted term of office. But inside his term, there might have been more trouble. Yes, he would have to be very careful, and Satan's warning was extremely well taken. Still, he did need to learn how to use the powers of the Hourglass. 'How do I nullify any of it?'

'Simply set the sand on yellow, then nudge it towards blue or red – red is best – so you're differing from normal time only slightly. Actually, I believe you can do it on your own backward time, but it is better to orient on Earth-normal when you're learning, so as to minimize the effect. That way you are dealing only with Earth's present motions, rather than with the added complication of Earth's past or future motions.'

'Uh, yes,' Norton agreed, labouring to grasp this. If Earth was presently flinging outwards from the universal centre at half the speed of light, and he voided the protective spell while moving forward in time, he could multiply the effect

122

and jump in space at several times the speed of light. He did not want to risk that! 'Why yellow?'

'That is the nullification mode. You wouldn't want it to happen while you were in another mode; you might travel in space by accident, disastrously. So you must make a very conscious effort, which is another protection for you. But you can get the other modes once you are in yellow.'

'Uh, yes. But what do I actually do, to – ?'

'Motion begets motion. You tilt the Hourglass towards the force you wish to negate. The greater the tilt, the greater the negation; right angles is full negation. But it's on a logarithmic scale, so the first part of the tilt provides comparatively little effect. Another protection against carelessness.'

Norton was coming to appreciate the qualities of the Hourglass even more. This thing had powers he had never dreamed of! He concentrated, willing the sand to turn yellow. In a moment it did. Then he tilted the Hourglass slightly away from him. Nothing happened.

'You have to put it in gear, as it were,' Satan said. 'Yellow is neutral, maintaining what you had before, which was white. Here in your mansion all visitors share your mode, and the Hourglass assumes you are merely demonstrating sand colours. But when you go to yellow, then to an additional colour, and then tilt, it knows you mean business.'

Norton concentrated, nudging the sand into a red tint. Then he paused. 'Why is red best? Why not green, to match universal time precisely?'

'Why, I hadn't thought of that,' Satan said. 'I suppose there could be a disadvantage to moving in space while phased in to the solid world.'

A disadvantage – such as smashing through a building while in the solid state! Norton knew he never wanted to travel on green. Meanwhile, sticking to his normal time seemed to make sense when he was learning. Satan was really being quite helpful. Maybe he was not as bad a sort as he had been painted.

Norton tilted the Hourglass about five degrees.

He shot forward like a cannonball. Quickly he reversed the tilt – and shot backwards even faster. He righted the Hourglass and found himself falling through the air, from a great height above the planet.

Evidently he had tilted too much. He had shot away from the surface of the Earth at a tangent, forwards and then backwards, leaving the ground behind. Ground? Since he had started from Purgatory – but he really didn't know where Purgatory was. Maybe it was near ground level, but part of another aspect of reality. Anyway, he had jumped right out of it. But why so much faster backwards than forwards, when he had tilted the Hourglass the same amount?

Because he was tapping into different forces. The ones Satan had described were surely not the only ones – and, of course, since a number of them were not straight-line forces, such as Earth's revolution around the sun, they would be constantly changing his orientation to the major motion, that of the universal expansion. So tilting the Hourglass in a given direction would produce a different degree of motion each time. He would always have to be careful! Even with a logarithmic scale, he could find himself travelling too many miles per second.

But now he had the Hourglass upright – and was plunging towards the ground increasingly rapidly. What was wrong?

Then he cursed himself for a fool. Gravity was wrong! He had popped into the sky and righted the Hourglass, so it was no longer moving him – but gravity was another matter. What would happen when he landed?

Well, he wasn't quite phased in to reality, so probably he would pass right through the ground without impact. That would leave him buried in rock, unable to see where he was going. As Satan had said, the Hourglass could not protect him from his own folly. He had to get moving – under control – before he lost control entirely.

He tried to return to the mansion. He tilted the Hourglass

slightly forward – and moved at a lesser velocity past the surface of the planet. But he did not seem to be getting closer to home, wherever that was. Actually, he would settle for a soft landing anywhere on the surface, where he could pause and take stock.

He took a moment to ponder, despite his inclination to react wildly. He could avoid plopping into the surface at the speed given by gravity simply by jolting himself a few million miles from the planet – but that didn't seem wise. What should he breathe? Also, he wasn't sure he could get into deep space, because magic was a planetary phenomenon.

He had set the sand on yellow, then tinted it pink. That should mean he was travelling forward in time, but not as fast as the normal Earthflow. He might be advancing at half the normal rate – did that make sense? – so each second of his matched only half a second of the world. Thus if he nullified the part of the spell that moved him along with the turning Earth, he might proceed, not at the thousand-or-so-mile-per-hour rate of rotation, but at half that, five hundred. Still a lot of velocity.

But he had not tilted the Hourglass all the way, so should have tapped into only a small fraction of that motion, no more than forty or fifty miles per hour. That was not the case; he had actually moved at more like five thousand miles per hour. The Earth's rotation couldn't account for that!

So he was using one of the far more powerful forces – and might have to draw on it again to return. But gravity had drawn him closer to the ground, so he couldn't simply reverse his prior course without going *through* a segment of the globe. In short, he was probably in trouble regardless of what he tried, unless he froze time completely. But that wouldn't get him home either.

'Sning!' he cried. 'Can you help me?'

Squeeze.

'Can you tell me how to return safely?'

Squeeze.

What a relief! He was now within a mile or so of the ground and still plummeting. 'Let's play hot and cold! Squeeze when I start to do the right thing!'

He focused on the Hourglass and considered tilting it marginally forward. Sning squeezed. So he did tilt it, very slightly – and started to move forward. He increased the tilt, encouraged by Sning, until he was travelling downwards at a forty-five degree angle, his forward motion equal to his descending motion. This was an improvement, but not enough to prevent him from passing through the ground in short order.

Should he tilt the Hourglass back the other way?

Squeeze, squeeze. Sning was telling him no.

What, then?

Squeeze.

'What do you mean, "yes"?!' Norton demanded. 'I don't know what to do!'

Squeeze, squeeze.

Approaching disaster, or at least discomfort, sharpened his thinking. 'You mean I know what to do, if only I think of it?'

Squeeze.

'But what I need is to stop falling, and I don't have any control for that!'

Squeeze, squeeze.

'I *do* have a control? But I can't tilt the Hourglass *up*, unless I just lift it – '

Squeeze.

He was almost at the ground, sliding into a small cultured lake where tourists were fishing from magic carpets. He jerked the Hourglass up – and shot up as if launched from a catapult. He wondered whether the tourists were staring, then realized they couldn't see him; he was not phased in to their time scale.

Hastily he corrected and, after yo-yoing a few times, got himself stabilized about a mile up.

So it was movement of the Hourglass, rather than tilt, that

did it – when it was in the yellow mode and in gear. Satan had misled him. No – probably Satan hadn't known. He had seen the prior Chronos – now who would that be? Himself, hence? – tilt and move off, so thought that was the only way it was done. There might be a lot that the Prince of Evil did not know about the office and accoutrements of Chronos, and it was best that Satan remain ignorant. All Satan's helpfulness might have been an effort to get to understand the workings of the Hourglass better, for no legitimate purpose.

With his broadened control and Sning's guidance, Norton finally made it back to the place and moment he had started from. Satan remained sitting; to him only a minute or so had passed. Let him never know how precarious a ride Norton had taken!

'So now you know how to do it,' Satan said with a friendly smile. 'No trouble at all, was it? Now you can take My minion to his interview.'

'I'm not sure – '

'Oh, yes, of course! Silly of Me to forget! You want to see the nature of My coin. I said I was prepared to pay well and indeed I shall.'

'No, I – '

'That's all right, Chronos. I will show it to you. It is an excursion to the aspect of the continuum you can't reach conveniently alone – distant space.'

'Space?' Satan had him off balance again, perhaps intentionally. What was he up to now?

'You control time, Chronos; that seems to overlap into space, but that is not strictly the case. You travel by standing still and permitting the world to pass by you in selected fashion. I can control space, for evil is everywhere. You can range to the ends of Eternity; I can range to the ends of the contemporary universe. This is what I offer you – travel in the universe, such as you have never known and cannot know on your own. Let Me show you – a sample of what I offer in exchange for the token favour I ask. I am sure you will agree it is a bargain.'

A bargain? Travel far beyond Earth was impossible, since magic was associated only with solid matter, like gravity, but did not have the infinite range of gravity. Five thousand miles or so above Earth, there was no magic – not until a person stepped on to some other planet and drew on *its* magic. Satan himself would have to use a matter transmitter to visit Mars or Venus.

Therefore this had to be an empty promise, a bluff.

Norton decided to call Satan's bluff. 'Yes, show me.'

7
Bem

Satan gestured – and suddenly Norton was zooming out through space at an accelerating rate that left the planet Earth far behind in a moment, and then the sun itself. He was in deep space, light-hours from his home planet, heading towards the centre of the Milky Way Galaxy, watching the stars streak by. He had no discomfort; he seemed to be magically protected, so that he felt pleasantly warm and could breathe; evidently the cloak was protecting him.

He had called Satan's bluff – and it hadn't been a bluff! How was that possible? Had he misunderstood the limitations of magic? It certainly seemed so!

There were moments of darkness as he passed through bands of galactic dust. Then he was in a channel of starless space, sliding along a glowing spiral arm of the galaxy, the individual stars shining along its curving length like jewels. He looked up and saw a globular cluster of stars passing overhead, a bright ball orbiting the centre of the galaxy at right angles to the plane of the great disc of it. Then he curved up towards that cluster, departing the galactic plane, spiralling in. The tiny cluster swelled enormously, becoming a miniature galaxy-ball itself, with something like a hundred thousand closely packed stars. What a spectacle!

As he came towards it, he decelerated. He entered it – but now it was evident how large it was – many light-years across, the stars thinning out at the edge, so that there really was a good deal of space between them. He coasted on in towards the centre, where day was eternal and stars virtually rubbed elbows. He came at last to a magnificent space station shaped like a giant spoked wheel, with tiny spaceships docked around the rim. But as he slowed and came closer, he discovered that these ships were not small, but large; the scale of the station dwarfed them. They were of many types, some being as sleek as needles, others resembling Earthly battleships floating in space, complete with layered armour and projecting cannon, and still others resembling collections of saucers.

It was to one of the needles Norton finally came. He phased through the hull in ghostly fashion and landed on a deck in what he took to be the control region. Windows or screens opened out to provide a panoramic view of the wheel station, the docked ships, and the myriad stars shining beyond.

A spaceman got up from the pilot's seat. He was tall, lanky, blonde, and handsome in a rugged prairie way; his legs bowed out slightly and he wore a blaster at his hip, holstered for a rapid draw. He eyed Norton appraisingly, a stalk of timothy grass projecting from the corner of his mouth. 'So you're my co-pilot,' he drawled, his lips thinning. 'You shore don't look like much, stranger! Any good with a blaster?'

'No,' Norton confessed. What had Satan got him into?

'Ever blast any buggers?'

'What?'

'Bems.'

'Bems?'

'You know – the Bug-Eyed-Monsters who're trying to take over the Glob. The Geniuses hired us to clean the Bems out of this sector of space. I lost my co on my last mission, but they said they'd send a replacement.' He grinned boyishly and chewed on his timothy. 'I was sorta hoping for a Femme.'

'Femme?'

'Pardner, where you been? You don't know what a Femme is? A human woman, or reasonable facsimile thereof, maybe twenty years old, shaped like that sand dingus you're holding, hot-blooded and not too smart.'

'Oh. There must be a mistake. Not only am I not a – a young female – I also know next to nothing about spaceships or monsters or Geniuses.'

'A mistake for sure!' the spaceman agreed. He hawked

disgustedly, looked about, found no spittoon, and finally swallowed it. 'We'll get this here nonsense cleared pronto!' He strode to a communications console and punched buttons with his dirty thumb.

A head appeared on the screen. The face was small and squeezed together, as if shoved aside by the hugely bulging braincase. The skull was hairless and traversed by purple veins and seemed almost to pulse with the overcapacity of grey matter it enclosed. This, surely, was a Genius – the end product of human evolution, virtually all mind and no body.

'Yes?' the head whispered. It seemed the vocal cords, too, had been largely displaced by brainstuff.

'Bat Dursten here, sir,' the spaceman drawled. 'My new co-pilot just moseyed in – but he says he don't know nothing about ships or blasters or Bems, and he sure don't look like much. Sending him – that musta been a glitch. I need a replacement pronto – maybe a nice li'l Femme.'

'There is no error, Dursten,' the Genius whispered sibilantly. 'Norton is to be your companion for this mission. He is competent.'

'But he's a greenhorn!' the spaceman protested. 'Never ever blasted a Bem!'

'He will suffice,' the Genius insisted, the veins in his forehead turning deeper purple.

'Gol-dang it, sir – ' Dursten started rebelliously.

But something strange was happening. The Genius was staring with his two bloodshot orbs intently at Dursten – and the spaceman's hair was lifting as if drawn by an unseen hand. Smoke began to curl from it, and his timothy wilted.

Dursten felt the heat. 'Ow!' he yelled as he slapped at his hair, spitting out the grass. 'Okay, okay, sir; he's the one! We'll make do somehow.'

'I rather thought you would see it my way,' the Genius said, smiling with his little pursed mouth as he faded offscreen.

'What happened?' Norton asked, amazed at this interchange. He could see a dark patch where the man's hair had frizzed.

'Aw, he used his psi on me,' Dursten said, rubbing out the last of the heat. 'They do that when they get riled.'

'Psi?'

'Don't you know *nothing*? All the Geniuses got psi power. They can't do nothing with their spindly li'l bodies, so they do it with their hotshot brains. That one tagged me with telekinesis and pyro. Just his way o' making his point. I'm stuck with you.'

'He lifted your hair and burned it – by sheer mind power?'

'That's what I said, Nort.'

'But he wasn't even present! He must be somewhere else on the Wheel.'

'Somewhere else in the Glob, you mean. Geniuses don't never risk their hides in space. Distance don't matter none to them; if a Genius can see you, he can tag you. If he'd been really mad at me, he'da stopped my heart.'

'If the Geniuses can do that, why do they hire mercenaries?' Norton asked. 'They should be able to stop the hearts of the Bems themselves.'

Bat Dursten sighed. 'You really *are* a greenhorn! Okay, since I'm stuck with you, reckon I'd better fill you in on the scene so you'll be able to cover my flank. The Geniuses share the Glob – that's this star cluster here – with the alien Bems. Things have been quiet for a century or two, but now the Bems are getting grabby. They rustled several human planets, raped the women, ate the men, and did mean things to the kids. They're trying to take over the whole dang Glob! Naturally the Geniuses don't like that – but Geniuses won't never leave their plush cells deep in their planets for nothing. So they've got to hire more regressive types of human critters like us. They pay pretty well, and I reckon it's a good cause, so we're for hire. Me, I sorta like blasting Bems anyway; wouldn't want none o' them to get fresh with my sister, for sure! But Bems are immune to the Genius psi, so we got to use old-fashioned weapons. Which is okay by me; real men don't use psi. We're massing for a big battle now; we're going to raid a Bem planet and give them buggers a taste o' their own snake oil.'

Norton was getting the picture, but still had trouble with an aspect of it. 'The Bems – if they're really bug-eyed monsters, their metabolism must be quite different from ours.'

'That's for sure!' the spaceman agreed readily. 'They're a cross atween bugs and cuttlefish, with huge eyes all over and tentacles and slime dripping. Real yucky!'

'Then how could they have any sexual interest in human women? Surely the women would be as repulsive to the Bems as the Bems are to the women.'

Dursten scratched his tousled head. 'Now that there's a puzzle, now I think on it. But it's a fact that Bems always chase Femmes, 'specially the luscious ones in bikinis. We got a lot o' pictures o' that, so we know it's so. If it wasn't for us noble spacers to rescue them dolls, there'd be no luscious ones left.' He paused thoughtfully. 'Strangest thing, though – some gals seem 'most as worried 'bout *us* as *them*.'

'There's no accounting for taste,' Norton said. 'I suppose if you want the girls for similar purposes – '

He was interrupted by a siren wail. Red lights flashed on the control panel.

'Yow, that there's the campaign alert,' Dursten said. 'Get your butt into that there co-pilot's seat, Nort. It'll just have to be on-the-job training. I shore hope you're a fast study.'

Norton got into the seat. Automatic safety clamps fastened him down. Dursten hit the castoff switch, and the ship dropped off its anchorage on the Wheel.

'Watch it, now. I'm throwing her into null-gee for man-oeuvring,' the spaceman warned. The weight left Norton; only the seat restraints kept him from floating away.

Then the ship accelerated, and he was thrown back against the seat. This needleship had plenty of power!

'One other thing I better tell you about the Bems, just in

case,' Dursten said as he concentrated on his piloting, getting his ship into formation. 'They're shape-changers.'

'What?'

'You heard me, Nort. They can take any form, just like that. So if you ain't certain, fire first.'

'But I don't have a blaster!' Norton said. 'Anyway, if I'm not sure it's a Bem – I mean, I wouldn't want to shoot one of our own people.'

'There is that,' Dursten agreed, as if he hadn't thought of it before. 'That's how my last pardner got it. After I plugged him, I realized he was only green from spacesickness, but it was too late. Had to deep-space him.'

'You killed your partner?' Norton asked, shocked.

The spaceman shrugged. 'I thought he was a Bem. These things happen when you got a quick trigger finger.'

Evidently so! 'I hope you don't make any similar little mistakes on this mission,' Norton said sincerely.

'Naw, no chance. You and me's the only people on this ship. So if you see anyone else, he's a Bem.'

'How do we know we're not Bems? I mean, for all I know, *you* could be one, or for all you know, *I* could.'

Again Dursten paused for a new thought. His hand twitched near his holstered blaster, giving Norton a horrible scare. But then the spaceman had another notion. 'Say, the robot can tell. Here, I'll check us out now. Hey, Clankcase!'

A robot trundled up, its feet evidently held to the deck by magnetism. 'You yelled, sir?' it rasped.

'Yeah, sure,' Dursten said. 'Check out Nort here. Is he human or Bem?'

The robot oriented on Norton. Its body was cubistic, with a television screen where its face should be. A pair of eyes appeared on the screen, and these inspected Norton closely, though not quite in focus. A nose appeared, and this sniffed him, its nostrils flaring. A mouth formed. 'Say "Ah",' it said.

'Argh,' Norton said, suddenly realizing that if the robot

134

decided he was a fake, he could not protect himself; he was bound to the chair.

An ear appeared, sliding to the centre of the screen to listen better, shoving the other features to the side. 'How's that again?' the mouth said from the border.

'A R G H H H H!' Norton repeated clearly.

The eyes slid back to the centre, squinting thoughtfully. 'He's human,' the mouth said. 'Probability of ninety-eight point three five per cent, plus or minus three per cent.'

'Plus or minus three per cent?' Norton asked, shivering with relief. 'Doesn't that mean ninety-five point three to one-hundred-one point three per cent?'

One eye drifted off the screen while the other bore unwaveringly on him. 'Correct,' the robot rasped blithely.

'Well, now check Mr Dursten.'

'Shux, I know *I'm* human!' the spaceman protested. But the machine clanked around to focus its screen face on him.

'Human,' Clankface agreed in due course. 'Ninety-six point one per cent probability, plus or minus the standard three per cent deviation.'

'What?' Dursten lipped thinly. 'You gave *him* a higher rating than *me*?' His finger itched towards his blaster.

'He is more human than you,' the robot explained.

'Get out of here, you bucket of bolts!' Dursten growled, and the robot dutifully retreated.

'I suppose you had better explain to me how to pilot this craft,' Norton said. 'Just in case.'

'You kidding?' the spaceman exclaimed derisively. 'I boned up on piloting for three years afore I even touched my first ship – and I wrecked that! Then it was two more years afore I touched another.'

There was a metallic rattle of laughter from the rear. 'That's why, you silly asteroid!' Clankcase chuckled.

'Get lost, you metal moron!' Dursten snapped.

'Lost? Honest?' the robot asked. 'A foolish man said that once to my cousin, and – '

'Cancel that there directive!' Dursten said quickly. Then privately to Norton: 'That "Little Lost Robot" got written up as a feature story in the tabloids. But that ain't part o' this here sequence.'

'Why do you put up with such perversity from the inanimate?'

The spaceman scratched his head, dislodging some dandruff. 'I sure don't know. It's just always been that way with robots. We need 'em for routine chores, so – ' He shrugged. 'Now I think of it, I'd trade Clankcase in a minute for a better assistant, like maybe a nice, plump Femme. A Femme would *really* be useful.'

Norton realized that opportunities for socializing were limited in space. The spaceman's mind naturally was on the distaff. 'About the piloting – I can't be a very good co-pilot if I don't know anything. Maybe if you just showed me how to signal for help – '

'Aw, I'll show you how to pilot,' Dursten said. 'It'll take 'bout ten minutes, give or take three per cent.'

And indeed, what had taken the spaceman five years to master was transmitted in ten minutes. It was mainly a matter of moving the steering stick and pushing the fire button when a target ship was in the cross hairs on the combat screen. The ship was largely automatic, and what little was not was handled by the robot. An idiot could pilot the ship – which was perhaps fortunate.

However, Dursten explained why it had taken so long for him to qualify. He had been easily distracted by available Femmes at the Academy. Femmes seemed to cause more trouble than Bems did!

The fleet drew into formation and warped through space at Woof-factor 5 towards the enemy planet. Stars streaked by the port like fireflies.

Suddenly a red light flashed. 'Oh, fudge!' Dursten swore. 'An enemy fleet is intercepting us. We'll have to fight.'

'But I thought you like blasting Bems,' Norton said.

The spaceman's handsome face lighted like a nova. 'Say, yeah! I forgot about that!'

The Bemships turned out to be warty boulders. They spread out to engage the human fleet. Soon the two formations degenerated into separate dogfights.

A Bem boulder loomed before their own needle, its ports resembling huge, faceted eyes. Light squirted from one of its warts. 'The danged zilch is shooting at us!' Dursten exclaimed indignantly. 'Well, just for that I'll blast it out o' space!' His features suffused with righteous anger, Bat Dursten concentrated on the obnoxious enemy craft, getting it in the cross hairs. His thumb jabbed the firing button. 'Take that, fertilizer-brain!' he raged.

A beam of light speared out. It struck the boulder. The boulder exploded into smithereens, soundlessly. Norton remembered that sound did not carry well through the vacuum of space.

'Got you, you alien bugger!' Dursten exalted.

But another boulder was bearing down on them. A spurt from a wart just missed their needleship. Quickly the spaceman reoriented, bringing the cross hairs to bear. He punched the button, and the enemy ship smithereened like the last one.

Norton checked the rearview screen. 'Bat, there's one on our tail!' he warned.

'You take it, Nort; I got to watch the front.'

So Norton oriented the aft laser gun, fumbling its cross hairs into place. He fired, but his beam missed. The enemy squeezed a wart back, coming closer. Norton, his hand shaking, got the wobbly cross hairs aligned and mashed the firing button so hard it bruised his finger.

This time he scored. The light lanced forth. The alien vessel burst apart, splatting some of its garbage on his viewscreen. Norton wrinkled his nose; he could almost smell the alien stench.

He turned back to Dursten – just in time to see a young woman approaching the spaceman. She was absolutely luscious in her scanty costume, and her flesh jiggled like gelatin as she walked.

The spaceman looked up at her. 'Say, sweetie – where'd you come from?' he asked, ogling her attributes.

'I replaced your robot,' she said with a phenomenal smile. 'How can I be of service?'

Dursten glanced at Norton. 'Say, co-pilot – why don't you take over the reins while I catch an errand in the back?' he suggested, unbuckling his safety harness.

'But – but how could there be a replacement when we're in deep space?' Norton asked.

The spaceman paused to scratch his head, his eyes remaining on the Femme. 'Say, I never thought o' that!'

'The Genius teleported me in, of course,' the Femme said. 'Did you think of a way I can serve you?'

'Well, as a matter o' fact – ' Dursten began, floating from his chair.

'I'll thank the Genius,' Norton said, touching the communicator. His brief course of instruction had included this, too. The panel had few controls besides an on-off switch.

'You do that,' Dursten agreed, drifting towards the back. He had forgotten to turn the gravity back on, so he had to hold on to the Femme for support.

The head of the Genius appeared on the screen. 'Yes, Norton,' the pursed lips said.

'Uh, sir, did you teleport a buxom young human woman to this ship? A, er, Femme?'

'Certainly not! Spaceman Dursten becomes combat-unready when distracted by temptations of fair flesh.'

An accurate assessment! 'But there's one here!'

The Genius frowned. 'Yes, now I detect an alien presence there. It is immune to my power. Destroy it immediately.' He faded out.

So the shape-changing Bems had infiltrated this fleet, and one was aboard this ship! Norton looked for a blaster, but found none. He spied a loose support rod in his chair,

138

evidence of slipshod construction, and wrenched it out. It would have to do as a weapon.

He set out for the rear of the ship – but his feet left the deck in the null-gee, just as Dursten's had. He didn't know how to turn on the gravity, so had to put up with it. Pilots, he thought irately, should wear magnetic shoes, just as the robots did! Clankcase had had no problem getting around.

Clankcase? The Femme said she had replaced the robot. And her feet had been firm on the deck. Bems, as he understood it, could not teleport or do other psi, but they could change shape. The Bem must have been in the shape of the robot before!

Norton grabbed his chair and pulled himself down close to the floor. Sure enough, there were moist sucker marks where robot and Femme had passed. No doubt about it – there was a Bem aboard.

Norton used the chair as a brace and shoved himself forcefully towards the rear of the ship. In a moment he sailed into the back chamber, where Dursten was in the process of scrambling out of his space suit while the voluptuous Femme giggled and jiggled gelatinously.

'Halt, alien!' Norton cried, brandishing his rod.

Dursten glanced about. '*What* alien?'

'That Femme,' Norton said. 'She's a Bem!'

'How can you say a mean thing like that!' the Femme cried.

Norton did feel like a heel, for she was an eye-popping morsel of pulchritude, but he had to answer. 'Because your sucker feet stick to the floor! *We* float in free-fall.'

She glanced down at her firmly anchored feet. 'Curses – foiled again!' she cried. She charged him, arms extended.

Norton knew he should hit her with his rod, but three things prevented him. First, she remained the most lusciously curvacious item of distaff flesh he had ever seen, and it was against his instinct to brutalize that. Second, when he tried to ready the rod, he lost his grip on the case of stored cans of beans that had anchored him, so he could not strike effectively. Third, she was on him before he could do anything.

Her mass carried him right back into the control room. She was naked now, and felt every bit as luscious as she looked. Her hand struck his rod and it flew free. Now he was weaponless!

Bat Dursten was unable to help; he was too busy climbing back into his space suit. 'To think – I almost kissed it!' the spaceman muttered, looking sick. 'A Bem-Femme!'

Norton was unable to gain any purchase, for the Bem-Femme had hold of him and lifted him aloft. This was easy enough for her to do, since he weighed nothing at the moment, while she had good sucker purchase on the deck. He found himself captive as the woman's shape melted beneath him. Her pretty face sagged into putty; her lovely breasts became great blisters of flesh. She metamorphosed into a mass of gelatin surmounted by three enormous bug eyes. Her two arms became three tentacles, still holding him tight. Her torso quivered in jellylike ripples, as it had before, but somehow the effect was less aesthetic.

'Just wait till I form some good, hard teeth!' she said from the gaping orifice that was all that was left of her once-human mouth. 'I'll chomp you to bits!'

Helpless, Norton stalled for time by engaging in dialogue, hoping Dursten would complete his dressing soon and recover his blaster. 'How did you get aboard, Bem?'

'I stowed away while the ship was in port,' she said. Already fierce teeth were growing in the orifice.

'Are there many of you in the fleet?'

'Sorry – that information is classified.'

How like a military creature! 'If you're going to consume me anyway, why can't you tell me?'

She scratched behind a bug eye with the tip of a free tentacle. 'I suppose it's because I don't know the answer.'

Oh. 'Why didn't you kill us before we suspected your identity?' Where was Dursten?

'Too risky to tackle two at once. I planned to eat Dursten

140

first, then do you when I got hungry again. It takes a while to digest a man; go too fast, and you get gas.'

Norton could see why a gelatinous creature would not want to get gas. 'But you could have eaten him when we were both strapped in our seats!'

The Bem blinked all three bug eyes. 'Say, I never thought of that! Why didn't you speak sooner?'

'Why didn't you eat him the moment you got him alone?'

'Well, he is a handsome man, and not too bright – '

'You mean you'd actually – ?' Norton asked, shocked.

'Oh, we do it all the time to beautiful Femme humans. I thought it would be a nice change to do it to a handsome Manne human this time.'

'But you're a completely different species!'

'True. But space duty does get dull, and novelty is the vinegar of life.'

'*Spice* of life.'

'Whatever. Now I'm ready to eat you.'

Norton, set back by the dialogue, could not think of another question. This was unfortunate, because now the teeth were thoroughly formed and the orifice was ready to commence consumption. 'Help, Bat!' he screamed.

'I can't get my foot into this $&%!! space boot!' the spaceman swore from the back room.

The Bem's orifice gaped. The huge, gleaming, new saw teeth glistened with saliva. The three tentacles hauled Norton down into the maw. 'Bat, forget the boot!' he yelled. 'The monster's eating me!'

'Be there in two shakes of a croggle's tail,' Dursten called back. 'My blaster floated away; got to find it.'

Norton struggled, but still had no purchase. He kicked the monster in an eye, shattering the orb.

'Oh, you mean thing!' the Bem complained. 'Why did you have to do that?'

'All's fair in war,' Norton said, trying to kick at another eye, but he could not get correctly aimed.

'Well, no matter,' the Bem said philosophically, blinking her two remaining eyes. 'I will grow a new one as soon as I digest you.' She sprouted several more tentacles to pin his extremities, rendering him completely helpless. The monster was surprisingly strong.

'Bat!' Norton yelled desperately, but heard only a muttered curse as the spaceman still searched for his missing blaster.

The descent into the maw resumed. In her natural shape, the Bem seemed larger; she really could consume him entire. He continued to think of the monster as female, because of the Femme form it had assumed. Was this the end?

The teeth closed on his boots and began to crunch through them. Saliva washed over the leather. Apparently the Bem could digest these, too.

Then Norton had an inspiration of sorts. 'Sning!' he cried. 'What should I do?'

Squeeze, squeeze, squeeze.

So much for that. 'Well, save yourself, anyway,' he said to the little snake. 'Get out of here before the maw reaches my hands and chews them and you up.'

Sning uncoiled and slid from Norton's finger. He floated a moment in air, also being subject to free-fall, then wriggled forward, using the air itself to slide against. He moved to Norton's pocket where the compressed Hourglass was and tapped it meaningfully with his nose.

The Hourglass! Of course! Would it work when folded away? According to Lachesis, it was unchanged, merely seeming different. Norton willed its sand to turn red. *Travel! In time!* he thought fiercely.

Suddenly he was in space, alone. He had travelled, but the ship had not. He realized that the ship was not a planet; the spell did not align him with it automatically. *The other way!* he thought, hoping this command sufficed.

Evidently it did. In a subjective moment, he was back in the ship, homing in on his prior situation. *Stop.*

He stopped. He was floating in the control room, behind

the two pilot seats. Dursten and Norton himself were discussing the mechanism for controlling the ship. Neither saw the new Norton. Neither robot nor Femme was in evidence; this must be the time right between their appearances.

The prospect of paradox overwhelmed him for the moment. Could he interfere with the events of his past self and change events he had already experienced? He had been told he was an entity apart, in control of time – but he had never consciously tested paradox. He might change the lives of other people – but how could he change his own? Yet if he did not, he would be consumed by the Bem. This did not appeal any more than the prospect of paradox did.

Now he saw the Femme approaching. Hastily he willed the sand and slid forward a few minutes, managing to keep his place within the ship. He floated behind the Bem as she held his former self aloft. *This* was what he had come to undo.

He remembered how he had been wrenched when he turned over the Hourglass, because that reversed his own timeline. Would it do that now, returning him to this point, or a point before the Bem had grabbed him? He had to try!

He turned the glass – and found himself moving backwards, along with the scene. The Bem retreated with her burden to the back room, while he –

He turned the Hourglass over again, and forward progress resumed. The Bem returned.

This wasn't getting him anywhere, because it wasn't changing reality, just his present perception of it. Reality was like a holo he could run forwards or backwards but could not change. But change was what he needed.

Still, if he could affect reality one way, he could affect it another. He concentrated on the Hourglass, turning the sand black.

The scene froze, except for himself. The Bem held the prior Norton aloft, both of them like statues.

Funny – he didn't remember being frozen before. But, of course, the objects were not aware of that, and his prior self was now an object. When they resumed action, they thought it had proceeded uninterrupted. So he could have been frozen . . .

Norton stepped forward, windmilling in air when his feet lacked traction, grabbed a tentacle, and wrenched it off his other self's arm. The tentacle was cold, slimy, and repulsive, but he was able to unwind it. Then he tackled the others. Soon he had his former self free. They were floating, the now-self animate, the then-self a statue.

Very well. He had rescued himself from the Bem. But how could he recombine?

One way to find out. He concentrated on the Hourglass, turning the sand white again. Normal time resumed.

The Bem waved her tentacles. 'Hey, where'd you go?' she exclaimed indignantly.

'I'm not sure,' the then-Norton said.

'Don't worry about it,' the now-Norton said. 'We've got to get rid of this monster before she eats us both!'

'My thought exactly,' the other Norton agreed. 'No sense giving her gas.' He floated to the drifting rod, grabbed it, and tried to stalk the Bem. This wasn't very successful.

Then the Bem helped. She shot out a tentacle and grabbed the other Norton around the waist. Thus anchored, then-Norton raised the rod with both hands and brought it down on what passed for the Bem's head. An eye shattered; now-Norton wasn't certain whether it was the one he had kicked in before, a new one, or whether this was happening before he had kicked that eye.

'Ooooh, that smarts!' the Bem exclaimed, retreating towards the control panel.

Then another strange thing happened. Norton's position jumped. He found himself in the other body, the tentacle around his waist, the rod in his hands.

He had recombined! Time had progressed beyond the point at which he had commenced his time travel, so now there was only one of him. His experience had combined, too;

144

he remembered being mysteriously freed from the clutch of the Bem, as well as remembering doing it while time was frozen. He had been in two halves, and now was whole again. One half was longer than the other, having never been frozen in time, but both were himself. That slight difference in the experience of the two selves gave him a special perspective, like binocular vision, providing a new perception of the depth of reality.

The Bem, however, was righteously angry about her shattered eye. 'You struck me!' she screamed. She shot out another tentacle to grab the rod and wrest it from Norton's grasp.

'I bashed your head in,' Norton said. 'How come you aren't unconscious?'

'I have no head,' the Bem explained. 'You hit my apex.'

Norton brought up his foot and kicked the monster in the crotch. But the Bem did not react. 'Why aren't you doubled over in pain?' he asked. 'Male or female, that should hurt!'

'I have no crotch,' the Bem said, gesturing with the rod. 'That's merely a nether bifurcation.'

Norton grabbed the rod back. The tentacles did not let go, so he wrestled the rod about until it was endways and shoved it violently through the jellylike central mass of the monster. Still there was no reaction.

'But I just stabbed you through the heart!' he cried.

'I have no heart,' the Bem said.

Three more tentacles whipped forward. One of them grabbed the Hourglass, which was now floating next to Norton. 'Hey, that's mine!' he shouted. 'Give it back!'

'Make me!' the Bem sneered.

But Norton couldn't make her, for she dangled the Hourglass just out of his reach. He couldn't change time, because he didn't have the Hourglass. He was in trouble again.

The Bem slid her maw forward until it intersected the rod that was still stuck through her body. Then she used the maw to spit out the rod. Being gelatinous certainly had its advantages!

'Now it's your turn,' the monster said, focusing a bug eye on Norton and hauling him in towards the maw again.

He kicked her in the teeth. Ouch! His whole foot felt numb from the shock. Furthermore, the maw caught his boot again and the teeth crunched into it.

There was a blast of terrible heat. 'Ooooh, you shouldn't have!' the Bem gasped, collapsing against the control panel.

Norton pulled his boot free of the crumbling teeth and twisted out of the failing grasp of the tentacles. Now he saw Bat Dursten, blaster in hand. The spaceman had finally got his boots on, his weapon back, and had blasted the Bem!

'In the nick o' time, as usual,' Dursten said, blowing the smoke from his muzzle and holstering his weapon with practised flair.

'I should have finished you when I had the chanmphnn,' the Bem said, trailing off into gibberish as her mouth melted. In fact, the entire monster was dissolving, her substance bubbling across the control panel and dripping to the floor.

'Nonsense,' Dursten said briskly. 'The good guys always win. It's in the script.' He glanced carelessly at Norton. 'You okay, Nort?'

'I think so.' Norton decided not to comment on the spaceman's inordinate delay in appearing.

'Well, let's get back into action,' Dursten said briskly. Then he looked at the control panel. 'Yaup! The cussed critter's melted into it! That gook'll ruin the wiring!'

The Bem marshalled enough animation to form a small mouth in the dribble near the floor. 'That's what happens, you klutz, when you blubb-drip-popple-ugh.' The rest of her plopped to the floor inertly.

'What did you call me?' the spaceman demanded ferociously.

One more bubble popped from the subsiding mass. 'Gludz!' it breathed, and was no more.

'Why, you sidewinding bugger!' Dursten shouted, stomping the gook with his boot. 'You take that back, hear?' But the muck only squished under his boot with the sound of a chuckle.

'How is it that the Bem falls to the floor, while we drift in free-fall?' Norton asked.

'Forget that!' Dursten snapped, drifting. 'The fool stuff's shorted the wiring! We're out of control! We'll crash on the dang alien planet!'

'But we're in deep space!' Norton protested. Then, as he peered out the front viewport, he saw that there was indeed a planet rushing up below.

'Hang on, pardner!' Dursten cried, grabbing on to the pilot's seat and hauling himself into it.

Norton followed suit, though a dribble of Bem had splatted across his chair. In a moment they were both securely buckled in, watching the ground rush up. Norton caught a glimpse of seas, continents, mountains, jungles, and shining prismatic cities. It looked very much like the kind of planet he'd like to visit – but not at this velocity.

There was a jolt that flung them forward against the restraints. 'The retros,' Dursten explained. 'They're on automatic, to brake us so we don't crash so hard.'

'That's nice,' Norton gasped. Indeed, they were no longer falling as fast – but the descent remained harrowing.

Then the ship crashed, and everything went up in smoke.

Norton shook his head, clearing it. He was hung up on the branch of a giant, serpentine, purple tree, miraculously unhurt. Bat Dursten was strewn over another branch. The wreckage of their needleship was below, sinking slowly into a bubbling grey-green bog. This was obviously a Bem landscape!

Dursten hauled himself upright. 'Looks like the Bem planet we came to raid,' he remarked. 'It's the scum of the Glob! Well, let's get going.'

'Get going where?' Norton asked.

'To hijack a Bemship and go home, of course.'

It seemed to Norton that would be easier said than done. On the other hand, he had no better suggestion.

They climbed down the tree to the ground. A giant antlike thing rushed up, its mandibles clacking menacingly. Dursten's hand was a blur as he drew his blaster and blasted the thing. It exploded, and pieces of it splatted into the trunk of the tree. 'Guess I fixed that creep,' the spaceman remarked, holstering his weapon.

'But how do you know it wasn't friendly?' Norton asked, appalled at the wanton killing.

'You kidding? Ain't nothing friendly on a bugger planet,' the spaceman assured him. He led the way away from the tree, scouting for a suitable enemy to hijack.

Norton followed. There still wasn't much else to do. He wished he could linger long enough to study the exotic alien wilderness, but Dursten wasn't waiting. Spacemen, it seemed, had no interest in wilderness.

They skirted an arm of the bog. The grey-green gook hissed, menacing them. Eyeballs sprouted all over it. Instantly Dursten's blaster was in his hand.

'Don't – ' Norton warned.

He was too late. The spaceman had hair-trigger reflexes. He fired. The gook puffed into noxious fog that spread out, threatening to envelop them. The eyeballs were hazier now, but still managed to focus on the prey.

Dursten backed off. 'That thing ain't dying!' he exclaimed. 'It's worse'n it was! Why didn't you say something, Nort?'

'I tried to warn – '

'Well, let's mosey on. We got a long way to go afore night.'

'But there's no night, here in the Glob,' Norton pointed out. 'Too many close stars – '

The spaceman scratched his head with the muzzle of his

blaster. 'There is that,' he opined. 'We'd better eat something so we don't get hungry.' He grabbed a rich red fruit from a nearby tree.

The fruit hissed and squirted brown juice at him. Dursten jumped back, but got some on his space suit. There was a sizzle, and smoke curled up as the acid etched channels in the material. 'Then again, I reckon I ain't that hungry yet.'

They came to a large, clear, glassy crystal standing on a block in the jungle. 'Wonder what this bauble is?' Dursten said, reaching out to tap it with the butt of his blaster.

'Don't – ' Norton cried.

Too late, of course. His protective reactions were just not as fast as the spaceman's whims. Dursten's butt touched the side of the crystal. The crystal vibrated. Light emanated from it. A humming sound developed, waxing and waning rhythmically as the light pulsed.

'Better get on out of here!' Dursten cried.

Norton's sentiments exactly! The two men fled as a Bem spaceball came into sight on the horizon.

'It was a signal station!' Norton gasped. 'Now they know we're here!'

Ahead loomed a huge saurian shape. It looked somewhat like a green carnivorous dinosaur with a toothache and somewhat like a twenty-ton grasshopper with teeth on its knees. It opened its ponderous and marbled jaws.

This time Norton did not cry warning. He grabbed Dursten by the collar and hauled him around behind the bright yellow trunk of a tree.

The saurhopper bounded forward – just as the pursuing Bem sailed up on its antigrav saucer. The two crashed together.

'This way!' Dursten cried, taking charge of the situation, undismayed by the sheer coincidence of their escape. He ran for the alien ship that now rested in a small glade to the rear.

'But suppose there are other Bems inside?' Norton asked.

'I'll plug 'em,' the spaceman said confidently. He was, of course, a man of action and quick decision.

Sure enough, a second Bem loomed in the irising door aperture. Dursten drew and fired in a single motion – but his blaster made a little, stupid *pfft!* and sagged in his hand. Its charge was gone.

The Bem had no hands, so it didn't carry a blaster. But it started to change shape.

'We'd better hide,' Norton said cautiously.

But stalwart Dursten was already charging the ship. Norton had to follow or let him go alone. He followed.

The Bem had sprouted half a dozen tentacles by the time they reached the ship. Dursten made a flying tackle that knocked the monster off its nether tentacles. Norton came up and shoved the mass out of the door-iris to the ground. He caught hold of one of the spaceman's legs and hauled him inside the ship.

'Thanks, pardner,' Dursten drawled as he got up and thumbed the button to close the iris. 'Next time I'll get me a six-shooter blaster so it don't poop out so fast.' He forged to the control section of the ship. 'Good thing I studied how to operate Bemships too,' he remarked.

To Norton, the controls looked similar to those of the needleship. He could probably operate them himself. Perhaps the Bems weren't, after all, so different from humans.

The acceleration couches were like saucers. Dursten and Norton seated themselves within them, and automatic safety harnesses came out to secure the men. Dursten punched buttons, and the ship lifted from the ground and hovered over the purple tree.

Another Bemball loomed close. Dursten's hand struck the firing button. A wart spat a shot of something – and the other ship exploded.

'Did you have to do that?' Norton demanded. 'We're in a Bemship now; maybe the other one was just being neighbourly.'

'The only good Bem is a blasted Bem,' the spaceman said, hawking and looking for a spittoon. As usual, there was none; this was, after all, the space age.

'Maybe if you just got to know a Bem, you'd find it pretty similar to our own kind. They speak our language and chase our women and breathe the same kind of air we do.'

Dursten scratched his head as he piloted the ship off-planet. 'Never thought of it that way. Got to admit that one on the needle was interesting when she took Femme form.'

That wasn't precisely what Norton had meant, but he let it pass. At least he had made progress.

Dursten glanced down at the dwindling disc of the planet. 'Well, I reckon it's time.' He slapped a red button.

'Time for what?'

'Time to blow up the planet, of course.'

'Blow up the planet!' Norton exclaimed, horrified.

'That's what we came for, you know, Nort.'

'But it would be so much better to – to conquer it and exploit its resources! Or to make a peace treaty with the Bems so they won't bother human planets any more. Maybe they could teach us how to shape-change.'

'There is that,' the spaceman agreed. 'Maybe I shouldn't have let that bomb drop.'

'Bomb?'

'Sure, the planetbuster bomb. It'll blow any moment now.'

'Any – ?' Norton said, freshly appalled.

Then the bomb detonated. There was a burst of light. The planet split into two halves that flew apart.

Norton stared, sheerly horrified. 'The planet's broken!'

'Sure,' Dursten drawled carelessly. 'Bems make good bombs, I'll say that for 'em.'

'But why would one of their own ships carry such a devastating weapon?'

Dursten shrugged. 'Guess they planned to use it on one o' ours. Now let's get on home, mission accomplished.'

Norton turned away, grief-stricken for the death of an

151

entire world and all the wilderness on it. He spied something behind them, in the ship, and blinked.

It was another Bem. But this one was small, with rather cute little tentacles and prettily shining eye facets. The spaceman was preoccupied by his task of setting course for home, so Norton unbuckled himself quietly and got out of his dish. He went to meet the little Bem. 'What are you doing here?'

'I'm Baby Bem,' the creature piped from a mouth that formed in the top part of its globe. As if to illustrate the point, it started sucking on a tentacle.

'You mean those were your folks who – ' Norton stopped.

'We're going on a family picnic,' Baby Bem said, blinking two or three wide eyes.

Not any more, Norton thought grimly. There was no longer a planet to picnic on, and no other Bems to picnic with. This baby was an orphan. 'Just a moment, Baby,' he said.

He turned to Dursten. 'How do you feel about orphans?'

'Poor things need a foster parent or something,' the spaceman said promptly. ''specially orphans o' the void.'

'Would you take care of an orphan child?'

'Me? I ain't no family man!'

'But you *are* a spaceman, embodying the best and brightest and noblest qualities of the human species.'

'There is that,' Dursten agreed.

'So if an orphan of any type needed protection – '

'Aw, sure, I reckon so.'

'Well, turn around and meet the orphan.'

Bat Dursten, the pride of the space fleet, started to turn.

Norton abruptly sailed through the wall of the ship and out into space. Helplessly he accelerated, feeling no physical discomfort. He zoomed between the stars of the globular cluster and on out into deep space, heading for the Galaxy-proper.

He was, he realized, on his way back to Earth; his sample excursion was over.

8
Clotho

Satan was awaiting him back in his mansion. 'Did you enjoy your visit, Chronos?'

It took Norton a moment to collect himself. 'I confess it was quite an experience! I did not realize your power extended so far!'

'My power is damn near universal,' the Prince of Evil said smugly.

'But one thing perplexes me. You know I live backwards, so outside my mansion here I have to make a special effort to align myself with normal people, if I want to interact with them. But in the Glob that was not the case.'

'Astute of you to notice,' Satan said.

'But how, then – ?'

The Father of Lies smiled winningly. 'Elementary, my dear associate. That is a CT globular cluster.'

'Cee Tee?' Norton asked blankly.

'Contraterrene. Antimatter. Where the atoms are made up of negatrons in the nucleus and orbiting positrons, the precise opposite of the local persuasion.'

'Oh. I've heard of it. But isn't such matter instantly annihilated by contact with normal matter?'

'Not when it's isolated. In a CT galaxy, our type of matter is abnormal. This happens to be a CT globular cluster orbiting our terrene-matter galaxy. No actual contact.'

'Very interesting. But since I belong to this galaxy – '

'You are a special case, Chronos. A very special case. You are an Incarnation, and not just a garden-variety one at that. You are the Incarnation of Time.'

'Yes, and I live backwards. Which is why – '

'But you see, my dear sir, contraterrene matter, being

opposite in charge, is also opposite in time. Therefore its frame is yours. That is why you, alone of all of us, are able to relate normally there.'

'Oh.' Norton would have to think about that. 'You mean that human beings have evolved there, just like us, though there has never been any connection between us? With the same language and everything?'

'It is called convergent evolution,' Satan said. 'And this is what I offer you, sir: a pleasant visit there whenever you choose.'

'A pleasant visit!' Norton exploded. 'I almost got wiped out!'

'Oh? I doubt it. As an Incarnation, you are fairly comprehensively protected from incidental mischief.'

'A Bem was going to eat me!'

'Bem?'

'Bug-Eyed-Monster, as if you didn't know! I was lucky to escape with my feet intact!'

'Oh, *that* kind of Bem. I assure you, you could not have been in genuine danger. The worst that could have happened would have been a premature termination of your visit. You would have returned here when your situation there became unplayable. I thought you understood that.'

'*Now* he tells me,' Norton muttered. But he had to admit, to himself, that it had indeed been an exciting adventure and change of pace. His wanderlust had always taken him to new sides of new mountains, and that CT Glob had been a really different mountain! 'You have other visiting spots?'

Satan gestured expansively. 'An entire universe of them, sir! A good many of them CT, aligned with your natural inclination, perfectly safe for you. Some are scientific, some fantastic, some mixed like our present world. There is some very nice material in the Magic-Lantern Clouds. And all I ask in return is this one trifling little favour.'

Norton still did not trust the motive of the Father of Lies, but found himself tempted. An entire CT framework to explore, with all types of people and cultures and planets, and no problem about reversed time! In retrospect, he discovered he had enjoyed the little adventure with Bat Dursten and the Bems, though it helped to know that he had not actually been in danger. If he ever returned there, he might use his power as Chronos to go back to the instant before Dursten released the planetbuster bomb and save the Bem planet from destruction. The least he could do now was listen to Satan's plea. 'Do you care to provide a little detail on that favour?'

'Certainly,' Satan said briskly. 'I would like to do a favour for a man about twenty years ago. I am in a position to know, because of hindsight, that a single choice of his had profound effects on his life. He made the wrong choice, and it led to his early demise. Had he made the right choice, it would have led to love and life with a beautiful and wealthy heiress, and phenomenal well-being for him. So now I would like to correct My error of omission and send a minion back to advise that man of the correct choice.'

'Why should you, the Prince of Evil, care to do a good deal for a mortal man?' Norton asked suspiciously.

Satan grinned disarmingly. 'I have My favourites too, Chronos. I try to reward those who help Me, and I am generous when pleased. In death, this man impressed Me favourably and rendered good service; now I wish to reward him by granting him, retroactively, the one thing he thought forever beyond his reach – an excellent life. He will probably go to Heaven thereafter, and so I shall lose him – but as I said, I am generous and I keep My promises.'

Norton wasn't sure he believed that, but he doubted there was any percentage in arguing with the Father of Lies. 'Give me his spacetime address.'

'Certainly!' Satan conjured a scroll on which was written neatly in blood a place and time.

'Kilvarough,' Norton read, taking the scroll. 'The Mess o' Pottage shop.' He looked up. 'What's that man's name?'

Satan scratched his head, a bit like Bat Dursten. 'Did I

omit that detail? How silly of Me! The name escapes Me at the moment – I do have countless clients, you know – but I will have My minions research it before we meet again. You will, of course, want to verify the situation yourself before you act on this and you can find the shop with the present information.'

'Yes,' Norton agreed. 'Understand, Satan – I'm making no promise. If I don't like the deal, I won't take your minion.'

'Understood of course. I know better than to attempt to deceive a person of your perspicacity.' Then Satan raised his finger, marking an afterthought. 'But until I locate that specific name, there could be confusion. Allow Me to provide you a ready way to contact Me, in case of need.' He curved his fingers, and abruptly a thin chain was there, anchored to an amulet. 'Accept this, sir, and blow it to summon Me. I will hear it, wherever and whenever, and come to your aid.'

'Well, I really don't think – ' But already Satan was pushing it into his hand. The amulet was a little horn with a flared rim, made of brass. Norton shrugged and put the chain on over his head. He didn't anticipate needing Satan's aid in anything, but there was no point in antagonizing him. He could simply ignore the amulet.

Sning squeezed twice, not liking even this gesture, but Norton felt that in this case expedience was preferable to affront. *Let it be*, he thought, and, reluctantly, Sning shut up.

Satan stood and saluted with one hand. 'Farewell, sir!' He vanished in a small puff of smoke.

Before Norton could organize his thoughts, the butler appeared. 'Another visitor, sir.'

'Who?' Norton asked shortly. He did not seem to be physically tired from the adventure in the CT Glob, but a great deal had happened recently, and he was about ready to call it a day.

'Clotho, sir.'

'Who?'

'An aspect of Fate, sir.'

156

'Oh.' Now it registered. He had seen only a flash of the youngest form of Fate and had been impressed, but the name had not made the same impression her body had. 'Show her in.' Fate was a remarkable woman, with her three forms.

Clotho stepped daintily in. She was not only young, she was lovely. She had done something to her hair so that it fell loosely to her shoulders in a gleaming cascade, and her dress was alluring. It was bright blue, with a peek-a-boo bodice that offered a startlingly intimate peek. 'Ready for this day's work, Chronos?' she asked.

'I think I've already had a day's work,' he replied.

'Oh? Will we do this tomorrow? It's my future and your past, remember. I assume I'm doing things in proper order for you, but it's easy to get confused.'

Norton laughed, relaxing. 'No, it's my confusion, not yours. You introduced me to my office and showed me how to function, and now we'll do more substantial work together as I learn the details of my job. I'm sure I'll get it all straight in due course. What I meant was that Satan has been here this morning – it *is* morning?'

'Midday,' she said. 'Time is normal for you, here in your mansion. But when I depart here, it will be earlier than I arrived. I'll have to avoid meeting myself, to prevent needless confusion.'

'I know the feeling!' Then something else occurred to him. 'It was afternoon when Satan came to visit me, and then – why did I think it was morning? It should be evening!'

'Probably you have spent the night,' she suggested. 'I plan to come to orient you tomorrow, in my Lachesis aspect, as that is your last day of office.'

'Yes, then a day has passed for me,' he agreed. 'But I don't remember it! Satan sent me to an – an alternate universe for an adventure, but – '

'How long were you there?'

'It's hard to tell. It seemed like an hour, but things fuzzed out when I was travelling, so – '

'So it could have been a day,' she finished. 'Satan is the master of deception. He can make an instant seem like an eternity, and vice versa. It is illusion, of course; only you can truly control time. But Satan's illusions can be doozies.'

'Yes, that must be it. I spent a day there, all told, and returned here. Anyway, Satan wants a favour, and – '

'Don't trust Satan!' Clotho said. 'He is the most sinister and devious of the Incarnations! He is always concocting mischief.'

'I don't plan to take anything he tells me at face value. But he has been helpful, so I will at least give him a hearing.'

'Well, leave me out of it,' Clotho said. 'I suppose we all have to learn about Satan in our own fashions. Now – let's get to work. Do you know how to use your Hourglass to read individual threads?'

'Not yet,' Norton admitted.

'Well, you were good enough at it yesterday, so I know you'll catch on readily.' She proceeded to teach him how to orient on the particular life-thread of a person, and how to fix on the exact place that thread had to be started, kinked, and cut. He was interested, but he kept being distracted by her peek-a-boo display that served as a backdrop for the threads as she held them up between her hands, and feared he seemed inattentive at times.

The start of each thread was a mortal birth, each kink was a key event in that life, and the cut end marked the termination of that life. These were only the special lives, Clotho explained; his staff and hers did most of the routine planning. Norton found it confusing at first, but soon he had the Hourglass ticking off indications rapidly. Each minuscule grain of sand, it seemed, was something like a mortal life, matching each of Fate's fine threads.

He glanced at his Hourglass with new appreciation. All those fine grains of sand – all of humanity, represented in this one instrument! Each single grain too small to perceive by itself, yet of total significance for its person. Did the cosmos care about any single grain of life-sand? About when or where it flowed, or the satisfaction of its tiny existence?

After several hours, Clotho paused and stretched, flexing the peek-a-boo. 'All work and no play,' she said and moved into his arms.

Startled, Norton froze. 'Is something wrong?' he asked.

'Oh, haven't we done this before, in your scheme?' she asked. 'I keep forgetting – you're coming from the other direction. This is new to you, isn't it?'

'Everything is new to me,' he agreed.

'Well, I think this is the time to begin, then, because in the recent past we have – ' She paused. 'But why should I spoil it for you by my memories? Come on, I'll lead you through.'

'Through what?'

'Silly boy! Why do you think I came as Clotho? I am the young man's – '

'Oh. You – Lachesis – did say something about – '

She cut him off with a kiss. She was a most attractive woman in this guise, but his painful memory of Orlene remained, and he wasn't ready for this. He drew away. 'I hardly know you!' he protested.

She laughed, unrebuffed. 'With any other person, I'd say you were joking! But that's all in your future, isn't it? Very well – what do you think is holding you back?'

Norton pondered. 'I don't suppose you'd care to believe anything about my not being a casual sort of person?'

She laughed merrily. 'You? You forget that I measured your thread before you assumed this office! You're fully casual with women!'

'You know me too well!' he agreed ruefully. He kept allowing himself to be deceived by appearances, when by now he ought to know better. Clotho had those deep eyes of Fate and she was no young or innocent damsel. No indeed! She was an Incarnation, with all the subtle power that implied. 'But all that stopped when I met Orlene. She was the first true love I experienced, and – '

159

'Oh, yes, of course – that's still fresh in your mind! How silly of me to forget! It is my position to help you get over that so you can focus without reservation on your office. Very well – we'll take time off to go see your mortal woman.'

'We?'

'Well, you could take me with you if you chose; it's in your magical power to do so. But I agree: for this, you'd better go alone.' She fished in her dark hair and drew forth a single strand. 'Here is Orlene's thread. Truncated, as you can see; only a third as long as it should have been. You can, of course, restore the full length, if you wish. The powers of the Incarnations are great, but none are absolute where they overlap those of other Incarnations. Orient your Glass on this, and you'll find her anywhere you choose.'

Norton had been learning the technique of thread orientation. He touched the Hourglass to the thread, then willed the sand blue.

The mansion vanished. He was zooming along the thread as if riding a cablecar. Events of the world rushed past, glimpsed momentarily. *Slow*, he thought, and progress eased, the glimpses becoming longer.

It was Orlene's life he was following, backwards. Her individual motions were too rapid for him to focus on, but her surroundings had more staying power. A building she had spent time in – perhaps a school – abruptly vanished. It had been unconstructed, and she moved on to a lesser school, more crowded. Trees around her home slowly shrank, their foliage flickering on and off through the seasons, the deciduous trees becoming suddenly clothed in bright leaves which then faded to green and eventually sucked back into the twigs and branches. The lawn grass kept jumping high, then smoothing down till nearly bald, then being mowed high again. The house became brightly painted, then abruptly turned dull.

He brought himself to a random halt. He was in a school class, looking at a girl about ten years old. The scene was strange; in a moment he realized this was because he was viewing it backwards. He had halted himself, not time, and now was living normally, for him. No one here was aware of him – but if he changed to match the world's time flow, he would become visible, disrupting the scene, so he let it be.

This was evidently a cooking class, with the teacher demonstrating how to bake a pie by using pyro-magic. Under her reversed guidance, the demonstration pie proceeded from brown to gold and on into pasty white. Norton watched the young Orlene, a pretty girl even at this age. Alas, she was not paying full attention, but was whispering with a female companion in girlish fashion. Her pie would probably be botched.

He turned the sand red and moved a few years into this Orlene's future, then watched her backwards again. This time she was lying on her bed at home, in jeans and a man's shirt – what was there about men's shirts that caused girls to prefer them to their own? – chatting into her holophone. It was a boy in the image, tousle-haired, animated, obviously full of the enthusiasm of the moment. Orlene was now about fifteen, and was assuming much of her adult beauty; he recognized some of her little mannerisms, as yet unperfected. He felt a surge of nostalgia; this girl was in the visible process of becoming the woman he had loved.

He moved three more years along her life, to her age eighteen. Now she was playing squash with a young man. It was a game that brought the active players into close proximity, since they shared the court as they slammed the ball against the wall, and therefore seemed to be popular for mixed couples. The man was obviously beating her, but the motions of her body as she strove for points were beautiful. The ball rebounded and flew at her, and she swung her racket backwards to intersect it, whereupon it flew back from her while she wore a look of expectant concentration. Orlene had matured into a healthy, lovely young woman, and it was sweetly painful for Norton to look at her. Those limbs, that torso, that face with the backward-flying hair – he had known them all intimately, in her present future. Those lips – he had kissed them, years hence. Orlene – he would love her and loved her still.

He followed her through to the beginning of the game, when she was fresh, clean, unglowing, and ready for anything. She bade hello to her opponent-date and strode backwards away from him to the female changing room. Norton hesitated, then decided not to pursue her there; he knew what her body was like, but this was inappropriate peeking.

He was not doing this just to be a voyeur. He wanted to rescue the woman he loved from her dreadful fate. Now he knew he could do it; his experience in rescuing himself from the Bem in the Glob had proved that. He was immune from paradox; he could change his own past and those of others without nullifying his present. He did not intend to abuse this power, but he did intend to spare her.

Where was the best place to act? *When* was best? Probably before he, Norton, had met her, so he would not have to interfere openly with himself. Would this nullify his association with her? Yes, surely it would – but that would be replaced by a new association, a better one. In fact, he could void the whole ghost marriage and marry her himself.

But first he had better make sure of his power. He wanted to interact with her in a noncritical period of her life, not to change anything, just to be sure he knew what he was doing. This was no ordinary person; this was Orlene!

He moved back along the thread to her childhood, to the time when she was seven years old, on her summer vacation after her first year of formal school. Now she was not using a holophone, because that instrument had not yet been commerically developed; the old sonic ones were still extant. Anyway, she was too young for social interchanges with interested boys; she was a wild-honey-haired spirit, running through one of the early city rooftop parks. The trees were still in big pots, and ramparts showed; true wilderness was a

162

thing of future parks. A lot of the bad old pollution and messiness remained in the world; soon the political climate would change, greatly facilitating improvement, but it had not happened at this moment.

She was with a party of children, but strayed from them, skipped happily down a bypath, and got lost. Worried, she gazed at the several bifurcations of the paved path, unsure which to take. Norton, having travelled past her immediate future, knew that she would be lost for a good thirty-five minutes, an eternity at that age, and be in tears before a park attendant rescued her from bewilderment and brought her back to her party. This was the appropriate time to approach her.

He tuned in to the beginning of her isolation and turned the sand green. Now he was in phase with her.

'Hello, Orlene,' he said gently. He was a grown man and she was a child, but he felt almost shy.

She stopped her nervous ambulation and turned quickly to face him. 'Oh – I didn't see you!' she exclaimed. 'Who are you, mister, in that funny dress?'

He was wearing the white robe of his office, of course. 'I am – ' He hesitated; he hadn't thought this through. He couldn't tell her he was Chronos; she would hardly understand. Neither could he tell her he was her future lover. 'A friend.'

'Can you tell me how to get back?'

'I'll try. I think it's this way.' He gestured towards the correct path, and they walked along it.

'How did you know my name?' Orlene asked brightly.

'I've seen you in school.'

'Oh, you're a teacher!' she exclaimed, as if it were the most important thing in the world.

'Well – ' But she was already skipping ahead, her piggy-braids flouncing.

I love her even as a child, he thought, surprised and somewhat awed at the extent of his own commitment. He had

163

been, as Clotho had chided him, free with women; this one had chained his soul. He followed after, trying to think of suitable comments to make or questions to ask.

Then Orlene made a glad little cry. 'There they are!' She ran to join her group.

The adult guide turned at the sound of her voice. Norton hastily shifted sand and faded out of contemporary view. Orlene was all right; she was an innocent child. She had been spared a bad half hour. He was glad he had been able to do her that small service. But adults were another matter. They would ask the wrong questions.

So his dialogue with Orlene had amounted to nothing. There had been no meaningful personal interaction.

No, not entirely true. She would probably forget the stranger in the white dress, but he had discovered the extent of his capacity. Now he knew he needed to rehearse himself better for questions. It had been a good practice session.

Should he go back those few minutes in time and replay it, trying to effect a more personal contact? He decided not to. He had verified what he wanted to; he could interact with her without wreaking havoc or generating paradox. Now he could proceed with confidence to change her life significantly.

He moved back and forth along her life-thread, sampling it here and there, zeroing in on the appropriate region. He traced, somewhat erratically, her life up to the point at which the family of Gawain the Ghost had contacted her and made her the offer she could not refuse. There had been other men in her young life – Norton spied on these passing relationships with a certain voyeuristic jealousy, though he knew from his own prior experience that she had been a virgin bride. Orlene had been looking for Mister Right and had not been able to choose among those who were handsome and stupid, smart but poor, or rich but degenerate. She, like any sensible girl, wanted perfection in a man, and it was hard to come by. Thus she was the perfect candidate for the ghost marriage: attractive, intelligent, pristine, and reasonably ambitious for security and creature comfort.

There was a period of about three months before Gawain's family came, when Orlene had no romantic attachment. This was ideal for Norton's purpose.

He located a day when she was home watching a dull holo rerun and phased in. He knew the young woman of twenty would not be even fractionally as accepting as the girl of seven had been, so he planned his approach more carefully. But he planned no deception; that would be the wrong way to start a relationship as important as this.

He knew she was alone today; that was a major reason he selected this time. Her father was away on a business trip, and her mother was on a shopping spree. So Orlene was minding the house. There would be a good six hours, if he managed it correctly – and if he did not, he would wind it back and try again. That was one huge advantage of his present office: he could replay scenes to correct errors. Of course, he would have to undergo the discomfort of reversing himself also, because he did not want several copies of himself competing for her attention. But with luck he would not make any bad errors, and would not have to run his own line backwards for more than a minute or so at a time.

He phased in outside her house and stepped up to the door. Again he felt something very like stage fright; his pulse way racing. But he kept a rein on himself and held his thumb on the pattern-recognition panel. In a moment Orlene's image appeared on the doorscreen. 'Sorry, we aren't buying,' she said pertly.

'I am not a salesman,' Norton said. 'I am a storyteller.' He had cadged many a meal that way in his past life; he had always told good stories that made people welcome him. This was the age of holo entertainment, but there was a special quality to genuine, live, personal narrative that still attracted people. The machines and the spells could never take over entirely!

'A what?'

'A storyteller. In this futuristic age, I revert to old-fashioned values. I tell stories by hand. By mouth, I mean.'

'You're selling holotapes?'

'No tapes. Just myself. Every narration an original! If you care to listen, I will – '

'Sorry,' she said, and the screen blanked.

He had blown it. She was, of course, not paying much attention to strangers. This was a sensible attitude for young women alone in houses.

He overturned the Hourglass and reversed time for himself and her, unwinding the prior sequence. Naturally she would not be aware of this; her life was erased to that extent.

'You're selling holotapes?' she asked as he resumed forward motion, thirty seconds back.

'No tapes. Stories. About young women who play pianos with rare skill and squash with lesser skill.'

She hesitated, surprised. He had described her, of course. 'What is this?'

'Stories about people who like picture puzzles,' he said. 'And walks in parks. And babies.'

She stared at him through the screen. 'Who are you, really?'

'I doubt you would believe that.'

'Try me.'

'I am Chronos – the human Incarnation of Time.'

She laughed. 'One for one! I certainly don't believe that!'

'I can show you tricks with time – '

'Don't bother, thank you.' The screen faded.

He rolled time back again. 'Try me,' she said.

'Your future associate. You will enter into a ghost marriage and – '

The screen faded.

He reversed time again. 'Try me,' she said.

He held up his left hand. 'Sning, show her.'

Sning uncoiled and slid into his palm. 'Oh, how cute!' Orlene exclaimed. 'I've got one just like it!'

'You gave me this,' Norton said. 'It's yours.'

'I did not! I have mine right here!' She paused, then brought up a duplicate snake ring.

This made Norton pause. Could Sning meet himself? Why not? Norton had met himself in the Glob. Sning had probably doubled up that time, too. 'Maybe they should meet.'

She put her ring on her finger and paused again, evidently thinking a question at it. After a moment she shrugged and opened the door. 'He says you're okay,' she said, almost apologetically. Norton entered, feeling somewhat the way he had felt when he first met her, almost three years hence. She was so lovely, and he so ordinary, and he wanted so much from her; how could he make known his ambition?

He touched the table with his left hand, and Sning slithered off to join the other snake. Apparently duplication of creatures was no problem, though he was sure paradox lurked in the shadows. How far did his immunity extend?

'May I get you something?' Orlene asked.

'No, thanks. I think I'd just better tell you what is on my mind.' He drew out a chair and sat down at the table.

She took a chair opposite. 'You certainly act as if you know me.'

'Let me show you my nature,' he said. 'What I have to say will be more credible, once you understand that.'

'Perhaps,' she agreed noncommittally. He wondered whether she was inspecting him for glow. Perhaps not; she was looking at him as an intriguing stranger, not as a marriage prospect, so the glow might not be in evidence – if, indeed, he was at this stage a good marriage prospect for her. Of that he could hardly be sure. He loved her, yes – but there was already more to this relationship than love.

'I am Chronos, the Incarnation of Time.' This time she did not retreat; she was intrigued enough to listen. 'I can reverse the flow of time, in part or in whole. Here.' He fished in his pocket for a pebble he had saved for its pretty form. Technically, he had been robbing the wilderness of Mars, but

167

he did not think that planet would mind. He dropped the red stone on the table. 'Note how it falls.'

'Straight down,' she said, raising an eyebrow, not sure of his point.

'I will reverse time for myself, for a moment,' he said. He held up the Hourglass, but did not invert it, he wanted only a limited effect. He turned the sand red, then willed the spot-reversal.

The sand reversed course, flowing from the base to the upper chamber of the Hourglass. A moment later the pebble on the table bounced, then lifted up to join his right hand. Then he turned the sand green, rejoining the normal world time. He had kept the reversal quite limited, so that Orlene had not been affected.

Orlene grabbed for her snake ring. In her haste she got both of them. One curled around one finger, the other around another. 'Is he of Satan?' she asked tersely.

Norton could not see the little snakes squeezing, but knew they were. 'Is he really Chronos?' she asked next. And finally: 'Then why does he wear an amulet of Satan?'

Startled, Norton glanced down at the little horn Satan had given him, suspended on its chain. 'Satan did give me this,' he said. 'But I am not his creature. He asked me to do him a favour, and this amulet was to summon him if I needed him.' He lifted the horn – and discovered that part of it was missing. There had been a flared rim; now there was only the basic horn. 'The rim must have fallen off during a prior phase-in to normal time.'

'Throw it away!' Orlene said.

Norton removed the chain and set the amulet on the table. 'If I threw it away here, it would remain in your vicinity. Better to destroy it. Do you have an incinerator?'

'Flames won't destroy a thing of the Devil!' she said. 'I have some holy water.' She rose to fetch it. Norton tried not to gaze at her too obviously; she was so lovely, so almost-familiar – yet he had seen her dead, years hence.

In a moment she returned with a vial. She shook a few drops on to the horn. It blackened and shivered, emitting a noxious stench. The chain wrestled itself around like a live thing, then puffed into a ring of smoke.

Orlene relaxed. 'I don't like Satan,' she said.

'Neither do I,' Norton agreed, his conviction strengthening because of hers. 'He is the Incarnation of Evil. I am the Incarnation of Time. I suppose I have to associate with him, but I don't really have to do him any favours.'

'Yes,' she said. She was about to put away the remaining holy water, then had an afterthought. She brought her left hand up and sprinkled holy water on her knuckles, dousing both snakes.

Norton jumped. Sning was of demonic origin!

Nothing happened. Orlene glanced at Norton. Wordlessly, he extended his own left hand, and she sprinkled a few drops on it, too. There was no reaction.

'Very well,' she said. 'I accept you as Time. What do you want with me?'

He wanted his whole life with her! But he couldn't say it.

Suddenly Norton made a connection. 'Sning!' he exclaimed. 'You tried to warn me about Satan's amulet, didn't you! You knew it wouldn't help me here!'

'Sning?' Orlene asked.

'That's what I call him. Contraction of Snake Ring. When you gave him to me, two years hence.'

She laughed. 'He says it is so! But he seemed to doubt the first thing you said, about the warning. I think he was thinking of something else, not me.'

'Well, it doesn't matter now, since we destroyed the amulet.'

Her brow furrowed. 'He's not so sure.' She shrugged. Oh, those little familiar mannerisms! 'Well, tell me why you came here, if you're going to meet me anyway in a couple of years. Certainly I wouldn't give you Sning if we weren't close friends.' She narrowed her gaze with mock distrust. 'Surely you're not going to warn me of your bad intentions!'

Norton started to laugh – and it froze in his throat. What was the distinction between bad intentions and bad results? Now he could tell her the truth – but he found his tongue balking.

If he told her, developed a relationship with her now, married her, and shared her life – ah, such joy in the mere contemplation! – so that the ghost marriage never took place – discounting any paradox, since he was immune – what kind of a life would it be? He was no longer an ordinary man; he was Chronos, living backwards, able to relate to ordinary people only by reversing his own life course temporarily. As a normal man, he could have done it; in his present capacity, there was really nothing he could offer her. He had been thinking only of himself, not of her.

'I thought I had something,' he said. 'I fear I do not.'

'Well, what were you going to tell me before you had second thoughts?'

He breathed deeply. She had asked; he should tell. 'I – in the near future – when I was still a normal man – I met you and loved you.' There; it was out.

'I had gathered as much,' she replied. 'The way you have been watching me, your possession of my ring, and the way you glow so brightly. It had to be love.'

Her candour set him back. 'Don't love me!' he blurted. 'I was the unwitting cause of your death!'

'My death!'

'It – it's a complicated story. I don't want that to happen – but the alternative I had in mind, of taking you away from that course now – that's no good either. I love you, but I can only hurt you.'

'Hurt me? No, you would not do that. The glow – '

'Ask Sning!'

She paused. 'My ring says no, you would not hurt me. But your ring says yes, you would.'

'They are the same ring – but mine has more experience. Do not associate with me when you meet me in two years. Then perhaps you will have a better life.'

'But if you are the one I am fated to love – '

'It's a cursed love!'

She shook her head, perplexed. 'You're not making much sense, you know.'

'Look at my choices. If I – if we have a relationship in two years, you will have a baby who dies and you will suicide. But if we have a relationship now, when I am Chronos – I live backwards! I could associate with you only for perhaps half an hour at a time, beginning now, and each time I met you, you would be younger. Not only would you not remember me, you would soon be too young for –' He spread his hands helplessly.

She nodded. 'Now you are making sense, and your ring confirms it. I think I would like you, and probably love you, since you do glow; but to keep meeting you for the first time when I was a teenager, and always having it happen when I was younger – I am not at all sure I could handle that. Though I remember meeting a strange man in a white cloak when I was a child, in a park – ' She shook her head. 'It is strange enough talking with you now!'

'Yes. If there were some way I could start with you now and continue forward – but the maximum that could last is about four years, because after that I became Chronos and turned backwards, and I can't step physically beyond my living time frame. I could look at you thereafter, but never interact with you, and you would never see me. It's no good; you deserve so much more! I love you and I want what's best for you, and your best life is without me.'

Slowly she nodded. 'Your ring agrees. I am sorry, but I can't argue with your case.'

He sighed. 'I – I'm sorry I bothered you. I should have left you entirely alone. Let me go now, and never deal with me again.' What a shambles reality had made of his aspiration!

'Here is your ring,' she said, returning one of the Snings.

Norton took the little snake and let him curl around his finger. 'Are you my Sning?' he inquired. Would it make any real difference if this were the other?

Squeeze.

Probably the two Snings would merge in Norton's present, anyway. 'Farewell, Orlene.'

She smiled. 'I don't usually do this sort of thing. But this once – ' She came to him and kissed him.

The sudden contact was ineffably sweet. Norton held himself frozen, knowing that if he let himself go to the slightest degree, he would enfold her in his arms and babble foolishness about somehow making it work, and thereby do her a colossal disservice. But for this timeless instant, his love was back with him, healing the abyss into which his heart had fallen. Orlene lived and, with luck, would pursue her normal, full life. It was better that she do it without him. Believing that, he could bear it.

She broke away and smiled; he recovered his volition and retreated out of the door. Before he could change his mind, he changed the sand and quickly phased away.

'Well, I bungled that,' he muttered aloud. 'But I suppose I just had to learn the hard way.'

Squeeze, squeeze.

'No?' But as he pondered the implications, he realized Sning was right. He had not handled it as well as he might have – but perhaps he had given Orlene the key that would save her life, and in the process he had immeasurably improved his own outlook.

Squeeze.

'Did you enjoy meeting your other self, Sning?'

Squeeze.

Norton smiled as he moved forwards through time. 'So maybe it was worthwhile after all. Now I am ready to accept the new reality and do my job as Chronos.'

Then he remembered the time-space address Satan had given him. He had not kept the parchment on which it was written, but retained the information. He had no intention of helping Satan; the dialogue with Orlene had firmed up the resolve. But his curiosity sharpened. Who was this person who commanded a favour from Satan Himself?

172

Norton traced down the address. It was not in Kilvarough itself, but in a floating city above it, a travelling shopping centre and fair. Flying carpets abounded in its vicinity, and the stores glittered with magic items. Below lay the sombre metropolis of Kilvarough, evidently one of the stops on the route of the floating complex. Gypsy cities, they were called.

The time was about twenty years before Norton's 'present'. He would be a teenager now – and he had no intention of looking himself up. It had been confusing enough with Orlene! He went to the Mess o' Pottage shop and watched it in his normal mode, the reverse of world time, so that no one was aware of him.

A man was inspecting magic stones. He had evidently decided on a large Wealthstone, the kind with a floating six-rayed star. As Norton watched, the man checked a Lovestone and then a Deathstone, then retreated from the store.

Norton jumped ahead to catch the man's recent future, after he bought the Wealthstone. By a series of jumps and pauses, Norton traced the man to his somewhat dingy apartment in Kilvarough. There the man discovered that his stone was not as good as represented; it produced only small change, not riches.

Norton jumped ahead three more hours, checked the man's apartment – and saw his body lying on the floor, blood pooled from a gunshot wound in the head.

So Satan was right. The man had made a bad choice and had therefore taken his own life. He had no future on Earth, literally. Satan planned to give him a better future – and what was wrong with that?

Norton moved back in world time, avoiding the actual suicide; he certainly didn't need to torment himself with that gory killing! More deeply perplexed at Satan's motive, he phased himself back to an episode he had only glimpsed in passing. A pretty young woman had had trouble with her carpet near a billboard advertising the supposed delights of Hell – what would Satan think of next? – and the proprietor of

173

the Mess o' Pottage shop had rescued her. Now Norton was able to re-create the detail: the client had spotted the woman by using the Lovestone, but the proprietor had foisted off a worthless stone and taken the woman for himself. It had been a highly profitable bit of flimflam, for as Norton traced their subsequent lives, he verified that the woman had made a significant difference. She was beautiful, wealthy, loving, and loyal – in fact, she was far better than the conniving shop-keeper deserved. If Satan interfered, so that the client chose the Lovestone to buy, the man would gain the woman for himself and have a deservedly better life – the kind of life Norton himself would have liked to have with Orlene.

Now Norton was in doubt. Should he, after all, do Satan this favour? He wanted to be fair, and it certainly seemed that Satan had a good cause this time. Maybe Norton could not grant himself a lifetime of romance, but he could do it for this other man and feel a vicarious satisfaction.

'Should I?' he asked Sning.

Squeeze, squeeze.

'Why not? I don't like Satan, but I do want to be fair. Shouldn't I support him when he's right?'

Squeeze, squeeze, squeeze.

Of course the little serpent could not answer such a comment directly! Well, Norton would think about it. The lives of ordinary people were governed by the threads of Fate; maybe he should ask her why she had allowed so gross an inequity in this case.

He set his Hourglass and travelled back home to his present time. He hoped Clotho would be awaiting him, but she wasn't. Apparently she had not properly coordinated things this time. Instead, Satan was there.

'Well?' the Prince of Evil asked.

'I checked your situation,' Norton said. 'I see nothing wrong with what you contemplate – but I haven't yet made up my mind.'

'My amulet,' Satan said, peering at him. 'Where is it?'

'Oh – it bothered someone I visited, so she destroyed it with holy water. Sorry about that.'

Satan seemed to swell. His face reddened, and a wisp of smoke drifted from one nostril. 'Destroyed one of My – !'

Then Satan got control of himself and settled down. 'It is of no consequence; it was only a trinket. So you are still considering My errand?'

'Yes.'

'Remember, I am prepared to pay well for such minor favours. Here, I will provide another sample.'

'Oh, you don't need to – '

But Satan gestured, and suddenly Norton was sailing through space, as he had done before, on his way to a contraterrene frame, where time flowed backwards. He hadn't protested quickly enough, it seemed.

9

Alicorn

He arrived this time at a different location, in a Magic-Lantern Cloud, coming to rest on the surface of a lovely Earthlike planet. Here space was not densely crowded with stars, so it was evident that distinct days and nights were feasible. Stately oak trees shaded the greensward, and daffodils grew in pleasant clusters.

Immediately before him stood a marvellously lovely young woman. Her hair was long but curly, like a mass of golden shavings, and she wore a long and modest dress that could not conceal her aesthetic contours. Her eyes were grey-blue, her lips red, and her hands and feet were quite dainty. She was staring at Norton with an attitude of faint surprise and dismay.

'Hello,' he said experimentally.

'But I meant to conjure a steed!' she exclaimed indignantly. She held up her right hand, one of whose delicate fingers bore a large and obviously magic ring.

'It seems your conjuration glitched,' Norton said apologetically. 'I'm just a man.'

'A demon, belike!' she snorted. She stamped her petite foot angrily. 'The magic works but once a day; now it is wasted, and I am stranded afoot. What use have I for a mere man?'

Why was it that the prettiest young women were the least interested in men? 'Uh, maybe I can help you find another steed.'

She studied him appraisingly, as if he might after all be of some use. 'Be that a magic ring you wear?'

He glanced at Sning. 'Yes, in a manner of speaking.'

'Then do you use it to conjure me a steed to replace the one you usurped,' she commanded imperiously.

'But it's not that kind of ring.'

Her eyes fairly flashed fire. 'What manner of man are you, to tease a maiden so? You owe me a steed!'

Norton wasn't sure about that, but she was so pretty and sure of herself that he really did not want to disappoint her. He would have to show her the nature of his ring. 'Sning – '

Sning uncoiled from his finger and slithered across his hand and dropped to the verdant ground. He expanded as he did so, becoming a regularly sized green snake, and then a python, and finally a monster a foot in diameter.

'Sirrah!' the Damsel exclaimed, drawing a gleaming dagger. 'Ye shall not consume me without a fight!'

'Oh, Sning doesn't eat people,' Norton said uncertainly. 'He's friendly. I think he's offering himself as a steed.' He was amazed at this development; he had never suspected that Sning could change size. Maybe it was a talent limited to visits to contraterrene worlds, where the rules might differ.

'Fool would I be indeed to trust my tender flesh to the back of that fell reptile!' she cried.

'I'm sure it's safe. Here, I'll show you.' Norton approached the monstrous Sning and climbed clumsily on to an elevated loop. The snake's flesh was firm and dry and slightly resilient, quite comfortable, and not slippery. Norton had no trouble maintaining his perch. 'See – Sning will carry you anywhere you need to go, Miss – '

'Excelsia,' she said. 'And who be ye?'

'Norton.' Fresh from his dialogue with Orlene, he did not care to go into the Chronos business yet. He wondered, irrelevantly, what her rule was for the use of 'you' and 'ye,' as it did not seem consistent.

'I'll not ride that creature alone, sirrah!'

Norton shrugged. 'I'll ride with you, of course.' He had not intended to separate from Sning anyway. 'You can take another coil.'

Warily she approached a loop behind his own. She mounted, sitting demurely sidesaddle. 'But where are the reins?'

'I think he's under voice control. Where are you going?'

She cocked her head prettily. 'Why, I had not decided.'

'You wanted to conjure a steed without having a destination?'

Cute annoyance fleeted across her face. 'Well, usually I fetch in a handsome unicorn, and we decide together.'

A unicorn. It figured. Back on Earth such creatures were hideously expensive, and the prospective owner had to show a pedigree as detailed as that of the animal before being permitted the purchase. Unicorns, like dragons, had gone underground during the so-called enlightened period, having their horns amputated, which, of course, robbed them of most of their magical powers. But they still bred true, and now there were some fine breeds openly displayed. It had been a similar story with winged horses. In time there would be greater numbers of them; but at present, rarity put a premium on all such magical steeds. Here, it seemed, such animals were more common.

'Why not go to the unicorn corral, or whatever, and fetch one now?'

Excelsia issued a tinkling peal of laughter. 'Sirrah, no one fetches a unicorn other than by compulsion of magic charm, and then it can only be accomplished by a lovely virgin like me.'

Oh. Just so. 'Well, maybe some other type of steed. One you can keep from day to day so you don't have to conjure a new one each time you want to ride.'

Again she cocked her head, considering. She did not seem to be unusually intelligent, but her beauty made up for that. 'There be only one magical steed a person can keep, and that one be already under the spell of the Evil Sorceress.'

'What steed is that?'

Her face became rapturous. 'The Alicorn.'

'The what?'

'He be a winged unicorn, the finest equine flesh extant, the adoration of every fair and innocent maiden. For that steed I would give anything.'

178

'Anything?'

She glanced sharply at him, making a moue. 'What was that thought, sirrah?'

Norton reddened. 'It's just that – as I understand it – if you gave that gift that only you can give, you wouldn't be able to keep the Alicorn.'

'True,' she agreed shortly. 'But it makes no nevermind, for no one can capture the Alicorn anyway.'

'Well, let's explore this. Exactly what are the barriers to acquisition?'

She frowned. 'What was that word?'

'Acquisition. That is, capturing the Alicorn.'

'Oh. First there be the Evil Sorceress, who must be slain ere the preserve be approached. Then – '

He didn't like this. 'Slain? Isn't there a gentler way?'

'Who intrudes on her territory but slays her not, she turns to slime.'

Point made! 'One can't reason with her?'

'Reason with that bi – ' She paused. 'I fear I know not the applicable term.'

'Of course you don't,' he agreed gently.

'Have you ever tried to reason with a woman?' she demanded challengingly.

'I'm sure I wouldn't get far,' he conceded, and that mollified her. 'Assuming we get by the Evil Sorceress, what other barriers are there?'

'The Evil Estate be fraught with hostile creatures and unkind spells. It be virtual death merely to set foot within it.'

She was serious, and that made him nervous, but he felt obliged to learn whatever he could about this. 'We might not set foot,' he said. 'We could ride Sning in, so only his coils would touch the ground.'

'There be that,' she agreed, pleased.

'Let's assume we get safely into the Evil Estate. Then what?'

'The Guardian Dragon,' she said.

'Dragon?' Gawain the Ghost had trained him in dragon slaying, but from that training Norton had gleaned a profound respect for the battle prowess of the species. It was best to avoid a dragon!

'Huge, enormous, and tremendous,' she said, her attractive eyes narrowing with anticipated horror. 'A big monster, very large, and of formidable size. He slays all who dast approach. He patrols the region around the Alicorn's pen, and none may pass unchallenged.' She glanced obliquely at him. 'Unless you, kind sir, perchance – ?'

'As it happens,' Norton said unwillingly, 'I've had some training in dragon fighting. But of course I've never actually –'

'Oh, joy!' she exclaimed, clapping her little hands with maidenly delight. 'Then we can pass the monster!'

Norton wanted to demur, but her expression of pleasure was so gratifying that he left the qualification unvoiced. It was very hard for a reasonable man to disappoint a lovely woman. 'So if we should somehow get to the Alicorn –'

'Then still be the victory not ours,' she said, 'for he be the wildest of creatures. Fire snorts from his nostrils and sparks from his mane, and were he not cruelly tethered in place, he would bound into the sky and vanish from human ken forever.' Her gaze lowered, a token of sorrow at the loss.

'Is there any way to tame him so he will stay voluntarily with you?'

'Aye, there be a Word of Power. Utter it, and he be tame.'

'What Word is that?'

She shrugged tragically. 'Alas, I know not!'

'Well, first things first. How does one kill the Evil Sorceress?'

'For that, methinks only the Enchanted Sword will do.'

That sounded good; it helped to have magic when interacting with a dragon. 'Where is that?'

She shrugged again. It was an intriguing motion, the way she performed it. 'I know not, sirrah. It is said that the Sword will appear only to a truly worthy Hero, lifted from deep water by a hidden hand.'

Norton sighed. He surely did not qualify for that Sword! He should have known there would be a catch. Also, he saw no water near – and if there had been any, how would he know *which* deep water, where?

Sning brought his head around to look at him. 'You have an answer?' Norton inquired. Then quickly: 'Don't answer in the usual way!'

Sning's face was not structured for smiling, but he tried. It would be some squeezing, in his present form! Then he nodded his huge head, once.

'You can lead us to the Enchanted Sword?'

Nod.

'Great! Go to it, then!'

Sning returned his head to the front and commenced motion. Now his coils undulated, so that Norton and Excelsia bobbled up and down as if on merry-go-round steeds – and sideways, too. At the bottom of a loop their feet dragged in the greensward, so Norton hefted his heels to the top of the coil and rode with his knees bent before him. Whatever magic kept him on seemed to have no trouble with that. But when Excelsia tried to lift her own feet higher, her voluminous skirt tended to fall away from her shapely legs, embarrassing her. Norton pretended not to notice; certainly she had no cause to be ashamed of flesh like that, however.

Sning coursed rapidly through the forest, field, and fen, and drew up at a large mud-puddle.

'This?' Norton asked, dismayed. 'No shining, still, mysterious, deep water lake?'

Sning pointed his nose firmly at the puddle.

How far reality differed from myth! Norton resigned himself and dismounted. He approached the puddle. His feet sank squishily into its margin, and he worried that it might be quicksand. 'Wait!' he told himself. 'I shouldn't be afraid of sand! It's the essence of the symbol of my office!'

181

'Office?' Excelsia inquired, perplexed.

'Never mind.' He brought out his Hourglass and waved it at the sand. Instantly his footing firmed. He put the Hourglass away again and trod on up to the marge of the puddle.

As his toes touched the obscure murk, there was a ripple in the centre. Slowly an object pushed up. It was a weed-strewn, filthy old sword with a rusty blade.

Well, he was no King Arthur; he probably didn't rate a first-class accommodation. Norton leaned forward and grasped the handle of the Sword. The thing seemed stuck, so he had to exert considerable force to lift it clear of the mud.

No wonder! The hand that had brought the weapon up did not let go. As Norton heaved, he drew forth not only the Sword but the mud-soaked little man holding it. The man was garbed in archaic clothing topped by a large, floppy hat. 'Who're you?' Norton asked, surprised, as he swung the Sword over land, dangling the man.

'I'm the Sword Elf, of course,' the man said grumpily. 'You sure took your time rescuing me.'

'Was that what I was doing?'

'Sure,' the Elf said, brushing ineffectively at his coating of mud. 'I only use the Sword as bait so someone will pull me out of that black hole.'

Myth was taking a further beating! 'How long have you been in there?'

'Oh, a century or two. Hard to keep proper track of time in the dark. But they sure don't make Heroes like they used to.'

'Are you telling me this Sword is a fake? That it's not enchanted?'

'It's enchanted, all right,' the Elf said. 'Do you think anyone would bother with a fake sword?'

'This will slay the Evil Sorceress?'

'Sure. That's what it's for.'

'How is it against dragons?'

'Adequate. Dragons have counterspells, diminishing the effect. Of course, it helps if you know how to use a sword and

182

how to tackle a dragon. The most devastatingly enchanted weapon in the world won't do much in the hands of an ignoramus.'

'Good enough.' Norton was willing to take things at face value, since this seemed to be a face-value world. He would have to trust in the quality of the training Gawain had provided him and in the potency of the Sword's enchantment. He walked back to Sning.

The Elf followed, mounting a third coil. It seemed Norton had picked up another companion.

'Well, let's tackle the Evil Sorceress,' Norton said. There didn't seem to be much else to do except carry on with the episode, and if he encountered something lethal – well, he would be returned to his mansion in Purgatory so that he could proceed with his job. But he was so constituted that he had to make an honest try to improve things here; he couldn't simply quit.

Sning got under way, zooming across hill and dale and around mountain and moor. Norton enjoyed the scenery; this was indeed his type of exploration. 'This be almost as good a ride as on a normal steed,' Excelsia confessed. She had found out how to tuck her skirt in around her bent knees so that nothing showed, unfortunately.

In due course the Evil Estate hove into view. On it stood a great old stone castle with a few window slits and tall, dark towers. Snow topped its lofty turrets, though the climate was pleasant enough at ground level. It was surrounded by giant, ugly trees. It looked like the bleakest and evillest of places.

They slid up to the ring of trees. Immediately a great, gnarled branch swung down menacingly. Norton swung his Sword up to intercept it – and the blade sliced through the wood as if it were soft cheese.

The tree made a groan as of bending in a cruel gale wind and whipped its stump away. Reddish sap dripped from the wound. Norton looked at the Sword with new respect. Where the contact with the wood had cleaned away the mud and rust, the blade virtually gleamed. This was, indeed, an excellent weapon!

They slithered on past the trees without further challenge. 'Serves ya right, woodhenge!' the Elf called back, and the trees shuddered woodenly with impotent rage.

But now they faced the gloomy Evil Castle itself. A chill draught seemed to issue from it. Norton wondered whether he really wanted to do this. By the look of it, this was no pleasant resort and no pleasant deed he had to perform. He might get trapped in there, unable either to complete or to terminate his mission, so he couldn't return to Earth. Could the Alicorn really be worth it?

But already Sning was drawing up to the sombre front portal. Then the snake shrank to his former size, forcing them to dismount. Norton put down his hand, and Sning slithered up and curled around his finger again. 'We have to go inside?' Norton asked with resignation.

Squeeze.

'We can't simply go around the castle and tackle the Dragon directly?'

Squeeze, squeeze.

Norton sighed. Probably there were guards in the castle who could riddle passers-by with arrows or spells. 'I don't much like this business.'

'But you are a Hero!' Excelsia protested brightly. 'Onward and Upward!'

'Suppose the Evil Sorceress turns us all to slime?'

'She can't do that while you hold the Enchanted Sword,' the Elf said. 'First she must disarm you.'

That was good to know. Norton braced himself and led the way to the front portcullis.

It lifted as he approached. 'Oh, it seems we're expected,' he said. That did not encourage him.

He stepped forward – but Sning squeezed his finger twice, rapidly, and he paused. 'A trap?'

Squeeze.

He glanced up at the gleaming spikes of the portcullis. 'What goes up can come down, I'm sure.'

Squeeze.

'Very well. I'll spring the trap.' He stepped up to the trough in the stone floor where the deadly iron spikes of the portcullis normally rested. Then he leaped across.

The spikes slammed down with horrible force. A cloud of rock dust billowed up. This was exactly what Norton had expected, but the sheer ferocity of it unnerved and angered him.

He turned and struck at the portcullis with his Sword, adrenalin giving him strength. Again the blade cut through as if touching only cooked noodles. In a moment he hacked out an opening, so the others could step through. Now more of his blade was clean and shining. His supposed Heroism was being recorded by the brilliance of the blade. The castle shuddered and groaned; its fangs had been cut.

They entered a dark and unpleasant hall. Light flickered from a guttering torch at the far end.

'Any more traps here?' Norton asked Sning.

Squeeze, squeeze, squeeze.

'Any immediate threat to life or limb?'

Squeeze, squeeze.

He decided to chance it. 'Keep close together,' he told the others.

Excelsia and the Elf were happy to oblige. They crowded in so close to him that he worried about insufficient elbow room if he had to use the Sword. He didn't want to cut any of his companions! On the other hand, Excelsia was an extremely attractive woman, pleasant to be this close to. Now that he had given up on Orlene, he was becoming more aware of that sort of thing – not that he had ever been *un*aware.

Then they heard the tromp, tromp, tromp of a giant. Damsel and Elf crowded in even closer. 'Sning are you *sure* . . . ?'

Squeeze.

The tromping came to the intersection of halls at the torch. Norton braced himself to face the giant – and saw nothing. The tromping continued towards them. No giant, just the noise of one.

No, not quite true. The boots of the giant were there. They were tromping along by themselves.

The three of them stared at the marching, empty boots. Was that footwear animated by magic or did it contain an invisible giant? It did make a difference. Mere shoes they could probably ignore, but an invisible giant was likely to be troublesome.

The boots halted immediately before them. The noise stopped. Now the boots looked exactly like discarded apparel.

Norton set himself and poked the point of his Sword towards the knee of the theoretical giant. He encountered no opposition. He sliced across the tops of both boots. Nothing. It seemed they were, after all, only boots.

He tucked the Sword in his belt and reached for a boot. He put his two hands on it and tried to pick it up. The thing would not budge; it was as if a giant did indeed have his foot in it.

Norton stood and turned back to the others. 'I suppose – '

He was interrupted by a swift kick in the rear. He was boosted into the air and moved a yard down the hall. One of the boots had booted him!

He caught his balance and rubbed his bruised posterior. The Elf was trying without complete success to restrain a smirk, and even innocent Excelsia seemed amused. Norton himself didn't happen to find it very funny, but realized that it would not profit him much to lose his temper. 'Let's just go around these.'

The Elf obliged, walking to the side. The boots came to life again, walking swiftly to get in front of the little man. The Elf stopped, not wanting to get kicked himself. Getting kicked oneself was never a laughing matter.

'Maybe if we jumped over,' Norton suggested.

'Sure,' the Elf agreed. 'You first.'

Norton considered where he would get kicked if caught in the act of jumping over the boot and decided not to risk it.

Excelsia tried another approach. She walked to the left, where no boot was. But suddenly a pair of giant gloves or gauntlets arrived, hovering in mid-air about head height. The right one closed in a fist before Excelsia's face, then extended its massive forefinger and waggled it warningly. She emitted a frightened squeak and stepped back.

Now the boots were before the Elf, to the right, and the gloves before the Damsel, to the left. Norton strode up the centre – and the right boot and left glove moved to close the gap. He, too, was blocked.

Well, at least it was clear what Sning had meant about there being no immediate threat or trap in the hall. The disembodied boots and gloves were neither – but they were effectively blocking progress. There would be no problem if the party simply retreated.

But retreat meant failure, and Norton had had enough of that. He became ornery. He drew his Sword again. 'Out of my way, objects, or pay the penalty!'

Nothing moved. He stepped forward – and the right boot swung up in a kick. Norton sliced down with the Sword and cut it in half. The two fragments fell to the floor and lay there, twisting about like a dismembered reptile.

'Ooo,' Excelsia said with sympathetic horror. 'You killed it!'

'I gave it fair warning,' Norton said. He stepped forward again and cut the fingers off the glove that grabbed for him. It, too, fell writhing to the floor. Excelsia twisted her own fair fingers as if afraid they would separate, but did not protest again. Even delicate Damsels had to yield to practicality on occasion.

The other boot and glove attacked. Norton got the boot, but the glove caught him in a stinging slap to the side of the head that sent him careening into a wall. The glove came at him again, forming a fist that aimed at his nose; this time he got the blade up, and the glove split itself against the Sword and plopped to the floor.

It took Norton a moment to recover his equilibrium, for that blow had had giant force! Next time he encountered something like this, he would act more ruthlessly.

'Ooo, you're hurt!' Excelsia said, dabbing at his face with a dainty handkerchief. The dabbing did not do much good for his face, but her attention uplifted his spirit.

They proceeded on to the torch. As they reached it, Sning squeezed Norton's finger three times: warning.

He paused. How he wished Sning could speak directly! 'Danger, maybe,' he said.

Elf and Damsel looked around. 'Where?' Excelsia asked.

Norton shrugged. 'Sning warned me. There's something.'

'Listen, Mac, we can't dawdle here forever,' the Elf said.

'You dawdled for a century in that mud-puddle,' Norton pointed out. 'What's the hurry now?'

'A critter can build up a lot of impatience in a century,' the Elf said. 'I'm going ahead.' He marched past the torch, into the cross-passage.

The torch flared monstrously, sending out blinding brilliance. Norton covered his eyes as he stumbled back, but the damage was done; for the moment he couldn't see a thing.

Gradually his sight cleared. He looked about – and found himself alone in the passage. Excelsia and the Elf were gone.

Alarmed, he looked for them – but they remained lost. The fragments of the boots and gloves were gone, too. That gave him a notion. 'Sning, am I in the same hall I was in before?'

Squeeze, squeeze.

'I blundered into another passage while blinded?'

Squeeze, squeeze, squeeze.

'I got moved to a new passage, or got closed off from the other passage?'

Squeeze.

'By the action of the Evil Sorceress?'

Squeeze.

'Are the others in immediate danger?'

Squeeze, squeeze, squeeze.

Damn those indefinite answers! 'Their safety – does it depend on what I do?'

Squeeze.

He was improving his touch! 'Can I find them?'

Squeeze, squeeze, squeeze.

'Not till I deal personally with the Sorceress?'

Squeeze.

That was what he had suspected. The Evil Sorceress had perceived him as the leader and had separated him from the others, and now intended to test him alone. Divide and conquer. If he prevailed, his companions would be safe; if he did not . . .

'Then I will deal with her immediately.'

Squeeze.

Norton strode ahead, past the torch, shielding his eyes as he did so, but this one did not flare up. However, as he entered this new hall he discovered a pack of half a dozen grotesque little monsters, gnarled goblin things. They charged.

The fastest one came at him first. It was globular in shape, with tiny legs and arms, its whole torso consisting of a ferocious face dominated by a huge mouth rimmed with inward-pointing teeth. No need to question the little monster's intent; it would chomp a bite out of any anatomy it reached.

Norton pointed his Sword at it, and the monster gaped its maw to swallow the Sword point first. The blade slid right through the back of its head-body, slitting it into halves. Defeated, the thing puffed into bad-smelling smoke.

But already the next two monsters were on him. Norton slapped at one with the side of his blade, knocking it into the other. The second gaped its maw and took a bite out of the first. In a moment the two had become one – and Norton ran his Sword through that one. These things were easy enough

189

to dispatch, but he was sure he would have been in painful trouble if either of them had got through to chomp him.

Soon he had polished off the remaining three, though one did take a piece out of his boot. He walked on down the hall, turned a corner – and there were five more little monsters and a hovering glow. He dispatched the monsters as they came at him, then stood before the glow. What was this?

Squeeze.

'Safe to touch?'

Squeeze, squeeze, squeeze.

'Safe to leave alone?'

Squeeze, squeeze.

So he reached out with his left hand, holding the Sword ready in his right, and touched the glow. It flickered – and became a round bed with a lovely woman draped on it. Her hair was shining silver, her eyes silver too, and so were her long nails. She wore a harem-style outfit that showed off precisely as much flesh as she wished it to, and it seemed she was generous in both anatomy and wish.

She gazed at him from beneath long silver lashes. 'Well, now, Hero,' she said huskily, inhaling.

'Uh – I take it you are the Evil Sorceress?'

'The same,' she breathed. She had remarkable breath control.

'And I found you by capturing the glow?'

'Naturally.' She shifted her décolletage.

'You don't seem so horrendous to me.'

'The legend was doubtless exaggerated.'

'But I must slay you, lest you turn me into slime?'

She nodded, sending a ripple through her flesh. 'However, there is no need to rush it, Hero.' She shifted position on the bed, and more flesh showed.

Sning squeezed his finger warningly. Yes, he was supposed to slay her.

'Here, I will bare the target for you,' she said, shrugging partway out of her upper clothing, so that her front was exposed. 'The point right here.' She touched a spot between her amazing breasts.

But how *could* he? This was no toothy little monster; this was a living, breathing (!) human being, lovely beyond belief, and he was no murderer.

SQUEEZE!

'I can't,' Norton said, dropping the Sword.

'I knew you couldn't do it,' the Evil Sorceress murmured as the Sword clattered on the floor. 'You are an innocent male fool.' She lifted one sleek arm, her forefinger coming to point at him.

Sning uncurled convulsively and sprang through the air to land on her outstretched hand. The little snake buried his tiny fangs in the Evil Sorceress' finger.

'Oh, snot!' she exclaimed, jerking her finger aside as she felt the puncture. A silvery flash jumped from it, just missing Norton, and struck the ceiling. Immediately the ceiling turned to slime and began to drool down towards the floor.

'Oooh, you little creep!' she screamed at Sning. 'I'll bite your head off!' And she brought her hand to her mouth, where sharply pointed teeth now showed between the blood-red lips.

But Sning was already wriggling away. He dropped to the bed and thrashed towards Norton. The Evil Sorceress slammed her fist down at the little snake's body and grabbed for him with her claws. She gouged out chunks of bedding, but Sning squiggled aside and off the bed, landing on the Sword. The Sorceress flopped on her front and grabbed for him again; the Sword glowed menacingly as her hand came near it, and she had to desist. She could not touch the Sword, so Sning was safe.

Already Sning's poison was taking effect. Norton had understood that the little snake's bite would not kill a human being, yet it seemed it was more potent against a truly evil person. The Evil Sorceress' finger glowed red and swelled like a sausage. But the change in the rest of her was more striking.

Her lovely facial features melted into homely ones. Her

breathtaking bare bosom became baggy, her stunning cleavage a wrinkled crevice. Her sleek arms and smooth-fleshed thighs became flabby limbs. Now, stripped of her enchantment, she was revealed as an ugly old crone.

Shocked, Norton watched as she died. This was almost as bad as the dissolution of the Bem had been during his visit to the space opera of the globular cluster, far away. He marvelled at the transformation from beauty to ugliness; how could he ever have found that thing attractive? Another part of him was more cerebral; why, he wondered, was it so much easier to watch an ugly old crone die than a lovely young woman? The two were separated only by age. He knew that goodness and evil could not be judged by appearance, yet his mind felt more comfortable now that he knew the Evil Sorceress was in reality ugly.

The transformation continued. After turning ugly, the Evil Sorceress began to melt. She dissolved into a puddle of slime, exactly as had the Bem.

Then the castle itself melted. Chunks of it dissolved and collapsed. Norton had to dodge a segment that fell from above. The walls thinned and sagged.

Hastily he scooped up Sning and the Enchanted Sword and scrambled to escape the developing ruin. Soon he was able to spot Excelsia and the Elf in their separate chamber; they had been hard pressed by the mouth-monsters, but had survived by diligent exercise of her stiletto and his active boots.

Norton forged across to join them. 'Come on – we've got to get out of here before the whole thing falls on us!'

'About time you showed up!' the Elf grumped. They scrambled out, dodging the slimy chunks. As they made it to the greensward at the rear patio, the entire remainder of the castle fell in with a grotesque sucking sound.

'Ugh!' Excelsia exclaimed expressively.

'Good thing you slew the Evil Sorceress,' the Elf said. 'I knew we were going to get slimed if she won.'

'I didn't slay her, actually,' Norton confessed. 'I lacked the nerve. Sning did it.'

The Damsel cocked her head at him. 'You are no Hero?'

'I'm afraid not.'

'But he's an honest man,' the Elf said. 'The Enchanted Sword goes for that kind, too, in a pinch.'

Unpersuaded, Excelsia turned away. Norton stood diminished in her eyes.

They continued into the estate. The land here was lovely, with pleasant little paths winding along among fruit trees. 'Oh, let's pause for refreshment!' Excelsia said, reaching for a bright red apple.

SQUEEZE, SQUEEZE!

Norton jumped across and dashed the apple from her hand. 'Poison!' he cried.

Indeed, the moment the apple touched ground, it smouldered as if being eaten from inside by some horrible acid, then burst into flame. Excelsia stared at it, wide-eyed. 'Yes, of course,' she agreed faintly. 'Everything belonging to the Evil Sorceress would be poison to ordinary folk. So silly of me to forget.'

'What about the Alicorn?' Norton asked.

'Oh, he does not belong to her,' she said quickly. 'He is her captive, not her creature.'

That seemed to make sense. They walked on through the poisonous orchard. Soon the terrain opened out into a circular valley whose centre was a mound. On the mound was a palisade – an enclosure surrounded by a tight fence of sharpened stakes that hid whatever was inside. But Excelsia knew. 'Therein – the Alicorn!' she breathed rapturously.

There was, however, a more immediate concern. From the far side of the mound galloped a horrendous red Dragon. This was one of the centipede variety; it had fourteen or sixteen pairs of legs and a long spiked tail, while black smoke snorted from its mouth.

Norton stepped forward. 'This is my job,' he said. It wasn't that he relished the prospect of doing battle with the Dragon; it was that he knew it was better to face the thing than to be run down from behind. Gawain had taught him that. 'Never let a dragon see your rear,' the ghost had cautioned. 'It will either toast it or take a bite out of it, or both.' Also, Norton was sure Excelsia would be easy and delectable prey for the Dragon, and he couldn't permit her to be hurt. If he got killed here, he would be wafted back to Earth, unharmed – he had the word of the Father of Lies on that. But the Damsel had no such assurance.

The word of the Father of Lies. There was something about that notion that bothered him.

The Dragon swerved to meet him head-on. It was therefore a stupid creature; the smart ones were more careful, taking time to scout and sniff, for scarce was the man who braved such a monster without the benefit of some potent enchantment. All the background Gawain had drilled into him was coming to the fore now, and for the first time he really appreciated it. So much of dragon fighting was tactics! One had to grasp the nature of the beast and exploit its weaknesses; a man was smarter than a reptile, usually, and that could count.

The Dragon was indeed large, as the Damsel had warned him. Its mass was elephantine. It blew out a tongue of orange flame – and Norton jumped aside. Gawain had prepared him for this, too; firebreathers always blasted first, hoping to toast their prey conveniently before coming within range of the prey's defences. This was virtually instinctive; they were not smart enough to reason it out. But they had to inhale deeply first – and so Norton had watched for the expansion of the torso and had moved the moment the contraction occurred. It was as if he had been in this business all his life, thanks to the ghost.

An instant after the fireshot, the Dragon was beside him, snapping at the spot where Norton had stood. Naturally Norton had dodged aside again, avoiding the teeth. It was amazing how easy it was. Of course, he had the benefit of much smaller mass, so could move much less predictably than the behemoth could. He knew what to do now; he rammed the point of the Sword into the monster's passing ear. This was intended to penetrate to the creature's token brain and kill it.

Unfortunately, Norton's reflexes weren't as good as his knowledge. He failed to allow sufficiently for the Dragon's velocity, and the Sword struck behind the ear and sliced away several scales and severed a neck muscle or two. Blood gouted as the Sword jerked clear of the wound.

Pain-maddened, the Dragon braked all fourteen or sixteen pairs of legs and screeched to a halt. Norton knew he was in for it; a careless man seldom got a chance for a second stroke. The Dragon whirled, becoming unconscionably agile for its mass, and brought its head about to snap at Norton's tasty rear.

Norton whirled himself, slicing desperately at the Dragon's nose. He scored, but not perfectly; the blade lopped off the tip. But that didn't stop the creature, which thrust the bloody snout at him and knocked him down.

On his back, Norton made one more attempt. He whipped the Sword up to stab at the monster's eye. This time his aim was good, for the Dragon was almost stationary. The point sank into the huge orb and found the tiny brain behind. One ordinary blade could not have done it, for the orb was surrounded by bony armour, but this one's enchantment sliced through the bone.

The Dragon went crazy. Its brain wasn't much, but it did need the thing to work its jaws and similar sundry tasks. It yanked its head up, blood jetting from the eye socket and splattering Norton. The great body threshed. Norton rolled out of the way. The creature flopped over on to its back and lay there, with all fourteen or sixteen pairs of legs twitching in the air. The Dragon was in its death throes – but its blind reflexes could still kill Norton.

'Oh, you're so brave, after all!' Excelsia exclaimed, clapping her hands. She approached Norton, evidently thinking to embrace him; then she saw the gore on him and desisted, wrinkling her pert nose distastefully. 'Couldn't you have done it a little more neatly?' she asked plaintively.

Norton brushed himself off as well as he could and slid the blade of the Sword along the greensward to clean it. Now it shone more brightly than ever, and he wasn't sure it was only the cleaning that accounted for this. It certainly was an excellent weapon.

'Well, one hurdle to go,' the Elf said briskly. 'Let's get on with it.'

Norton, battered, tired, and gunked with gore, would have preferred a rest break. Heroism wasn't an ideal life!

The final challenge – the steed no one could tame! He hoped the Damsel wasn't headed for disappointment. Women liked horses – but a unicorn was no ordinary horse, and the Alicorn was no ordinary unicorn. This creature could be more dangerous than the Dragon.

They marched up the mound to the palisade. There was no gate in it; the wall of stakes formed a tight enclosure. Inside was grim silence.

'Sirrah, use your blade to open a gate,' Excelsia told Norton. 'I shall not be barred from my steed!'

Norton put his hand on the hilt of the Sword, then hesitated. 'A gate that let us in would also let the Alicorn out,' he said. 'Maybe we should peek over the top first.'

'That's using your noggin,' the Elf agreed. 'In fact, let's poke up a hat.'

'A hat?' Excelsia asked, her fair brow furrowing.

The Elf removed his hat from his head. His skull was almost bald, now that it showed. 'Balance it on the end of the Sword.' Norton extended the Sword, and the Elf set the hat on the tip.

Norton lifted the hat slowly up beside the palisade, while Excelsia tapped her dainty foot impatiently. 'This be sheerest nonsense, sirrah! What think ye a hat can see?'

196

The palisade points were about eight feet above the ground. Norton elevated the hat beyond that point – and abruptly there was a ferocious squeal, and a spear thrust through the hat and withdrew.

Spear? No, that was the horn of the Alicorn!

Norton brought down the hat, lifted it from the Sword, and gravely handed it back to the Elf. The Elf held it before his little face and sighted through the twin holes in it at the Damsel. No one spoke.

That was one unfriendly equine creature in there!

They retreated a reasonable distance and considered. 'Probably the Evil Sorceress abused him,' Norton suggested. 'That made the Alicorn mean.'

'Nay, he be merely untame,' Excelsia said, but her voice lacked conviction. That strike had been too swift and sure, too vicious, after such complete silence. The Alicorn had to have been listening to them, pacing them, biding his time, concealing his awareness until he had the chance to strike. Had he been able to understand their dialogue, he would have known the hat trick was coming, but he was only a cunning animal. Cunning and savage.

'That animal will kill ye, lassie,' the Elf warned her.

'Oh, no, unicorns never harm my kind,' she insisted.

'This be no ordinary unicorn,' he reminded her.

The Damsel acknowledged this logic by bursting into maidenly tears. 'Oh, woe!' she cried. 'How may I tame the untamable?'

Norton exchanged a glance with the Elf. Obviously they had to come up with something. 'Isn't there supposed to be a magic Word?' Norton asked.

Excelsia brightened instantly. 'The Word! We must find the Word!'

The Elf frowned. 'If there be a Word, why did not the Evil Sorceress use it to tame the beast?'

'She didn't know it!' Excelsia said.

'Neither do we.'

'But we shall find it!'

Norton sighed to himself. The Evil Sorceress had had years to search out the Word and had evidently failed. How could they succeed in an hour?

But the Damsel was threatening to cloud up again. 'I guess we'll just have to guess at it,' he said. 'We can stand outside the enclosure and shout words until we come to the right one.'

'Why didn't the Evil Sorceress do that?' the Elf asked.

'She didn't think of it!' Excelsia said eagerly.

Again Norton was doubtful. The Evil Sorceress had struck him as smart and ruthless. She had surely wanted to ride the Alicorn, otherwise she would not have held him captive. Her power would have been enhanced if she could have used that magical steed. Yet she had failed.

Was there really a magic Word? Or was that only a myth?

He looked at Excelsia and knew he couldn't tell her there was no Word. So they would have to try it.

They stood in a line and called words at random. 'Valour!' the Elf cried bravely. 'Beauty!' Excelsia bespoke prettily. 'Uncertainty . . .' Norton muttered doubtfully.

The other two glanced sharply at him, and he was abashed.

They tried another round. 'Courage!' the Elf cried. 'Modesty,' Excelsia murmured. 'Time,' Norton said.

Again the other two glanced askance at him. 'Well,' he said awkwardly, 'the Word could be anything. Maybe the Sorceress only tried conventional words. How do we know? Maybe "time" was it.'

Indeed, the silence continued inside the enclosure. 'We are at risk of taming him without knowing it,' the Elf said. 'We must test it.'

'We know how,' Norton said. He borrowed the Elf's hat again and poked it up above the palisade.

Nothing happened. 'Can it be?' Excelsia asked, her eyes glowing and her bosom heaving with hope.

Norton wasn't sure. 'Let's try something else.' He cast

about, and finally removed his shirt and draped it on the blade of the Sword. Then he poked that up, wiggling it to make it seem lifelike.

The horn speared it.

'That infernal creature tried to trick us!' the Elf said indignantly. 'He pretended to be tame and then struck.'

'And he was too canny to fall for the same lure twice,' Norton agreed. 'We have a real problem here.'

Even the Damsel was sobered by this. 'We must get closer to him,' she decided. 'So we can see him react to our words.'

It was a good suggestion, but impractical. They could not see the Alicorn without entering this enclosure, and that would be suicidal before they discovered the Word.

'Why does not the beast break down the wall?' the Elf asked irritably. 'He plainly has the means.'

Excellent question! If the Alicorn could spear a target above the palisade, he could surely spear the palisade itself.

But Excelsia had the answer. 'He be tethered, of course. So he can't fly out.'

'Then why have an enclosure at all?' the Elf asked. He seemed to have a considerable practical streak.

Excelsia cocked her head and shrugged.

But this time Norton had the answer. 'To keep the Dragon out. The Evil Sorceress wouldn't have wanted those two creatures fighting. With the Alicorn tethered, he would be at a disadvantage against the Dragon and might get eaten. That must be why he doesn't punch holes in the fence or kick it down. He doesn't want the fires of the Dragon to come in. Not while he can't escape. And the Dragon was too stupid to realize *he* could bash or burn down the palisade.'

The Elf nodded. 'Then we can take down the wall.'

No sooner realized than done. Norton hacked out a section and stood clear as it fell outward with a resounding crash. Now at last they had a view of the interior.

The Alicorn stood there – and a magnificent creature he was. He stood about seventeen hands at the shoulder, with two enormous white wings rising from that shoulder region and a gleaming black horn at his forehead. The rest of him was a burnished red, not the shade of blood but the hue of fire. He fairly gleamed, and his eyes stared back at them with a disconcerting awareness. Dumb animal? Unlikely!

He was indeed tethered. A silver chain was locked to his right hind leg and anchored to a silver stake. Silver, of course, was resistant to magic; that was why the Alicorn could not break it. The Evil Sorceress had stooped to mundane means to pen him.

'Oh, you Noble Creature!' Excelsia exclaimed, walking towards the Alicorn with arms outstretched. 'All my young, pretty, innocent, and genteel life I have longed for the like of you!'

'Don't do that!' Norton cried, suddenly realizing that the Damsel was mesmerized by the beauty of the beast. But she was already stepping within range.

The Alicorn never hesitated. He lowered his horn and leaped to the limit of his tether. The terrible horn stabbed right through the Damsel's body and withdrew so rapidly that the Alicorn seemed hardly to have moved. But now there was blood on the horn, and Excelsia collapsed, her blood pouring out. She had been speared neatly through her maidenly heart.

Norton was frozen for an instant in shock. Then he drew his Sword and charged the Alicorn.

'Don't do that!' the Elf cried, exactly as Norton had. But he, too, was too late. Norton stepped within range.

The Alicorn charged, the deadly horn levelling. The Sword sliced down. The blade severed the horn at its midpoint.

Blood gouted from the stump of the horn. The creature stiffened, then collapsed beside the woman, mixing his blood with hers.

'You fool!' the Elf cried. 'Now ye have two deaths for one – and what be gained?'

Norton gazed at the bodies. For a moment he seemed to see Orlene, collapsed at her piano. What had he gained, indeed! He had been as much a fool as Excelsia had been and had only magnified the damage by his thoughtless violence. This gallant quest of his – he had converted it to disaster. Some fantasy hero he was!

Of course, he realized that he was *not* a fantasy hero. He was Chronos, Master of Time, with a job to do back on Earth. Why had he allowed the Devil to distract him like this? He should never have deluded himself about his position.

Chronos? Of course – there was the answer!

He brought out the Hourglass and turned the sand red. He reversed time for the immediate region and willed the sand to flow up. That left himself out of the change.

The Alicorn trembled, then righted himself, collapsing to his feet. Blood gouted back into his horn. The severed end of the horn flew back into place. A moment later, the Damsel was unpunctured, and walked blithely backwards out of the compound. Then the palisade became unhacked. Since Norton had excluded himself from this reversal, he was both standing apart and participating, backwards. So he moved to rejoin his prior self, merging, then stilled the sand and returned to normal time. All was well again.

'Never have I seen the like!' the Elf exclaimed. 'You are a Sorcerer!'

Oops – he had forgotten to include the Elf in the reversal. The little man had seen it all and remembered it. Well, it wasn't as if there was supposed to be any secret. 'I'm not a sorcerer, I'm Chronos.'

'What are you talking about?' Excelsia demanded.

'It's complicated to explain,' Norton said.

'Then don't bother. Go ahead and hack down the wall.'

The Elf pursed his lips in a soundless whistle. 'Damsel, ye know not what ye ask.'

'I want to see that divine steed!' she insisted.

'I don't think that's wise,' Norton said.

'But we know he's tethered!'

'Better explain, Wizard,' the Elf said.

'Wizard?' Excelsia demanded. 'Riddles again, belike?'

'I am afraid,' Norton said carefully, 'that if I open this wall and let you see the Alicorn, you will be so smitten by him that you will walk right into his horn and perish.'

She opened her mouth for an angry retort, but stalled out before speaking. Evidently this was the type of thing she knew she was prone to do.

'Still, we do need to see this creature,' the Elf said, his practical streak taking hold again, 'so we can verify the Word. Maybe if we tie her up – '

'What?' Excelsia screeched undaintily.

'Perhaps if she merely promises not to go near the Alicorn until we're sure it's safe,' Norton suggested diplomatically.

Excelsia pouted. 'Oh, all right!'

The Elf shook his head bemusedly. 'If only ye knew, Damsel!'

'Never mind,' Norton said quickly. 'It never happened.'

'*What* never happened?' she demanded.

'I'll bring down the fence,' Norton said. 'Remember, Excelsia, you promised – '

''Tis a mess of foolishness o'er naught,' she grumped.

Nevertheless, he chopped much more carefully at the wall than he had before, so as to open a smaller hole and be on guard against her passage.

The Alicorn stood as before. To the stallion, this *was* before; no awareness of his prior fate remained in his memory. The double disaster had been undone. The beast was still magnificent – but now Norton and the Elf had firsthand evidence as to why the Evil Sorceress had not approached him. Without the Word, approach was death.

What *was* that Word? They had to come up with it – and Norton was sure that no random search would do it. If there was a Word, it had to be well hidden.

Excelsia peeked through the hole and saw the Alicorn. 'Ooooo!' she exclaimed melodiously, starting forward.

Norton moved to intercept her, and she stopped. 'I was not

202

going in there,' she said somewhat insincerely. 'He's so beautiful. All my young, pretty, innocent life – '

'Let's try words again,' the Elf suggested. 'Do we have any better way?'

'Do we?' Norton echoed. He was not pleased with himself. He had met the Damsel, acquired the Enchanted Sword, slain the Evil Sorceress – approximately – and the Dragon, and now was balked by what should have been the simplest aspect of this adventure: speaking a Word to an animal.

Squeeze.

Could it be? 'Sning – you say there is?'

Squeeze.

'You know it?'

Squeeze.

'A way we can learn the Word quickly?'

Squeeze.

'Well, let's get to it!' He looked up at the other two. 'Sning can help us find the Word. All I have to do is find the right questions to ask him.'

'That's one mighty useful snake,' the Elf remarked.

'Even if he weren't, I would value him,' Norton said. 'He was given to me by one I – '

SQUEEZE! SQUEEZE! SQUEEZE!

Norton froze. He trusted Sning's warning – but what was its nature? Had he been about to say something wrong?

Squeeze.

Oh, yes – he kept forgetting that he did not have to speak his questions aloud. *You object to my speaking of your value to me?* he thought.

Squeeze, squeeze.

Is there some other threat?

Squeeze.

Some new monster approaching?

Squeeze, squeeze.

Norton pondered. The Elf and the Damsel watched him,

mutually perplexed. They judged him to be an odd one. *Some error in what I'm saying?*

Squeeze, squeeze, squeeze.

This was difficult! *Something all right to think, but not to speak?*

Sning hesitated, then gave one squeeze.

What could that be? Norton glanced at the Elf. 'I was about to say something wrong, so Sning warned me. But I haven't figured out what – '

'The Word,' the Elf said wisely.

'The Word!' Norton and Excelsia repeated together, and Sning squeezed affirmatively.

'But why should it be wrong to – ?'

'Ah, we have all been fools!' the Elf cried. 'Know ye not that the power of a Word adheres to him who speaks it? If you had spoken it – '

Now Norton understood. 'Then the Alicorn would be tamed by me – '

'And by no one else,' the Elf agreed. 'I knew, but I forgot. A century of mud on my brain may have dulled it. 'Tis folly for us all to be crying out words; only the lass must speak that one to the steed. She be the one who wants him.'

'I had somehow thought the Alicorn would be completely tamed,' Norton said. 'So anyone could approach him.'

The Elf spat to the side. 'Who would want a completely tame steed? That were as tasteless as a completely tame woman! He must be tame only for his master. Mistress.'

Norton nodded. A steed no one could steal, who would be as wild to strangers as he was now, unless cautioned by the one he respected. That did make sense. Perhaps the Alicorn was tame now for a former master, who had died or got lost. 'If I discover the Word and whisper it to Excelsia, and then she speaks it aloud to the Alicorn – ?'

Squeeze.

Now he had it straight. But one thing still bothered him. 'If Sning knows the Word, the Evil Sorceress must have known

204

it, too. I mean, she *was* a Sorceress and she had magical sources of information. Yet she never used the Word. She must have had reason.'

Excelsia had stood silently all the while, adoring the Alicorn through the hole in the fence. Now she looked at Norton. 'She surely would have used it if she could!'

'True Sning?'

Squeeze.

'She knew it and could not say it?'

Squeeze.

'There's no actual danger in using the Word – apart from making sure the right person uses it?'

Squeeze.

'And once that person uses it, it can't be used again, so no one else can take away the Alicorn's loyalty?'

Squeeze.

Until, perhaps, that person died, leaving the Alicorn free again. It was a firm commitment.

Squeeze.

Norton shook his head. 'The Evil Sorceress certainly would have *wanted* to use it. Was she physically incapable of pronouncing it?'

Squeeze, squeeze.

'Emotionally incapable?'

Squeeze.

'Ah!' Excelsia exclaimed, clapping her hands. 'I can guess what Word she could not say! The one that countered her nature!'

'She was a creature of hate,' the Elf agreed.

Norton thought back to the moment of Sning's first warning on this subject. He had been commenting about Sning, who had been given to him by Orlene, the one he –

Excelsia marched up to the Alicorn. The beast braced, ready for his devastating attack. 'Love!' she cried.

The Alicorn shuddered. Then he furled his wings and

bowed his head until the terrible horn touched the battered earth.

'It could be a ruse!' Norton warned.

Squeeze, squeeze.

Excelsia approached the stallion and put her small fair hand on his muscular shoulder near where one of his wings sprouted. 'Love,' she repeated softly. He lifted his head and brought his nose around to nuzzle her neck. He had indeed been tamed.

She stooped to untie the knotted silver chain from his hind leg. Her human hands could do what neither his hooves nor his horn could. In a moment he was free – but he did not move. He waited for her directive.

The Elf walked towards them. Instantly the Alicorn was alert. His wings unfurled and his horn took a bead on the intruder. A small puff of fire showed at his nostrils.

'It's all right, Alicorn,' Excelsia said. 'These are my friends.'

The creature relaxed. If she said it was all right, it was all right, for her word was his law. But woe betide the one she did not speak for!

Excelsia jumped up on the steed's back, managing to achieve a sidesaddle position though there was no saddle. Norton knew how difficult it could be to mount a standing horse without the aid of a stirrup. Perhaps she had a little magic of her own – the magic of Damsel with Equine.

'Oh, I'm so happy!' Excelsia cried, waving to Norton and the Elf. 'Onward and upward, Alicorn!'

The Alicorn spread his great white wings, pumped them, and launched himself into the air. There was hardly any downdraft; most of his impetus was magic. In moments Damsel and stallion were high aloft.

'Well, the job's done, the adventure complete,' the Elf remarked. He held out his hand. 'You won't be needing the Enchanted Sword any more.'

Norton stared at the diminishing speck in the sky. Some-

206

how he had expected more thanks for his effort than this. 'I suppose not.' He handed the Sword over.

The Elf took it by mid-blade and held it up over his head, horizontally. A mud-puddle began to form around his feet. Slowly he sank into it.

'But I thought you didn't like mud!' Norton protested.

'I don't,' the Elf agreed, sinking further. 'But that's fantasy for you. The Damsel gets to fly, while the Elf gets stuck in the mud.'

Something caught the corner of Norton's eye. He looked around. The slain Dragon was reviving!

'Hey, wait, Elf! I have further use for that Sword!'

The Elf's descent into the widening puddle paused. 'What for? You're finished with the Quest.'

'The Dragon! He's not quite dead!'

'Of course he's not quite dead! He's immortal! He dies only for an hour, then he resumes his post. Naturally he'll be somewhat irritated by the loss of the Alicorn he guarded – but that's a new Quest.'

'But that means I need a weapon!'

'Nah. You won't be staying long. Otherwise you'd be worrying about when the Evil Sorceress revives. It takes her two hours, 'cause she's worse; but when she does, hoo man!'

Norton looked wildly at the fallen castle. Sure enough, it was beginning to re-form from the mound of slime. 'None of this destruction was permanent? It's all coming back?'

There was no response. He looked – and the Elf was gone. Only his hat and the Enchanted Sword remained above the mud, and in a moment they, too, sank out of sight.

Norton felt very much alone. Now he was without weapon or companions – and the Dragon was climbing to its fourteen or sixteen pairs of legs, larger than ever and quite annoyed. Norton would have to cross the Dragon's path to escape this region.

Squeeze.

Suddenly he felt better. 'Sning! I've still got you!'

Then he drifted from the planet and zoomed back towards his own realm. This visit was over – none too soon.

10

Gaea

Satan was waiting for him again as he returned. 'Did you enjoy yourself?' the Prince of Evil inquired politely.

Norton looked at him narrowly. 'You don't know?'

'My dear associate! How could I?'

'You sent me there. You ought to be able to tell how things are. Otherwise how could you be sure you weren't sending me to my doom?'

'One Incarnation cannot harm another.'

'Without the other's consent. If you placed me in a challenging situation and I failed to meet that challenge, would that constitute my consent for harm?'

'There is no danger to you in the fantasy scheme! It is nothing but a living adventure.'

'I thought that was rather convenient,' Norton said. 'I arrive just in time for a classic fantasy adventure, complete with Damsel in Distress, Enchanted Sword, sturdy Elf, Evil Sorceress, Dragon, and Alicorn. True chance would have had me land in a barren wilderness. And my prior trip, too – with spaceman, Bem, psi powers, shape-changing, and wreck on an alient planet. Another arranged adventure.'

'Well, My clients would not be interested in dull vacations,' Satan pointed out. 'I try to reward them well for their services to Me. Heaven, you know, is a pretty dull place; My settings have the excitement of challenge and success.'

'So others have interacted with Bat Dursten and his Bems, and with Excelsia and her Alicorn?'

Satan looked modestly uncomfortable. 'Or reasonable fac-similes thereof,' he agreed. 'There is no harm in it, and a scripted adventure is, after all, an aspect of My speciality: an interesting and amusing fabrication.'

'Yes, I remember. You are the Father of Lies.'

'Certainly. Fiction is but an accepted lie, and so it is My business. People have been brainwashed into supposing that there can be no benefit in lies, but lies of this nature can be exceptionally rewarding. If you would care to visit other settings, such as the Wild West, or Mystery Sleuth, or Complex Historical, or Torrid Romance – '

'The antimatter frame has quite a spread of habitats!'

'Indeed. Plenty of room for all My favoured friends.' Satan leaned forward persuasively. 'There are many scenarios within each setting, too. If, for example, you found Excelsia attractive, We could arrange for her to – '

'Never mind that.' Norton had indeed found her attractive, but didn't care to have Satan know it. 'If you have such an excellent way to reward your minions, why do you need to bother with me? Your friend in your past – '

'Ah, you checked him? Did you discover any flaw in the life I contemplate for him?'

'No. I just don't follow your motive. Why not send him to delights in the globular cluster or the Magic-Lantern Cloud, instead of taking all this trouble with me?'

Satan shrugged. 'I suppose I could. But I have promised him a happy life in this world and I always keep My promises.'

Norton hesitated. He did not trust the Father of Lies, yet this particular case did seem to check out. 'I'll give it further consideration.'

Satan stood. 'As you wish, Chronos.' He turned about in place and, somehow, by the time he completed the turn, he was gone.

Norton took a meal and a snooze. He wasn't sure how much objective time had passed, in whatever direction, or what day it might now be beyond his mansion, but he himself had been quite active.

In due course Clotho showed up. She stepped into his arms immediately and kissed him, then hesitated. 'Or is this too soon for you now, in your lifeline?'

Norton realized that there had been, or would be – depending on viewpoint – a romance between them. He still loved Orlene but knew that was over. He had been intrigued by Excelsia, but did not want to get involved in such fashion with a creature who played roles for Satan. Clotho he trusted. 'I think it is right for me now,' he said. 'But it's newer to me than to you.'

'There was a time when it was otherwise,' she said, smiling. 'This will be my pleasure.'

Indeed, she led him through a quite satisfactory liaison, for she was conversant with what pleased him, including some things he hadn't known before would please him. He realized he was going to enjoy experiencing the other encounters she remembered. His separation from his past was now virtually complete. Clotho was excellent medicine . . . except for those knowing eyes.

Then they set up for the day's work. For this, Clotho shifted to Lachesis, who glanced at him obliquely while pretending to be ignorant of what her other aspect had just been doing. Then she put her spread-fingered hands together to draw out the first cat's cradle of crossed threads. She paused. 'That's odd.'

'You have a tangle?'

'A crossed set, where there shouldn't be.' She frowned, trying to make it out.

'That reminds me. Satan wants a favour, and I checked it, and it seems all right. But maybe I should consult with you, just in case it disturbs your threads.'

She looked up from her network. 'That would be wise. Satan must never be trusted. He builds deceit upon deceit, until reality disappears.'

'It's a favour for a man about twenty years in your past. He had a chance to meet and marry a lovely and wealthy young woman, but missed it and committed suicide instead. Satan wants to reverse that so the man can have a good life.'

'Suicide,' she said. She shifted to Atropos. 'That's my

211

department,' the old woman said. 'And Thanatos'. I schedule the terminations, he executes them.' She moved her fingers in intricate patterns, conjuring threads. 'Specific space-time address?'

Norton gave it. She zeroed in. 'Got it. There's the severed thread. He – great Heaven!'

'What's the matter?'

'That's Thanatos!'

'Yes, he would have collected the soul.'

'Not that. This life – it's the mortal man who assumed the current office of Thanatos, just as you assumed the office of Chronos. He didn't suicide; he killed the prior officeholder. That's how that office changes hands.'

'They murder their predecessors?' Norton asked with horror.

'Thanatos deals in death,' she said grimly. 'Nevertheless, the current Thanatos is a good one – perhaps one of the best. He cares for his clients in a way that others of his office did not; and he did balk Satan in a critical situation, thereby preserving the scheme of the world as we know it. It would be disastrous to allow Satan to eliminate him!'

'I thought Satan couldn't harm other Incarnations!'

She collapsed her network of threads and put one withered hand on his. 'Dear boy,' Atropos said. 'Satan never allows himself to be bound by any law he can circumvent, and he is the ultimate master of circumvention. There are ways and ways.'

'But how – ?'

'If you take his minion to that nexus and the minion persuades the man named Zane to buy the Lovestone and win the lovely young woman – ' Her old eyes seemed to sparkle. 'You young men do like lovely young women, don't you! I can't imagine what for.' When he did not respond, she resumed making her point. 'Then he will indeed be happy. He will have an excellent life. But he will, by the same token, not assume the office of Thanatos. Then Thanatos will not save the Magician's daughter Luna from Satan's mischief, and she will not be on hand to balk him in that most critical political nexus not far hence.'

'I don't remember any – '

'It is, I believe, beyond your assumption of the office. Satan thought to use your ignorance to facilitate his ploy. Since you also have not met Thanatos – '

'I met him – before I become Chronos. But his face was a skull; I wouldn't know him in mundane life.'

Atropos pondered momentarily. 'I think you must meet him formally now – and Luna, too, so that Satan cannot again deceive you about them.'

Norton's head was spinning. What a disaster he had almost precipitated! The elimination of the Thanatos he had encountered, who had so kindly explained to him about the baby. Thanatos had cared about him; it would have been the cruellest irony to remove him from his office in return!

Atropos spun threads in her hands and manipulated them. 'This way,' she said. 'Adjust your time; we'll be entering the normal world.'

Norton brought out the Hourglass to turn the sand green. He was surprised to discover that it was already green. That didn't make any difference here in his mansion, but he didn't remember putting the Glass on that setting. 'It is ready.'

Suddenly they were sliding along cables strung through chaos. Norton's eyes could not follow any one of them to its end; all seemed to extend to infinity. They filled the universe in a multidimensional splay of coloured lines. He felt somewhat as a tiny bug might, caught in an endless array of tumbled pickup sticks.

Then the universe firmed again. They were at the entrance to a wealthy estate. 'He's visiting her now,' Atropos explained. 'I dislike interrupting their tryst, but this is important.' She knocked on one of the bars of the gate with a wrinkled knuckle.

Immediately two griffins charged to the gate from the other

side. They had muscular lions' bodies and fierce eagles' heads and wings. But their savagery abated as they spied Atropos; evidently they had encountered her before. 'This is a friend,' she told them, much as Excelsia had told the Alicorn. 'Show us in.'

They turned their beaks towards Norton. Nervously he held up the shining Hourglass. Immediately they relaxed; this, too, they had seen before.

Now Atropos opened the gate, and Norton followed her in. The two griffins paced them, forming an escort. 'Actually, neither of us is in any danger; it is to protect the griffins that I introduced you.'

'To protect *them*?'

'Your cloak, as an extension of the Hourglass, will instantly age-to-oblivion anything that attacks you. Only your good will deactivates it.' She smiled toothily. 'Fortunately for those who might happen to touch you.'

Such as Clotho, who had touched him most intimately. He had not realized his misty cloak had such power; it would have been terrible if he had inadvertently aged Clotho to Atropos during their liaison!

They approached the door to the house. It opened. Thanatos stood there, with a comely woman of perhaps forty beside him. 'Welcome, Incarnations!' Thanatos said.

'Perhaps you did not realize,' Atropos told him, 'that there has been a change. This is the new Chronos.'

Thanatos looked at Norton. 'You jest, Thread-Cutter! This is the Master of Time I have known twenty years, since he helped me understand my own office.'

'Uh – whom you *will* know,' Norton said. 'That is – '

Thanatos laughed and took his hand. 'Of course, friend! You live backwards. So this is when you meet me! Twenty years after I met you.'

'Yes,' Norton agreed. 'But we also met when I was, uh, mortal. You came to collect a baby – '

Thanatos peered at him more closely. 'Oh, yes! I remember now! The demon ring! I did not make the connection; you appear different in your robe of office.'

'Not more so than you do,' Norton said.

They all laughed. 'I am hoist in my own petard, as Mars would say.' Thanatos drew back his dark hood, and now the features of the customer at the Mess o' Pottage shop emerged. 'Well, welcome to the office, old friend!'

Atropos took Norton's arm and drew him towards the other occupant of the house. 'And this is Luna Kaftan.'

The woman smiled. 'I, too, am glad to have you meet me at last, Chronos, though we have been friends all this time. You saved my life, long ago.'

'Uh – I'm really not clear what – '

'Of course you don't remember! I had been slain by a dragon, and you turned time back to unslay me.'

As he had done for Excelsia. 'Uh, good,' he said inadequately.

'Come in, friend,' Luna said, taking his arm and drawing him to the centre of the room. 'We realize we owe you explanations. We have grown accustomed to your knowledge, forgetting it needs an origin. You have been an excellent friend to all of us, and it is time for us to clarify things for you.'

And clarify they did. Luna, born the daughter of a powerful Magician who had foreseen the first of Satan's current series of efforts to subvert the system, was now a Senator, influential in Congress; it was understood that she would in the near future be instrumental in balking Satan's plan to take over the government and influence the nation and the world enough to swing the total balance towards evil and make him the final victor over God. No one knew exactly what Satan planned to do, but all knew that Luna was the key to stopping it. She had to be protected. There had already been horrendous episodes. But Chronos' role was to be critical, for he alone could literally change history. Everything else that had happened could become invalid, and all their memories and experiences

215

could change – if Chronos did not hold firm against the wiles and guiles of Satan. What Chronos had done – would do – to balk Satan was not clear to any of them; evidently much of it had been erased by changes in reality already. But if he won, they would remain as they were now, ready to defeat Satan.

'But I must have won,' he said. 'Since you are here!'

Luna shook her head. 'No. We are at the moment only a theoretical present; our reality is subject to your action. We sincerely hope you will prevail, but we are largely helpless to assist you in that effort.'

Atropos told Thanatos and Luna of Satan's latest trick – trying to get Thanatos vacated before he even assumed the office. 'Because Chronos didn't know – at his beginning,' she concluded. 'Satan was striking at the outset – and he almost bypassed us all.'

'The last shall be first,' Luna agreed. 'We have been napping in that respect, but it seems that ploy was foiled because Chronos did not take the minion there, and now knows better. Yet my stones indicate that Satan is not through with him, and the issue remains in serious doubt.'

How blithely she talked of her own potential defeat or nonexistence! 'What can Satan do, now that I am alert?' Norton asked.

'I'm not sure,' Luna said. 'But there is something.'

'It is impossible for any of us to be sure,' Atropos said, 'when our own history is being changed.'

'But I haven't changed any!' Norton protested. 'I won't – '

Atropos shook her head. 'There is something,' she said, repeating Luna's words. She brought forth her threads. 'That strange crossing – and now I think it's not coincidental.' She concentrated, peering closely at her network. 'Can't seem to spot it specifically.'

'Satan couldn't have done anything in any past time without Chronos' cooperation,' Luna said. 'And Chronos has not cooperated – and as he progresses into our past, he'll be increasingly careful, so Satan will have no opportunity to fool him. If Satan hasn't managed anything yet, he'll never have the chance – as well he knows.'

Now Thanatos turned his hollow-skull gaze on Norton. Even though Norton knew this was merely the effect of the hood, which the man had drawn close again, it remained disconcerting. 'Are you certain Satan's minion did not accompany you to the past?'

'No demon went with me,' Norton said. 'Unless you mean Sning?' He held up his hand, showing the snake ring.

'He is not of Satan,' Thanatos said. 'I meant something Satan might have given you, that you accepted. You have to accept it; that is the nature of this. Evil can never touch the person who refuses to accept it. But evil can be subtle. Satan might have concealed the minion's nature and purpose.

'All Satan gave me was a scroll with the address, which I didn't keep – I memorized it – and an amulet to – ' Norton stiffened. 'Oh, no!'

'The demon!' Luna agreed. 'Satan knew you would want to investigate, and once you carried his minion there – '

'How could I have been such a fool!' Norton cried in an agony of conscience. 'Sning tried to warn me, but I didn't understand. Satan said it was just a little horn – '

Thanatos nodded. 'The horn of a demon,' he said. 'Do not blame yourself unduly, Chronos; all of us have been deceived by the guiles of the Father of Lies. All of us have learned the hard way. Once he almost convinced me my magic was gone.'

'But your life is not changed, Thanatos,' Atropos said. 'I checked that first; the snarl is not there.'

The Deathhead grinned. 'Obviously.'

'No, I didn't take the horn there,' Norton said. His knees felt weak. 'I could have eliminated you, Thanatos, without ever realizing! You who were so kind to me when you took the baby! When you took the time to explain. I feel terrible! It was just blind luck that I didn't – '

'You two met before?' Luna asked. 'Perhaps, then, it wasn't luck. Paradox may have been brought into play.'

'I thought I was immune,' Norton said.

'You are. But there are special cases. When did you meet Thanatos – in our time?'

'About a year and a half ago, maybe less. Before I became Chronos. It was partly because of Thanatos that I took the office. I knew, because of him, that it was possible for a good person to function as an Incarnation.'

'He is a good person, isn't he?' Luna said, bestowing on Thanatos a momentary gaze of such love and respect that her beauty was intensified. Then she turned back to Norton. 'Had you had no connection with Thanatos, you could have eliminated him without consequence to yourself. But you met him and were influenced by him; thus your elimination of him would have constituted a variety of paradox, even though the result occurred later in your own life. He had to be there to talk with you in your normal life – and I know from my own experience why he did it and that a different man in that office would not have done it.' She smiled at the Death-figure.

'Well, he noticed my ring – '

'I have a houseful of similar enchantments.' She turned and reached to a shelf, picking up a tiny elephant formed from a single blue topaz stone. In her hand the elephant came to life and trumpeted faintly. 'He would not have found your ring remarkable.'

Norton looked at Thanatos, who did not react. 'Then why – ?'

Luna took Thanatos' bone-arm, showing no aversion to its form. 'Because he saw that you were suffering, and he had compassion. Few in his office have had that quality, and of course Satan doesn't comprehend it.' She turned again to Thanatos. 'I went with him first because I was required to, but when I grasped his inner nature I loved him. He saved my life – as all the Incarnations have – but I would have loved him anyway.'

'That other woman,' Norton said. 'The one he would have married, had he not become Thanatos instead – she was

218

beautiful and wealthy and good – but so are you! He lost nothing!'

'Nothing!' Thanatos agreed.

'So you could not readily eliminate Thanatos,' Luna concluded. 'Paradox did help there.'

'Not – readily?'

'It is possible,' she explained. 'Paradox is not absolute for you. You will tend to avoid it, rather than confront it head-on, even when only mortals are involved. Incarnations are much more difficult to change, so paradox is stronger with them. But if you *do* meet it directly, it cannot stop you. So you could have eliminated Thanatos without consequence to yourself, but it would have required a more specific effort.'

'I made no effort!' Norton said.

'Yes. So you avoided eliminating him, for a reason Satan was not equipped to understand. Satan's ruse malfunctioned by seeming coincidence. That is the way such things operate; without your will, paradox will not be abused, even when only normal people are involved. What happened to Satan's horn?'

'I visited – the woman I loved,' Norton said, abruptly aware that Atropos was merely another form of Clotho, with whom he had so recently made love. 'She made me destroy the thing.'

'There is the seeming coicidence,' Luna said.

Atropos shook her head. 'Still, there is something. Did you go anywhere before then?'

'Yes. I visited her when she was a child. And, you know, somewhere along the way part of the horn was lost – '

'Not lost,' Luna said. 'Departed. The part that was the messenger-demon took off to do its mischief.'

'When?' Atropos demanded of Norton.

'When Orlene was ten years old – or maybe seven – that's the first stop I made – call it about fifteen years ago, your time. No, more like seventeen. I entered normal time to chat with her in a park. That could be where it left.'

Atropos explored her threads. 'Nothing in that period.'

219

'Actually, I paused at a number of places in her life. But I didn't phase in to normal time – '

'Probably that wasn't necessary. The demon could have dropped off while you were travelling.' She continued to check. 'There does seem to be something eight or nine years ago.' She put her old eye close. 'Yes, threads I never crossed, in that general range.'

'The minion, for sure,' Luna said. 'It made a change. It couldn't get to the primary target, so took a secondary one. Now we must discover what that is.'

'A change in the past, to get rid of you – without touching Thanatos?' Norton asked.

'Or to nullify me,' Luna said. 'I am the real target, not Thanatos – and in this case I am easier to get at, since I am mortal and you never before interacted with me. In any event, Satan does not care how he gets his way – as long as he does.'

'But you are the same – I mean, you haven't changed, have you? Or would you know if you had changed?'

Luna smiled. 'I understand your concern, Chronos. But no, I don't believe I have changed – yet. My stones indicate that Good retains the advantage over Evil, and that would not be the case if Satan had his way. Still, mischief is in the making. We should be able to undo it if we act correctly and promptly.'

'First we must discover what the damage is,' Thanatos said. 'Perhaps this is merely a diversion.'

'It's oddly minor,' Atropos said, still peering in perplexity at her threads. 'Nothing significant, really. No one was killed, harmed, or even frightened.'

'Keep looking,' Luna said. 'Satan is devious, but we can be sure he knows how to score.'

'I'm afraid I still don't understand,' Norton said. 'If the demon did something to change the future – our present – why isn't it finished now? And if it isn't, why can't I simply go back to fix it? If Atropos can just pinpoint the moment – '

'It's the three-person limit,' Atropos said, still tracing her threads. 'An aspect of the paradox resistance.' She glanced up to spy Norton's look of bafflement. 'Thanatos, you understand it, don't you? Explain it to him, for Chronos certainly has the need to know.'

Both Thanatos and Luna chuckled. 'Indeed, he explained it to me many years ago, when I was new in office,' Thanatos said. He opened his cloak and removed it; with that action, he became a completely ordinary young man, the one called Zane. Twenty years had not aged him at all; evidently Incarnations did not age the way normal people did. That aligned with Norton's observation of the prior Chronos: it had been an adult man, not a newborn baby, who brought the Hourglass. So he himself would probably remain his present physiological age until his term expired. 'Chronos was kind to me,' Zane continued. 'Now I shall be kind to him at *his* commencement.' And he settled down and explained it so that Norton could understand.

The reason no change had occurred in the present was that it had not yet occurred in the past. Whatever the demon of Satan had done was quiescent, evoking no change in the life of any human being. But that was merely a delayed implementation, a literal time bomb that would in due course have its effect on human events. The moment it did, the future from that point on would change, in whatever manner the initial alteration determined. That would surely include Luna; if she were not eliminated as a person, she would certainly be nullified as a force to balk Satan. So they had to locate and nullify that change before it touched the human fabric; only in that manner could they be assured of success.

'But how long – ?' Norton asked.

'Atropos is trying to determine that,' Thanatos said. 'She can trace living threads readily, but inanimate threads are more devious. It could be five more minutes – or five more years.'

Norton felt another chill. Time bomb indeed! 'Maybe I

can go back and destroy the demon before it escapes. It was in my possession, after all.'

Thanatos shook his head. 'You cannot. That is the other aspect of Satan's mischief. The three-person limit prevents you.' And he explained about that.

Chronos was the only entity who could travel in time and he was largely immune from paradox – but there were limits. His easiest way was simply to proceed along his natural life course, backwards to the date of his birth. It required magical effort to reverse his direction and match that of ordinary people, as he was doing now, more effort to travel through historical time, and more yet to take physical form and act in such a time. But the magic of the Hourglass made it possible, and he could indeed change reality by changing the past. But in such cases, he was there in two persons – himself in his original, normal life, and himself in his return as Chronos. Doubling himself was in his power; it had to be, for him to use his power effectively. But tripling himself was another matter; then he was making a third appearance at a given time, interfering with himself as Chronos, and the potential for paradox magnified exponentially.

No one could interfere with an Incarnation with impunity – not even if that Incarnation was himself. That strained the power of the Hourglass, for it was itself being doubled and was opposing itself. It was theoretically possible for this to occur, but so awkward that it was hardly worthwhile to try. If he did try, most likely he would bounce off and land in a time when there was no duplication, possibly doing incidental mischief in the process. In short, the risks were probably greater than the likely benefits; mischief in time was the most awkward to undo – because of the three-person limit. Chronos could do damage that Chronos could not correct.

'And Satan knew that!' Norton exclaimed. 'He knew I could not change my mind once I changed the past – even if it was inadvertent.'

'True,' Thanatos agreed. 'Had you taken the demon to the

Mess o' Pottage shop, you would have nullified the best efforts of Atropos and myself, for in such interactions Chronos is more powerful than Thanatos. The rest of us can double only by your action – and we can be rendered nonexistent by your action, too. Only God and Satan, the true Eternals, are exempt from that.'

Something about this explanation bothered Norton, but he was not able to pin it down. 'Then there is no way to stop what Satan's minion has done?' he asked. 'If I can't return to stop the demon –'

'There should be a way,' Luna said. 'Satan's minions do not endure long apart from him. That demon must have done its deed and expired. If we can identify what he did and nullify it before it impinges on human events, then the victory will be ours. We probably have time, because Satan sought to distract you; he would not have bothered, had the deed been truly irrevocable.'

'It was some distraction!' Norton admitted ruefully. 'He said he was showing me the nature of his bribe to encourage me to take his minion to the Mess o' Pottage. All the time he knew this was pointless or impossible. He was certainly angry when he learned I'd destroyed the horn, though; he must have thought the mission had been a complete failure.'

'We were lucky,' Luna said. 'We could have been lost before we had a chance to fight back. But that secondary mission can still destroy us. How is it coming, Atropos?'

'I have almost pinpointed the time and place,' Atropos said. 'But not the deed. I only know that when it manifests, it will give Satan the victory. My threads have tension on them that threatens haywire shifting. I need to comprehend it further.'

Norton's mind had been running back over his recent experiences with Satan. The globular cluster, the Magic-Lantern Cloud, and his adventures there – suddenly the thing that had bothered him came clear. He had doubled himself in those adventures, rescuing himself from the Bem and saving Excelsia from the Alicorn. It had been not only possible but easy. How, then, could the three-person limit be such a formidable force? Did it exist at all?

'Gaea,' Luna said.

'I will take Atropos to her,' Thanatos said, rising and resuming his cloak.

'Take us all,' Luna said. 'Chronos must meet her, too.'

'Gaea – another Incarnation?' Norton asked. It seemed to him he had heard that name before; Gawain the Ghost had said –

'The Green Mother,' Luna explained. 'Nature.'

Yes, that was it; Gaea had changed the baby for Gawain and thereby had caused terrible mischief. The memory of that banished Norton's three-person speculation from his attention; he wanted to meet this powerful yet fallible entity.

The four of them walked out to the estate parking lot, paced by the guardian griffins. They were certainly beautiful animals! Beside the parking lot there was a small, verdant pasture. A handsome stallion of pale hue grazed there.

'Mortis,' Thanatos called.

The pale horse perked up his ears and trotted over. He was a truly splendid animal, with a sleek hide and firm muscles; had he had wings and a horn, he could have passed for another Alicorn. This was, Norton remembered, the Death-horse – the steed who carried Thanatos to his appointments.

'We need transportation for four – to the Green Mother,' Thanatos said to the horse.

Mortis stepped on to the pavement – and shifted into the form of a pale limousine. Norton gaped. 'That – but that's a machine!' he protested.

Thanatos drew his cloak about him more tightly; as the hood closed, the skull-face manifested with its gruesome grin. 'Mortis is an excellent steed – but perhaps no more remarkable than your little ring.' He opened a door for the ladies.

Squeeze. Sning liked that comparison. He was another creature who converted from living to dead, or vice versa.

Norton walked around the car, noting that the tag in the

224

back said, MORTIS. And he had thought the Alicorn was remarkable! When magic and science were one, such miracles were commonplace. He opened a door and climbed in.

He found himself in the back seat beside Clotho. She shrugged at his startled glance. 'I want to be presentable for Ge,' she explained.

Of course. Fate changed bodies the way others changed clothes. This made it seem like a double date, for Thanatos and Luna were companions, while he and Clotho – well, what did it matter? His old existence as a mortal was behind him.

The car started smoothly, driving itself. It turned about – and abruptly it was zooming through space and matter. The world was rushing past in a smear of colour. Then this slowed, and they were driving into the gate of a truly sumptuous estate with luxuriant trees of many varieties and a sparkling lake. It was the kind of place that could charge tourists for visits.

A huge shape loomed in the sky ahead. Norton peered through the windshield. 'That – that's a – '

'A roc,' Luna said calmly. 'The largest of birds. Ge has made her estate into a preserve for rare and magical creatures. It's hard to imagine how she salvaged the rocs.'

The roc swooped towards them, its wings seeming to span the whole horizon. It pounced on the car, its monstrous talons poking into the windows and vents, and picked up the vehicle together with its occupants as if this were no more than a mouse. In moments they were dangling high in the air.

One talon was near Norton's face, projecting from the top of the window to the ceiling of the car. The talon was like fine blue steel, an inch in diameter at the window and tapering to a needle point. What a bird!

Luna turned to Thanatos, unruffled. 'Ge is testing us,' she remarked. 'Perhaps you had better perform a token, just to reassure her.'

'Gently,' Clotho cautioned him. 'We are fairly high at the moment.'

'Gently,' Thanatos agreed. He reached up and touched a talon with a skeletal finger.

The bird shuddered – and so did the car. The roc had felt the touch of Death, and that was a touch no creature ignored. The roc spiralled down to the ground and set the car gently back on the road. Then it hastily departed.

Norton realized why caution had been advisable. Thanatos could have stunned or killed the big bird – but that would have led to a crash landing. So he had merely given warning – and the roc, recognizing a power more sinister than its own, had yielded.

But a new problem loomed. A cloud formed, and rain slanted down from it, turning rapidly to sleet and then snow. From the right puffed smoke and steam; then a vent opened and molten rock poured out. The lava was not moving rapidly, but it was hideously hot; the vegetation it touched burst instantly into flame. The snow, on the other side, was already piling so deep that the car could not plough through it.

Clotho shook her head. 'Ge.' She sighed as if addressing a naughty child. 'Mortis, follow my thread.' She flicked a finger, and a thread flew out, passing through the windshield without touching it and extending in front of the car, glowing.

Mortis followed it. The thread wound through the slush melted by the lava, left the road, travelled along a ridge that held the lava temporarily at bay, and went across a narrow channel that concentrated the lava. The car speeded up to hurdle the ditch, then slewed about to follow the curving thread towards the main mass of lava. This seemed hazardous indeed to Norton, particularly since the traction was treacherous and the visibility almost nil, but the thread of Fate knew exactly where to go. That, of course, was part of Fate's business – to know the intricacies of man's interaction with Nature. They threaded their way successfully between snow and lava, sometimes with each close enough to touch on either side from a window, sometimes pausing, then scooting forward, avoiding a minor avalanche, and emerged on to a firm, dry road. Fate had foiled Nature.

Then Norton experienced an urgent need to relieve himself. His gut knotted and his bladder swelled. 'Uh, if we could stop a moment . . .' he said.

Luna fidgeted. 'Ge again; we all feel it. No way to avoid it, and stopping won't relieve it. It's her speciality for intruders: instant flu.' Her cheek seemed greenish.

Indeed, now Norton's stomach roiled. Beside him, Clotho looked seasick, and Thanatos seemed about as sick as a skeleton could be.

Clotho turned to him. 'Your turn, Chronos.'

Oh. Norton lifted the Hourglass, turned the sand blue, and willed the immediate region to be included in a short hop. There was a small jump, and the discomfort abated.

He had brought the car and occupants five minutes into the past, which was his future, before the illness commenced.

Clotho took a deep breath. 'Thank you, Chronos. A girl doesn't like to look sick in public.' She brought out a small mirror and checked her young and pretty face.

He had not violated the three-person rule, since he had not duplicated himself. Well, perhaps he had, because he had been phased in to real-world time. The others and the car would be duplicated for five minutes, but by the time the other carful of them caught up to this spot on the road, *this* car would be gone, and so there should be no problem. The other carful would fade out, leaving this one.

Or could the other carful have been retroactively erased? That would avoid the three-person problem. There was still a lot he did not understand about his office.

Now the mansion of the Green Mother Nature was before them. It seemed to be formed of vegetation, its thick wood alive and leafy, with a streamlet flowing from level to level in the manner of a fountain. Animals peeped from crannies –

bunnies, wrens, lizards, and perhaps an elf or two. This was indeed the handiwork of the Earth-Mother.

The car parked, they got out, and Mortis reconverted to equine form and set about grazing beside the mansion. Had they really been inside a horse all this time? Norton shook his head, filing the matter as another wonder to be pondered at leisure at such time as he was alone with a campfire. The four walked up to the entrance.

Gaea met them there. She was a stoutish woman of middle age with a crown of woven leaves and vines and a dress of leaves and pine needles; green was certainly her colour. She seemed to Norton to possess an aura of competence and power; this was no innocuous creature.

If green was Nature's colour, he reflected, then surely black was Thanatos', and white his own. But what would be Fate's colour?

'We're in trouble, Ge,' Clotho said without preamble. 'Satan tricked Chronos into taking a demon back in time to eliminate Luna. That was partly balked by paradox, but there's a sleeper. I can't quite track it down.'

Gaea glanced at Norton. 'My apology for my error,' she murmured.

No confusion there! She was referring to the problem with Orlene's baby. 'Accepted,' he said. He knew she had helped facilitate his present office as compensation for that error.

Gaea turned to Clotho. 'Let me see it.'

Clotho held out her hands, the network of threads between them. Gaea peered. 'May I?' she asked.

'You may,' Clotho replied.

Gaea made a little gesture with a hand near the threads. They changed – and the environment changed. The threads became curling green vines with sprouting leaves – and the five human figures in the mansion seemed to be standing in an enormous garden, existing on the scale of insects.

The vine-threads wove through the fabric of this new reality in an amazingly complex scheme. Everything seemed to relate, in some obvious or devious fashion, to everything else. Of course, that was the nature of reality, or the reality of nature, and of fate, and this manifestation was hardly surprising, since these were the very Incarnations of Nature and Fate.

Gaea walked along a vine. 'Here it is,' she said. 'Here is where the threads were crossed.'

The others crowded close. Norton saw that a tiny stem, something like a section of fine straw, had been moved, so that it crossed the main vine in a slightly different place. The change hardly seemed significant.

Clotho concentrated – and the vines expanded, until the large vine seemed to be the diameter of the height of a man and the small stem was three inches through. 'I will analyse the small one,' Gaea said. 'That one's dead, but I believe it holds the key.' She gestured. A glow formed about the small vine and the place from which it had been moved. Coloured light radiated from that region, separating into prismatic components, bathing them all in rainbow hues.

'There,' Gaea said, pointing to a dark band amidst the coloured light. 'The spectrograph shows it. Contamination.'

'Dangerous?' Clotho asked.

Gaea frowned. 'No. It's cyanide, but that was there before the interference. It has been chemically nullified, so that its effect on a human being would be minimal. A few hours of queasiness, no more.'

'Why should Satan act to nullify an existing poison?' Thanatos asked.

Clotho inspected the larger vine. 'Oops,' she said. 'Now at last I fathom it. What an insidious plot!'

Gaea looked at her expectantly. 'You had slated a poisoning?'

'Not exactly,' Clotho said. 'Here, Lachesis can explain it better.' She shifted to middle-aged form. 'I do not slate people for doom any more than Thanatos kills them,' Lachesis said. 'I merely weave the threads in necessary

229

patterns. Some mortals must prosper and some must decline, and there is no guaranteed personal justice in this. My concern is not for individuals, but for the pattern as a whole. In this case, a certain older man of indifferent qualities had to be woven out in order to make way for a young woman of superior qualities. So – he was accidentally poisoned, mostly by his own carelessness. He swallowed a pill contaminated by cyanide and died at the age of sixty-two. It was small loss for the world, though he was politically prominent.'

'Cyanide,' Luna said thoughtfully. 'I remember – '

'The same,' Lachesis agreed.

'I don't understand,' Norton said.

Lachesis faced him. 'This remains in your future – but you do need to know now. The senior Senator from Luna's state died in office, so a special election was scheduled. Luna ran for that office with the support of the Forces of Good and won. This is the office she now holds.'

'Luna is a Senator?' Norton asked, surprised. He might have heard about it before, but it hadn't sunk in.

'And an excellent one,' Thanatos said with a certain possessive pride. 'At the moment, the Senate isn't in session, so she's not in the news, but normally she is. She was first elected eight years ago and is now well established with a firm base of support. She may one day become our first female President.'

'I haven't decided to run yet!' Luna protested, embarrassed.

Norton was embarrassed too. He had been so much out of touch with contemporary affairs that he had never heard of Senator Kaftan during his ordinary life.

'But after you balk Satan in that critical showdown, you will be the front runner,' Lachesis said. 'I see it in the threads.'

No wonder Satan didn't like Luna! A powerful female political figure, allied with the Incarnations themselves, possessed of a legacy of magic from her Magician father – she would be in an excellent position to balk any political ploy the Prince of Evil tried! Obviously he had something in mind and needed her out of office so she couldn't interfere. 'Then the demon I took back in time – '

'Went and nullified the contaminated capsule that the original Senator was destined to take,' Lachesis concluded. 'So when he takes it, he won't die and will remain in office, and there will be no special election for Luna to win. She will remain a lesser officeholder and not become a Senator, and will not be in a position to foil him politically at the critical moment.'

Subtle indeed! 'But couldn't she win the office in a normal election?'

'Against an incumbent? No chance! The Senator has to be dead before giving up his seat.' Lachesis grimaced. 'And even if she did manage to oust him, it wouldn't be the same. Taking office four years later, she wouldn't have the same seniority. That's important for key committees and influence – especially the committee chairmanship that will give her the specific authority she needs. No, Luna has to win that seat when she did – which means we have to restore that capsule before the Senator takes it.'

'But this is murder!' Norton cried, aghast.

'We do deal in life and death,' Gaea said, with a significant glance at Thanatos.

'But in their proper pattern,' Lachesis said. 'Is it really murder to restore the events of the past to their original settings?'

Norton was confused and unhappy. 'To poison a person knowingly – '

'Have you any notion,' Lachesis asked grimly, 'how many people will knowingly be poisoned – and tortured, murdered, and literally damned to Hell – if the minions of Satan win political power on Earth?'

'No,' Norton said.

'With political power, Satan can and will make the worship

of God a crime punishable by torture until recantation. Thus all those who are not good enough or strong enough to resist such torture – and that is the majority – will become worshippers of Satan, and the balance of power will shift to Him. He will have His way with both Life and Afterlife, and there will be no reprieve from Evil. On that day, the death of one corrupt Senator will not even be noticed, for Good itself will be dead.'

'But – you are saying the end justifies the means!' Norton was still deeply troubled. 'If we do evil in the name of good – '

'Why don't you step into Hell and see what Satan's power is like?' Gaea asked him. Her eyes were like blue skies with roiling clouds in the background.

'I can do that? Visit Hell?'

'You are an Incarnation. You can do what you choose. Even Satan cannot deny you that.'

Norton considered – and found that he did not need to visit Hell to know that Satan was evil. He did not like killing, but it was true that the ethics of his revising the past were problematical. Was he guilty of murder if he did not set about revising history to eliminate every death that had occurred during his projected term of office? If he decided to let history stand as it was, deaths included, was it right to allow Satan to make the decision about which person should be spared by a spot revision? Viewed that way, the sacrifice of the Senator seemed to be the lesser of evils. He did not like becoming the instrument of the Senator's demise, but he preferred that to the evil Satan would generate if the Senator lived. It seemed he had to choose among flawed means to achieve the smallest total evil for the society, cutting one thread for the benefit of the majority. He had to respect the judgment of the other Incarnations, who had been in office longer than he had and who had had more experience with the machinations of Satan. 'No, I will help you to restore the original past. I will take you back to when the demon changed – ' He broke off, remembering the three-person barrier. 'Except you tell me I can't go back there, having been there once before as Chronos.'

'There is a way,' Gaea said. 'But it is not easy.'

'None of this is easy,' Norton agreed.

'None of it is,' Gaea agreed. 'You cannot return directly to that time. But you can return to a spot on the timeline that is no longer than your elapsed personal time, and anchor yourself then, and – '

'Wait! Wait! I'm hopelessly confused! No closer than what?'

Luna came and took his hand. 'You are new in office, however long we have known you in it. We keep forgetting, because you have been so knowledgeable in our past. I will explain, while they narrow down the precise coordinates of the demon's interference.' She guided him to another huge vine, and they sat down on its resilient surface. She had a remarkably compelling presence and a quiet air of authority and she was, despite her age, a beautiful woman. Norton could understand how Death himself loved her.

'Time is objective,' Luna said, 'and subjective. It passes in the world and it passes for you – and though your normal course is opposite to that of the world, time is equally real for both of you. When you live a day, the world lives a day, and this ratio holds regardless of direction. So, since it has been about six hours from when you loosed Satan's minion on Earth, in terms of your life, the same amount of time has passed on Earth since the change. You can no more return to a spot within that six hours than you can duplicate yourself; it is an aspect of the same limit.'

Norton shook his head. 'It almost seems to make sense when you say it.'

She smiled. 'Almost! It will make more sense to you as you mature in office.'

'Nonetheless, I can't accept all of it.'

'What can't you accept?'

'First, I *can* duplicate myself; I have already done so more than once. So – '

'Duplicate once, yes; it is the second duplication that is the barrier.'

'Yes. But since my original life counts as one, and my present backward life as another – '

'Did we say that? That was a misunderstanding. Your prior, mortal life is excluded. Only your present Incarnation relates. You have no further connection with your mortal existence; that is one reason you are immune from any paradox involving it. So your normal backward course is one, and your jump to our past is another.'

'But I have doubled up, and interfered with my prior Chronos self – in fact, once I rescued my prior self from destruction.'

She pursed her lips. 'That's interesting! But it does not violate the three-person rule. It does not matter whether your doubles are together or far apart; you cannot conveniently go triple.'

He nodded. 'Yes, I see how it applies now. But the other thing is this business of six hours. It has been a lot longer than that since – '

'I calculated it,' Lachesis called, overhearing him. 'Your time in Satan's frame doesn't count for this, only your time in this one. You slept for three hours, talked with Satan for half an hour, and spoke with me for an hour and a half before we realized the problem and went to join the other Incarnations an hour ago. Six hours total.'

'I see,' Norton said, surprised at the accuracy of her assessment. But, of course, she was Fate, the Mistress of the Threads of Life; this was her business.

'At the moment,' Luna said gently, 'it is enough for you to know that these six hours are barred to you by direct effort, but that you can penetrate them by an extraordinary measure.'

'I land seven hours later and – what?'

'And turn back the clock,' she said. 'You must reverse time and take the whole world with you. That will put you in the same category as you were – would be – *will* be, for you –

234

when you live through that period as Chronos. You will pre-empt that period.'

'You mean, by that device I'll actually erase whatever I was doing in my normal course then?'

'We believe so. There is a risk, if that normal course covers something important, but Lachesis sees no problem in her threads. Perhaps that period has never happened for you, because of your pre-emption, so nothing is lost.'

Norton's head was spinning again. 'How do you know my so-called normal Chronos self will go?' he asked. 'Maybe I'll actually be tripling myself. That's theoretically possible, isn't it?'

'I suppose it is,' she agreed with a certain reservation. 'There may be an infinite progression, like a picture within a picture, or mirrors facing each other. But it is convenient for us to call it the three-person limit. Our understanding is more restricted than yours will be; perhaps we understand only part of your nature. At any rate, we are reasonably certain that if you reverse time for the world, for those six or seven hours, you will be able to reach the moment the demon acted, despite your prior trip there, and to nullify the demon just before it acts. Then you can relax, with the world returned to its original course, the damage undone – and protected by the same three-person limit that at the moment is causing us so much difficulty. Reversing Satan's ploy.'

'But what, when – ?'

'When you come to that period in your normal life? I believe you will simply jump over it, having already lived it pre-emptively. The three-person limit should not harm you, but merely cause you that inconvenience – if we judge it correctly.'

'It seems reasonable enough to me,' he said. 'Thank you, Senator – '

'Luna.'

'Luna. Now I think I know what I'm doing.'

235

'Thank *you*,' she said, touching the back of his hand with her cool, delicate fingers. 'It is my career you are preserving.'

Norton looked across at the others. Lachesis was facing him. 'We have now pinpointed it exactly,' she said. 'We can give you precise coordinates. Are you ready to save the world from Satan, Chronos?'

Norton breathed deeply. 'I hope so,' he said.

11
Drawkcab

They took him to the spot where the deed had been done –
not the contamination, but the decontamination of the capsule. The capsule was already in a bottle in the Senator's
suburban residence, in storage for later use. It was an irony of
the type Satan specialized in that this Senator had acted to
block more effective regulation of the production and market-
ing of exactly such products as this, so that slipshod quality
control was practised in the interests of cost-economy, and
many people were harmed by such contamination. But now it
suited Satan's purpose to preserve the life of the Senator, so
he had acted.

The demon had simply come, denaturized the capsule, and
expired. Norton would have to catch the demon just before it
did the job and cause it to expire early. That was all. Gaea had
provided him with a vial of holy water for the purpose. Norton
had donned a conventional suit, concealing his white cloak, so
that he would not seem remarkable among the mortals.

The room was empty and dusty now; the Senator's house
had been sold after he died, and this wing of it was in disuse.
Of course, it might remain empty if Satan's ploy worked, for
in eight years the Senator could have died of natural causes.
Satan didn't care about the Senator; he just wanted to see that
Luna was not the person who replaced him.

Norton concentrated on the Hourglass, turning the sand
blue, and zoomed through time to the designated moment.
The other Incarnations could not come with him for this
mission; they had to maintain their own positions in this
historical period so that Satan would not suspect what effort
was being made here.

He arrived at the designated time and slowed to his normal

pace. He raised the Hourglass, about to invoke the major magical attempt of his brief career, when he noticed something. He had overshot his target time by a few minutes and come within the six-hour limit. That was readily fixed; he would simply back up till he was clear, before engaging the rest of the world. He had not yet phased in to reality, so there would be no three-person complication. But there was another thing – something that jarred.

He was in the same room he had started from, a generous eight years hence, but now it was filled with supplies: bottles of bourbon, smoked hams, cans of caviar, and other signals of rich living. The Senator evidently believed in taking care of Number One first. One high shelf was devoted to medicines – more than one man should need in a lifetime. Among these was *the* bottle; Lachesis had described it precisely, so Norton would know it without fail. All this he had anticipated. But there was another presence, and that was what had made him pause.

Sitting across from the key bottle and watching it intently was a small demon. The creature was so small it could have been a figurine, with little snub-horns, red shoe-button eyes, and a leathery forked tail. But it was no figurine; it was a living – if that term applied – minion of Satan.

Had the demon survived its mission? No, the other Incarnations should not have been wrong about a detail like that. This must be another demon, a contemporary one, assigned to guard the capsule until it was used. That could only mean that Satan was aware of this counterplot after all. The Satan of this time, eight years before Norton's present. Since Satan did not live backwards, he could not know what his future self had done – but he surely had recognized his minion. So he must have assumed, correctly, that his future self was up to something nefarious and he was seeing that no one interfered with whatever that was. He would not know *why* the demon from the future had nullified the contamination, but he would know there was good, or rather evil, reason. Satan was evil, but not stupid.

238

This posed a problem for Norton. The little demon could not perceive him at the moment, for Chronos was not obvious in his normal state. The demon was existing forward, while Chronos existed backwards. Only when he phased in to the world – or made the world phase in to him – was he apparent to others. But when he did reverse the world, he would be apparent to this demon. That would tip off Satan, the Satan of this time, and there could be all manner of trouble. In fact, that might be this demon's purpose – to catch Chronos himself when he approached the capsule and balk his effort.

Mischief indeed! He had to do something about that guardian demon, for the creature would surely interfere with him one way or another. If it summoned its master to this spot, Norton's little vial of holy water would be relegated to the status of mere annoyance. Holy water destroyed the things of Satan but could not touch Satan himself, just as Satan's minions could spread mischief in the world but not touch God Himself or directly harm other Incarnations. Maybe the demon would not be able to stop Norton, because, of course, the world would be proceeding backwards. But he didn't care to take the risk. Why should Satan post a demon, if it couldn't do anything?

But if Norton phased in and tackled the demon, extinguishing it with the holy water – wouldn't that action alert Satan? Again Norton wasn't quite sure, and hesitated to gamble. Too much was at stake.

He pondered, then decided that the best thing to do was to avoid the demon. If the creature never knew Chronos was present, it would never give its master the alarm. Satan would assume that all was well (ill) – until it was too late (early). Norton would approach the capsule only at its moment of change, then use his holy water. A swift, surgical strike – and victory.

He walked away from the chamber, passing through the wall. In his normal mode, the universe was hardly aware of him, and he could ignore it to the extent he found convenient.

He was very much like a ghost. He emerged on to a busy street, one of those old-fashioned kinds with concrete sidewalks, asphalt road surface, and ornamental shrubs planted along the sides. Most suburban streets, even on this day eight years in the past, were travelling composition sheets that carried both people and vehicles to and from their residences, just as they did in the nether levels. Evidently the Senator was conservative and had prevented modernization of his region. It was a status symbol to live primitively when the common man lived modernistically; it was also a type of posturing – the humble servant of the people. This should be a good place for Norton to phase in to; he could lose himself in the throng, and the demon in the house would never know.

Norton reddened the sand and moved fifteen minutes forward in the world's time. This put him safely beyond the six-hour limit. There was a large clock on the facade of a store, another archaic affectation; its hands jumped from 11:03 to 11:18 A.M.

Now he turned the sand white, for his normal progress backwards. And he concentrated – and caused the sand to reverse, flowing up to the top chamber, causing the outside world to match his timeflow. He had once thought that the falling sand measured his own passing life, but now knew that was only approximate. The sand measured – everything.

He willed the magic to include the entire world and felt the massive engagement of magic as the spell of the Hourglass took hold. This was potent sorcery and represented the limit of what the Hourglass could do. A significant portion of the magic power of the planet was being drawn on here, chanelled to this purpose. He knew he would have to give the instrument a rest, once this mission was over, so it could cool and recharge.

The white sand flowed up and the world phased in to Chronos' timeline. The facade clock started to tick backwards; the breeze reversed – and so did the people. A car had been approaching Norton on the street; now that car was moving backwards. Pedestrians walked backwards. Some of them looked startled.

Startled? Norton had not expected this! These people were aware! They realized that they had reversed, though they were powerless to prevent it. This was a new wrinkle. Would it make a difference?

He glanced at the Senator's mansion. Was that a face looking out of the window? Probably just a perplexed servant – but it could be the demon. Norton decided to get out of sight of the building. He strode down the street.

Now a problem manifested. He was moving with the flow of pedestrian traffic – but the other people were walking backwards. Norton was following a young man – but the man was facing him. To the man, Norton realized, it was as if he, Norton, were striding backwards. Certainly Norton differed from others here.

How much easier this would have been on a normal moving belt! Then he could simply have stood in place, facing back, and not attracted attention.

No help for it. The man before him was starting to gawk. Perhaps this one did not realize he was now living backwards, so saw Norton, who travelled forward into the past, as a freak. Norton turned about and proceeded to walk backwards.

Unfortunately, this was not his natural mode. The others could walk backwards at speed with confidence, because they were reversing a course already travelled; Norton was not. He was new to this scene. He tripped on a crevice and stumbled, windmilling his arms. This was no good either!

He looked back at the Senator's mansion. Someone was emerging from it, he thought. The little demon?

Norton ducked into an alley, just wanting to get out of sight. Now he didn't bother to walk backwards; that was too much trouble and not much for either safety or concealment.

He heard a groan. He went to the source – and found an old man lying in a pile of garbage, bleeding from the head. He had evidently been mugged and needed help. Norton started

241

towards him – and suddenly another man charged backwards towards them, holding a wallet.

Norton paused, uncertain what was happening. The running man went right to the fallen one, bent to tuck the wallet into his back pocket, turned him over, and retreated a step while the victim hunched himself back to his feet. The other man brought out a blunt instrument, unclubbing the victim's head. Then he retreated, while the victim, his head unbruised, scalp untorn, proceeded blithely backwards after him at a slower pace, just as if nothing had happened.

Norton, furious, charged the mugger. He caught the man's blunt-instrument arm and swung him about. Startled, the mugger cried, '!yeH'

'You mugged him!' Norton accused.

The man stared at him. '!gniog er'uoy erehw hctaW' he exclaimed.

Norton paused. Backward speech! Another complication! No doubt the people of the world were able to understand one another, since they were all living backwards, but he, Norton, was living forwards. Their speech was gibberish to him. He should have anticipated this, but had had no prior experience, since he had to phase in on green to interact with normals. Physical involvement was different from aloof observation!

Frustrated, he wrenched the blunt instrument from the man's grip and threw it away. 'Get out of here, you criminal!' he cried, shoving the man away.

The man, surprised, ran backwards away from him, disappearing around a corner. Norton stood, trying to get oriented. Had he disarmed a mugger just after – just before the mugging and prevented the crime – or had he merely witnessed it? The man had had the blunt instrument at the time of the act. Obviously he had completed the crime before time reversed; would he be balked when time reversed again, after (before) Norton's mission ended (began)? Norton hoped so. Therefore a perfect replay of prior events wasn't possible, with his interference. Maybe he had saved an innocent victim some trouble.

He looked around for that victim, thinking to warn him of the danger, but the man had gone. He must have taken another route. Anyway, the mugging hadn't happened yet.

Norton walked along the alley. He was in the unsightly service area where garbage cans sat and the pavement was dirty. Garbage cans? This was another aspect of the past that wasn't all that aesthetic! Far better to use a modern banishing-spell for that sort of thing! But, of course, such spells were expensive, and not every person was able to invoke them properly; sometimes a bungled spell brought extra garbage into a house instead.

He glanced up and saw a magic carpet fly backwards high above the buildings, the only present evidence of the good modern life. This was not two hundred years ago, even though it might seem like it.

He found a back step and sat down. He had time to pass, away from observation by the demon, and this was as good a place as any. It was private because it was ugly; crowds did not seek this particular region out.

His wandering eye spied graffiti on the opposite wall. Idly curious, Norton studied them. Most were in male hand, large, dark, and crude in both execution and concept: four letter words describing sexual and scatological concepts, as if mankind were hopelessly enraged at the universe and determined to demean it. These graffiti were basically rapes of the viewers, assaults on whatever sensitivities passers-by might possess. No beauty or gentleness or caring here, just ugliness. Norton felt ashamed to be a man. But he noted one thing; the words were not backwards. Time was reversed, but not space. So if he really had to talk with someone, he could do it by writing. Lachesis had done that at the outset of his career as Chronos; she had known. Now he realized the significance of that approach.

Nestled below the male efforts were a few female offerings.

These were small, neat, and polite, and seemed to represent genuine efforts to communicate. 'My John avoids me, but I still love him. What should I do?' one asked plaintively. Below it was an answer in a different feminine hand: 'Mine, too; it hurts.' And another: 'Stay the course, sister; he'll get tired of the tart.' And another: 'Who wants him, then? Used goods.' And a final one: 'Who you calling a tart?' Norton had to smile, somewhat wanly. He liked the company of these anonymous but distressed women better than he did that of his own kind; at least they seemed sensitive and human.

He noticed that nothing on the wall had been erased. All contributors and readers seemed to honour this rule: thou shalt not erase another person's message. It was all right to talk back to a message by writing a contradicting one, but not to destroy the original, no matter how crowded the wall got. Small messages were written within large ones; there was much overlapping, but no actual molesting. Here was the ultimate free society!

Norton knew that all men were not loud, crass boors and all women were not sweet and troubled innocents. They just came across that way on walls. Perhaps it would be the same if the rest of society were similarly free and anonymous; the constraints of civilization did have a lot to offer. The graffiti were the exposed underside of society, just as this service alley, with its garbage cans, was the backside of the town. Both sides, actually, were probably necessary.

Moved by a curious emotion, he got up, went to the wall, scrounged in the debris at its foot for a fragment of chalk, and wrote below the feminine messages: 'This John loves you, not the tart.'

He returned to the step. Would the original woman ever see his offering? Would it mean anything to her? Or would it be blotted out by the excretions of mocking male graffiti? He probably would never know. That was the problem with anonymity. But he had had to speak, however feebly, for his kind.

244

He looked at the wall, tracing to the place where his own contribution was – and his graffito was gone. Startled, he peered closer – then realized that its absence was explicable. He and the world were moving backwards in time, so his present situation preceded his message on the wall. His words would appear in due course, when time resumed its normal flow.

But the message had not been there when he first sat down! How could he explain that?

He pondered and worked it out. He was not an ordinary member of this scene. He had not been here on the original go-round. What he did was not a reversal of what he had done before; it was new. So he was, in fact, changing reality in some small degree. His graffito had not existed before he had made it, but did exist now – or *would* exist when normal time resumed, though he probably would not retrace his course to make it. He was exempt from paradox. He did what he did and it was done – though a normal person could not have done it that way. Normal rules did not apply to Incarnations. He was continuing to learn his trade.

To the right, a desultory mongrel dog wandered up, tail-first. The animal meandered to a pile of refuse and paused, partially squatting. Sausage-shaped chunks of the refuse lifted from the ground and squeezed into the dog's waiting posterior. Norton watched, disgusted but fascinated. Of course biology was backwards too! The dog, a mere animal, did not realize what had happened – but how would a human being react to this particular necessity of life?

The dog, satisfied, trotted backwards on past Norton to a garbage can to the left. The lid was off and the contents partially scattered. The dog went and neatened it up; fragments of garbage jumped into the can, and then the lid sailed to seal it as the dog removed its nose.

Then a demon appeared, walking backwards. This one was larger than the one by the capsule bottle. They *were* searching for him! That meant Satan did have some notion of what was going on. The backward flow of time had surely given him the hint! How he planned to stop Chronos was a mystery – but Satan's craft and power were great, and Norton did not want to meet that challenge directly. He had to avoid the demon!

The thing was regressing down the street, tail-first, peering from side to side. Soon it would spot Norton. And – there was another backing in from the opposite side! They had him cornered.

Norton jumped up and turned the old-fashioned round-knob handle of the door behind his step. The door opened; evidently the occupants were not worried about intrusions from this direction – or maybe they were simply careless, or believed they had nothing worth stealing.

The doorway opened directly into a kitchen. A woman sat there eating a snack. She was a housewife in her thirties, not yet past the age of sex appeal, but frowsy in her curlers and housecoat. She was not aware of Norton, and this was not surprising, because she had distractions of her own. She was consuming her snack backwards, and this evidently bothered her, but she couldn't stop it. What she had eaten had to be uneaten.

The cup of coffee was not bad; she brought it to her mouth and tilted it, and the flow of fluid into the cup was hardly visible. Her throat worked, bringing up a swallow. Then she set down the cup, its level of coffee raised, and stared at it with dismay.

Next she put her hand to her lips and spat out a few indelicate crumbs. Then she opened her mouth wide and ejected a bite of coffee cake. This was followed by another, and another, until the full cake was there. She stared at it with odd horror. '?gniod I ma tahW' she asked out loud.

'It's all right,' Norton answered, closing the door behind him so the demons wouldn't see him. 'Time is backwards.'

Startled, she looked at him. '?uoy era ohW' she demanded, drawing her housecoat open to reveal her bosom.

246

Her reactions were, of course, reversed; she had intended to conceal herself.

'Don't be concerned,' Norton said. 'I'm hiding from – ' But he paused as he realized that his words were gibberish to her, as hers were to him. Each was living backwards relative to the other, though they moved in time together. She could see him and hear him, but could not understand him.

The woman scrambled from her chair – and almost fell, again because of her backward reactions. Norton hurried across to steady her, and this alarmed her even more. '!em hcuot t'noD' she cried, colliding with the wall. A dish rose from the floor, where it had evidently shattered, and nudged back to the jostled shelf with its companions.

He had to reassure her! Norton found a pad of notepaper on the table, and a pencil; she had perhaps intended to make out a grocery list. I AM A FRIEND, he wrote.

She stared at the sheet. He knew what her problem was: in a normal time sequence, his reassurance would have occurred before her fright that caused him to write it, and this cause-after-effect was difficult for her to accept. But she was living backwards now, so his actions changed her reality. She was remembering what had happened in the immediate future.

Best to take her mind off the incipient paradox. I'M HIDING FROM DEMONS, he wrote on the sheet.

',snomeD' she repeated doubtfully.

'Snomed,' he agreed, imitating her pronunciation. It was amazing how alien ordinary human speech sounded when prounced backwards! Then, on paper: I'M UNDER A SPELL. I SPEAK BACKWARDS.

',hO' she said, her face brightening with comprehension. 'sdrawkcaB'

'.Sdrawkcab,' he agreed, aware that he was mangling the pronunciation and punctuation. He wrote: THE WORLD IS GOING BACKWARDS.

She nodded agreement, her glance flickering warily past the unconsumed coffee and cake. Perhaps, he realized, she had thought she was being sick. Now she knew it was merely a different reality.

'?yhW' she asked.

Norton tried to phrase an answer she would be able to understand and accept, but found himself at a loss. How could he tell her that he was responsible, and be believed? To prove it, he would have to reverse the effect – and that he refused to do.

He was spared the awkwardness of answering by the arrival of another person. A man ambled into the kitchen backwards, tilting a bottle of beer in his mouth. He was evidently the woman's husband, for she evinced only boredom at his presence. He was in baggy trousers and undershirt, his hair tousled, his face unshaven for this day. What he was doing home at this hour Norton didn't know; maybe this was one of the intermittent periods of underemployment the society suffered, so this family was subsisting on state funds while waiting for the economy to improve. The man unpoured the last drop of beer into the bottle as the final bubble descended into his mouth, then capped it and set the bottle into the refrigerator. Then he noticed Norton.

Norton held up his last sign: THE WORLD IS GOING BACKWARDS, hoping to forestall a jealous-husband reaction. The woman tried to pull herself together again, and again succeeded only in further displaying her private flesh. ',sdrawkcab gnivil er'eW' she said.

'?eh si lleh eht ohW' the man demanded, glaring at Norton.

',snomed morf gnidih s'eH' she explained.

' – lleW' he began, then paused. '?sdrawkcaB'

',sdrawkcaB' she agreed firmly.

'!top eht ffo tog tsuj I tuB' he said, annoyed.

The woman looked at her unconsumed repast. '?did uoY' she asked, making a connection. ' – snaem taht nehT'

'!taht toN' he exclaimed. '!t'nseod ti ,on ,hO'

Norton had by this time figured out what 'top' translated to. He repressed a smile, remembering the dog in the alley.

'!ereh fo tuo gnitteg m'I' the man cried, charging backwards out of the kitchen. But his reflexes, like those of the woman, betrayed him. Their dialogue had evidently been in sensible order for them, but their actions remained reversed. And though their individual phrases or sentences were backwards, their separate verbal exchanges seemed to be more in the order of present consciousness. Norton's presence altered their reality to a degree, but not enough to reverse them totally or to provide them true self-determination. The man, despite his horror, was backing towards what looked to be the bathroom.

Well, Norton thought, this was a necessary consequence of reverse biology. What was ejected from the body in the form of coffee, cake, or whatever had to be taken in in some other fashion. The biology of men and animals did not differ that much.

'!oN !oN' the man screamed from the hidden room. There was the sound of a toilet flushing backwards. A pause, then a scream of sheer horror and outrage. It seemed the job had been done – or undone, as the case might be.

Norton decided to vacate the premises before the man returned to the kitchen, as he might be in an ugly mood after taking on that ugly load. Norton cracked the door open and peeked.

The demons were gone. He had slipped their net. He slid out, leaving the family to its adjustments. The last thing he saw as he glanced back inside was the woman's face as she looked towards the bathroom. She wore a somewhat smug expression, as if she thought the man had got what he deserved.

Norton made his way across the street, then walked carefully backwards to a small park. There he selected an isolated bench and sat on it. That way, he seemed no different from the normal people and did not attract unwelcome attention.

Perhaps an hour had passed; it was now, according to the

249

park clock, just after 10 A.M. Norton watched the clock click back to the hour and heard it bong ten times. Even the bongs were in reverse: !GNOB ,GNOB He saw the squirrels leaping backwards from branch to branch and assembling nuts from scattered shells and regurgitated interiors. Periodically a person would back past, attracting the whole peanuts to his swinging hand and depositing them in a bag.

A young couple backed past Norton and into the bushes behind his bench. They were not aware of him, intent on their liaison. But they became conscious of the reversal, and this seemed to affect their lovemaking. Norton listened unashamedly, trying to visualize what was happening. To experience the gratification first, followed by the buildup – that might be unsettling. Sure enough, after a while the couple backed away from the bushes with perplexed expressions.

The sun moved slowly eastward. Morning was arriving. Rush-hour traffic developed on the street, the cars and carpets crowding crazily backwards at a hazardous velocity. People hurried back past the park without noticing it, paying no attention to Norton. He was just a character on a bench, not rating either a backward or a forward glance.

But he became aware of another problem. The progress of time was not perfect. At first he thought it was his own boredom stretching things out, but when he checked his watch, which measured his personal time, against the park clock, he discovered that the clock was taking a minute and a half to back up one minute. What was wrong?

The question prompted the answer: the magic was weakening. The Hourglass was powerful but not omnipotent, and the reversal of the whole world was a considerable chore. After two hours, the Hourglass was losing its edge, processing the enormous magic less efficiently.

He concentrated, willing the magic back to full potency. This was effective; the normal pace of time resumed. But now he had to keep his mind on it, because, when his attention slipped, so did time. He could not simply wait for the key

250

moment to arrive; he had to will its arrival. Fortunately, this was not difficult; it was like holding on to a suitcase. It did require effort, but the effort became automatic.

The clock bonged past nine and started towards eight-thirty. Then it bonged nine again. Norton jumped up, alarmed. He had started nodding, and time had not only slowed, it had resumed forward progress. That was no good! He concentrated again, and the clock bonged nine a third time and proceeded safely on backwards.

Norton paced around the park, afraid to sit down again, lest he lose concentration. He had several hours to go and he meant to see it through.

He started into an intersection of paths near a backward-spouting fountain – and saw a demon on the intersecting path. The creature was approaching backwards, so didn't see Norton; that was the second time he had been in luck this way. He was walking forward when others were not near to see, pausing when they were. But if he paused here, the demon would come back far enough to spy him, and that could not be allowed. Norton retreated hastily the way he had come. He hid behind a tree and watched the demon pass. Surely the thing was looking for him; Satan did not send his minions out in public without good reason, for people tended to react negatively to demons. It wasn't that Satan cared how human beings felt, but he did not like them getting jolted back to righteous living that would cost him souls. So he kept his operators covert, except for his continual ad campaign to convince people that Hell was in fact a fun place. No one with any sense believed that – but there were a lot of stupid people in the world. Satan also maintained discreet recruitment stations, but no demons were ever in evidence there; it was strictly soft sell.

But all this walking and skulking about was making Norton tired. He wanted to rest his feet – but didn't dare. Then his eyes fell on his ring. 'Sning!' he said happily. 'Will you warn me if I start to lose concentration?'

251

Squeeze.

Gratefully he sank on to a bench. Oh, that relaxation felt good to his legs!

Fifteen minutes later, Sning gave him a good, hard double squeeze. He snapped alert. 'Thanks, Sning,' he said. 'I needed that. Stay on the job.'

In this manner he endured till 8 A.M. Then he got up and walked some more. He had to make it to just after five in the morning; he was halfway there.

He spied another demon and avoided it. They were really cruising the area! Fortunately, they were handicapped by having to proceed backwards. But they would probably be thickest at the time and place of the capsule nullification; how would he get there without being caught by them?

It was getting harder to keep time on track. He had to concentrate more intently, making up for the slowly fading power of the Hourglass. He felt as if he were running a marathon; the miles were passing, but his strength was depleting. Would he be able to make it to the end? He had to! But it was not going to be easy. He had not practised willing before; he had no muscles for the purpose and wasn't sure even how to tell the nature of fatigue of the will.

He went to the public facility for a routine call of nature. His own biology was forward, but the other men were retreating from the urinals with distinctly uncomfortable expressions. They had no real choice about using the facilities, but he couldn't blame them for not liking what happened there. Normal processes did not seem aesthetic when reversed. There was probably some philosophy to be gleaned from that realization, but right now he was too busy keeping time moving to cogitate on that. He used the facilities, hoping no one would notice that he was not reversed, then backed away, adopting the appropriate disgruntled expression.

Sning squeezed his finger more frequently, but he made it to 7 A.M. without significant incident. Two more hours!

Now doubt was seeping in, clogging the channels of his

252

concentration. Could he make it to 5 A.M.? His effort of will was not the same as a physical effort, yet he felt himself tiring. The Hourglass continued to fade, so that he had to fill in with more will, and his will was becoming exhausted. The park clock began wavering again, and the people and vehicles performed a strange kind of dance, moving backwards and forwards and backwards again as the flow of time fluxed. Sning's squeezes were almost continuous, and these, too, were losing effect. Norton was sweating, though he was standing still. This was awful!

'Sir, may I pleh uoy?'

Norton looked dully at the speaker. It was an attractive young woman who leaned towards him and away from him as time wavered. 'No, I – ' he began, then felt a surge of dizziness.

She caught his arm, steadying him. '?era you ilL' she asked solicitously. 'Here, tis nwod. m'I a nurse.'

Her speech was phasing backwards and forwards, too, as time changed. He had to get it back on track! He put forth a special effort, and the normal backflow resumed.

'?ytilaer degnahc siht ti sI' she inquired. '.sselmrah s'ti tub ,ot tsujda ot drah s'ti wonk I'

Norton was getting better at comprehending backward speech, though this was far from perfect. The woman had caught on to the fact of the backward flow of time and was trying to reassure him. She assumed that it was the shock of reversal that was making him ill. Well, in a way it was.

'Thank you,' he said.

She glanced at him, startled. '?aisahpA' she inquired.

Oops – he had dazzled her with his own backwards speech. She thought it was aphasia. Well, again it was close enough. 'Yes,' he said.

'!suoires si sihT !nam roop uoY' she exclaimed.

Norton scraped a section clear in the dirt beside the bench and leaned down to scratch a message with his forefinger. IT'S ONLY VERBAL, he wrote.

She rummaged in her purse for some paper and a pen. CAN YOU READ THIS? she wrote.

He nodded yes.

',thgir lla er'uoy sseug I nehT' she said. She stood, ready to depart.

Then Norton spied another demon. The creature was walking rapidly backwards; no chance to avoid it.

Norton put his face in his hands, hoping he would not be recognized.

'!kcis er'uoy ,hO' the girl exclaimed, bending to assist him. She had a nice figure, and her body helped conceal him from the gaze of the demon. But time wavered again as he lost concentration. He corrected that, and the demon retreated on past.

',uoy evael dluohs I kniht t'nod I' the woman said.

The truth was that he appreciated her help, misguided as it was. He borrowed her pencil and paper. WHAT'S YOUR NAME?

'.elgeH ?eman yM'

'Agleh,' he repeated carefully, and she smiled. He was conquering his verbal aphasia!

Agleh took him to her apartment at the edge of the park and made him comfortable on her couch, from where he could see her wall clock. She was perplexed by his being so intent on the clock when he had a watch of his own, but she humoured him. She was, it developed, a single girl, working at a local hospital, and this was her day off. She had a tender heart and could not refrain from helping people who were in trouble. He told her his name, Notron, and explained that he wasn't really sick, but was pursued by demons. She looked at him with increased sympathy and didn't argue. He wasn't sure that was a good sign, but let it go.

She offered him breakfast at quarter to seven. Norton tried to demur, but she insisted, certain that food would be good for him. But she had for the moment forgotten the new reality of eating.

She brought dirty dishes from the sink and set them on the

table, then sat down and delicately disgorged a poached egg and a glass of milk.

Norton did not eat. He could not, for she had given him nothing. Why should she? She had adjusted nicely to living backwards and was replaying in reverse her morning meal; she expected him to do likewise.

Norton sighed. He had not intended to deceive her about this matter or his nature. Words were unlikely to persuade her, so action would have to do.

He took her pristine egg and milk before she could prepare them and return them to her refrigerator, and he consumed them both. They were very good, for he was indeed hungry.

Agleh stared. Then she laughed. '!sdrawkcab er'uoY' she exclaimed.

'I'm backwards,' he agreed.

'? – woH'

He wrote it on her pad. I AM CHRONOS, THE INCARNATION OF TIME. MY LIFE PROCEEDS BACKWARDS.

She looked again at the empty dishes, and again at him. She shrugged. ' – siht tub ,yad ym ni cigam nees d'I thguoht I' she exclaimed. '!esle gnihtemos er'uoY'

'Sey,' he agreed, again speaking carefully to get it right. He brought out the Hourglass, with its white sand flowing upwards, and showed her how the instrument followed him when he set it down in mid-air.

'?taht ees I yaM' she asked.

He handed her the Hourglass – but when she tried to take it, she could not. Her hand passed right through it. To her, it was a ghost-object.

That surprised him as much as it did her. He remembered how the Bem had grabbed it in the globular cluster. Had it been in a different state then?

Agleh looked at the empty dishes. He knew what she was thinking: where had that food come from? She had uneaten it and he had eaten it; when time went forward again, it

255

would be the other way around. When and how was that meal ever prepared?

She glanced again at the shining Hourglass. '. . . xodaraP'

I AM IMMUNE FROM PARADOX, he reassured her in writing. Then, in the course of the next half hour, he clarified his nature for her, including the manner in which his presence changed reality. She was not reversing her life precisely now, for he had not been with her on her forward living through the morning. Now she was living backwards, but interacting with him. She could remember her recent future – since meeting him.

'!thgir s'tahT' she exclaimed. '!rebmemer od I'

He explained how he was trying to balk Satan's ploy, but had run low on willpower to keep the reversal going. Now, thanks to her support, he was doing better; time wasn't wavering.

I'M IN *YOUR* reality, she wrote, getting it straight. Actually, she put a new sheet of paper on the pad, with the words already there, then went over them from right to left with her pencil, and they disappeared as she did so. When the sheet was blank, she brought another to set over it, with new words. At first she had been startled, watching herself do this, but now she accepted it as a matter of course. Norton realized that his way of writing must appear similarly strange to her.

However, the novelty of this situation carried Norton only so far. The power of the Hourglass was still fading, and it required horrendous mental effort for him to keep time flowing backwards. At six-fifteen time wavered again.

Fortunately, Agleh now understood. '!nataS thgif tsum uoY' she said. '.uoy pleh lliw I' Her backward expressions were organized only by phrase or sentence; beyond that, his time frame took over. Probably, he realized, the rest of the world was speaking completely backwards; near him, the effect was distorted by his own counterlife. That could also account for the way people seemed to come aware of their situation in his presence; elsewhere they might not know that there had been any change at all. He was sure that his presence would have generated many minor paradoxes, like eddy currents in the contrasting time flows, if he had not been immune.

But he did not see how Agleh could help him, generous as her offer was. He tried to explain the problem: his will had to brace the Hourglass, and his will was giving out.

Her brow furrowed in concentration as he collapsed the Hourglass and put it away. ',emiT' she said. '.emit era yllaer uoY'

CHRONOS, he wrote again. IT IS AN OFFICE.

She glanced at him sidelong. '?nam lamron a era uoy nehT'

'Sey,' he agreed wryly.

'sdrawkcab gnivil tuB'

'Sey.'

She wrote again: BUT OUR WILLS ARE THE SAME.

He shrugged, not seeing the relevance.

LET MY WILL SUPPORT YOURS, she wrote.

Norton's mouth fell open. Was that possible?

They tried it. Norton relaxed his will, and when time wavered, Agleh concentrated on the objective. It worked – but her will was only a fraction as effective as his. She could buttress him, but could not carry the load alone. Still, that was a great help; it extended the period he could operate.

She touched him, putting her hand on his arm, but proximity did not seem to make a difference to the Hourglass. She was doing all she could, simply by sharing his will.

But now they were standing close together. Agleh ran her tongue over her lip. '?ekil eb dluow ti tahw rednow I'

Norton frowned. 'What *what* would be like? Satan's victory?'

A slight flush crossed her face. ' – wonk uoy – namow a – nam A'

Norton figured it out. A woman – a man. Now it was his turn to blush. One moving in one direction in time; the other, the other. Was it possible?

',rednow I' she repeated, licking her lips again.

She was a pretty woman, and though he had known her only briefly, he liked her and sincerely appreciated her help. He wondered too – what would sex be like in such conditions?

But then time wavered badly, the sand shifting back and forth in the Hourglass. Agleh's support had tided him through almost an hour, but this thought was distracting!

',emit rehto emoS' Agleh said. She was as quick as he to realize that if her will could support his, it could also detract from his.

'Some other time,' Norton agreed ruefully. He found himself disappointed, but the flow of time did firm again. He benefited from her support – to a degree.

She backed away from him. Then she shrugged and came back. He half-spread his arms, concentrating on the Hour-glass so that time would not waver. She came into them with a kind of half-turning motion, as if being reeled in, and slowly brought her face up to meet his. Gradually they kissed, and it was like any other kiss: pleasant but not strange. They were in phase for this.

Time wavered. He concentrated to return the flow. Then he lifted his head and looked at her face for a moment before releasing her. She opened her eyes and stepped away from him.

They had kissed, and it had been backwards for at least one of them – and yet the same.

'?efil ruoy ni nemow rehto neeb evah erehT' she asked.

'Other women,' he agreed. 'But the one I loved – died.'

',deiD' she repeated.

'I think she was – like you.'

'.uoy knahT'

'I – ' he began, but hesitated. Then he used the paper to explain, though it took a while: that he not only lived backwards but didn't even belong in this period of time; that his normal existence was eight years in her future; that in due course he would return to this present time but would have to hurdle it, so as not to reduplicate himself. Thus this meeting of theirs was all there was or could be. If he encountered her in his normal progress, they would be travelling in opposite directions. There was, literally, no future for them.

But, she inquired alertly, what of his prior life, before he assumed the office of Chronos?

Norton did a quick reassessment. Eight years ago, in his original life, he had been thirty, in one of the duller periods of employment. He had finally given up the mundane existence entirely, to hike the parks and tell stories for his supper. But suppose he had met a woman such as this? Would he then not have met Orlene?

And not have caused Orlene's death?

'Here is my address of that time,' he said abruptly, writing it out on the paper. If such an encounter turned out to be paradoxical, then it simply wouldn't occur; he didn't have to worry about that. 'But I'm younger then, and know nothing of my future as Chronos. Maybe it would be better not to tell me.'

',dnatsrednu I' she agreed.

It was at that point he became fully aware of the futility of trying to have any continuing relationship with a normal woman. He had run up against this with Orlene, but that had been a special case. Now he realized it was not a special case; backward existence prevented any close relationship with any normal person. This was the penalty he paid for his office. Clotho had known, and had provided him with an alternate fulfillment. Clotho understood the problem of the Incarnations, who were human yet unhuman, himself most of all. As another Incarnation, Clotho could handle it. But Agleh –

',rettel a uoy etirw ll'I' she said.

'A letter, yes,' he agreed, surprised.

'?ti dnes I dluohs erehW'

'Where?' Norton pondered. 'To Chronos, I suppose, in care of Purgatory.' Did the mail service deliver mail to Purgatory? It seemed to him that Thanatos had mentioned that it did, in the course of their last conversation. He wrote

259

the letter out for her: CHRONOS, C/O PURGATORY. 'But I can't be sure the letter will reach me or that I'll be able to answer. And if it does reach me, I don't know *when*.' Perhaps two years before she wrote it? Reverse time had its pitfalls.

Now it was close to six in the morning. He had come within striking time of his mission. Soon after 5 A.M. . . .

A.M. – how significant each marker of that had become! A. for Ante, M. for Meridian – before the meridian of noon. A convenient contraction. It had never seemed very important to him before.

But it was time for him to orient on the conclusion of his mission. He had avoided the questing demons – yet how could he reach the right capsule at the key moment without alerting them? They would be clustering close, and though, as an Incarnation, he was theoretically immune to molestation by Hell's minions, he wasn't sure they couldn't balk him on this. After all, he was the one trying to change reality or to unchange it. The advantage probably lay with the present status quo.

',pleh ll'I' Agleh volunteered.

Involve her with the minions of Satan? Norton didn't like that. NO. DANGEROUS, he wrote.

WHAT IF SATAN WINS? she wrote back.

She had him there. 'Hell on Earth,' he muttered.

',htraE no lleH' she repeated. And, on paper: CAN YOU DO IT ALONE?

Norton considered. Probably he would have to wait till the last moment, then charge in and hope that nothing balked him. It was a one-chance effort. What were his chances for success? Fifty-fifty? With the fate of the world at issue, he did not like that. But how could he improve the odds?

YOU CAN'T she wrote.

He sighed. She was probably right. But he wasn't sure how she could help. He certainly didn't want her getting involved with demons; she was too nice a girl. 'I'll just have to try it by myself,' he told her firmly.

She started to protest, but he was firm. The memory of Orlene and her fate bothered him, and he was determined not to be responsible for any more mischief to a mortal.

Agleh relented reluctantly. She wrote: COME BACK IF –

'I will,' Norton promised, hoping he wouldn't have to return here. He squeezed her hand and left.

He was getting better at walking backwards, though his leg muscles protested. Much could be done with peripheral vision and careful attention to sound. By walking ahead of another person, he could be reasonably certain there were no obstacles in the immediate vicinity, because in forward time he would have been following that person, and the other naturally avoided problems of terrain. In any event, he was now familiar with this region, and that helped.

His plan was to get as close to the key room as he could without being observed and hide until the proper moment. He would catch the demon just after it changed the capsule – which would be just *before* in normal time – and douse it with the holy water before it retreated back to its association with his prior self. Of course, that would not prevent it from rejoining him, but that was not the point; this would prevent it from messing with the capsule. If he timed his action precisely, the watching demons from this present time might not be able to balk him.

He backed to the shelter of a tree and paused there as if resting. A bird-dropping jumped up from before him to rejoin its origin; good thing he hadn't been standing there! The other pedestrians continued on by, retreating towards their homes without paying him any attention. It was early morning now; the sun was no longer beaming down. When he believed no one was watching, Norton backed slantwise across the lawn to another tree, and thence to a side gate into the Senator's estate. Now he was in a walled-in garden, a pleasant place. A child was there, just unpicking a flower; the stem became whole as she placed the severed ends together.

What was she doing here at this hour? The flower wasn't even open yet; it was waiting for a direct ray of sun.

',olleh ,hO' she said, becoming aware of Norton.

'Olleh,' he replied, then essayed a question. 'Ereh evil uoy od?'

She glanced at him, her brow quirking at his odd pronunciation and emphasis. '.rotisiv a fo rueffuahc eht fo rethguad eht m'I .oN'

Norton found this too much to assimilate, so he just smiled. He wanted to get away from her and into the house. 'Gnol os,' he said, beginning to back away nonchalantly.

'!ynnuf er'uoY' she said.

Norton proceeded through the garden, handicapped by its unfamiliarity. He stumbled against the footing for a potted tree. Well, now he was alone; he turned about and walked forward.

A man stepped out before him from an alcove in the estate wall. '.sonorhC'

Norton froze. This man recognized him! 'Who – ?'

The man only smiled. Then Norton saw his eyes. They were like glassy lenses, with dim red lights behind. Demon eyes!

He had been caught by a demon lurking in human form. Now, in the immediate vicinity of Chronos, the demon could interact somewhat on his terms. '!yortseD' it said and grabbed for Norton.

That was warning enough. Norton let his cloak spread out beyond his suit. The man-demon's hands aged and weakened as they came into contact with that cloak. Hastily he hauled them back, cursing backwards.

'.olleH'

Both men turned. It was the little girl. She had followed Norton, perhaps curious about the odd man.

The demon leaped for her. The girl shrieked but was caught. '!lliK' the demon cried. He drew a wicked-looking knife and held it poised near the child's face while his other hand held her by the hair.

Norton knew he would not be able to disarm the demon

262

before the girl was stabbed. She was a hostage – and the demon would not hesitate to kill her. True demons were minor incarnations of evil, serving only the major Incarnation.

'What do you want?' Norton asked.

',ereh yats tsuJ' the demon said.

Stay here – until it was too late – or early – to stop the other demon's change of the capsule. Or until the last power of the Hourglass gave out. Either way, Satan's victory. He could not tolerate that.

But if he acted, the child would die. He couldn't tolerate that either.

Time wavered – and that gave him a notion. He concentrated, or rather relaxed, letting time flow forward.

The demon put away his knife and let the girl go, bounding back to Norton's vicinity. This time Norton grabbed the demon, his white cloak extended, and held him fast.

The demon screamed. 'You're killing my body!'

Indeed the body was ageing. The skin wrinkled; the clothing rotted and fell away. In moments the shrivelled body collapsed. It had died of old age.

Norton dropped it. The girl was staring, horror-stricken. 'You dried him up!' she cried.

'I had to. He was going to hurt you.'

'Say – you don't talk funny any more!'

Norton remembered. He concentrated, reversing time again. It was like picking up a monstrous load after inadequate respite.

'!erom yna ynnuf klat t'nod uoy – yaS' the girl exclaimed.

Norton took her by the arm and led her away. He knew the demon, now separated from the ambience of Chronos, would not recover – except that that execution would be undone by the resumed retreat of time. Avoidance was therefore best.

'!pu mih deird uoY' the girl cried, horrified.

Something nagged at Norton. It was the demon's last cry: 'You're killing my body!' Of course that was literally true; a demon could not take physical form on Earth. Only in very special circumstances did that happen. The demons he had seen before were mere evil spirits, with no substance. This one had had substance – because it had taken possession of a living being.

That meant the demons could act physically here. They could not hurt him, Norton – but they could harm others. That made Norton vulnerable. They could take hostages.

This was too much for him to handle alone. He had dispatched one demon – or at least sent it back to Hell by destroying its living host – but he couldn't afford to chance that again. He had rescued the child, but there were too many other potential victims, and he knew that the minions of Satan would use them. He didn't worry about destroying the living hosts, for he knew that a demon could enter a human body only when invited, and that only the worst elements of society would ever do that inviting. But he couldn't stand to have the blood of one innocent victim on his conscience.

'Go home,' he urged the girl. 'Find your family and get far away from here. Fast. There is evil afoot.'

Wordlessly, the child nodded. Then she ran, taking off backwards so fast her hair flung out behind her head, in the direction of her flight.

Norton, reluctantly, returned to Agleh. 'You were right,' he admitted. 'I can't handle it alone. Those demons are taking possession of human bodies and they are unscrupulous. But I'm still not at all certain you can help, and I don't want to risk – '

She waved aside his incomprehensible explanation. TELL ME THE DETAILS, she wrote.

His eye fell on his ring. 'Okay, Sning?' he asked.

Squeeze.

'She can really help?'

Squeeze.

Agleh pointed to the ring. '?cigaM' she asked.

'Cigam,' he agreed. And explained briefly about Sning.

'?pleh I nac woh ,gninS' she asked the ring.

264

Squeeze, squeeze, squeeze.

'He can't answer that sort of question,' Norton explained. Then, on paper: YES-NO ANSWERS ONLY.

'.yrroS .hO' She considered for a moment, then wrote: CAN SNING HELP?

Squeeze. It seemed Snign could read.

Norton was startled. 'Directly? Physical action?'

Squeeze.

Time was running short. Together they worked out a campaign. The problem, Sning explained when they found the correct questions, was that demons could emulate human beings by taking possession of human hosts. The minions of Satan could no longer be readily distinguished from innocent people. Norton and Agleh had to find a simple way to tell humans and demons apart, so that they could leave the former alone and eliminate or avoid the latter.

Sning's poison could make a human being very sick, but should have no effect on a true demon, since that was only a spirit. The spirit demons were patrolling the area, trying to spot Chronos, while the demon-possessed bodies were acting to block him physically. There was no telling how many of each there were, but probably enough to do the job. Satan would have sent in the largest number immediately after the capsule was changed, as that was the critical moment; the network six hours after the event had been relatively thin.

Norton had presumed that the possessed people were worshippers of Satan, doomed to Hell and not worth his sympathy. But now he wondered: could demons somehow borrow the bodies of good people too? Sning reassured him; they could not. Goodness was anathema to the creatures of Hell. But his concern about the hostaging of innocent people in the area was valid, Sning agreed. Only the Senator himself was free of that threat, as Satan would not harm the man whose life he was trying to save for worse things.

Norton couldn't tell the innocents from the possessed, at a distance, and he couldn't afford to get up close without

265

knowing. How could he identify the possessed ahead of time and get by them?

'The regular demons are really thickening,' Norton remarked, glancing out of the window. 'There's one patrolling the street now.'

Agleh looked. '?erehW'

He pointed. 'There.'

She squinted. '.gnihtyna ees t'nod I'

The demon was quite plain. Sning squeezed three times. 'You mean she can't see it?' Norton asked, startled.

Squeeze.

He turned to her. 'There's a spirit demon there – but you can't see it.'

',ti ees t'nac I' she agreed.

'But there *is* one there. Sning can tell you.'

She looked doubtful, so Sning uncurled and crossed to Agleh's waiting hand. Like Orlene, she was not afraid of small serpents. '!etuc woh ,hO' she exclaimed.

Sning curled around one of her fingers. 'Ask him a yes-no question,' Norton said.

'?ereht nomed a ereht sI' she asked. Then she jumped. '!em dezeeuqs eH'

'How many times?'

',ecnO' she said, holding up one finger.

'That means yes. Sey.'

'.ees I ,hO' She was pleased. '!mih peek dluoc I hsiw I'

Keep Sning? 'Well, you might borrow him – so you can spot the demons. I can see them without Sning's help.' That seemed to be another power conferred on him by the mantle of Chronos.

',seY' she agreed.

Now it jelled. Agleh and Sning would scout the Senator's estate, locating all the demons and possessed people. The minions of Satan would not suspect them, because Agleh was obviously a normal person, not an Incarnation. She would report to Norton, who would then move in to the capsule at the critical time, avoiding the pre-spotted demons. Sning would warn Agleh of any threat to her. With luck, there would be no trouble, and the deed would be done before Satan knew it.

Then at last Norton would be able to relax. He could return to his own time – and never see Agleh again. That he regretted; these few hours had brightened when she appeared.

He knew he shouldn't, but he asked her anyway, on the paper: DO YOU LIKE WILDERNESS?

She replied: I LOVE IT.

Why did he torment himself?

'!og s'teL' she said briskly, heading for the door.

Norton started to go with her, then stopped. He couldn't show his face near the Senator's estate until they had the demons posted. 'I'll wait here,' he said somewhat lamely.

',eyB' she agreed and backed out.

Norton watched at the window as she went out on the lighted street. The demon was still patrolling, but paid Agleh no attention. He relaxed slightly; it was working!

He watched Agleh out of sight, then paced restlessly. The woman had passed the demon, and that was good – but now he wondered just how many of Satan's minions in whatever form mingled with the living human beings regularly. Did the Prince of Evil normally keep an eye on the affairs of the mundane world? How could any person ever be sure that evil was not just around the corner? It was a disquieting notion.

The clock on the wall wavered, and he refocused his concentration; he was tiring, or the Hourglass was, and now that he had nothing to rev him up, it was becoming more difficult to keep the reverse flow going. He seemed to have periods when it went automatically and periods when it required all his effort. But he felt his resources giving out; it was as if he had been driving all night or running all day. He had only an hour to go, but now it seemed like more than the time that had passed.

He continued to pace, fighting to maintain control, but the clock wavered more frequently. He no longer had Agleh's direct support of will; maybe that was making a difference. He was in danger of giving the victory to Satan by default.

Now he wondered: was it really worth the effort? Would it be all that bad if Satan won? It would be so easy just to let it slide, to let the normal flow of time resume. He realized his attitude was similar to that of a freezing man who just wanted to sleep – a sleep that would never end – but somehow he didn't care. He was so tired; his will was exhausted.

He relaxed, heedless of the changing of the clock. He sank into a chair, his eyes glazing. This apartment reminded him of Orlene's – she who had loved her baby too well and died of it, because of the evil in the family genes of Gawain the Ghost. That evil, travelling down the lineage, taking its dreadful toll of each generation. Where had it originated? Where would it end?

Evil? It had, of course, originated with the Prince of Evil. It would end there, too. From Evil came evil, and to Evil it returned. Without the Demon of Evil, the D-Evil, the Devil, it would not exist, for he was the Incarnation of it. From him and to him –

Something coalesced. The evil that had been responsible for Orlene's death – it had had to come from Satan!

Suddenly Norton was up and alert. Satan had cost him Orlene – and he owed Satan for that. Now he had a chance to repay the Prince of Evil by foiling this present mischief.

The flow of time reversed again. The clock resumed its backward march. Norton knew he would make it through now. Hate would accomplish what duty could not.

At 5:25 A.M. Agleh returned. '!lla meht dettops evah eW' she exclaimed. And she grabbed pen and paper and sketched a map, showing both spirits and possessed by marking their locations with little S's and P's.

Just in time! 'I've got to get into that building soon,' Norton said, aware that she could not follow all his backward words,

268

but would pick up the sense of them. 'I need to know every demon!'

',lufrednow saw gninS' she said, perfecting the map.

Norton studied the pattern of S's and P's. 'But if they're moving, they won't be in the same places,' he said, concerned.

She figured this out. ',staeb klaw yehT' she explained, sketching in light lines to mark territories. '.htrof dna kcaB'

'Oh.' Walking beats – yes, of course. So there would be fair continuity. All he had to do was time his passage. It was like a maze or a video game; if he manoeuvred deftly enough, he should score.

He concentrated on the map, aligning the details with what he knew of the region, memorizing the pattern. It wasn't difficult; there were only six possessed and six spirits, and his fatigue of will was not fatigue of mind. Six and six – of course. 666 was Satan's personal number. But where was the third six?

Well, he judged that he could make the run in about six minutes. Maybe he'd better plan on that. It might have the effect of completing Satan's number, so that there would be no infernal alarm. The period of backward time was also scheduled for six hours. One way or another, it matched.

Six minutes – that would leave him no margin for error. Any significant delay would cost him the mission. But as he pondered it, he became more certain this was the key. Play it by Satan's rules – and Satan's defeat would be complete.

He explained this to Agleh, writing out essential words to be sure she had it straight. ',uoy htiw og ll'I' she said.

'I don't think that's wise. You've been there, scouting it. If the demons see you again, so close to the zero hour, they'll be alerted.'

',rebmemer t'now yehT' she pointed out.

'They won't remember,' he repeated thoughtfully. But he wasn't sure of that. Most people seemed hardly aware of their backward progress, but the ones in his immediate vicinity were, and those ones had backward memory, as Agleh herself did. Also, these were not people, but Satan's demons and spirits, assigned to watch for him. If Agleh was seen with him now, the demons might manage to remember backwards just enough to make trouble.

He pointed this out to her. Reluctantly, she agreed. Then she brightened. '!noisrevid a sa tca ll'I' she said.

A diversion. That could indeed make it easier for him – but it would be risky for her.

'!tsisni I' she said.

He looked at his watch. Time was shortening; his final six minutes were almost upon him. He didn't have time to argue.

',pleh lliw gninS' she said, holding up her hand with Sning.

He had forgotten to take the little serpent back! But it was true; Sning could be a big help to her, since the little snake could detect invisible spirits. Norton could recover his ring once the mission was done. 'Okay,' he said with some misgiving.

'!yakO' she echoed. She gave him another kiss somewhat less backward; she was getting used to these interactions.

It was time. They moved out smartly. Agleh set out ahead to intercept the first possessed. Sning would signal her if she needed to distract the man; if not, she would simply proceed to the second, in effect running interference. Norton followed more slowly, trying to look like a casual passer-by.

The problem was that they both had to walk backwards, so he couldn't see what happened to Agleh. He just had to assume that his way would be open, thanks to her and Sning.

He entered the first possessed's beat and backed through it without challenge. This was on the main street, and normal people were occasionally passing – early risers catching the local matter-mitter before the throng. He hoped he seemed like one of them. It was working – so far.

Now he was entering the beat of a spirit. According to his estimate, the spirit should be at the far side of it, facing away, so wouldn't see him. Sure enough – he spied the spirit's tail as the creature backed towards him. He schooled himself to make no overt reaction; that would be a giveaway, since ordinary people could not see such creatures. Of course the spirit would recognize him anyway, if it turned and saw him – but it was unlikely to turn, because of the regularity of its beat. Evil spirits, as he understood it, did not have much imagination or initiative. Only strange behaviour on his part would cause them to break their routine – such as reacting to the sight of one.

He reached the estate. Though there were twelve of Satan's minions on patrol, they were not all in one place; they were spread fairly thin through and about the estate, to cover all of it. They knew he would exploit any gap in their coverage. He had only three to worry about along this route, and now he had navigated two. The third was another spirit in the hall beyond the side entrance. He probably could not avoid that one – but with only two minutes remaining till zero-time, maybe that one could not spread the alarm in time to do Satan much good. This was the chancy part!

He opened the door behind him and backed in. This was a servants' entrance, and there weren't many servants about at this early hour. Norton turned and proceeded forward; it was more comfortable, and he knew he would not fool the spirit anyway. He moved through the labyrinth of the servants' region, guessing where the spirit would be and avoiding that region.

He guessed wrong. The spirit appeared, did a double take, and fled through the wall. Norton was not reassured. Ninety seconds remained – was it too much time? Could the spirit summon overwhelming counterforce before zero-moment? Had he given Satan too much leeway?

He entered the pantry where the bottle of capsules was stored. No spirit guarded it now; he had spooked that one away. He looked at the bottle –

There were six horned, barbtailed feline creatures there. Hell-cats – that was the final complement of the 666!

The Hellcats spied him and snarled. They formed a

271

semicircle near the shelf of the capsule, tails switching. Each had sabre-toothed tusks and great blood red claws. They looked deadly.

But this was Earth, not Hell, Norton reminded himself. No true Hellcats existed here. These had to be spirit cats, powerless against any living person physically, and impotent against Chronos in any way. They represented another lie from the Father of Lies, a bluff to confuse Chronos. All they could do was attempt to distract him – and that would fail.

One minute. He was early after all, but he would prevail.

Then he heard approaching noises. Was the original capsule demon arriving? Norton brought out his vial of holy water and stood ready. The demon would have to be given the chance to unhex the capsule; then Norton had to douse it.

Figures appeared. Norton stared, stunned. A possessed – and Agleh. They had taken her hostage!

The possessed held the woman's right arm wrenched cruelly behind her, while his left hand clasped a gleaming knife menacing her face. '!seid ehS' he grunted eagerly.

Norton held the holy water. He could throw it at the pair of them; it would not hurt Agleh, but it would banish the evil spirit from the possessed man. One flick of his wrist –

'!ti od t'noD' Agleh cried, divining his intent.

Angrily the possessed brought the knife to her neck. She caught at his hand with her left hand, but she had neither his strength nor his leverage. '!seid ehS' he repeated.

Norton stared at those two hands – his big hairy one, clasping the wicked knife; her delicate fair one with Sning on the middle finger. Now he understood the ploy; if he used the holy water to save Agleh, he would not have it to foil the capsule demon, and Satan would win. But if he did not save Agleh –

He heard something to his side. The six impotent Hellcats had vanished, and in their place was a coalescing cloud of smoke. In seconds it cleared, revealing a tiny solid demon with a single large horn. This was the capsule demon.

The possessed made an incoherent grunt and nudged the blade in to touch Agleh's throat. Norton couldn't let her die!

Then he had an inspiration. 'Sning!' he cried.

Immediately the little snake uncoiled and struck at the adjacent hand of the possessed. The tiny fangs sank into the hairy skin. The man grunted, feeling the sting.

Norton turned to watch the capsule demon. The thing was standing below the capsule bottle. Suddenly it rose up to land on the shelf. It touched the bottle, and there was a small flash of light. Then the demon began to climb down the shelving. The hex had been undone.

Norton hurled the holy water at the little demon. The water struck – and the demon puffed into smoke, exactly as before – but a critical minute earlier in normal time.

He turned back to Agleh and the possessed. The man was leaning against the wall, bafflement on his face. Agleh stood alone, massaging her sore right arm, otherwise all right.

Norton relaxed. 'It's over,' he said. 'The demon no longer possesses the man, and my mission is complete.'

'I thought it was a good deal,' the unpossessed muttered. 'But when that evil spirit actually took control – God! I mean that literally – I'm turning to God, while there's still time!'

'It's over,' Agleh agreed. Time was now normal; they were all talking comprehensibly.

Then she vanished. Norton stood alone in the deserted and dusty house. What had happened?

In a moment he knew. He was back in his present. The power of the Hourglass had been exhausted, causing him to revert when his will no longer supported the fading magic of the instrument. Or it might be that when he tried to live in normal time flow, allowing himself to be carried along by the world current, he had run afoul of the three-person barrier and been bounced out. Either way, it was over, and he had foiled Satan.

He looked at his bare hand. With a shock he realized that he had lost Sning. Agleh had been wearing him when it

273

happened. Sning had saved her by poisoning the possessed and forcing the evil spirit to leave. Apparently the spirit had thought the man was going to die, so had instantly deserted the sinking ship – and there had been no chance for her to give the ring back to Norton. She had intended to, but his sudden return had prevented it.

Norton sighed. That was a telling loss! But he missed Agleh, too. She had loyally helped him, and must have been chagrined when he deserted her so abruptly.

Well, perhaps it was only fair for her to retain a token of the experience. Chronos was gone, but Sning would comfort her.

Norton left the deserted estate, feeling lonely. On impulse he walked to Agleh's apartment – but found the neighbourhood changed. In the intervening eight years the oasis of primitive life had been abolished, having no regressive Senator to preserve it. The building had been replaced by a warehouse. He could not find her or anything of hers there.

He used the Hourglass to return to his mansion in Purgatory. The instrument performed sluggishly; it was tired. So was he; the success of his mission provided him little elation.

He checked his mailbox. There was a single package in it, a small one. He opened it immediately, curious what anyone would send to Chronos – and discovered Sning!

A brief note was enclosed, in feminine script. *Chronos – I couldn't keep Sning; he's yours. He told me this would reach you. Best wishes, Helga.*

Norton stared at the message until it blurred. What a fine woman! Was there no way he could thank her?

Sning uncoiled, slid across his hand, and curled around his finger. Squeeze.

The separation had been brief, in Norton's terms, but eight years in another sense and an eternity emotionally. 'Oh, Sning, I'm so glad to have you back! You say I can thank Agleh?'

Right there, in the Twenty Questions fashion, Sning told

274

him. All he had to do was make a quick trip to a moment just before his interaction with her time and mail her a letter – Sning had the address, which he could explicate by squeezing as Norton pointed to letter and numbers on a sheet of paper – that would reach her after their separation. Theoretically, the mails were magically enhanced to give one-day service, but in practice it was seldom so; there would be no paradox of premature delivery. He could even make it a package, containing some suitable gift that would please her.

'Yes,' Norton agreed. Suddenly he felt much more positive. He would shop for an appropriate gift; Sning would help.

He glanced once more at the note before putting it away. *Best wishes, Helga*

Helga – her name forwards, of course.

Now he remembered; he had known Helga in his younger days, while still employed within the system. She had come to him, inquiring, 'Haven't we met before?' And he had been so flattered by the come-on from such a pretty and sensible woman that he had not demurred. They had kept company for a couple of years before the exigencies of his wanderlust and her professional nursing career had required an amicable separation. She had been his dearest female friend, prior to Orlene, and he felt a lingering fondness as he thought of her, even these six years later.

Odd that he hadn't thought about her before, or recognized her when he encountered her in his guise of Chronos. Obviously she had remembered him, thereafter, though she hadn't said so.

Odd? No, not odd at all! He had not known her in his first experience; she had been added to his experience as Chronos. His past had been changed – without paradox.

Ironic that he should have that wonderful experience of her company only in memory, not in reality. Yet for her, surely, it had been fully real, and perhaps that had been her reward for helping him balk Satan. She had kept his secret, too; never had she mentioned Chronos, or spoken any backward word.

He still owed her. He would send her a really nice gift.

Whistling, he walked on into his mansion.

12

Quest

'You have a caller, sir,' the butler informed him.

'I'm not at home to callers at the moment,' Norton said. 'I've just had a very wearing session; the Hourglass and I must rest.'

'Sir, he will not be denied. He is angry.'

Norton paused. 'Satan? I'm not surprised. All right. I'll tell him to go to Hell myself.'

The Prince of Evil was literally fuming. A haze of sulphur smoke surrounded him, and his horns were showing. 'You interfered with My demons!' he rasped, a small tongue of fire showing at his lips as he spoke.

'They interfered with my business,' Norton said curtly. 'Now you get out of my mansion; I have no use for you.'

'You are messing up My whole programme!'

'Good for me! I don't like being deceived or used for evil purpose.'

'I will have satisfaction!' Satan said, his eyes flaming as he drew off one of his red gloves. He did not look at all benign now!

But Norton was fed up. 'Go to Hell!'

Fire puffed out of Satan's ears. He raised his fist to Norton, clenching his glove.

Norton extended his white cloak. 'Hit me,' he invited.

'No,' Satan snarled past lengthening tusks. He was enraged, but not foolish; he knew the defence of Time. Instead he hurled his glove directly at Norton's face. 'You will go – without return!'

Norton ducked the glove, though he knew it couldn't hurt him. But it puffed into smoke, and the smoke surrounded him. He could see nothing. He stepped to the side, out of it.

He found himself on a green planet, looking at a Glob spaceship. He was back in the antimatter cluster!

'Damn it, how does he do that?' Norton demanded. 'I didn't ask to come here again!'

Squeeze, squeeze, squeeze.

Norton chuckled grimly. 'Well, at least I have you with me, Sning! Do you know how I can return promptly home?'

Squeeze, squeeze, squeeze.

'You're not sure? But I understood Satan couldn't do anything to me without my consent.'

Squeeze.

'But I didn't consent to this!'

Squeeze, squeeze.

That made him pause. Was Sning agreeing or disagreeing? 'You say I did consent, tacitly?'

Squeeze.

'This time you're wrong, Sning! What could possibly interest me here?'

Then he spied a shape in the air. He squinted, and discovered a winged unicorn bearing a lovely young woman. Excelsia on the Alicorn, both looking splendid, coming here.

Squeeze.

Norton sighed. 'Point made,' he agreed ruefully. Excelsia was a lovely young woman with whom he could interact on a continuing basis, since her time flow matched his. That did indeed appeal to him! 'This must be the Magic-Lantern Cloud, instead of the globular cluster – as good a place to relax as any.'

Squeeze, squeeze.

'You say no? You mean Satan is up to something new?'

Squeeze.

'And he figures to keep me here so he can perform his mischief without my opposition?'

Squeeze.

'Then I'd better return immediately!'

Squeeze, squeeze, squeeze.

278

The Alicorn landed, Excelsia bounced off and ran towards him. Her gown this time was filmy white and low cut, and she was better endowed than he had realized; Norton found that run fascinating. 'O Sir Norton!' she panted, her bosom heaving prettily. 'I never thanked you properly for your valiant assistance – and when I returned, you were gone! I have searched all over the planet for you!'

'Well, I – '

She reached him and flung her arms about him. 'Now at last I have found you!' She planted a delightful kiss on his mouth. He felt as if his feet were leaving the ground. 'Thank you so much!' she breathed.

'You're welcome,' he said. What an armful she was! 'But I regret I must depart, because – '

Her pretty face misted over. 'Depart?'

'There is pressing business back on Earth, and – '

Two big, shining tears formed in her lovely eyes. 'But, Sir Norton, I have so much to show you!'

He gulped. How much he wanted to see what she had to show! But he had learned the hard way not to ignore Satan's mischief. 'Uh, can I take a rain check?'

'A rain check!' she flared. There was a crack of thunder nearby, and rain began to threaten from a ballooning grey cloud.

Excelsia wrenched herself from his arms and fled towards her steed. 'You can have a deluge for all I care, sirrah!'

Norton ran after her, sadly out of sorts. 'Wait, Excelsia! I didn't mean it like that! It's just that – '

She reached the Alicorn, who brought his horn about to bear directly on Norton. Norton drew up short, not comfortable with that, though probably this creature could not hurt him. He didn't want to hurt the Alicorn, either.

'I'm sure you don't need to explain yourself to *me*,' Excelsia said primly. 'Go on home right now, sirrah, and I wish the other woman good fortune hunting!'

'There *is* no other woman!' Norton protested. But it

occurred to him that, had Agleh been in his time frame, she would have been an excellent prospect; indeed, in the past she *had* been – well, never mind that. And of course he still felt love for Orlene, and there was always Clotho, the one who really understood, so he wasn't being quite candid.

'Then you will stay?' Excelsia said, brightening.

How much harm could there be in a short stay? He had wanted to rest for a while, anyway.

Squeeze, squeeze.

'Shut up!' Norton snapped guiltily.

'Well!' Excelsia said, affronted.

'No, I didn't mean you!' Norton protested, taking a step towards her. But the Alicorn snorted and levelled his horn again, stopping that. 'I was talking to Sning!'

The Damsel frowned attractively. 'I remember Sning, the good adviser and strange steed. Does he tell you I be not good enough for you, sirrah?'

'No, of course not! He tells me there will be great trouble back on Earth if I don't return at once.'

She mollified. 'Then perchance you must go, Sir Norton. I regret my dainty outburst of temper. I will wait somewhat patiently for your return.'

Would Satan ever let him come back here, after he had once again balked whatever mischief Satan was hatching now? Norton brushed that thought aside. 'Thank you,' he said gratefully. 'I really wish I could be with you right now, but it must be duty before pleasure.' He concentrated, willing himself home.

Nothing happened. Excelsia watched him with curiosity. 'Belike you have mislaid your way?'

Norton realized that he had never made this trip on his own volition; Satan had conducted him each way. He didn't know how to return! 'I seem to have done that,' he admitted, abashed.

The space blob had been sitting quiescently all this time. Now it irised open a wart. A man emerged. It was Bat

Dursten. 'Say, get a glimmer o' that there Femme!' he exclaimed.

The little Bem followed the spaceman out. It had grown some, but remained cute as a bug eye. It changed into a wheeled robot in the shape of a motorcycle. Dursten mounted, and the robot-Bem-cycle churned across to join the party.

The Alicorn reared with alarm, spreading his wings. 'What manner of thing be this?' Excelsia demanded, drawing her knife.

The Bemcycle angled its faceted headlamp to cover them as it proceeded. 'Uh, it's okay,' Norton said quickly. 'It's just Bat Dursten, spaceman galore. And his Bem.'

Her fair brow wrinkled with perplexity. 'Bum?'

'Bem. An acronym for Bug-Eyed-Monster.'

Dursten arrived and jumped off his vehicle. 'Bemme,' he clarified. 'She's a Femme-Bem. 'Course, she's still young, not for messing with – but ain't she pretty?'

The little Bemme shifted back to normal form, a blob with tentacles and huge insectoid eyes.

Excelsia screamed, and the Alicorn snorted fire.

Norton hastily interposed himself. 'They're from the space opera frame,' he said – and paused. 'How can that be? This is the heroic fantasy frame!'

'Fantasy, smantasy!' Dursten exclaimed. 'We got caught in a space warp and woof and had to make landfall on the closest green planet, to give the ship a chance to repair itself.' He nodded towards the blob. 'These Bemballs look like rotten eggs, but they're not bad when you get to know 'em. They can pretty well take care o' themselves, given half a chance. But what in space are *you* doing here, pardner? Last time I saw you, you'd vanished. I figured the Genius 'ported you away.'

'Close enough,' Norton said. 'Now I've been, uh, teleported here. But this is a fantasy world you've landed on, where magic works, just as it does on my home world of Earth. Excelsia and I had quite an adventure – '

Bat eyed the woman. 'Yeah, I'll bet. Man, I'd sure like to take that there Femme myself and – '

'Go eat a slimeblob, you utter cretin!' Excelsia snapped.

'Listen, you bare-boobed broad!' Bat retorted. 'I don't take no shipment from – '

'All a misunderstanding,' Norton cut in before things could proceed to mayhem. Already the Bemme and the Alicorn were squaring off, loyal to their associates. The Alicorn had lowered his horn, while the Bemme had assumed the form of a giant pencil sharpener. 'You're from two different worlds – '

The Bemme sprouted an eyeball on a stem and squinted at him. '*Three* different worlds,' Norton corrected himself. 'Naturally, conventions differ. We have to be tolerant.'

Excelsia shrugged gracefully. 'Very well, since you ask it, Sir Norton. I can tolerate the presence of a cretin when absolutely necessary.'

The spaceman grinned. 'And I sort of go for bare bo – '

'Agreed!' Norton interrupted. 'If you will just explain to the creatures.'

'Certainly,' Excelsia said. 'Bemme, if you can get along with that spacelout, I'm sure we females can – '

'Sure,' Dursten agreed. 'Alicorn, if a horny horsehead like you can put up with that dizzy Femme, you and me can shore – '

But already the Alicorn and the Bemme were making up. She was batting huge faceted eyes at him and he was snorting an appreciative puff of smoke.

'Maybe you can help me, Bat,' Norton said, relaxing. 'I need to return home in a hurry, but I don't know how. Do you think you could contact a Genius and inquire?'

'Why, shore,' the spaceman agreed laconically, glancing again at Excelsia's décolletage. 'You can ship right home, and I'll take that there doll and . . .'

Excelsia huffed up to make an angry response, almost bursting out of her gown, but again Norton intercepted it. 'And I'll return when my job on Earth is done.'

282

'That, too,' Dursten agreed without complete enthusiasm.

They proceeded to the blob spaceship. The Bemme assumed the form of a petite female Alicorn and trotted along beside the real one, exchanging nickers.

Excelsia was fascinated and somewhat awed by the ship. 'What magic mirror be this?' she inquired as the vidscreen lighted.

'Magic mirror!' Dursten echoed. 'That's great!'

The Bemme was showing the Alicorn the food synthesizer, producing delicious alfalfa hay for the animals to munch on.

The head of a Genius appeared on the screen. 'Yes?' the wizened entity inquired.

'Ooo, a goblin!' Excelsia murmured with distaste.

'My friend Norton here did dang good service for you, and you never paid him,' Dursten said. 'Now he needs a little – '

'We do not exchange favours,' the Genius said coldly. 'We are strictly business.'

'Maybe we can do business, then,' Norton said. 'All I need is some advice.'

The veined eyeballs swivelled to orient on him. Norton felt his hair getting hot. Quickly he extended his cloak ambience and was cool. The Genius' orbs widened a trifle. 'You counter my power?'

'I'm not from your cluster,' Norton explained. 'You should have that information in your records, from my last visit with spaceman Dursten.'

'Records are suspect. You may be a Bem agent. You do occupy an alien ship.'

'Captured,' Dursten said quickly. 'No Bems here.'

The cruel eyes flicked to cover the Bemme. 'What is that?'

'That ain't no Bem,' Dursten insisted. Fortunately, the Bemme had retained her little Alicorn mare form in order to chew on the hay.

The Genius' eyes narrowed. Behind his back, Dursten

made a signal. The Bemme jumped in the air, did a somersault, and landed on her back, shuddering and lying still.

'Oh, the poor thing!' Excelsia exclaimed, hurrying to the Bemme. She shot an angry glance at the Genius. 'You mean goblin, you killed her with a spell!'

'Ixnay,' Dursten muttered under his breath.

Unmoved, the Genius returned his gaze to Norton. 'Business?'

Norton was appalled by the creature's callousness, but he knew he could not afford to pass up any chance to return to Earth before Satan completed his mischief. 'I need to go back to my own world promptly. Can you transport me there, or tell me how to return on my own?'

'I am unable to read your mind,' The Genius said, as if this were a defect in the subject. It seemed the cloak of time protected Norton from this form of psi power, too. 'Where is your world?'

'It's in the terrene section of the galaxy. Time moves forward there – the reverse of yours. It's called Earth.'

The Genius frowned. 'Let me check our listing . . . yes, Earth is as you describe. A backward planet on the periphery of the main disc. It is fifty-seven thousand light-years distant. That would represent a considerable expenditure of psychic energy.'

'That must be why I can't get there myself,' Norton agreed.

'You will have to perform an equivalent service for me.'

'Well, I can try,' Norton said cautiously.

'You are currently on the fantasy world of *i*. The Evil Sorceress resides there.'

'Not any more,' Norton said. 'We destroyed her.'

'Destruction is seldom permanent in the magic realms.' But the Genius checked his records again. 'True, you did discomfit her for two hours. She recovered, but during that period of incapacity she suffered certain losses.'

'The Alicorn,' Norton said.

284

'And the nefarious null-psi amulet that prevents us from following her activities. Her more powerful sister, the Eviler Sorceress, now possesses it. Fetch me that amulet.'

A Sorceress worse than the one he had encountered? Norton didn't like that. 'That sounds risky to me! She would hardly give up such a prize voluntarily.'

'True. That is my price for your return to Earth.'

'But it could take me a long time to get such a thing, if I didn't get slimed on the way!'

'I suggest you move expeditiously.'

Norton sighed. What an uncompromising tyrant! 'I'll try.'

The owlish head faded out. Dursten turned off the screen. 'Okay, Bemme,' he said.

The Bemme recovered instantly, flipping back onto her hooves, startling Excelsia. 'You were pretending!' the Damsel exclaimed.

'Shore, I taught her tricks, like how to play dead,' Dursten said cheerily. 'Figured it'd come in handy someday. Sure faked out the Genius, didn't it!'

Excelsia's brow furrowed. 'But why?'

'Why else, twit? So the Genius don't catch on she's immune to psi, that's why.'

Norton remembered. 'Geniuses can't touch Bems! That's why they hire mercenaries to do it!'

'Shore,' the spaceman agreed. 'If he'd zapped her, and it bounced, he'da known. So she played possum, and he figured she was a normal critter.'

'But you told him no Bems were here – '

'Right. Bems are male. Didn't say nothin' 'bout Bemmes.'

Norton realized that Dursten was more canny than he looked. He had indeed saved the Bemme from discovery and thus enabled Norton to deal. 'I thought you didn't like Bems,' he said, aware that an exception had been made.

'Well, I know this one,' the spaceman said, embarrassed. 'She's an orphan, you know, and a good kid. Real smart, too.'

There, of course, was the secret to peace; people did not

hurt creatures they knew well. Strangers were fair game, but not associates. 'It seems I've got a chore to do,' Norton said. 'Anyone happen to know where the castle of the Eviler Sorceress is?'

'Oh, you wouldn't want to go there!' Excelsia protested.

'I've just got to get that amulet – the sooner the better. So if you'll tell me where the castle is, I'll be on my way.'

'Only a heroic fool would brave the Eviler Sorceress in her lair!' the Damsel warned, wringing her hands.

'Surely so.'

'I can't let you go alone, Sir Norton,' she said troubled. 'I will go with you.'

'Aw, shux, I'll come too,' Dursten said then, scuffling his feet. 'You helped me afore, after all.'

'But it may be dangerous,' Norton reminded them. 'I don't want you to take such a risk on my behalf.'

'You helped us, we'll help you,' Excelsia said, her marvellous bosom heaving with emotion. 'It's only right.'

'Yeah,' Dursten agreed, his eyes goggling with each heave.

'Thank you both,' Norton said, moved.

Excelsia described the locale, and Dursten piloted the Bemship there, circling the planet and setting down outside the castle. The Damsel was suitably impressed with the strange flying vehicle, but the Alicorn snorted with something like jealousy.

The abode of the Eviler Sorceress was a gloomy thing, with dark turrets, a dismal moat, and a wolf baying at the wall. A plaque over the front gate proclaimed: ABANDON HOPE.

Norton gulped. 'Well, thanks, folks,' he said. 'I'll take it from here.'

Excelsia looked at the castle. Her fair features seemed greenish at the moment. 'I'll – I will go with you, Sir Norton,' she said with tremulous bravery.

'Shux, me too,' Dursten said, though he looked none too confident himself. Perhaps he had hoped the Damsel would

286

let Norton go alone. 'I don't hold with none o' this fantasy shimmer nohow.'

'I really appreciate this,' Norton said, feeling even more grateful than before. Satan had once assured him that he faced no genuine personal danger here, but now Satan was angry. 'The Alicorn and the Bemme can wait in the spaceship – '

The Alicorn snorted. 'He's coming too,' Excelsia said.

The Bemme became a small humanoid robot. 'Me too,' the screen face said, the screen showing a small feminine mouth.

'But you two aren't even human!' Norton protested. 'You have no call to risk your lives for us!'

The Alicorn made a series of snorts. 'He says the Latins called him *Cornu*, horn, before they ever saw the rest of him,' Excelsia translated. 'The Italians added the article, calling him *Licorne*, the horn. The Arabs added their article, calling him *Alicorno*, THE the horn. Now he is the Alicorn, and he says he has associated with human beings as long as human beings have existed – maybe longer. That is, with those who know the magic word to tame him temporarily. You have no authority to tell him not to associate now. He can use his horn to detoxify much of the poison of the Eviler Sorceress.'

'Well,' the Bemme robot spoke up, 'my kind has fought the bone-fleshed kind ever since our two species went to space and discovered the delights of interstellar war. We even named your kind, MAN '

'You did?' Norton asked, surprised.

'Of course. MAN – an acronym.' The mouth on the screen quirked with obscure humour.

'Oh? What do the letters stand for?'

'Multi-Appendaged-Numbskull, of course. Every creature who is worthy of the title of sapience knows that.'

'What?' Dursten exclaimed indignantly. 'It can't be that!'

The Bemme fidgeted, and the screen mouth frowned. 'I did clean it up a little for mixed company.' Two eyes formed on the screen, glancing at the Alicorn.

'What's the danged original?' the spaceman demanded.

287

'Mucky-Arsed – '

'We'd better get moving,' Norton said quickly.

Dursten hesitated, then decided to let the acronym pass. After all, he had asked for it.

They advanced on the drear castle. This one, like the other, was wide open for entry, as if daring strangers to try it. These Evil Sorceresses were entirely too confident! The other one had nearly finished Norton; only Sning's intercession had saved him.

That reminded him. 'Am I doing the right thing, Sning?'

Squeeze, squeeze, squeeze.

He didn't like that answer. It meant he could go either way, and he wanted to go the correct way. 'Is it right to seek the null-psi amulet?'

Squeeze, squeeze, squeeze.

How he wished Sning could talk to him directly! 'Well, warn me when I start to go wrong.'

Squeeze.

They crossed the drawbridge and entered the dark aperture of the front gate. There was no sound; it was like a crypt. The air was cool and smelled faintly of earth.

'Ho!' Dursten called. 'Anything in there?'

He was answered by a gust of wind that reeked like the flatulence of a corpse, and a low moan, as of breath sighing through deserted chambers.

Excelsia shivered. She wasn't wearing much, but her torso was excellently padded; her chill was more of the spirit than of the flesh. 'I wish we had a candle,' she said.

'You could conjure one,' Norton suggested. 'Aren't you entitled to one conjuration a day?'

She brightened. 'Candle!' she exclaimed, and one appeared in her hand. It was a big taper, already burning, and it spread a fine light.

'Say, that there's a real good parlour trick,' Dursten said. 'Too bad you couldn'ta produced a laser fluoroscope, so we could spy the null-psi dingus through the walls.'

The Damsel shrugged, not understanding his language. But Norton realized that the candle probably had been foolish, for she could indeed have conjured something far more effective for either illumination or protection. Well, he should have thought of that before he spoke; now her conjuration was done, and that was that. They would have to make do with what they had. The light of the candle was comforting, anyway. There was something about a flickering lamp.

They entered the dark hole. The Alicorn led, since he could see and smell in the dark, was largely immune to poisonous magic, and had his weapon always ready. Excelsia followed with her candle, illuminating the passage for the rest of them. Her gauzy gown tended to become translucent when the light was on the far side. Norton admired the effect, but wished it wasn't occurring right at this time; he needed to be alert to the hazards of the castle.

Next came Norton, followed by Dursten, with the Bemme in her natural form bringing up the rear. She, too, could see pretty well in the dark because of her huge eyes. As Norton glanced back, he could see a thousand miniature candles reflected in the jewel like facets of her orbs. He doubted the Bemme would overlook anything!

The passage proceeded directly in towards the centre of the castle. It was about eight feet square in cross section, lined on all sides by clammy, mortared stones. In fact, those walls sweated tiny driblets of water that gleamed in the candlelight. The whole thing was dank and oppressive. Norton began to feel claustrophobic, for no good reason.

The Alicorn came to a blank wall cutting off the passage. The light of the Damsel's candle showed smaller tunnels exiting at right angles to the left and right.

'Which way should we go?' Norton asked Sning.

Squeeze, squeeze, squeeze.

This was getting annoying! 'Don't you have opinions any more?'

Squeeze.

'You mean I'm not asking the right questions?'

Squeeze.

Norton sighed. Maybe on a better day he would have been able to come up with the right questions and cut through this nuisance instantly; right now he was too distracted by the exigencies of the moment. It had been a long time since he had had a chance to relax and recuperate.

'Maybe we could split our party, and – ' Dursten began.

'No!' Norton and Excelsia said together. They remembered getting separated in the castle of the other Sorceress.

Dursten shrugged. 'Suit yourself. Pick a tube.'

Norton chose randomly. He pointed right. 'That one.'

There was no warning squeeze from Sning, so they proceeded. This passage was narrower, only four feet across. It made another right-angle turn left and debouched into a chamber whose cross section was about twenty-five feet and whose ceiling arched high above. The candle hardly lighted it all. Its far end, fifty feet distant, seemed to have another tunnel exit.

They spread out and started across.

Squeeze, squeeze.

'Hold it!' Norton said. 'Sning just gave warning!'

The Alicorn dipped his head to point with his horn. There was a line crossing the chamber about ten feet from the entrance.

'Trap door?' Dursten asked, peering at the line.

Squeeze, squeeze.

'No,' Norton said. 'I think we're not supposed to cross that line.'

'Hell with that noise!' Dursten said impatiently. 'Nobody corrals *me* like that nohow!' And he stepped across the line.

From the far side of the chamber a dozen blobs of drainpipe garbage appeared. Each one floated a foot above the floor, trailing drools of hair and slime. They fired clogs of jellylike stuff across the chamber as they advanced.

'Ooo, ugh!' Excelsia exclaimed, dodging a missile. Evidently she had been braced for routine things like knives or empty boots, but not for this.

'I'll get them gunks!' Dursten said gallantly. He drew his blaster and popped away with excellent aim. All spacemen, of course, were crack shots. As he scored on each gunk, it exploded, spraying coffee grounds and potato peels at the ceiling. In a moment the chamber was clear – and messy.

Dursten blew off his smoking muzzle and holstered his blaster. 'Told you I'd upgrade my shooter,' he said. 'I never liked gunks nohow.'

They continued on through the chamber, through the passage beyond, and into another blank wall with channels to the right and left. 'Right again,' Norton said. They turned right, and around another right-angle turn, and came into a chamber similar to the first, with another line across it. Dursten drew his blaster and stepped over the line.

More gunks appeared. One gunk splatted just behind Norton as he dodged. He turned to look at its impact on the wall – and discovered that the stone was smoking. 'That's acid!'

'Sure, them gunks don't mean us no good,' Dursten said philosophically, blasting away at them. His aim remained uncanny; in a moment all gunks were refuse.

They passed on through into another passage, met another T-intersection, and turned right again. A left elbow brought them to a third chamber.

'Are we getting anywhere?' Excelsia inquired, waving her candle impatiently.

'Sure, we're blasting lots o' gunks,' Dursten answered, stepping across the line and proceeding to blast away.

'Is that all there is to human life – blasting gunks?' the Bemme asked, forming a mouth for the speech.

'Ain't that enough?' Dursten asked.

The Bemme shrugged gelatinously and followed. But the question nagged Norton. He didn't want to continue blasting gunks indefinitely; he wanted to locate the Eviler Sorceress and get the amulet from her. He would be happy to bypass the gunks entirely.

They blasted through two more chambers. 'Are these all different?' Norton asked.

Squeeze, squeeze.

'You mean we're repeating chambers?'

Squeeze.

'Let me check this.' Norton walked back to the beginning of the last chamber they had cleared of flying gunks and turned about. He stepped back across the line.

Twelve new gunks appeared. The other folk, caught by surprise, scurried to avoid them. Dursten got busy and blasted them all.

'Crossing the line does it,' Norton said. 'Watch.' And, when they were out of the way, he crossed the line a third time – and twelve more gunks appeared.

Dursten mopped them up. The charge in his upgraded blaster seemed indefatigable.

'Just what are we accomplishing?' Norton asked, frustrated. 'We're repeating chambers and blasting things that are triggered into existence by a line!'

Dursten considered. 'Never thought o' that,' he admitted. 'This here thing's just a maze.'

A maze – of course! Their object was not to blast innumerable gunks, but to find their way through the maze to the Eviler Sorceress. 'So we aren't getting anywhere,' Norton concluded. 'Is that why you had no answer before, Sning?'

Squeeze.

'Can you direct us through this maze?'

Sning hesitated, then slowly squeezed once.

Still those odd reactions! They had not yet fathomed the whole truth about this sinister place! 'Very well. Should we turn left at the next T?'

Squeeze.

They moved through the maze, following Sning's directions. Each new chamber brought a dozen new gunks for the spaceman to blast. Then, abruptly, they came to a chamber that was different. It was small, only eight feet on a side, and had no exit. At Sning's behest, they crowded inside.

The entrance door slid closed. Then the chamber descended. Excelsia screamed, thinking they were falling to their doom, and clutched Dursten desperately.

'Say, now,' the spaceman said, pleased. 'I guess I reckon there *are* better things'n blasting gunks!'

'It's only an elevator,' Norton said. 'Sning wouldn't send us into a trap.'

'Not doom?' Excelsia asked, wide-eyed.

'Not even discomfort,' Norton assured her.

'That's okay, cutie,' Dursten said. 'How 'bout a li'l kiss while we're at it?'

The Damsel realized where she was. 'Oaf!' she shrieked, slapping him smartly and stepping indignantly away.

The spaceman shook his head. 'Femmes – who needs 'em?'

The elevator's motion stopped. The door slid open. Beyond was a green passage.

'A new maze,' Norton said, stepping out. 'Can you guide us through this one, too, Sning?'

Again the response was a slow squeeze.

'I wish I knew what's bothering you!' Norton exclaimed. 'Is there danger we can't handle?'

Squeeze, squeeze.

'Then let's move on through.'

They threaded the second maze. This one was curvy rather than angular, and the walls were green plaster. The chambers were ovals with bloated purple glitches attacking on cue. These were resistive to Dursten's blaster, but popped like bubbles when pricked by Excelsia's knife point or the Alicorn's horn. 'Just as well,' Dursten said gruffly. 'My blaster's charge ain't forever.'

Sning guided them through the labyrinth to a second elevator. They entered and descended to a third level – which turned out to be a yellow maze. The creatures in it were icks, like soft bowling balls with eyes where the holes should be. They rolled up, threatening to crush everything in their paths, but Dursten's blaster caused them to go all to pieces.

Then the charge gave out. The last ick was only winged. It spun out of control and banged into a wall. 'Oh, the poor thing!' Excelsia exclaimed. 'It's hurt!' She dashed to it and put her arms about it.

'Crazy dame! What about my blaster?' Dursten demanded.

'Oh, shove your – ' But she was too ladylike to be able to complete a thought like that.

'Maybe I can stomp the ick,' he said.

'Leave it alone!' she flared, cuddling the bowling ball. 'Can't you see it's suffering?'

The spaceman shot a baffled glance at Norton. 'Femmes! Can *you* figger 'em?'

'Not me,' Norton said, though in truth he had some sympathy with the ick. It was perhaps a variety of wilderness creature, forced to serve as cannon fodder for the Sorceress. He bore no special ill will for the soldiers of the front, who tended to be victims of circumstances no matter which side they fought on.

But this delay gave him an opportunity to ponder the situation again. These multilayered mazes – were they any different from the endless mazes on any one level, if a person proceeded randomly? Was there any more point in threading endless mazes than there was in blasting endless gunks, glitches, and icks? Especially considering that Dursten's blaster had pooped out? Well, he would find out. 'Is there?' he asked Sning.

Squeeze, squeeze.

'Is that why you've been hesitant? You can guide us through the mazes, but there's not much point?'

Squeeze.

'Do you know an alternative?'

Squeeze, squeeze, squeeze.

He had been afraid of that. 'So we've still got to muddle through ourselves?'

A reluctant squeeze. Sning was doing his best, and he was very helpful, but his limit of information had been reached; this castle maze was too complex.

The Eviler Sorceress, Norton realized, didn't have to kill them directly. She could simply let them wear themselves out in interminable mazes until they were too tired to bother her, or until they made some mistakes and got creamed by whatever monsters defended the level they were on. They were fools to play the Sorceress' game – yet Sning lacked the power to penetrate that larger riddle.

'Hick says there's a secret room,' Excelsia announced.

'Hick?' Norton asked.

'The icks are named by letters. This is H ick. He says if he'd known how nice we are, he wouldn't have tried to roll us.'

Norton had an idea. 'That room – does it have anything we can use – like maybe the amulet?'

'Hick doesn't know,' the Damsel said.

'Sning, can you tell?'

Squeeze.

They were back in business! 'It has the amulet?'

Squeeze, squeeze.

Sigh. Somehow things never turned out easy! 'But it does have something that will help us shorten this rat race?'

Squeeze.

'Let's find it, then!' He turned to Excelsia. 'Will Hick show us that room?'

The Damsel talked to the ick by tapping on its surface with her delicate knuckle. The ick answered by making little off-centre rolls. 'He says he'll try,' she repeated. 'But the way is difficult.'

'It always is,' Norton said with resignation. 'We'll get through somehow. Lead the way.'

The ick rolled to the side of the chamber, somewhat

295

awkwardly because of its – his? – injury, and stopped. 'He says through there,' Excelsia said.

Norton contemplated the wall. It looked very solid. Well, Hick had warned that the way was difficult! 'We have to break a hole?'

Squeeze.

Norton tapped the yellow wall with his knuckle. It was of the same substance as the ick, slightly resilient but quite solid, like padded plastic. He struck it with his fist, and made no impression. Just as he had suspected – soft but strong.

'A danged padded cell!' Dursten said, disgusted. 'Bemme, shape up and try it.'

The Bemme formed into a robot with a sledgehammer fist. She pounded this at the wall. The fist bounced off harmlessly. She changed form to that of a small crane with a dangling wrecking ball. This, too, bounced off harmlessly.

Norton saw the problem. 'A brittle surface would crack, but this padding absorbs most of the shock.'

'Hick says *he* could do it,' Excelsia reported. 'If he weren't injured.'

'It figgers,' Dursten said wryly.

The Alicorn poked at the wall with his horn. He succeeded in making a hole, but the horn got stuck and he had to wrench it out. He couldn't break through either.

Norton pondered. 'If the icks can do it – too bad we can't get their cooperation. Or can we, Sning?'

Squeeze, squeeze, squeeze.

Well, he could understand the little snake's problem. The creatures of the Sorceress answered to the Sorceress, so it was difficult for Sning to predict their reactions.

'Shux,' Dursten opined. 'We don't need them things to agree. We can trick 'em into helping.'

Squeeze.

'Sning says that's it,' Norton reported.

'Sure it is,' the spaceman agreed complacently.

'But how – ?'

'Aw, Bemme can do it. Bemme, trick 'em.'

The Bemme pondered a moment, then slid to the wall, formed a dripping-ink appendage, and painted a tunnel opening on it. The picture was very realistic; the Bemme was a fair artist. Then she slid to the centre of the chamber and formed into a wooden barricade with an arrow pointing to the wall and a printed sign saying: DETOUR.

'Say, that's neat!' Dursten said. 'You're doing okay, Bemme.' The wooden barricade purred.

The spaceman walked to the line, crossed it, and then stepped back towards the centre of the chamber.

A dozen new icks rolled out of the opposite passage. They advanced on the barricade, hesitated, then made a right-angle turn and took off towards the wall. One by one, they plunged into the painted passage.

The first one struck the wall roundly and smithereened. Hot on its tail, the second struck the same spot, denting the wall and in the process fracturing itself. Rapidly the others followed, and with each impact the dent grew deeper, until the last ick crashed on through. There was a faint whistling sound, followed seconds later by a distant thunk.

The Alicorn trotted up to the hole in the wall and poked his head through. He neighed with surprise and withdrew.

Norton looked next. Only a little light came through from Excelsia's candle; that showed beyond the wall a void – a crevasse whose height and depth were lost in darkness. There seemed to be no way around it; it paralleled the wall.

Excelsia brought her candle and joined him. The candle-light showed another wall about ten feet beyond – evidently the confinement for the next chamber.

'Where do we go from here?' Excelsia asked. 'We don't need to break into another ick chamber, do we? We could get into that by going through the tunnels.'

True. This was apparently the interstice between the chambers of the maze, and since the secret chamber they sought was outside the maze, this was where they wanted to be. But it seemed impossible to pass!

'Well, we must have to follow this, uh, space to the key chamber,' Norton said. 'If the Alicorn can fly it – '

'He can fly it,' Excelsia said confidently. 'He will carry anyone I ask him to. But he can bear only one person.'

'If he could ferry us across one at a time – '

'But he doesn't know where to go,' she said.

'The ick knows,' Dursten said. 'Take the ick first.'

The Damsel nodded. 'And return for the rest of us once he knows the way. Spaceman, you aren't quite as stupid as you seem.'

'Thank you, gal,' Dursten said, scuffling his feet.

'Nor as ugly as you look,' the Bemme added. The space-man patted her on a bug eye affectionately.

They rigged a harness from Dursten's shirt to fasten Hick to the Alicorn's back. Then the Alicorn scrambled through the hole, fell into the void, spread his wings, righted himself, and flew upwards. His wing tips brushed the walls on either side, despite a considerably shortened stroke; he was cramped but remained airborne. He disappeared to the right.

The others waited anxiously. Would the ick lead them the right way? If the creature had only been pretending to join them, it could guide them right into disaster – or simply deprive them of the Alicorn by leading the animal into a trap. How could they be sure?

Squeeze.

That was a relief. Sning might not be able to fathom the labyrinth of the castle interstices, but he had confidence in Hick.

The Alicorn returned, wearing the empty harness. They put the Bemme in it, and the winged unicorn departed again. It seemed that the Bemme could assume the form of an Alicorn, but could not actually fly like one; that was a matter of muscle and magic, not mere appearance.

'Say, pardner,' Dursten drawled, getting bored with the

298

wait; he had a short attention span. 'Do you have all this shipment in your world?'

'I suppose we do,' Norton answered. 'We have both science and magic, so there could be castles like this, though I never encountered any myself.' Something about his own statement bothered him, but he couldn't quite nail it down.

''Cept you live backwards,' the spaceman said.

'Backwards?' Excelsia asked, her fair brow furrowing in the pretty way it had.

'Mine is a terrene-matter world,' Norton explained. 'Yours is contraterrene, otherwise known as antimatter, so your time is reversed.'

'But we are together!' she protested.

'That's because I am Chronos. I live backwards. In my own world, everyone else is going the other way.'

'That must be very awkward for you,' she said.

'It is, on occasion. It does interfere with continuing social relations.'

'There be no such problem here,' she pointed out.

He looked at her. She was lovely. How nice it would be to have a continuing relationship with her, forever searching out new enchantments. But his world was in trouble, and he had to go back as soon as he could manage.

The Alicorn returned, and Excelsia boarded. Now Norton and Dursten waited, watching her candlelight recede. They were in darkness.

'I ain't so dumb I can't see how she likes you, Nort,' Dursten said. 'If I was in your britches, I'd sure stick around!'

Norton sighed. 'I'm sure that's what Satan has in mind. If I am tempted to remain here, he can have his will with Earth.'

'Who's Satan?'

'The Incarnation of Evil. You have no Devil here?'

'Hell, no! I'm a science man myself. I don't believe none o' that ship.'

'Perhaps he doesn't exist here.'

'Must be,' Dursten agreed. 'We ain't superstitious.' He

299

glanced at the hole; Norton could tell by the sound of his body moving. 'I sure hope that there animal don't get lost in the dark, knock on wood.' He tapped the plastic floor.

Then they heard the beat of great wings and relaxed. The spaceman's nonsuperstitious knocking must have helped.

Dursten was next. 'We'd never a needed this, Nort, if my danged spaceship had fitted in here,' he remarked as he mounted invisibly. 'But I gotta admit, this sure's a good horse.' Then they were through the hole and gone, and Norton was alone.

Now the darkness seemed to press in on him. He was an adult, but he didn't like this. He liked to see where he was and he liked company. He really felt the isolation of his office! This antimatter Cloud was indeed tempting, because of the companionship it allowed. To be able to interact with a woman like Excelsia, who seemed much more interested in him than she had been on the prior adventure, and to have her remember in the same sequence he did; to touch her, love her –

Touch her? Again he felt a wrongness. What was it? Not merely that Satan was tempting him; he knew that. Not that Excelsia would be unwilling; she was virginal but ready to be wooed. Not that there was any insurmountable difference between their cultures; they were remarkably similar. He loved the wilderness; she was a creature of it, not even knowing the city life. They had the same language –

Same language? How could that be? There had never been any contact between the people of the Glob or those of the Magic-Lantern Cloud and the people of the normal galaxy! There couldn't be, because matter and antimatter could not touch. When the two came together, they annihilated each other, dissolving into total energy with an explosion that dwarfed any nuclear detonation.

Explosion? Total conversion? Then how was he able to exist here? He was normal matter; he knew that. He had lived most of his life normally, until taking the Hourglass. After that he lived backwards – but he remained terrene, for he had touched normal people, such as Agleh, and normal Incarnations, such as Clotho, and could phase in with them any time.

Well, his magic white cloak protected him from attack, and might also protect him from the ravage of contact with antimatter. But he kept that cloak shield withdrawn when interacting with friends – which meant it wasn't operating.

The more he pondered, the more certain he became that Satan had lied to him. This was no contraterrene frame! It couldn't be! He had kissed Excelsia, and neither of them had exploded. There had to have been social contact between Earth and these other worlds before. The Alicorn had referred to the Latins, Italians, and Arabs, and it was simply not to be believed that there could have been similar names in a frame having no contact with Earth. Without the antimatter aspect, such contact became feasible.

But how was it, then, that the time scale was backward?

He heard the wingbeats of the Alicorn's return, and his thought was interrupted. But he remained shaken. There was definitely something about this too-similar-to-Earth setting that didn't mesh, but he did not yet comprehend the full nature of Satan's lie. And why should he? Satan was the Father of Lies, the ultimate professional in deception, while Norton was only a man, not long experienced in his present office. Still, now he was sure there *was* a lie to decipher! That was a significant revelation, and he would go on from there.

The Alicorn came to him in the dark, and Norton fumbled to a mounting. He braced his legs against the firm front anchorage of the great wings and grabbed two handfuls of mane. 'Let's go, gallant beast!' he said.

They squeezed through the hole and dropped into the void. The wings beat, and the Alicorn forged, as Excelsia would put it, onward and upward. They were flying – and it was a wonderful feeling! Little jets of flame showed at the creature's nostrils as the Alicorn exerted himself, and the flame lighted the region dimly. No wonder the beast could handle himself

301

in the dark; his own breath gave him just enough light to aid his excellent vision. This was certainly the finest of steeds!

They flew swiftly through the dark reaches, then cruised around a corner where two voids intersected. Norton saw dimly how massive arches of substance crossed from wall to wall, requiring the Alicorn to travel above or below; these would be the casings for the passages between chambers of the regular mazes. This castle was twice as complicated as he had thought! Then they flew down to a cold nether pass, up to a warm high pass, and into the view of Excelsia's flickering candle. The Alicorn landed neatly on a high, strong ledge where the rest of the party waited.

'You're safe, Sir Norton!' Excelsia exclaimed, almost singeing his ear with the candle flame as she flung her arms about him. She planted a moist kiss on him.

Contraterrene? Not likely!

The ledge was the edge of a sloping surface that proceeded towards a dim glow inland. Hick rolled confidently down, and the others followed.

The glow expanded as they approached. It turned out to be a hot section of the pavement before a passage into a mound. The ick rolled to a stop at the edge of the glow.

'In there?' Norton asked, unpleased.

'Hick says yes,' Excelsia said. It was unclear how she communicated with either ick or Alicorn, as she did not always tap the former or touch the latter, but obviously she understood them. 'He can't go there; the heat would melt him. And it would singe Ali's wings, too; he can't escape it in that low tunnel.'

'How far in is the chamber?' Norton asked.

'Hick says not far. About fifty feet.'

This frame had the same measurements as Earth, too. Feet, inches. Everything was the same! 'Then Hick and the Alicorn can wait here while the rest of us go in.'

The Damsel tested the air near the passage by extending her hand. 'Ooo, that would burn my tender flesh!'

She was correct. The ambience was too hot for any of them. 'I'll go alone,' Norton decided. 'If I can find a way.'

Squeeze.

'There is a way?' Yet again he was frustrated by Sning's inability to speak. 'Some way I can be protected from the heat?'

Squeeze.

Norton looked around, but saw nothing. 'Sning says I can be protected – though I don't know how.'

The Bemme slid up. She settled into a furry puddle about eight feet in diameter. 'Her?' Norton asked, and received Sning's squeeze in response.

'Oh, I get it,' Dursten said. 'She's a heat shield. Put her on.'

'Put her on?' Norton repeated dubiously.

The spaceman bent to pick up the thin material. It flopped and folded in his hands like a quilt. He held it out to Norton. 'Yep. She's good at this – she superinsulates, when she wants to. The perfect blanket.' The blanket purred.

Norton tentatively took hold of the Bemme cloth. It felt like furry silk. He draped it over his head and shoulders. It was really quite comfortable. 'This will really shield me from the heat?'

Squeeze.

'Okay, I'll try it. I'll return this way once I have what I need from the chamber.'

The others nodded. It struck him what an odd group they were – a swashbuckling spaceman, a voluptuous, innocent Damsel, a winged unicorn, and an animate bowling ball. But he liked them all; they were dedicating themselves to his welfare.

He turned and stepped on to the hot pavement. His solid shoes protected him from the immediate heat of it, and his Bemme-cloak shielded him from the ambient heat. It was working!

Nevertheless, he hurried. He ran through the tunnel towards a greener glow ahead – with luck, the chamber.

It was; in moments he burst into it, and the heat abated. But he kept the cloak draped over his shoulder, just in case.

He looked around. Four people stood in lighted alcoves: an old grey-robed, grey-bearded man; a stoutish, middle-aged woman in a business suit; a strikingly beautiful young woman in a bursting bikini; and a boy of about six with a moderately arrogant curl to his lip. They were all quite still, as if in suspended animation; perhaps they were in storage, awaiting whatever use the Eviler Sorceress might choose to make of them at her convenience.

What now? He had not known what to expect, and now did not know what to do with what he had found. 'One of them can help me?' he asked Sning.

Squeeze.

'Can give me the amulet?'

Squeeze, squeeze.

Perhaps that had been too much to hope for. 'Can you indicate which one?'

Squeeze, squeeze.

Still too complex for the little snake. Human beings were far more devious than mazes! Well, he couldn't expect Sning to handle everything.

Norton went to stand before the old man. He saw now that the man's robe was mail, linked and woven metal to protect him from attack. He wore a small iron crown, and his face was set in a half-sneer of authority. Surely he was some great king or warlord. 'Uh, hello,' Norton essayed.

'Speak up, youngster!' the man said, coming to life in the alcove. His voice had a fine timbre. 'Do you accept my gift?'

'I'm not sure. Who are you? What is your gift?'

'I am Ozymandius, King of Kings,' the king said grandly. 'Look on my works, ye mighty, and despair. My gift is Power.'

'Power?' Norton looked around, but saw no works he could safely attribute to the king.

'Power, lad. I can make you the master of all you survey, with authority to extirpate lives by your merest whim.'

Norton pondered. 'Do you know anything about this, Sning?'

Squeeze, squeeze.

Again, he would have to decide for himself. He remained uncertain, but had no alternative. 'Can you give me power over the null-psi amulet?'

'Certainly,' the king said.

But Norton decided to try one more question. 'Can you give me power over the whole contraterrene frame?'

'Indubitably,' the king assured him.

Just so. Norton moved on to the next person. Now he saw that the middle-aged woman's suit was of woven gold, and she wore a necklace and bracelets formed of brilliant precious stones. 'Hello, ma'am.'

'A greeting, young man,' the woman said, coming to life as the old king had. Evidently this was another rote address, as Norton was not really young. 'Do you accept my gift?' Diamonds sparkled at her ears as she moved her head.

'Who are you, and what is your gift?'

'I am Mrs Croesus, widow of the fabulous King of Lydia, who was the father of coinage. My gift is Wealth.' She extended her arm so that her sleeve pulled back to reveal additional bracelets of gold, platinum, and emeralds. She opened her jacket to show inner pockets stuffed with bright gold coins.

'Enough wealth to buy the null-psi amulet?'

'Certainly.' She moved her leg, and an anklet of sparkling opals showed.

'Enough to buy the contraterrene frame?'

'Assuredly.'

Norton went on to the next. 'Hello.'

The lovely young woman animated. 'Oh, aren't you the handsome one!' she cooed. 'I am Circe. Let me delight you with my gift.'

'What is your gift?' Norton had heard of the lovely sorceress Circe and didn't trust her.

'Romance,' she breathed ecstatically. 'I can bring you to fantastic heights of passion and fulfillment such as you can hardly imagine, let alone endure!'

'A height sufficient to make me forget about the null-psi amulet?'

'Of course!' she agreed, leaning forward.

Norton blinked. It took him a moment to remember his next question. 'More passion than elsewhere in the contraterrene – ?'

'Oh, yes!' she sighed. Her bikini halter was beginning to fray from the tension on it.

Norton took one last look, gulped, and moved regretfully on to the boy. 'Hello.'

'What's it to ya?' the lad snapped impertinently. 'Ya want my furshlugginer gift or don't ya, creep?'

'What is your gift?'

'I can tell ya where anything is. Now get lost, jerk.'

'Anything in the contraterrene cluster?'

The boy stared at him. '*What* CT cluster, dodo?'

'How about the Magic-Lantern Cloud? It's CT, too.'

The boy shook his head. 'Mister, you're dreaming! Ain't no CT here!'

Finally one who spoke the truth, however insolently! 'I will accept your gift.'

'What, when ya coulda had power, pelf, or sex? Ya nuts, moron?'

'Tell me where the amulet of null-psi is.'

'Ah, ya don't want that thing! It don't do nothin'.'

'I do want it.'

The boy eyed him with new appreciation. 'Ya got a death wish, dumbbell?'

'I need it to make a deal with a Genius.'

'You're crazy, numbskull! Them bulbheads will screw ya every time!'

'You mean they don't honour agreements?'

'Oh, they stick to the letter, sorta, but they use the loopholes to weasel out anyway. Ya ain't going to get nothing you want from no skullbrain.'

'I don't seem to have much choice. Where is the amulet?'

'Aw, Eve's got it.'

'Eve?'

'The Eviler Sorceress, dolt! Ya can't get near that bitch, and if ya could, she'd zap ya before she'd let ya get that thing.'

'Zap me?'

'Ya know. Turn ya to mush, like her sista useta. She ain't going to give ya no amulet, that's for sure, stupe.'

'I will have to take that chance. Tell me where the Sorceress is.'

'Aw, she moves about all the time. Ya gotta reach her through channels.'

'Then show me the channel.'

'It's another chamber, first off, where they can get a bead on the route. But it's real hard to get there. Ya gotta pass the animals.'

'I'll find a way.' And Norton listened while the impertinent boy described the route in his particular vernacular. Then the boy returned to immobility in his alcove, and Norton redraped his Bemme heat shield and ran back to rejoin the others.

'We have to find another chamber,' he reported, doffing the Bemme, who re-formed her natural shape as he set her on the pavement. 'You were great, Bemme! I hardly sweated.' She blushed pink with pleasure all over.

'Well, let's mosey on, then,' Dursten said, rolling himself a cigarette and touching it to one of the hot coals in the ground to light it.

They moseyed on, following the route the boy had described. 'But we have to watch out for pieharps,' Norton said.

'What's a pieharp?' Excelsia asked. 'Something to eat, or something to play?'

'I'm not sure,' Norton admitted. 'But I fear it's something that will try to eat or play *us*.'

The ledge they were following circled the mound and cooled. It broadened, becoming a darkling plain on which thick, dark stalks grew, bearing long, thin leaves. Excelsia held her candle close to one, peering at it. 'This looks familiar.'

'Watch it, gal,' Dursten warned. 'It might eat you.'

'No, it's harmless,' she decided. The Alicorn sniffed a plant, then began eating it avidly. Excelsia clapped her hands. 'Oh, I know! 'Tis flying carpet reed!'

'Why, so it is,' Norton agreed, startled. 'I've seen the same thing back on Earth. They strip the long fibres and weave them into magic carpets.'

'Yes, that is done here, too,' she said.

Squeeze.

Norton glanced at Sning. 'A warning?'

Squeeze.

'Danger coming?' When Sning agreed, Norton relayed the warning to the others.

'By land or by space?' Dursten asked.

It turned out to be both. 'Then we better get us a ship,' the spaceman decided. 'You say these here weeds can fly?'

'They must first be stripped and cured,' Excelsia said. 'In their natural state they are too wild.'

'We don't have time for that,' Dursten said. 'I can tame a wild ship; I'm the best durned pilot in this neck o' space. Hold your light here, gal; I'll make us a ship.' He began tearing plants out of the ground.

Dursten seemed to know what he was doing. Norton and the Bemme helped him harvest the plants and weave them into a crude and shaggy mat. True to the Damsel's warning, the thing was extremely unruly. It bucked and tossed ferociously, threatening to fall apart. Finally the Bemme formed herself into an endless rope and wrapped herself about the mat, holding it together. Dursten clambered on it, braced his feet in rough-hewn stirrups the Bemme formed, and hauled on vine reins. 'Yahoo!'

There was a sound ahead of them – raucous screeching, as of a flock of unruly birds. Sning gave Norton another

308

warning squeeze. 'That's it,' he told the others. 'The danger!'

'Well, we can stand and fight,' Dursten said. 'But with my blaster dead – '

Squeeze, squeeze.

'Sning says fighting's no good,' Norton reported. 'We'd better try to avoid this threat.' He asked Sning, 'Can we outrun it, then?'

Squeeze, squeeze.

He glanced at the bucking carpet, not thrilled with that prospect. 'Outfly it?'

Squeeze, squeeze, squeeze.

What did that mean? Neither yes nor no! But the birds were coming too fast; there was no time for twenty questions. 'We'd better try to outfly it!'

'Then get aboard, Nort!' Dursten cried.

Norton grabbed on to the back half of the bucking bundle of plants. Some carpet! He hauled himself up behind the spaceman and hung on gracelessly. Excelsia mounted the Alicorn. In a moment all of them were airborne except the ick. There simply was no way to carry that creature this time. 'Hide, Hick!' Norton called to it, and Hick rolled away.

The menace arrived. Norton saw them in the unreliable light of Excelsia's candle – fantastic crossbreeds with the lower bodies of human beings and the upper torsos and heads of gross birds. 'Pieharps?' Excelsia cried, horrified.

Norton figured it out. Human tops and bird bottoms were harpies; bird tops and human bottoms were pieharps. They looked and sounded vicious.

The pieharps were running along the ground, using their powerful legs. But when they saw their prey escaping, they spread their dark wings and launched into the air. They were big, hairy, and fast – faster in the air than either carpet or Alicorn. Sning's warning had been well advised. But Sning had also hinted that they might somehow outfly the menace – or at least, Sning had not denied the possibility.

'I'm ready to hotshot it!' Dursten cried. 'Hang on, Nort, while I buzz them there birds!'

Norton hung on. There was nothing else he could do. He had never been aboard an uncured carpet before and hoped never to repeat the experience. Under the spaceman's guidance, the carpet bucked, then slued around to charge the pieharps.

The bird-men squawked and scattered, caught by surprise. 'Get along, li'l dogies!' Dursten called, pursuing them. The weed-steed swooped and reared, kicking up its leaves, bashing into the posteriors of the fleeing pieharps.

Norton was amazed. The pieharps obviously had the more formidable force, but the antics of the carpet kept them disorganized. Thus, without either outflying or outfighting the bird-men, the spaceman was nullifying them.

Norton looked up and saw Excelsia on the Alicorn, hovering above. There was blood on the animal's horn and hooves; evidently he had fought off some pieharps. But now the pieharps had forgotten about him, because of the distraction of the men on the carpet. Sning's ambiguous response was making sense.

'Hang on, pardner!' Dursten cried. What did he think Norton had been doing? Now the rug made a vertical loop. The surroundings whirled around dizzily, a universe in chaos, a dream-world.

A dream-world . . .

This whole adventure lacked credibility as an objective situation. Maybe convergent evolution was possible, as Satan had described it – but if the Glob and the Cloud really were flowing backwards in time, what were the chances of their people matching Earth's so closely, even in slang, right at this moment? This planet of *i* should be either more primitive or more advanced than Earth, not just the same. Who, in his right mind, would believe in this coincidence? This frame *couldn't* be opposite in time flow to Earth!

But a dream-world, now – made up for Norton's benefit

within his own mind – *that* could be believed. That would require no galactic travel, no contraterrene frame, no reverse time flow or phenomenal coincidences. A dream-world was so obvious – how could he have overlooked it? Satan, the Father of Lies – naturally he would use an easy lie in preference to a difficult truth to gain his nefarious designs.

But if this was a dream – why couldn't Norton simply break out of it? He had tried to will himself home at the outset and had failed. Was he drugged, so that he was locked in until the drug wore off? No, Satan could not have done that to another Incarnation. There had to be a trick of some sort, something Norton did not yet understand. This was another type of puzzle, and to solve it he had to find the key to its solution.

Sning, do you know?

Squeeze, squeeze.

In the end, the mischief of Satan had to be a greater thing than a little magic snake could compass. Sning was like a pocket calculator, very useful for spot answers, but not for the formulation of questions about the nature of ultimate reality.

Squeeze.

'Which way from here, pardner?' Dursten cried.

Norton's question, precisely! But until he found his private personal key to escape, he would have to play the game he was locked into. He gave instructions, and the galloping rug charged and disrupted another wave of pieharps. Then it lifted and swung on to course. The pieharps were now so disorganized they didn't even follow right away; possibly they thought the rug was about to loop back on them.

Too disorganized to follow – again, an analogy of his own condition. Satan was keeping him so occupied with challenges of the moment that he couldn't figure out the grand design. Obviously, Satan's finger was in this adventure, as it had been throughout; since fiction was the highest form of lie, naturally the Father of Lies was skilled at it. Challenge, adventure, humour – Norton had to admit it was a good presentation.

They zoomed on towards the next station. The wind caught

up Excelsia's skirt, so that her legs flashed, still draped sidesaddle. *Sex appeal*, Norton added mentally to his list of fictive qualities. Everything was here – and, frustrating as it was, Norton had to admit to himself that he liked it. This sort of thing surely *was* a reward for Satan's minions. But Norton knew he could not afford to allow himself to remain locked in it.

The pieharps re-formed. They pounded after carpet and Alicorn, their hairy bare legs dangling. They were gaining; soon the fight would resume.

'Them birdbrains won't leave off,' Dursten muttered, glancing back. 'I sure wish I had a recharge on my blaster! Didn't you say there are caves in between? With stag-tites and stuff?'

'Stalactites,' Norton agreed. 'You can distinguish them from stalagmites mnemonically by thinking of the C in stalactite as standing for ceiling, and the G in Stalagmite as standing for ground. So the stalactite hangs from the – '

'Just tell me where they are!' the spaceman snapped. 'Afore them barefoots catch us!'

He had a point. 'But it's not safe to go near them in the air in this dark. Those things are solid onyx, like giant icicles – '

'It's them or the featherfaces!' Dursten cried.

Indeed, the bird-men were closing in rapidly, screaming belligerently. They were flapping in at the carpet, pecking at it. Norton tried to kick them away, but it was futile; he was too busy just hanging on.

Then the party approached the cave region. All of this was inside the castle, of course, between the walls confining the regular functions. There seemed to be an extraordinary amount of waste space here.

The Alicorn flew beside the cave entrance, hovering while Excelsia's candlelight played across it. The stalactites were there. Icicles? No, they were more like jagged teeth! The polished onyx gleamed reflectively, wet like saliva in the mouth of that orifice. Inside the cave, behind the first row,

312

Norton could see the points of endless backup rows of them. If the C stood for ceiling, surely the T stood for teeth! Norton didn't want to fly through that!

'Yore squeeze dingus,' the spaceman said as he absent-mindedly clubbed a pieharp on the beak with the butt of his blaster. 'Can it call out stag-mites?'

'I suppose so,' Norton said, giving up on the lesson in pronunciation. 'But what – ?'

'Call 'em out, 'cause we're going through!' And the carpet charged the cave.

'But it takes time to get that sort of information! Sning can only – '

'Just tell me when one's dead ahead and close!'

Squeeze. 'Now!' Norton cried, knowing in his heart that they would crash into a tooth and fall helplessly to the rising stalagmites below.

The carpet swerved. In the faintly flickering and distant illumination of Excelsia's candle, he saw the stalactite pass just to their left. Two pieharps, too hot in pursuit, crashed into it. They screamed and dropped out of sight, for that had been a high-speed collision. In seconds their descending screams cut off abruptly. They had struck the spires below. But many more still pursued.

Squeeze. 'Another!' Norton cried. He was terrified by this suicidal flight.

The carpet swerved left – and three more pieharps were caught by the column on the right. They weren't looking where they were going; of course, the darkness made it easy to err.

'Ain't this fun?' Dursten demanded exuberantly. 'I ain't flown like this since I threaded the head of a comet on a dare!' He sobered momentarily. ''Course, I did lose my ship on that one . . .'

That was indeed the problem on this sort of thing! But Dursten certainly was an able pilot. He swished the carpet past half a dozen columns, taking out most of the pieharps. In the dark, the bird-men were unable to manoeuvre as effectively as the Sning-guided carpet.

Abruptly they were at the next stage of the trip – the deep caves. These were much smaller than the prior ones, with no stalactites or stalagmites, and had many rounded tunnels that wound through the rock. It was necessary to traverse these to reach the second chamber.

The Alicorn came to land on the ledge. He had taken an easier route through the caves – the space between the points of the stalactites and stalagmites. But had Dursten done that, the pieharps would have pursued them unscathed. Norton had to admit that the spaceman had known what he was doing; he was indeed a hotshot pilot.

There was a new problem, however. The caves were large enough for all of them to walk, including the Alicorn, but not to fly. There were no impassable crevices or heated stones. But these caves were occupied. As soon as the group entered them, Excelsia's candle showed the antennae of giant insects.

They were monstrous termites, predators of the castle interstices. The ones in front were warriors, with grotesque armour and huge pincers. They scuffled along the tunnels, familiar with the labyrinth, for it was the termites that had carved out these warrens. In time they would hollow out so much of the castle that it would collapse. But that was in the future, while the problem of passage was now. How was it possible to get by?

Squeeze.

'Sning says there is a way,' Norton reported.

'Does that there thing know my blaster's dead?'

Squeeze. 'Sning knows. Can we fight through?'

Squeeze, squeeze.

'Sneak through?' Dursten put in.

Squeeze, squeeze.

'Bluff through?' Excelsia asked.

Squeeze, squeeze.

'You shore that thing's got all its batteries?'

'If Sning says there's a way, there's a way.'

'Well, he better tell us real soon, 'cause them termites are mighty hungry!'

Indeed the termite warriors were nudging forward in the process of deciding that the intruders were edible. The Bemme was holding them back temporarily by forming pincers even larger than theirs, but Norton knew this would not fool them very long. Once the termites reached a firm conclusion, this would be no safe place!

'Is there something we can do to make it safe?' Norton asked, trying to cudgel his mind for the right answers.

Squeeze.

Aha! 'As a group?'

Squeeze, squeeze, squeeze.

'Damn! 'One of us?'

Squeeze.

'To make it safe for all of us?'

Squeeze.

A warrior termite marched up more aggressively. The Bemme was balking the ones on the left, but this one was on the right. The Alicorn moved to intercept it, but it was obvious that, when the overt hostilities commenced, the termites would overwhelm them by sheer numbers. 'Get a wiggle on, Nort!' Dursten murmured.

'Which one of us?' Norton asked Sning. 'Me?'

Squeeze, squeeze.

'Dursten?'

Squeeze, squeeze.

'Excelsia?'

Squeeze.

The Damsel's head turned quickly. 'Oh, I cannot fight such monsters, sirrah!' she protested, her candle wavering. 'I am but a helpless feminine creature!'

Exactly. What was Sning thinking of? 'Some magic she can do? Maybe a conjuration?'

Squeeze, squeeze

This was baffling. 'The way she looks?'

Squeeze, squeeze.

A third termite warrior was advancing between the ones blocked by the Bemme and the Alicorn, coming disconcertingly close. Dursten stood before it, pointing his blaster. This did make the insect pause – but for how long?

'Something about her?' Norton asked.

Squeeze.

'Something specific?'

Squeeze.

'Uh, can you show me? Hot-cold?'

Squeeze.

Norton walked quickly to Excelsia, who stood with her delicate knuckles in her mouth, nervously watching the closest termite. He pointed his finger at her pert nose. Sning did not comment. He pointed to her heaving bosom. No reaction. Then he tried her purse – and that was it.

In a moment they were sorting through the items in her purse. She had the usual assortment of inconsequentials. The object turned out to be a little bottle of perfume.

'Perfume?' Norton asked blankly.

Squeeze, Sning replied patiently.

'You mean it destroys monsters, like holy water?'

Squeeze, squeeze.

'Repels termites?'

Squeeze, squeeze.

'Well, then, what good is it?'

Squeeze, squeeze, squeeze.

Excelsia's lips quirked. 'It be good for wearing, belike.' She opened the bottle and dabbed some behind her ears.

The nearest termite paused. It seemed confused.

Dursten snorted. 'That there thing's sniffing the bottle!'

'The smell!' Norton cried. 'It pacifies termites?'

Squeeze, squeeze, squeeze.

'Well, it does something to them! Should we all put it on?'

Squeeze.

316

So they all dabbed perfume on themselves and on the Alicorn, and the termites did not attack. They walked on through the warrens, and the termites ignored them.

'I get it!' Dursten said. 'The smell o' the hive! We've got the dang smell o' the hive!'

It seemed that Excelsia's perfume was precisely that flavour, or had it as a component. The termites were odour-oriented, and now regarded the intruders as other termites.

They arrived at the second chamber. This one was easy to enter; it had glass facing and resembled an executive office, the kind that allowed the boss to keep an eye on every employee without stirring from his desk.

Of course, the employees could also see in. Excelsia's candle showed the interior clearly. There were four alcoves – but all were empty.

'An empty room?' Norton asked, dismayed.

'The jokers musta skedaddled when they heard us coming,' Dursten said disgustedly.

'But the only way out is through the termite warren,' Norton said. 'We should have seen them.'

'Unless this is another magic levitator,' Excelsia suggested.

Levitator? Oh – *elevator*! 'If so, maybe we can use it to follow them.'

They all entered and looked around. There seemed to be no control buttons, and the floor of the glassed-in chamber was that of termite-hewn rock. It did not seem to be an elevator.

Dursten poked around the first alcove. 'Sure coulda been somebody standing here once,' he said. 'See, his footprints are right here.' He stepped into the alcove, planting his space boots where indicated.

Abruptly, he stiffened. His breathing stopped, and his face was frozen in an expression of mild surprise. He had become a statue.

'It's a trap!' Norton exclaimed, horrified.

Squeeze, squeeze.

'Not a trap? But look at him! He's petrified!'

Squeeze, squeeze, squeeze.

'Sning says there's something about this,' Norton said to Excelsia, who was, of course, biting her knuckles in mute helplessness.

He went to stand before the petrified spaceman. 'Can you hear me, Dursten?'

Dursten came alive again. 'I ain't exactly him any more,' he said. 'You want my advice, sport?'

Norton hesitated. Had the spaceman become the exhibit? If so, care was essential. 'I'm not sure. How competent is your advice?'

'Well, I reckon that's for you to find out, Nort.'

What Norton really wanted to ascertain was whether he was, in fact, in a dream world that he could simply awaken from. If he was not, his 'awakening' might be disastrous. A person who decided, when about to step off the brink of a cliff, that it was all a dream and didn't matter would be in trouble if wrong. But if right, he could step off the cliff and force the dream to end. Norton had to be *sure*. What conceivable question could he ask of a dream-figure that would settle that?

That internal question brought its answer: he needed to find someone who knew more than he did on some subject. Only that way could he be sure the answers were not coming from his own mind. For that purpose, it didn't matter whether Bat Dursten was himself or an alcove-figure; if he could not show knowledge beyond Norton's own, he was not enough. Presumably if all four alcove-figures manifested, and none could prove individuality, then Norton could reasonably assume he was locked in a dream of his own. How he would manage to awaken from it he didn't know; somehow, committing suicide here didn't appeal. But first he had to be sure what he was dealing with.

Squeeze.

So Sning agreed! But, of course, if this were a dream,

Sning himself was probably part of it, a dream-snake whose advice was suspect. Likewise the Hourglass; now he remembered how the original, adult Bem had snatched it from him. In real life that was not possible; the Hourglass had passed right through Agleh's hand. But that did not guarantee this was a dream-world; Satan could simply have arranged the illusion that the Hourglass had been snatched. Norton knew he could trust nothing until it proved to be independent of his imagination.

Merely talking with the alcove-spaceman would not do the job. Asking Dursten's name and sentiments would produce only answers that were obvious or not subject to verification. So he would have to get technical, posing the riddles that had always baffled him; the point was to get beyond his own knowledge in such a way that he remained assured the information was valid. Only through scientific logic could he do that.

Norton pondered, then addressed the spaceman. 'Let me ask you a sample question before I decide.'

'Why, shore, pardner. Ask away!'

'There is a story about Galileo, back on my home planet. He was supposed to have climbed to the top of the famous Leaning Tower of Pisa and dropped several objects to the ground. I forget what they were, but that doesn't matter. Let's assume they were a penny, a ping-pong ball, and a cannon-ball. He discovered that they all fell at the same rate, contrary to popular opinion, the small and the large. Popular wisdom had had it that larger and heavier objects would fall faster than small ones. From this experiment he deduced the theory of gravity – that all objects in the universe attracted one another with a force directly proportional to their mass and inversely proportional to their separation from one another. Can you accept that story?'

'Well, I ain't never been to the Tower of Pizza – '

'Any Tower will do,' Norton said patiently. 'The point is, what about the objects falling?'

'Why, sure,' the spaceman said. 'That's gravity, sure 'nuff. You find it around planets and things.'

Norton controlled his irritation. 'What about air resistance?'

'Oh, yeah, there's that. I don't mess with atmosphere so much; planets are a bother. That there ping-pong ball would fall slower in air. And so would the penny, 'cause it's flat, catches the air.'

'Very well. Let's repeat the experiment on an airless planet. Absolutely no atmosphere. Now do they fall at the same rate?'

'Shore,' the spaceman agreed amicably. 'Weight 'n density don't matter none in a perfect vacuum. A dang feather would fall as fast as a lead shot.'

'But the theory says that objects attract one another in direct proportion to their masses. Since the cannonball is more massive than the ping-pong ball, shouldn't it fall faster?'

Dursten scratched his head. 'You know, I never thought o' that! I'll go try it sometime.'

'Does this suggest to you that Galileo could not have performed the experiment attributed to him – or that if he did, and got the results claimed, he would not have derived that particular theory from it?'

'Yeah, shore does, now you put it that there way.'

Norton sighed inwardly. The spaceman had not been able to take it any further than Norton himself had. He had questioned the Leaning Tower story at the outset, as a child, and been sure that Galileo's experiment must have been misrepresented in some way. For example, magic could have distorted the results. None of the other children had thought so, however, and they had ridiculed him for questioning it. Norton himself had never been quite certain whether he had a valid argument or was merely finding fault with what he did not properly understand. Had Dursten been able to offer a better explanation, he could have been accepted as an

320

independent entity. But the spaceman knew, if anything, less than Norton himself did – and that was no proof he was not a figment of a dream.

'Thank you, Bat. I'm afraid I must decline to accept your advice. This does not imply any criticism of – '

'That's okay, Nort. Can I step down now?'

'By all means.'

The spaceman stepped out of the alcove. 'Say, that shore was funny!' he said. 'For a while there I felt like I was somebody else!'

'Let me try that,' Excelsia said. She stepped into the second alcove, placing her dainty feet where indicated.

She froze. 'Say, she's pretty as a pitcher!' Dursten remarked appreciatively.

She was indeed, Norton reflected. Pretty as a fine porcelain pitcher with a classic picture painted on it. He went to stand directly before her. 'Hello, Excelsia.'

'Oh, hello, Sir Norton,' she replied, reanimating sweetly. 'But I'm not exactly the Damsel at the moment.'

'She sure looks like a Damsel to me!' Dursten remarked.

'I understand,' Norton said.

'Will you accept my advice, O noble querent?'

'First may I try a sample?'

Her fair brow furrowed. 'A sample of *what*, sirrah?'

'Of your advice, of course.'

'Oh.' Her brow cleared. 'Certainly, Sir Norton.'

'If the universe and everything in it doubled in size in an instant, would anybody notice anything different?' This was another question that had frustrated him, because his answer had differed from that of everyone else. Such differings had set him apart from his peer group, perhaps putting him on a path to self-isolation in the wilderness, where philosophy and reality were one. He believed this was another good question for the occasion.

Excelsia pondered prettily. 'I don't think so,' she said. 'I mean, sirrah, if everything were twice as big, including the

321

yardsticks and people, there really wouldn't be any change, would there?'

That was the standard answer. 'But what about the square-cube ratio?'

'The what?' she asked, perplexed.

'The surface area of objects increases by the square, while volume increases by the cube,' he explained. 'If you doubled the diameter of the planet and the height of the man standing on it, his mass would multiply by a factor of eight and the mass of the planet by a similar factor, so his actual weight would be something like sixty-four times as much as before, while the cross section of his legs would be only four times as much. The burden on each square inch of his feet would be about sixteen times the prior burden – without strengthening his flesh. He would collapse and die in short order; it would be like standing on Jupiter – '

'Oh,' she said blankly. 'I've never been to Jupiter. Are you sure?'

'It's why ants aren't the size of elephants. The square-cube ratio prevents them from achieving such great size without changing form radically.'

'But the big termites – '

Excellent point! Scientifically, those monsters were impossible! But he had the answer. 'Magic changes things, of course. Without magic, those huge termites could not exist.'

'Then – with magic, the universe could double!'

Another nice point; she was certainly smarter than Dursten. But her point was flawed. 'Magic is limited to planetary range. Sections of the universe are not magic; these would perish. The laws of science, in contrast, are universal, so science is what applies here. Thus, where magic overrides science, as here, huge termites are possible, but the doubling of the universe remains impossible.'

'That's for shore!' Dursten agreed. 'I never had no truck with none o' that there magic.'

Norton had eliminated Excelsia as an independent thinker;

she, like Dursten, knew less than he did. The dream-world hypothesis, so far, was two for two. 'You may step down, Damsel.'

She stepped out of the alcove, seeming perfectly normal now that her interview was over. She brought out a little mirror and checked her makeup.

'Must be your turn,' Norton said to the Alicorn. 'Want to try an alcove?'

'An Alicove!' Dursten said, chuckling.

The Alicorn shrugged and stepped into the third. This one turned out to be larger than it looked; there was room. He put his forehooves on the footprints and froze.

'Hello, Alicorn,' Norton said. 'Can you speak?'

The Alicorn animated. *Telepathically*, he projected. *But I am not exactly the animal at the moment.*

'I understand.'

'I sure don't,' Dursten said. 'What in space is going on?'

'The Alicorn is telepathic,' Excelsia said. 'Everyone knows that.'

The spaceman was silent, embarrassed. Obviously he hadn't known – and neither had Norton. It seemed the Alicorn generally didn't bother to communicate that way to people with whom he was not tame.

Will you accept my advice?

'First I must question you.'

Proceed.

'This is a scientific question. You are a magical creature. Can you handle it?'

In this guise I can.

'It is said, scientifically, that the mass of an object increases as that object is accelerated towards the velocity of light. Thus nothing can actually reach the speed of light, because its mass would become infinite.'

True.

'But what, then, of light itself? Doesn't its mass become infinite – thus preventing it from achieving its set velocity?'

Light is massless, so is not affected.

'But it bends around stars. It is affected by gravity, and gravity is the force that acts on mass. Light must have mass.'

The Alicorn sent no thought; he was unable to answer.

Norton dismissed him and moved to the final alcove. The Bemme entered it, settling her base on the footprints. She froze.

He went through the ritual, animating her in the new office. He asked her his most difficult question. 'Are you conversant with the scientific theory of relativity?'

'Naturally. We Bems grasped it long before Man did.'

'Then you know that when a spaceman takes off from Earth and accelerates to a significant fraction of the velocity of light, he experiences the phenonemon of time dilation. For him and his ship, time seems to slow, so that at the end of a trip of perhaps a month, he returns from the far reaches of the galaxy to discover that the folk back on Earth have aged maybe centuries and all his friends are gone.'

'Shore, any fool knows that!' Dursten put in. 'Happens all the time. That's why a true spaceman's got to love 'em and leave 'em; they're old hags when he makes port again.'

'Continue,' the Bemme said.

'But a prime tenet of special relativity is that everything is relevant; there is no absolute standard of rest. So, while from Earth the spaceman seems to be travelling at nearly light-speed and suffering time dilation, the effect is opposite from the spaceman's view. To him, Earth is travelling at nearly light speed and suffering the time dilation. So when he rejoins Earth, he should discover that the folk on Earth have aged only a fraction as much as he has. How do you resolve this paradox?'

'There is no paradox,' the Bemme said. 'Though for a while each party perceives the other as functioning more slowly than itself, this is largely a matter of perspective.'

'Perspective? They can't both be right!'

'Perspective,' she repeated firmly. 'If you are on one

324

spaceship, and I am on another, and our ships drift apart in space, to each of us the other's ship will appear smaller than his own, together with the people in it. The instruments of each will measure that diminution of size in the other. Each viewer is correct – but this is perspective, not paradox.'

'Say, I never thought of it that way!' Norton exclaimed.

'Me neither,' Dursten said.

'The human species does tend to cogitate shallowly,' the Bemme agreed politely.

'Hey, watch it with them dirty words!' the spaceman said.

'But does this mean,' Norton asked, wrestling with the paradox of perspective, 'that when the spaceman returns to Earth, there will be no difference in their time frames? Once the distortion of perspective is eliminated?'

'No, there will indeed be a difference, though not as great as perspective made it seem. The spaceman will have aged less than the folk on Earth.'

'But then the principle of relativity – the apparent slowing of the Earth, from the spaceman's viewpoint – '

'Perspective does not change reality,' the Bemme said patiently. 'Despite your planet's apparent slowing, from the spaceman's perspective, there is a distinction. He ages less.'

'Now I can't accept that just on your say-so! What dis – '

'The distinction of acceleration. The spaceman experiences it; Earth does not. To each party, the other is retreating at increasing velocity, but only the spaceman *feels* the extra gees. This distinguishes his condition from that of Earth or the rest of the universe; his time is slowed.'

'Acceleration? Why should that – ?'

'Besides,' Dursten put in, 'he decelerates when he comes home, so it cancels out.' He seemed to have forgotten which side of the issue he was on.

'There is no such thing as deceleration,' the Bemme said. 'There is only negative acceleration, which is to say, acceleration in the opposite direction. The spaceman accelerates twice – when he is departing from Earth and when he returns to it.'

'Very well,' Norton said. 'So he accelerates twice. What has that to do with time?'

'Everything. It is easier to understand in the frame of general relativity, which relates to gravity. Gravity slows time, literally – and the effects of gravity are indistinguishable from those of acceleration. So when the spaceman accelerates, or as Dursten so quaintly puts it, decelerates, his time slows – regardless of the temporary effects of perspective.'

'Gravity slows time?' Norton asked dully.

'Certainly. The effect reaches its extreme at the so-called event horizon of a so-called black hole, which is a stellar object of such density and mass that gravity increases to the point at which light itself cannot escape, and time slows to eternity. Thus the spaceman bold enough to travel there would become truly timeless.'

'But nothing escapes from a black hole!' Norton protested. 'How can we ever know what goes on there?'

'Three ways. First, we have worked it out theoretically, in the form of the general theory of relativity. Second, we have tested it by experimenting with lesser levels of acceleration and gravity; it has been verified that the intensity of gravity does affect a clock. Third, we have explored black holes magically and recorded the effects there. In this manner, magic, far from opposing science, facilitates it.'

'So there is no clock paradox?' Norton asked weakly.

'Correct,' the Bemme agreed. 'And, I might add, your other questions were somewhat deficient in aptness. You confused the theoretical work of Galileo with that of Newton and misstated their conclusions; and as for the infinite mass of anything travelling at light-speed, you failed to take cognizance of the fact that an infinite series can have a finite total. Mass and energy are merely different aspects of the same reality; mass is merely solidified energy. So when an object accelerates towards C, or light-speed, the energy required to – '

'Enough!' Norton cried, his mind spinning. The Bemme

obviously knew more than he did, and was teaching him things he had never grasped before and could not now dismiss as nonsense. This was the mind he had been seeking. 'I will accept your advice.'

'An excellent decision,' the Bemme said, stepping out of the alcove. 'What is your problem?'

'I'm stuck in this frame and I need to get back to Earth. How do I return?'

'You never left Earth,' she told him. 'That should have been obvious to you the moment you remembered that magic is limited to planetary scale; you cannot tour the universe by magic.'

'You mean I *am* in a dream? Then how do I wake?'

'You are not in a dream. You are in an illusion fostered by the Father of Illusion. You must find a way to perceive reality with certainty; that will vanquish the illusion.'

'An illusion?' Norton asked, still reeling. 'Are *you* an – ?'

'No. I am what I seem – a creature alien to your planet. I needed a job, and your Figure of Evil hired me for this role.'

Norton looked at the others. 'And they – ?'

'They, too, are role players – but they don't know it. For them, the roles have become reality. This is perhaps just as well, for it prevents them from realizing they are damned.'

'And you are not?'

'I am not of your socio-political-religious frame. I have no attachment to your Incarnative figures of Good or Evil. I deal with them on a purely practical basis. Your damnation does not relate to me. When I tire of this job, I will seek some other.'

'How do I perceive reality, then?'

'That I cannot tell you. I can describe reality to you in superlatively accurate detail, but only you can perceive it. As with any natural function, you must do it yourself.'

Surely true! 'But if I am on Earth, why do I perceive the make-believe world of the Magic-Lantern Cloud? I mean, now that I know – '

'I have some difficulty grasping the irrationalities of your species,' the Bemme confessed. 'I presume you find some private satisfaction in the perceptions you maintain, and the Lord of Buzzbugs caters to this innate propensity.'

'Buzzbugs?'

'I think you call them flies. Small creatures with pretty eyes. On my planet we call them buzzbugs, because their tentacles buzz as they levitate.'

The Bemme was a real font of information! Perhaps almost too much information. 'Um, Sning – do you know how I can break out?'

Squeeze.

'But I have to figure out how, so you can confirm it?'

Squeeze.

Norton sighed. He had made significant progress, but it seemed he had a long way to go yet.

He pondered a moment. 'Would getting the null-psi amulet the Genius wants help me?'

'No,' the Bemme said, while Sning squeezed once.

Oops – opposite signals! Which one should he trust? Well, he would ask. 'Sning says the amulet would help me, but you say it wouldn't. How can I tell which of you is right?'

'We're both right,' the Bemme said, and Sning squeezed once.

'But you can't be! Your answers are opposite!'

'I shall explain, since you seem to have some difficulty grasping selective aspects of truth. If you get the amulet and take it to the Genius, he will use psi to transport you back to the real world. In that sense the amulet will help you. But that process will take so long, because of the hurdles you must pass to reach and win the amulet, that by the time you return to reality, Satan will have completed his designs and your effort to balk him will be wasted. In addition, he will still be able to send you back into this illusion at will, forcing you to obtain the amulet again to get out, playing by his rules. Therefore the amulet will not help you in the way you need; it

328

will merely give you the illusion of help. Sning is less sophisticated than I am and lacks the superior objectivity of being alien, so could only provide you with the limited immediate truth. When you ask an inadequate question, he is at a disadvantage.'

SQUEEZE!

Norton winced; that had been a sharp constriction! He realized that he had been giving Sning trouble all along, asking wrong questions, so that the little snake had had to give hesitant yeses or noes, or throw up his nonexistent hands with triple squeezes.

'Then how can I return to reality fast enough to balk Satan?' he asked after a pause.

'Here I have the disadvantage of being alien,' the Bemme said, though she did not seem perturbed about it. '*I* have no problem perceiving reality, but, of course, I have better eyes than you do. I cannot reach into your mind and change your perception. Because I am immune to psi, I have none myself. All I can do is give you my intelligent advice when you ask for it.'

'Do you know how I can return, Sning?'

Squeeze.

There it was again; the one who could speak could not give him the answer, while the one who had the answer could not speak. Satan, if he happened to be watching this, probably found the irony delicious. If the occasion ever came for Chronos to torment Satan the way Satan had tormented him . . .

'Well, maybe the others can help,' Norton said without much hope. He turned to the group, who had been ignoring this dialogue. 'Have any of you any notion how I can return to, uh, Earth quickly?'

'Why, shore, pardner,' Dursten said. 'Just put that there squeeze dingus on the Bemme and let 'em talk in overdrive. They're both a heap smarter'n we are.'

Norton gaped. So obvious a solution! 'Okay, Sning?'

Squeeze.

Norton held out his hand, and the Bemme held out a tentacle. Sning uncurled, crawled across, and curled around her appendage.

There followed a wait, while the Bemme and Sning communicated. Then she held out her tentacle, and the little snake returned to Norton.

'We must proceed to the third chamber,' the Bemme said, and Sning squeezed.

'But that's the route for finding the amulet!' Norton cried. 'You just told me the amulet wouldn't – '

'It *looks* as if we're searching for the amulet,' the Bemme explained. 'That will keep the Eviler Sorceress off our tentacles until we accomplish our purpose.'

Good notion! 'Very well – let's go to the third chamber.'

'A precaution will be necessary,' the Bemme said. 'You must be deprived of your senses.'

'What?' Norton demanded, partly outraged, partly nervous.

'In your culture there is the narrative of your historical figure Odysseus,' she said. 'He wished to see and listen to the sirens, but to do so was death, for he would then throw himself into the savage sea and drown or wreck his ship with all aboard, trying to reach them. So his crewmen tied him to the mast, while they blocked their own hearing. In that fashion he heard the sirens and survived. Human beings are very foolish.'

'You mean I will see and hear things that will madden me?'

'And smell, taste, and feel them,' the Bemme added. 'The Eviler Sorceress has saved her worst for last.'

'But we're outside her formal maze! Between the walls! There shouldn't be any – '

'We are merely in another aspect of it. We never left this maze.'

'Oh. But this business about – '

'Temporary. I will cover your head, shielding you from the blandishments, allowing only oxygen to pass in. You will don

Bat Dursten's space gauntlets. That will protect you from the worst of it. You will ride the Alicorn, and Dursten and Excelsia will guard your flanks. That should get you through, if you heed Sning's warnings.'

'But if it's that dangerous, what about the rest of you?'

'We are all role players, here to facilitate your diversion. You are the target; the effects will not affect us.'

'This is the way it has to be, Sning?'

Squeeze.

Sning and the Bemme had certainly worked it out in that brief interval of private dialogue!

The Bemme assumed the form of a hood, which Norton put over his head. He was afraid it would feel suffocating, but she was true to her word: there was pure, sweet oxygen inside.

He donned the gauntlets, which were designed to protect hands from interstellar vacuum, and mounted the Alicorn with a boost from someone. He felt like a condemned criminal being hauled to the gallows.

The Alicorn moved. For a few paces everything was routine. Norton was aware only of motion, for no sound, light, or smell penetrated the living hood. Then the atmosphere changed.

First, something seemed to touch his gauntleted hands. It was the merest hint, filtered through the impermeable material, yet it suggested the sleek body of a beautiful and vibrant woman or the controls of a finely machined, high-performance racing car. He wanted to get a better feel, so he started to draw off one gauntlet.

Squeeze, squeeze!

Oh. The temptation of Odysseus was upon him! For the first time in his life Norton experienced some sympathy for the ancient Greek warrior. But he left the gloves alone.

Then something brushed about his head. It was a hint of perfumed music, ineffably sweet, as of a lovely garden glade with flowers blooming and a damsel with a dulcimer – the kind of place he longed to enter and remain in. But he could not perceive it clearly through the hood. So he reached up to pull it off –

SQUEEZE! SQUEEZE!

Damn! He had to desist, but he was furious at what he was giving up. That garden of delights –

The beast moved on – and somehow Norton felt the presence of a book or wise man or computer terminal containing the answers to all the most perplexing and fascinating riddles of the universe. All the myriad little mysteries that had nagged at him, from the punch line to a joke others had found uproarious and he had not quite heard, to the nature of Ultimate Reality. He had to see that book! He –

SQUEEZE! SQUEEZE!

'The hell with you!' he snapped, wrenching at the hood.

Something fettered his arms, so he could not pull, and the hood clenched itself stiflingly close about his head. He heaved off the encumbrances and grabbed the hood with both hands. It stretched like taffy, but did not come off. He clawed at it in a frenzy, but his gauntlets made him clumsy. Feverishly he tore them off.

The Alicorn leaped, almost dislodging him. He had to grab for the mane for support. That delayed his attack on the hood, and in a moment the desire waned.

Now the hood relaxed. It slid away from his face, coursed down to the ground, and re-formed into the Bemme.

'We made it!' Dursten said. 'But you shore fought that there hood, Nort, like you was suffocating!'

Norton's head cleared. 'If that was the filtered siren song, I never would have made it through the unfiltered one! Even now, I'd like to go back and – '

Squeeze, squeeze.

'Shux, Nort, it's just quicksand and maggots there,' Dursten said. 'You'd just sink in over your head.'

'I can't believe that! That beautiful music – '

'Here, I'll show you. Bemme, make like a danged floodlight.'

The Bemme convoluted into a floodlight mounted on a stand. The spaceman flicked the switch to ON and the beam of light speared out, striking a distant wall. Dursten swivelled the beam down to the ground where the tracks of the Alicorn showed.

A hundred feet back, those traces disappeared into a monstrous roiling bog. Tiny highlights of white showed, wriggling in and out of the muck – the maggots.

'We had to walk right through that. Ugh!' Excelsia said, wrinkling her nose. 'Fortunately, the Alicorn was able to pick the shallowest point to cross. He couldn't fly, because we had to stay close enough to stop you from taking off the hood. One misstep, and we all would have been drowned in it.'

Now Norton saw the caked, maggoty mud on their legs and shoes. They had done it, all right. Excelsia and the Alicorn especially had made a sacrifice, for otherwise they could have flown over the muck. 'Thank you, friends!' he said humbly.

'We're not really your friends,' the Bemme murmured. 'We are simply playing our assigned roles.'

'Maybe you are,' Norton replied. 'But *they* don't realize they are playing roles, you said. So they're as good friends as any other kind, aren't they?'

'I stand corrected,' the alien agreed. 'It is a human nuance of interpretation.'

Norton turned to face the other way. There was the third chamber; a door in a wall was marked: 3-d chamber. 'Well, let's go in.'

'This you must do alone,' the Bemme said, returning to her natural bug-eyed state. She had spoken before from a speaker grille in the floodlight. 'Our perceptions are not precisely yours. Even Sning's are not yours, though he understands what you perceive. You must align your perception of reality yourself by your own effort; only then will you be in control. We wish you well.'

'Shore do,' Dursten said.

'If you succeed,' Excelsia said, 'promise you will return at least to say good-bye.' There was a delicate tear in her eye.

'I will,' Norton agreed.

He put his hand on the knob and turned it. The round door opened in the old-fashioned way, swivelling out on hinges. Beyond the circular port that was revealed was only blackness.

He stepped through – and found himself suspended in deep space as the door swung closed behind him. Its closure cut off Excelsia's candlelight; with the darkness, the stars shone all around with preternatural clarity, and the ribbon of the Milky Way wound its snaky course in a great circle. To the rear, where the door had been, the sun blazed – but somehow it did not wipe out the other stars. He could see everything in a way never before possible.

'What do I do now?' he asked, noting that his cloak had spread out to protect him from the vacuum and radiation of deep space. It didn't seem to matter whether he was in reality or illusion; he was comfortable.

Squeeze, squeeze, squeeze.

Oh, yes – he had to figure it out for himself. 'But I am safe here, whatever I do?'

Squeeze.

What he had to do was align his perception to reality. Evidently this chamber provided the mechanism, if only he could figure out how to use it.

Well, this was the naked universe. He was Chronos. He could take a better look at it, travelling in time. Since he knew he would have to travel far to see any significant change, he willed the Hourglass to virtually maximum effect, turning the sand to its most intense red. 'Forward in time – to the end of the universe!' he proclaimed grandly. 'Sning, give me a squeeze when each billion years passes, just so I know.'

He started off. The location-spell remained on, so he remained where he was in the galaxy – but it changed about him. Individual stars waxed and waned, some becoming brighter, some dimmer, and their constellations distorted into unrecognizability. New constellations formed, flexed, and dissolved. He knew it was all in his perspective, as stars shifted positions relative to his location, but it did make for an effect of almost-living animation.

Every so often there were supernovas, flashing with phenomenal brilliance and vanishing. He realized that his accelerated time travel made them as brief to him as the flashes of flashbulbs, but still they were bright in passing! He began to perceive a pattern to the changing positions of the more stable stars, patches of stars, and clouds of gas and dust. The galaxy was rotating, turning more rapidly in the centre than at the edge, as if stirred by a cosmic spoon. Once he realized that, his perception became truly three-dimensional, and he saw himself as part of the giant, viscous mix of material. The galaxy had seemed stationary when he had been fixed in time; now he saw it as a porridge of stars and dust. In fact, the dust was stretched out in great spirals, moving outward from the centre, and at the fringes of those bands of dust the stars were thickest and brightest, for the dust was their raw material. Stars did not form from mere contractions of gas amidst vacuum; they were squeezed into life by the tidal fluxes of the galaxy itself, like eddy whorls against the shifting dust.

Squeeze.

Oh, yes – a billion years had passed! Entranced, he continued to watch. Having analysed the pattern of the great rotating galactic disc, he was now able to perceive the broader universe beyond, the neighbouring galaxies, moving and spinning in their own courses and gradually drawing together. Stars kept moving in on their dust banks and disappearing into them, while the bands themselves snaked out towards the extremes. The galactic centres grew brighter.

Squeeze.

Another billion years already! He was still accelerating in time, but also becoming more absorbed by the wonder of the universe about him, so that time seemed to pass faster, anyway. Objective, subjective – what was the truer definition of time? Fascinated by the moving panorama of space, Norton began to trace the patterns of whole galactic clusters. His perspective kept expanding as he came to understand the more fundamental motions of the universe.

Squeeze.

Now it was easier to see how the galaxies were all converging on a single region of space, like shining pinwheels rolling in to a rendezvous. And the galaxies themselves were changing as they went, their centres becoming brighter despite the flow of dust and stars out from them.

Squeeze.

After that he pretty much ignored the squeeze markers, for they were coming faster as his sphere of awareness expanded. It almost seemed as if the universe were shrinking.

Suddenly a band of dust and gas passed across his region, momentarily blotting out his vision. When it passed, the sun was gone. Startled, he cast about for it; he had tuned it out in his effort to perceive the patterns of motion of the farther galactic clusters. It was definitely gone.

Well, how many billions of years had passed now? Six, eight? Mankind would not feel the loss! He let the sun go with momentary regret and refocused on the universe at large, which was really more interesting.

It was definitely shrinking. He verified this by fixing his attention on one particular spot and gauging the contraction of galactic groups around it. His perception seemed to have accommodated the enormous distances separating galaxies, so that he could know where they were even though, theoretically, it took billions of years for the light of the farthest ones to reach him. Perhaps this was because he himself was travelling rapidly in time; he didn't have to wait on the normal speed of light. Or maybe it was simply another facet of the magic of the Hourglass.

Shrinking? How could that be? The universe was supposed to be expanding!

Yet as the billions of years squeezed by, ten, eleven, twelve, he became certain; the universe was indeed contracting. It became small enough for him to see completely, then smaller yet. Dismayed and enthralled, he watched it form into a giant globe perhaps four billion light-years across. The galaxies were becoming quasars, with hugely radiating centres and tenuous umbras of dust and gas, and these dissolved into formless waves, much as the individual stars had dissolved into the dust clouds before. The universe became a great ball of gases and energy that then compressed into a mass of plasma less than a billion light-years in diameter, a super-duper nova.

It shrank into the size of a single quasar, then, so rapidly it was an eyeblink, into the size of a single planet, and disappeared.

Norton stared at the distant point of nothingness. If this was to be the way the universe ended, winking out in fifteen billion years or so, how did that differ from the manner in which it had begun? Perplexed, Norton reversed directions, turning the sand its most intense blue, and willed himself back in time.

The universe reversed. The ball of plasma reappeared from nothing, expanding ferociously. He was unable to distinguish energy radiation from matter; they were inextricably mixed. Now Norton noticed some things he had missed before. In this version, a great deal of energy seemed to be forming from nothing, even as the expansion occurred, so that, though the ball was exploding at light-speed, the universe itself was multiplying much faster than that. It was as if a shock wave were travelling out ahead of the light, triggering the condensation of energy from whatever unknowable recess it had hidden in. But, of course, he was travelling backward in time now, which meant that that energy had actually converted into nothing before the remainder squeezed into the singularity of the black hole and winked out entirely.

How could that be? He had understood that matter and energy were fairly permanent, and here they were dis-existing freely. In the ripples of energy as he now perceived them, matter coalesced, as if light were being bent around so tightly that it rolled up against itself and formed tiny balls of energy that developed a certain stability of their own. But when two balls touched each other, one of them spinning in one direction, the other in another, they burst like soap bubbles and vanished in total energy. Thus the forming matter was promptly destroying itself, renewing the explosion, generating more turbulence and eddies that spun out more bits of matter. Except that in actuality, he reminded himself again, it was the other way around; energy was forming matter implosively, and the implosive condensation then unwrapped to form new beams of energy that arrowed in towards the final extinction of singularity, of nonexistence. This was nonsense!

He continued to watch as billions of years squeezed back. The turbulence of the explosion imparted a slight rotation, and this spin caused the majority of the lightballs to curl up in one direction, so that soon all of the opposite-spinning balls were eliminated by cancellation and matter stopped destroying itself. The remaining matter coalesced into dusty masses, still rushing outward from the common centre. The masses had their own rotations and formed into crude discs that solidified in the centres, compressing until the pressure was so great that ignition occurred, and suddenly they were quasars. Still the centres intensified, until they became black holes that expanded, swallowing much of the brilliance and sucking additional matter in long spiral trails. Now they were galaxies, structured as spiralling fodder for their central appetites. There was no hunger in the universe like that of a black hole!

Except, again, that this was backwards. How could a black hole spew out matter continuously like that, until it disappeared? That simply was not the nature of such things! A black hole, with certain very limited exceptions, was strictly a one-way affair. What went in did not come out. Except, the Bemme had said, in the case of magic. And the force of magic did not reach out on galactic scale; it was confined to the radius of a typical planet, like Earth. Everyone knew that. That was why they used matter transmitters for interplanetary travel. Even ghosts had to use such modern conveniences, as Gawain had. Had the Bemme told him wrong?

This bothered him. If the alien had lied or been in error, he, Norton, had placed his trust in the wrong entity. He was reluctant to believe that, partly because he liked the Bemme and partly because that would leave him back on circle one. How, then, could he rationalize her statement about magic and black holes?

Aha! Black holes come in all sizes, from supergalactic to pinhead. A pinhead black hole could be used for experimental purpose, even moved about, provided one did not do anything foolish like poking a finger at it. The better laboratories had pinholes. Certainly it was possible to test magic on a hole. So the Bemme had not been refuted. That was a relief, and he could proceed with his current tour.

How could a black hole be reversed? Answer: not this way! Theoretically, a black hole could become overheated so that it exploded, but it could not pay out material a bit at a time. So either what he was seeing was wrong, or –

Or he was, in fact, seeing it backwards.

He looked at the Hourglass. The sand was intense blue. He was supposed to be travelling backwards, from normal future to normal past – but was he?

Then he had another revelation. Satan was the Father of Lies and the Master of Illusion; why couldn't he craft an illusion that changed the colours of the sand of the Hourglass? Obvious answer: he could – and he would! That would be far, far easier than creating a whole world that ran backwards. That explained how Norton was able to relate one-to-one with the role players here – they were living forward, while he was living backwards – for him.

He remembered how the sand of the Hourglass had shown green upon his return from a prior visit – the colour of universal time. He had not set it there – not consciously. Obviously he *had* set it there – thinking the colour was white, his normal backward course. Satan had tricked him into supposing green was white and red was blue. Black and yellow seemed to have been left alone; that change would have been too obvious. If he had gone to black to freeze time, and found himself careering through space instead, he would have known something was wrong. So only the directions of time had been changed – the normal and accelerated modes. Very neatly done; it had certainly fooled him. Each visit to the 'the contraterrene' frame must, in fact, have been a reversal of time he had just spent on Earth. Satan had had to free him before he overlapped a prior reversal and ran afoul of the three-person limit.

How long did he have this time? He wasn't sure, because he had been operating in the drawkcab mode, undoing Satan's damage of eight years in the past. He had been about six hours between the departure of Satan's minion horn-demon and the onset of his effort to neutralize that minion; did these periods cancel out or add on, in the present? Evidently the latter, since he lived subjectively through both of them. But didn't some of that time already overlap his adventure with Excelsia and the Alicorn and the Sword Elf? He wasn't sure how to figure it, but suspected that Satan had made sure to allow enough time for this present diversion so that Norton would arrive back on Earth too late to foil his mischief. Probably if he got the null-psi amulet and took it to the Genius, the Genius would agree to transport him back to Earth just as his allotted time was up, anyway. What a conniving rogue was Satan!

Now he was zooming along the temporal length of the universe and knew that his perception of the sand of the Hourglass was wrong. Yet nothing had changed. How could he cancel the illusion?

Probably he had to be absolutely certain he was right, for uncertainty was the grist for exploitation by Satan. At the moment, he was not at all certain. He had figured out a theory to account for the discrepancies he had noted, but a theory was not a fact. He needed solid corroborative data.

Well, what in the universe was more solid than the universe itself? Suppose he explored it to the very end of time and satisfied himself that he knew its directions in time – shouldn't that be enough for certainty? If it wasn't, what was?

If he could not believe in the universe, he could not believe in anything. This chamber might be part of an illusion, but he suspected it was also a window to reality. He would travel to the end of the universe he saw here, seeking certainty.

He willed the sand to turn an even more intense blue, knowing that was reverse in colour but correct in thrust. The universe accelerated, and Sning's squeezes came more and more rapidly, until the billions of years were passing in seconds and Sning became more of a shudder than a series of squeezes. The universe flew apart at an awesome rate, the galaxies separating so rapidly they appeared blurred. Soon the local section of space was clear. In a sphere ten billion light-years across, there was no longer any matter at all, and very little energy. The hole in the torus.

Norton turned his attention to the retreating outer fringe. Again he was able to adapt, to spread his awareness to perceive objects on a vaster scale than any human being had perceived them before. The torus of galactic motes was now a hundred billion light-years out, and still expanding. This was an open universe, seemingly without end.

But those galaxies were still evolving themselves, getting consumed by their black-hole centres. The process was slow while the available free matter diminished, but it continued. In due course the ring of galaxies became a ring of black holes, each spaced a hundred billion light-years or more from its nearest neighbour. The holes were detectable only by their declining halos of radiation, and even that was doomed.

Finally nothing was visible; Norton knew their paths only by inference. A trillion light-years out, and still the torus expanded, for there was nothing to stop it. Would it ever end?

Then something happened. In the far, far, far distance he perceived a detonation. It was another Big Bang, the explosion of a monstrous black hole. A new universe was forming!

He realized that this Bang had occurred directly in the path of one of the local universe's far-flung holes. They had collided and over-heated and burst apart. New energy and matter were generating in the region of this flux, as they had done so before.

He also realized that, just as some holes were pinhead size, so were some universe size. They were scattered through space (though space did not really exist in the absence of matter or energy – a quibble), rendered ever larger by the accumulation of stray radiation and dust and the debris from other worn-out universes, perhaps billions of such toruses. On occasion, a swiftly travelling galactic hole would collide with such a universe hole, like a neutron ploughing into the nucleus of a uranium atom, and the impact would shatter both holes and cause the most massive possible explosion, augmented by the stress of space itself. In this manner were new universes born, his own included.

He continued to work it out as he watched the distant universe expand. Obviously not all galaxies became neutrons, and not all neutrons would strike larger holes head-on with sufficient force to shatter them. Most would be captured in orbit about the larger holes and eventually swallowed peacefully. Thus the masses of larger holes would steadily increase as their number diminished. Perhaps there was a critical mass, beyond which a hole became unstable, ready to be detonated. Thus the detonation of new universes would be a regular thing, occurring every trillion years or less, each expiring in a grand flash of a few tens of billions of years before its black-hole ashes were absorbed by still-accumulating universes. Perhaps new universes were flowing continuously, scattered over such a wide region that no entity could perceive more than one at a time, not even Chronos. Surely his own universe had developed in that fashion, not remarkable at all, just a single brief spark in eternity.

All it took was a little matter and antimatter – that was why the secondary explosions occurred around a new universe, because of the dexter and the sinister curls of matter formation – and time. Time.

And he was Chronos, the Incarnation of Time. The one entity permitted to grasp the true nature of reality.

Norton shook his head. 'Satan, compared to this truth, your lies are of no consequence!'

It was time to return to his own tiny portion of his particular spark. He brought out the Hourglass and focused on its flowing sand. He was still travelling forward, and the sand was still blue – but as he looked at that lie, the colour changed to red and he saw truly at last. He had penetrated Satan's illusion and knew that he would never again be vulnerable to it.

He willed the sand blue again, this time to true blue, and the progress of time reversed. The distant universe began to contract. He wondered idly whether it had sapient creatures within it, living, loving, warring, and dreaming, performing minor exploits of science and magic, and whether any part of his long-gone physical body was incorporated into it, on the off chance that his own Milky Way Galaxy happened to be the neutron hole that had triggered this new effort. Perhaps a quark or two of him was there! 'Good luck, you who follow us!' he cried.

Then that universe contracted back to its origin, and the hole from his own universe was ejected from it. It – and he – was on its way home.

Mars

Sning advised him when he arrived at his own time. He set the sand on green and reached for the sun. His hand caught a sunspot, and the sun clicked and swung outward, showing the walls beyond. He stepped out and closed the door behind him.

Dursten, Excelsia, the Alicorn, and the Bemme were there, watching him. They looked the same, but their surroundings did not. The walls were props, painted and buttressed, and outside the immediate stage area the paraphernalia of the set were visible.

He beckoned the Bemme, and she slid forward for a private dialogue. 'I have penetrated the illusion,' he told her. 'Do the others know?'

'No.'

'Would it be kind to tell them my version of reality?'

'No.'

'May I visit any of you again, after this?'

'Since you live opposite to us in time, such opportunity is limited. We have to be briefed for each new act, because you return before we experience the last one. Soon we shall be beyond the time of your accession to office, and you will be able to visit us only discarnately.'

Norton found himself mildly shaken. Of course they could not have experienced his three visits in the same order he had! So they would proceed next to his Alicorn adventure, and finally to the space adventure, never telling him. Truly, he did not belong here! 'Then I will bid appropriate farewell now,' he decided. 'I thank you, Bemme, for your invaluable advice.'

'I only play my role according to the rules,' she said. 'You played and won when you had the wit to select me for advice and to fathom truth in the third chamber.'

'All the same, I would like to call you friend.'

'Friend,' she agreed. 'I do not have many of those among your kind. I understand you will do me a favour.'

'Favour?'

'In the third act. Saving me from destruction by the spaceman. My briefing suggests something of the sort.'

'Oh. Yes,' Norton agreed awkwardly, remembering how he had talked Dursten into adopting the orphan. But he also remembered the cause of the Bemme's orphaning and winced. It was all a play, yet . . . 'I wish I could take you away from this.'

'You do have that power, Chronos. But that would be pointless, for my service to you is finished from your perspective, and, if I departed this frame, who would take care of Dursten? When the occasion is appropriate, I will depart of my own accord.'

She made uncompromising sense. 'Good-bye, then, friend,' he said sadly, shaking her tentacle.

He turned to Dursten. 'Bat, I have found the way back to my planet of Earth. I thank you for risking your gallant life to help me, and wish you every success here.'

'Shux, 'twern't nothing,' the spaceman said, abashed in his handsome, rough-hewn, manly way. His eyes flicked towards the woman. 'You ain't coming back?'

In a sense he was, since his space scene was in Dursten's future. But that wasn't the essence. 'I'm not coming back,' Norton agreed. 'I'm trusting you to keep an eye on Excelsia.'

'Shore will!' Dursten said enthusiastically.

Norton turned to the Alicorn. 'Thank you for carrying me those two times,' he said. 'Without that help, I couldn't have made it through.'

The Alicorn snorted, swished his tail, and fluttered his wings, embarrassed. Then he nuzzled Norton's ear with his velvety-soft nose. *Trot well, good man!*

Now it was Excelsia's turn. Norton took her in his arms and kissed her. She was a bit like Heaven itself, though her destiny lay closer to Hell; but, as with Orlene and Agleh, he knew he could not continue with her.

The Damsel smiled through her tears as they separated. That was all; she understood.

Then he turned and walked along the wall until he came to the edge of the prop. He circled it and found himself in a motion-picture studio, with cameras, workmen, a director, and a general atmosphere of rushed chaos.

An attractive, mature woman approached him. 'You were a fine star, Chronos,' she said. 'I am only sorry the play did not reach its climactic scene.'

'The confrontation with – ?'

'The Eviler Sorceress,' she said. 'Yours Truly. I was to seduce you and strip you of your magic ring so you could not escape my clutches. I'm not sure the latter would have been successful, but the former would have been intriguing.'

Indeed it might have been, for she had a figure very like his Hourglass and was obviously an experienced star. 'Better luck with the next leading man,' he said.

'It's hardly luck,' she breathed. 'It's magic.'

He moved on past the personnel and props, finding the exit. When he left the building , he turned back to read the sign above it: SATANIC STUDIOS. Yes, that was what he had thought.

This was Hollywood, of course, where Satan could field excellent actors and facilities and be able to operate freely without interference. Probably there were some pretty good motion pictures released under the Satanic imprint, for he was certainly adept at invention. It had been quite an experience, and the Father of Lies' expertise was impressive, but now Norton had broken free of the deception and would be able to balk whatever plot the Prince of Evil had brewing.

He turned the sand of the Hourglass yellow and travelled spacially to his mansion in Purgatory. What a relief to be home!

346

But he couldn't rest yet; he had to find out what the Father of Lies was up to, which made the absence of Chronos so important. 'Summon Lachesis,' he told the butler. 'I'd like to talk to her at her earliest convenience.' He noted that the mansion clock showed him to be back at the time he had started the third antimatter adventure; the three-person limitation had prevented him from living those hours a third time and slid him smoothly past them.

'Immediately, sir,' the butler siad.

Indeed, a spider was swinging down along a thread when he entered the sitting room. She expanded and formed into Lachesis as Norton sat in his easy chair. 'Something special on your mind, Chronos?' she asked.

'I've been away a few hours,' he told her. 'I understand Satan is planning something, and I hurried back to balk his mischief. Do you know what it is?'

She glanced at him with evident perplexity. 'Why should Satan do anything to disturb the status quo?'

'Are you teasing me? He wants to win political power on Earth!'

'But he already has the inside track on that. All he needs to do is wait.'

'He *has* it? When did he get it?'

'Sometimes it is difficult for me to untangle my skein enough to isolate significant threads. But the key is political. In about two years there will be a crucial vote in Congress – and though it will be close, it seems Satan has the votes to prevail. From then on, things will go his way, and there is nothing we can do that won't simply make the situation worse. Satan knows that, which is why he isn't worried.'

'But what about Luna? *She* won't support him, and –'

'Who?'

'Luna. Senator Kaftan. Thanatos' woman.'

'Oh, her. I had forgotten her name. Yes, that woman does keep company with Thanatos, but she's no Senator. She runs a magic shop in Kilvarough.'

Norton stared at her. 'Not a Senator?'

'Never was. Never held any political office at all. Are you sure you have the right name?'

Norton realized that something was seriously amiss. 'I must have misremembered. I'm sorry I bothered you for nothing.'

She smiled and became Clotho, in a revealing gown. 'You don't need to use a pretext, Chronos. I understand your situation.'

Oops. 'This time it was an honest confusion. Let's postpone it for a few hours. I have an errand of business I must attend to first.'

'Business before pleasure,' she agreed. 'I have a backlog of my own, and no excuse now not to get to it.' She shifted back to arachnid form, ascended her thread, and vanished.

Luna not a Senator! Satan must have struck – but how could he have done this without the aid of Chronos?

He travelled to Kilvarough and knocked on Luna's door. The two griffins ignored him; it seemed he would be here often enough in his future, so they knew him.

Luna was home, and looked pretty much as he remembered her. 'Why, welcome, Chronos!' she exclaimed. 'Thanatos isn't here at the moment – '

'I don't want to intrude, but I must verify something – '

'By all means. Come in.'

Inside, he asked her point-blank: 'When did you leave political office?'

Her brow furrowed. 'I never held political office, Chronos. You know that.'

'You forget I live backwards, when not deliberately phasing in to your frame, as now.' He indicated the green sand. 'I do not know your past.'

She considered. 'Well, I did run for office eighteen years ago. But a tremendous campaign of vilification was waged against me, so that I lost, and I have never cared to repeat the experience. That was my closest approach to office.'

Eighteen years ago! 'Luna, I know this will sound strange to you, but not long ago I knew you as a Senator destined to balk Satan's major ploy for political power on Earth. Can you believe that?'

'Naturally,' she said. 'See, the Truthstones support you.' She gestured at small gems on the mantel, which were glowing pleasantly. 'But I assure you, this is not *my* reality.'

'Reality seems to have changed,' he said. 'Satan must have done it. If only I could figure out how!'

'Satan was surely behind the campaign against me,' she agreed. 'But that was so long ago, and he has ignored me since.'

'He must have sent another minion back in time to set things up. But *how*, without my cooperation?'

'You mean that if he had not done so, I might have won that election and commenced a political career?'

'I mean exactly that! You would today be a prominent Senator. And somehow I must restore that career to you, for the sake of humanity! But first I must figure out how he did it. Then I can act to cancel his ploy.'

Luna went to a cupboard and fetched another stone. 'Perhaps I can help. This is an evil-detector, very sensitive to the presence of the artifacts of Satan.' She brought it near him, and it flickered. 'There has been evil near you recently, or it will be near you soon, but it is not present now.'

'I was in Satan's environment in your near future – '

'No, this is a specific thing you carried with you, close to your body.' She moved the stone. It flickered more brightly near his folded Hourglass.

He opened out the Hourglass again so she could inspect it – and the stone flickered more brightly yet. 'There was a demon associated with this,' she said. 'Or will be. It seems to have hidden in the base for a while.'

The illusion of colour change – a demon had been there, doing it! Naturally Satan had not been able to follow him on his tour of eternity; Norton had to have carried a minion there. And he had never noticed! 'It – must have had a spell of invisibility,' he said, appalled. 'So that I took it whenever I went – and I went the full length of time itself!'

'That would seem to cover the situation,' she agreed. 'Satan's demons can be very small, like pinheads. There could have been a dozen or a hundred here – and some dropped off at a selected spot in prior time, while others remained to preserve the spell.'

'That must have been it,' he acknowledged ruefully. 'I finally abolished the spell in the farthest future – but I did travel backwards in time first. Satan tricked me again!'

'He is the master of guile,' she pointed out.

'So he managed to drop at least one demon off to give the demons of that time the word – they do cooperate with one another – and they destroyed your chance to get elected. I'll have to go back and intercept – '

'There could have been a dozen demons dropped off there,' she reminded him gently. 'If you have intercepted one of Satan's minions before and neutralized it, I'm sure he would be more careful on his next attempt. You could never intercept them all – not with the three-person limit. Some would get through.'

'You're probably right,' he said glumly. 'But I can't just let him win!'

'Perhaps Thanatos can advise you better than I can,' she suggested. 'Or one of the other Incarnations. Lachesis is wise in the ways of – '

'I've already talked to her. The other Incarnations have been affected by the new reality; only I am aware of the change.'

'And Satan,' she said. 'He surely knows the nature of his mischief.'

'Yes. He surely does, damn him!'

'Have you talked to Mars?'

'Mars, the Incarnation of War? No, I haven't met him.'

'It occurs to me we are at war – and war is what Mars best understands.'

Norton smiled grimly. 'Good point, Luna. I will seek him out. Only – ' He hesitated. 'I don't know how.'

She smiled. 'Here is a stone attuned to him. It will glow as you approach, and fade as you move away from him. Take it and use it, Chronos.'

He accepted the stone. 'You are a very helpful woman, Luna.'

Again she smiled, and the moonstone she wore at her neck glowed. 'So Thanatos informs me.' She was about Norton's own age or a little older, beyond the joy of youth, but her features were finely structured and she was a handsome person with excellent poise. She credited her magic stones with providing her an understanding of his situation, an understanding no other person in this reality would have had, but it was more than that. She was a woman of special qualities, experience, and tact. The sort of woman that he, Norton, would have liked to build a relationship with – that perhaps Orlene would have become at this age. The sort that he, Norton, could never have a continuing relationship with.

Once again he felt the burden of his office. How little he had understood the subtle sacrifice of Incarnation! But he could not afford self-pity at the moment; he had a job to do. 'Thank you, Luna; I hope Mars can help.'

He walked in a circle, watching the stone. When he had determined the direction of brightest glow, he turned the sand yellow. 'Farewell!'

She waved, and he was off. He zoomed across the face of the Earth, through buildings and mountains as if they were illusions, becoming more skilled in spacial motion, zeroing in on the Incarnation of War.

He found Mars on a battlefield in mountainous terrain somewhere on the Eurasian continent. Norton hadn't kept track of the landmarks, and the location really didn't matter; he just wanted to talk to the Incarnation.

Tanks were charging a mountain retreat that seemed to be guarded by Oriental dragons. Science against magic – and the two were surprisingly similar. The dragons spurted fire – but so did the flame-throwers of the tanks. There were aeroplanes, too – but flying dragons were meeting them. The sides seemed even.

Mars was perched on a ledge, watching with detached interest. He was a small man, dressed in faded fatigues. Norton was surprised; he had somehow anticipated a robust giant in Roman-style armour.

Norton phased in beside Mars. 'If you have a moment – '

The man looked around. 'Oh, hello, Chronos. I always have a moment for you, you know that. What's up?'

'Um, from my view, this is our first meeting.'

'Oh, sure, you live backwards. I didn't realize this was your beginning.' He put out his right hand, and Norton took it. 'I'm Mars, Incarnation of War. You're Chronos, Incarnation of Time. We have a long and benevolent association, with mutual respect, ever since you helped this stutterer get started.'

Stutterer? Mars wasn't stuttering now! 'I – '

'I don't suppose you want to hear my rationale for war as a necessary cauterization of society and stimulus to progress, so I'll spare you that this time. If you're ill at ease, don't be; we're old friends.'

'That's nice to know,' Norton said awkwardly. 'I really haven't got the whole hang of living backwards yet, though at least the other Incarnations seem to understand.'

'Yeah, I guess it's hell on romance; when you're coming, she's going.'

Aptly if unkindly put! 'I think I need your advice, if you have the time.'

Mars squinted at the tanks and dragons. '*You* have the time, no pun; you can freeze the world and leave just the two of us to talk. But this is a minor and inconclusive operation. Pointless, really – but where there's battle, I have to supervise. You know how it is. Spill the beans.'

'Uh, yes.' And Norton, somewhat haltingly, explained the

situation. 'So Luna thought you might have a better insight, since this is a war with Satan,' he concluded.

Mars nodded. 'I have fought Satan myself, and I fear his deviousness prevailed. I am well aware how formidable an opponent he is. I can't tell you how to reverse what he has done, for this is not my MOS, but – '

'MOS?'

'Military-Occupation-Speciality. But I can suggest broad principles of battle strategy that may apply.'

Norton had hoped for something more specific, but took this in stride. 'Maybe that will help.'

'First you have to analyse the patterns of strength – yours and the enemy's. That way you can arrange to attack his weak flank with your strongest force. Force is vitally important and must be understood in detail.'

'Force,' Norton agreed without much enthusiasm.

'Force,' Mars repeated emphatically. He gestured towards the indecisive battle. 'See how those fools are opposing force with similar force? They're slaughtering each other and destroying equipment and animals pointlessly. If either side had approached the issue with proper professionalism – ' He shook his head sadly. 'I hate to see things bungled by amateurs. War is too important for bungling! Now you – you are up against a real professional, the ultimate Master of Deceit, who has already won the battle. It is your task to reverse the outcome after the fact – and that is a considerable challenge.'

'Amen!' Norton agreed.

'But you are by no means powerless. You must use what you have – and you have the single most potent tool that exists.'

'But – '

'You doubt? Watch.' Suddenly a monstrous sword was in Mars' hand. He swung it at Norton. Norton, without thinking, blocked it with the Hourglass.

The blade rebounded. Undismayed, Mars put it away. 'To

others, your instrument is without substance, but my Sword represents the essence of war and cannot be blunted or avoided. Therefore the two instruments meet and balk each other; neither can hurt the other. Force against force, pointlessly. But, properly applied, my Sword is matchless – as is your Hourglass. Not even Satan can stand against these tools, or against the Scythe of Thanatos or the Threads of Fate or the Will of Gaea – if they attack his weaknesses. Only by guile did he nullify my effort to balk his plot to assume political power on Earth, and only by guile did he foil you.'

'True. But – '

'You talk too much, Chronos,' Mars said with a smile. He produced a clipboard and pen and began marking the sheet of paper. 'Now, we know there are only five intrinsic forces in our reality. Let's list them in nominal order of strength.' He printed: NUCLEAR STRONG, ELECTROMAGNETIC, NUCLEAR WEAK, GRAVITY, MAGIC. 'If you set the first at unity for convenience, or 10^0, the others are 10^{-3}, 10^{-5}, 10^{-38}, and 10^{-41}.'

'Now, wait!' Norton protested. 'The whole universe is dominated by gravity; it is the single most compelling factor in the evolution of matter! How can it be rated so weak in comparison with the others? And magic – '

Mars smiled, as if a feint had been effective. 'That does seem odd, doesn't it! But sometimes the last shall be first, and the meek do inherit the Earth. Range is the key. The strong nuclear force has a range of about the diameter of a neutron. If another neutron were just one millimetre distant, it would never feel that force, any more than your Hourglass would feel the impact of my Sword if it were just out of range of my swing. That force binds our most basic substance together, and is indeed essential to the integrity of matter, but on our macroscopic scale we don't even feel it. The weak nuclear force is even more limited, having a range only one-hundredth as far. Yet the disruption of these forces leads to nuclear explosions or lethal radiation. They are potent in their proper applications. Electromagnetic force falls in between the strong and the weak nuclear forces in power – but its range is infinite, so we can experience it on our scale. Indeed, we use it for our vision, radio, electricity, magnetism – our civilization would collapse without it.'

He gestured towards the ongoing battle. 'The motors of those tanks utilize magnetism for their power, for example. But it has one critical limitation: it acts *as a force* only on charged particles. The most potent magnetic field has no direct effect on wood or human flesh. So magnetism is limited though infinite. Gravity, in contrast, not only has infinite range, it is accumulative and acts on all matter. So, despite its low rating – and 10^{-38} is almost unimaginably small – on the scale of the universe it becomes the overwhelming force, as you pointed out. The last has become first, because of its nature. Of course the ratings are distorted; if the significance of range was factored in, gravity would be the strongest, if most diffuse, force.'

'Yes, I have seen it in action,' Norton replied, thinking of the black holes and the way they governed the universes. What was a black hole but a gravity sink? 'So its effective force – '

'Effective force,' Mars repeated. 'There is another key concept. Think of a tiger and a million ants. The tiger has much more force than any ant, or any hundred or thousand ants. But the tiny force of the ants is accumulative and cooperative; together they swarm over the tiger and destroy him, as gravity swarms over the universe. *Effective* force – you must retain that concept, for it certainly counts most in battle.'

'Um, yes, I suppose.' Norton was not entirely satisfied with this argument, since it seemed that his Hourglass was the tiger and the minions of Satan were the million ants. 'But then magic – '

'A thousand times as feeble as gravity! So weak that for a time scientists doubted its existence!' Mars chuckled, as if it were a great joke. 'Can you imagine that? Not believing in magic, simply because you can't detect it in a single molecule? It's pretty hard to detect gravity in a single molecule, too, but they never doubted gravity! The magic in the molecule is overwhelmed by the gravity there; that doesn't mean the magic doesn't exist. But magic has a range of about 10^7 metres, or about the diameter of Earth. So we can experience it quite conveniently on our scale, without noting any effect on the larger universe. It's like the strong nuclear force, acting only on the neutron touching it; but since all of us are touching Earth, we're in its range. It is true it is weak in absolute terms, but not only is it accumulative, it is focusable, so that the magic inherent in a cubic kilometre of the planet can be brought to bear in concentrated form at a microscopically small point. Think of it as sunlight being focused by a magnifying glass, able to burn holes in solid wood. Thus its malleability causes magic to become, when properly applied, a force more potent than even the strongest of the other forces. The right magic, concentrated 10^{42} times, can separate the nucleus of an atom nonexplosively, which accounts for the transmutation of lead into gold; or it can interfere with the internal workings of a small black hole.' Mars paused to waggle his finger in mock warning. 'Now don't you try it with a *large* black hole! Anywhere the magicons can reach – '

'Don't you mean "magicians"?' Norton asked.

'I do not. The strong nuclear force is carried by gluons, the weak by intermediate vector bosons of several varieties, the electromagnetic by photons, gravity by gravitons, and magic by magicons. Of course, all these basic forces are united by the Reunified Field Theorem – '

'You're getting too technical for me,' Norton protested. 'I never did understand nuclear physics very well.'

'Certainly. My business is force, so I understand forces; your business is time, so you understand aspects of time that would baffle me. It is enough for you to accept that, for you, time *is* force. Your Hourglass focuses magic more potently

356

than does any other instrument. The Hourglass has the power to balk Satan – if you use it properly.'

'That's good to know! But how should I use it?'

Mars spread his hands. 'That I cannot tell you, for time is not my speciality. I can only assure you that the potential is there. My force analysis makes this quite clear.' He showed Norton the paper, now filled out with a neat chart of the five intrinsic forces with their strengths, ranges, and carrier particles. 'Take this with you; maybe it will help your strategy of battle.'

'Uh, thank you,' Norton said, uncertain about that.

'Remember, Chronos: fight, never give in, and you shall win. You have the instrument Satan cannot overcome. He is Goliath; you are David.'

'I'll try,' Norton agreed weakly and moved out. If he had to bet on a return match, he would bet on Goliath.

He went back to his mansion in Purgatory, deeply troubled. Mars had expressed confidence in him – but was it justified? It hardly mattered how powerful the Hourglass was or how vulnerable Satan might be – if he did not know how to apply his force to Satan's weakness, what good was it?

When he entered, the butler informed him that he had a caller. No rest for the weary! It was Satan, the last entity he wanted to see at the moment. 'Get out, Beelzebub!' he snapped.

'Now, don't be that way, my dear associate,' Satan said graciously. 'I have glimpsed an alternate reality in which we had a very stimulating encounter. Now it is over, and there need be no hard feelings. I am really not a bad fellow, when you give Me a chance. For example, there is lagniappe for you.' He gestured to the television set, and it came on, showing a woman with a healthy baby.

Norton stared. The woman was Orlene! Alive and well!

'In this reality, she survives,' Satan said. 'Gaea was more alert and refused to do the favour for the foolish ghost. Her baby is not flawed, favours you, and will live to inherit the estate. You may readily verify this for yourself. Go to her, Chronos; she loves you.'

With that, Satan opened his suit jacket, revealing emptiness inside. The emptiness expanded as he drew the lapels back around him, until only his two hands holding the lapel remained; then they, too, disappeared, and he was gone.

Orlene! After Norton had given her up for lost – to have her back! To have joy return to his life!

Then he wondered whether it was right. It was true that he loved her, she loved him, and their baby had a fine future awaiting him. But Satan was actually proffering a bribe – settle for this reality and have this reward. At what cost? If he went along with it, he would be acquiescing in Satan's victory on Earth. In fact, because he, Chronos, had unwittingly enabled Satan to bring about this reality, he had become one of the agents of the Prince of Evil.

He watched Orlene's image on the screen as she cooed to her baby. How he wanted her and wanted her to be alive and happy! But could he accept these things – as payment for facilitating evil?

He stood, and slowly his vision blurred; an intangible yet terrible weight settled upon him. 'Forgive me, Orlene,' he whispered. 'I cannot.'

The television snapped off. She was gone, in every sense. Norton stared at the blank screen, feeling a wash of grief for what might have been. He had thought he was over Orlene; now he knew he would never be over her. Yet he had denied her. He would have to live out his life with the knowledge that he could have saved her – and had not. He had condemned her back to agony and death. What price, conscience?

That was assuming he found a way to reverse what Satan had done. Did he really want to do that now? Knowing what was right was not the same as completely desiring it. But even if he found no way, and this present reality stood, he would always know that he had in the end rejected the

358

woman he loved. She had not, in the final analysis, been the most important thing in his life. He had chosen principle instead.

Principle tasted like ashes.

Satan had found a fiendish way to torture him, by showing him Orlene! Satan certainly knew how to exploit a person's weakness.

Then he had another thought – why had Satan bothered? Surely the Prince of Evil had worse things to do than torment a defeated foe. Satan had a world to organize, preparing for his final victory on Earth just a few years hence. It did not make sense for him to trouble himself with trifles.

Unless he was not teasing Norton. Suppose the bribe was real – that it had definite justification, by Satan's logic? That it was necessary to change the outcome of a battle that was not yet quite over? This suggested that Chronos could indeed reverse what Satan had done, and Satan knew it. So Satan was trying to sap Norton's will to fight.

Mars had told him to keep fighting and never give up. Mars had believed Chronos could win, because of the supreme potency of the magical force he controlled. Was Mars a fool? Surely not about battle!

Norton brought out the chart Mars had made. There was magic, the weakest of the intrinsic forces, yet the strongest when properly utilized. Here was the Hourglass, capable of utilizing magic most properly. Satan was Goliath, seemingly all-powerful; Norton was David, with only one weapon. But it was the one weapon that could do the job.

It seemed that Goliath knew of his own vulnerability, so he had tried to bribe David not to use his weapon. 'Here, David, you're a plucky lad – let me give you this beautiful woman Delilah for that little sling of yours.' No, Delilah was from another legend, and Orlene was no temptress. Still, it fitted. Satan wanted him to quit. Therefore he should fight on. His enemy had confirmed his power.

Now another thing occurred to him. He could not have

Orlene anyway, for the same reasons as before; he lived backwards and, if he reversed himself to join her, he would soon come up against the date of his acquisition of the office of Chronos and have to leave her. So Satan's offer was largely illusion, anyway.

Norton was glad he had made his decision of conscience before realizing that. It made him feel a little better about himself.

Of course, it would be better to have Orlene and the baby alive than tragically dead. Or would it? What kind of life would they have in a world dominated by Satan? The Prince of Evil had been proceeding carefully, not interfering unduly in the affairs of the world until he could consolidate his power. Evil had infinite patience! But once the critical nexus passed and he was victorious, what then? Surely he would change everything to suit himself, and it would be literally Hell on Earth. Orlene would suffer that, and her baby, and everyone else. Evil would triumph everywhere, making all decent people miserable. No, Satan had offered no bargain at all!

If only it could be possible for every person in the world to see the future Satan offered – to remember his future as he remembered his past, and to appreciate how that future declined as Evil gained. That would shake things up and make Satan's victory impossible. But that could not be done.

Or could it?

Norton brought out the Hourglass and contemplated its flowing white sand. *He* lived backwards; the future was familiar to him, as far as it went. But the Hourglass could also affect others when he willed it to. It could transport others in time, or even cause the whole world to live backwards for a few hours. Truly, it was the most potent of all magic instruments, as Mars had said. But could it make ordinary people see a future they had not yet experienced?

Squeeze.

'Sning!' he exclaimed. 'I forgot you! How I need your

360

advice now!' He realized that, though he had called others friends and loved a woman, Sning had been his truest companion throughout, the one who was best able to share his experience.

Squeeze.

'You say the Hourglass can make others see the future?'

Squeeze, squeeze, squeeze.

Um. He had to narrow down the circumstances. 'It can, but it's limited? Such as to – to the time I assumed the office, since I have no worldly power beyond then?'

Squeeze.

But that was only a few days. Not much good. He needed a decade or so. In fact, he needed eighteen years – the time since Satan had foiled Luna's entry into political office.

Squeeze.

'We can do it – for eighteen years?' he asked excitedly.

Squeeze.

'I can go back to that time – just before she loses the election – and show the world what it is heading for?'

Squeeze.

But now he saw a serious flaw. The world had not become a horror in those eighteen years. The horror would not occur until Satan could assume power openly – and that was after (before) Norton's assumption of office. He could not show the world that, and certainly Satan would not make his mischief known before then. The Father of Lies wanted complete order and peace until he was ready, just as a hunter wanted no disruption until the wild animal he stalked came within his sights. All Norton could show people was a fairly normal progression.

Squeeze.

'But that won't work! Because there's no horror.'

Squeeze, squeeze.

'It *will* work?'

Squeeze.

'You're sure?'

Squeeze.

'Okay, Sning. Your information has always been good before. How do I do it? Do I turn the sand a new colour?'

Squeeze.

'Which colour? Purple? Gold? Plaid? Orange? Grey? Violet? Brown?'

Sning had not squeezed at any of the colours, but after brown he squeezed three times. Norton scratched his head. 'None of those, but brown does have its points?'

Squeeze.

'But I've really guessed all the basic colours and several shades. You act as if no colour or combination – '

Squeeze.

'No colour? But you said – '

Squeeze.

'Ah – no colour! Transparent. Clear.'

Squeeze.

'Representing the future, not for living but for seeing. Or remembering, the way I do. The veil of opacity made permeable.'

Squeeze.

'Well, let's try it!' he said, excited.

He turned the sand to yellow and travelled in space to the spot on Earth where Sning indicated Luna would be found after the election. This was in the city of Kilvarough, at her estate.

'Her estate?' he asked, surprised.

Squeeze.

'Um, let me do one thing, then, before I get on it.' He turned the sand green and knocked on her door.

She answered immediately. Naturally she wasn't away from home much, since she had no office to attend to. In the other reality she had been Senator, but had arranged to be home to meet him; Lachesis had surely facilitated that. Behind her, this time, stood Thanatos – and Mars, Atropos, and Gaea.

362

'My stones informed me you were going to try,' she said. 'We wish you success.'

He had thought he was about to inform her; obviously there had been no need. 'You understand – if I succeed – you will no longer exist as you do now. You won't even remember this life. None of you will.'

'We understand, Chronos,' Luna said. 'Your power in this respect is greater than any other.' She took his hand, drew him forward, and kissed him on the cheek. She was not young, but she was a lovely woman.

Norton brought out the Hourglass. 'Well, farewell, all,' he said awkwardly.

They merely waited expectantly. He was touched by their acceptance of this significant change that could abolish their past eighteen years of experience. Surely it was not easy!

He turned the sand blue and willed himself into the past.

Sning gave a warning squeeze as he neared the date and another as he came to the hour. Finally he settled on the minute and stopped, turning the sand green.

Luna stood there, Thanatos beside her. She was wiping her face, evidently repairing the damage wrought by tears. She was eighteen years younger than he had seen her a moment ago, about half her prior age, or at any rate in her early twenties, and stunningly beautiful despite her misery. Her dull brown hair was now bright chestnut, shoulder-length and luxurious, and her eyes were like windows on Heaven. She was breathtakingly slender and well formed, in a green gown reminiscent of her namesake, the luna moth, and her bright moonstone shone at her bosom. A jewel she wore – and a jewel she was, surely! She looked up, startled, as Norton manifested.

'Chronos! Certainly you don't wish to share this unfortunate moment!'

'Not exactly,' Norton said.

'She is about to go out to make her concession speech,' Thanatos said.

'I – I would like to address the world first,' Norton said, conscious of how preposterous this sounded.

'You?' Surprise did not register well on the Deathhead. 'This is not your concern, Chronos!'

'I'm afraid it *is* my concern,' Norton said. 'I was inadvertently responsible for Luna's loss. Now I must try to undo the damage.'

Thanatos shook his head. 'Her reputation has been sullied beyond repair. The minions of Satan have used innuendo, outright lies – even ballot-box stuffing. Satan's work – but the people were fooled, and now it's over.'

'I beg your indulgence,' Norton said. 'Let me try to undo what I can. If I fail, she can still concede.'

Luna put her hand on Thanatos' shoulder. 'See the Truthstones,' she murmured.

Indeed, the stones on the mantel were shining like little stars. 'I yield,' Thanatos said.

They went outside to the front gate, beyond the range of the griffins. Television cameras and a magic mirror were set up there. The world was watching – or at least that minor portion of it that cared to tune in on this particular concession speech. Most people were probably more interested in Luna's beauty than in her politics, anyway.

Luna stepped up to the focus on the media. In this year, mechanical microphones were still in use for sound pickup. 'Before I speak, my friend Chronos will address you,' she said.

'Hey, what's this?' a man protested, pushing forward. His eyes blazed with the inner fire of the possessed – an agent of Satan. 'We came to hear the harlot drop out!'

Thanatos started forward in cold fury. But Norton moved first. He shoved the Hourglass in the possessed's face. The man fell back, stunned.

'The minions of Satan have wronged this fine woman,' Norton said. 'Now I will show you your future if this wrong stands.'

364

He turned the sand transparent and willed it into action, to embrace the whole world. He felt the immense power channelling through the Hourglass, the weakest force becoming the strongest. Nothing changed, physically; this was magic of the mind only.

There was a hush as the effect took hold. Then a cameraman lurched away, dropping his camera. 'I'm gonna die!' he screamed. 'Next year, covering a hostage crisis, bomb goes off – I *remember!* I'm getting out of here!'

A female reporter turned and slapped a news director. 'You're going to throw me over for that hussy!' she cried indignantly. 'Well, you can just forget about tonight, you sneak!'

The director could not deny it, for he remembered, too. Indeed, he seemed preoccupied, seeing farther into his own future. 'AIDS?' he said, bewildered and horrified. 'Me? But I'm not part of that culture!'

'Evidently the hussy is,' the driver next to him said. 'That stuff's spreading fast, now that it's out of the special groups. My uncle's gonna get it, too, and die – ' He broke off, horrified as he realized what he was saying.

'Leukemia?' a bystander asked, chagrined. 'How can I remember having that, when it's five years in the future? I'm going to do some research and change that before it happens!'

In moments the street was empty, as every person attending the concession speech sought to avoid the horrors of his own future. Each person in the world was going to suffer tragedy and death sooner or later – and no person enjoyed the prospect. Everyone was trying to change his life to avoid the mischief he foresaw – and, of course, that changed his future and that of those he interacted with and gave him new visions of the inevitable. Humanity was in chaos.

Satan himself arrived. Most of his minions could not take solid form on Earth, but he himself was an Incarnation, as real as the others. 'Give over, Chronos!' he cried, fire showing inside his mouth in lieu of a tongue. 'I sought no quarrel with you!'

'Not this year,' Norton said. The sand remained clear. 'But in a future year – '

'You are generating utter chaos!' the Prince of Evil protested, smoke rising from him.

Norton glanced up and down the street. 'Am I?'

'It's impossible for anyone to function in this!'

'Even you, Satan?' Norton inquired pleasantly. He was coming to understand the impact of his action. Satan's ultimate evil did not need to be manifest within eighteen years; the ordinary lives, loves, and deaths of people sufficed. The sudden knowledge of the specific circumstance and time of his own misfortune or death drove the average person into a frenzy like that of a drowning man. The veil that shrouded the future was in fact a blessing, and now it had been rent.

'I am a Creature of order!' Satan said. 'I have plans – '

Norton merely looked at him inquiringly.

'I can't accomplish anything if they remember – '

Norton waited.

'What do you want, Chronos?' the Prince of Evil demanded.

'Need you ask, sirrah?'

Satan stomped about, his horns turning red with frustration and emitting sparks. 'All right, Chronos! The bitch shall have her office!'

'The who?'

The sparks became larger, and a small zap of lightning flashed between Satan's horns. 'The good woman!'

Norton allowed the sand to return to its underlying green. Sometime he would have to explore the mechanism that enabled him to remain in the green while the sand turned clear, but there was no hurry; obviously there were sophistications of the Hourglass that would require careful study for full comprehension, but which protected him in his ignorance. 'I trust you to honour your word, my dear associate,' he said.

'Your trust is misplaced, fool!' Satan said, gesturing.

Abruptly the two of them were in Hell. Opaque smoke surrounded them, obscuring the details, but there was no question about the location. 'Now try your little trick,' Satan said grimly. 'I'm sure My demons will enjoy seeing their futures.'

Norton lifted the Hourglass – but now the sand was fogged out by smoke, and he could not see the colour. It wasn't illusion; it was genuine smoke; he couldn't abolish it by concentrating.

Satan couldn't hold him, of course. The Prince of Evil was merely setting up another diversion, trying to salvage his campaign to win power on Earth. The three-person limit would prevent Norton from returning here; he had to accomplish his mission now.

Norton had had enough of this. He owed Satan. *Sning,* he thought. *Can you help me fix him once and for all?*

Squeeze.

What colour? Transparent?

Squeeze, squeeze.

'Did you really think you could oppose me, Chronos?' Satan asked, sneering. Sulphurous smoke was curling up from his nose.

Black?

Squeeze, squeeze.

Desperately he tried the colour they hadn't used before. *Brown?*

'Enough of this,' Satan said. His arm shot forward, his hand landing on Norton's. There was a jolt of current – and Sning was in Satan's grasp. 'This rogue demon is Mine!'

Norton felt as if he had been skewered. He had lost his most vital adviser! Satan could not touch the Hourglass, but Sning had no such protection.

Norton willed the sand brown, the colour of Luna's hair, knowing the Hourglass would respond, though the smoke obscured it.

Satan paused, surprised. The smoke was curling down to his nose.

Norton was similarly surprised. What had he done?

Satan turned about abruptly. Flame shot into his mouth, and sparks zapped from the air to his horns. He lashed his tail. '?lleh eht tahW' he demanded.

He was living backwards! But no one else was; the demons of Hell showed through the smoke now, glancing at their Master with curiosity. The brown sand reversed time for Satan alone.

The Father of Lies would break out of this predicament soon enough. That was not the point. Norton had shown Satan that Chronos could make him just as uncomfortable as he could make Chronos.

Norton reached for Satan's hand to take Sning back. Satan tried to snatch the ring away, but his reversed reflex caused him to shove it directly at Norton instead. Norton took the snake and returned the ring to his finger.

Sque-he-he-heze! Sning seemed to be laughing.

Norton walked away – and Satan's illusion dissolved around him. He was still on the street, and Thanatos and Luna were waiting. 'We saw the smoke, but decided to let you deal with Satan in your own way,' Thanatos explained. 'Every Incarnation must come to his own terms with Satan.'

'True,' Norton agreed. He turned to face Satan, who was now on the street but still locked in reverse. 'I trust you will behave now, Lord of Flies. I wouldn't want to have to invoke my power again. Or is my trust misplaced?'

Satan became so hot he suffered a phenomenal implosion of flame and winked out like a reversed nova.

Norton experienced a great relief and satisfaction. He had at last faced Satan directly and held him off! Mars' advice to him had been right; all he had needed to do was keep fighting.

He turned to Luna. 'Notice of the recount should be broadcast soon, and your reputation will be restored. You have begun your political career.'

'Thank you, Chronos,' she said faintly.

Thanatos stepped forward, extending his skeletal hand. 'I knew you had power, Chronos; I never suspected its extent.'

'Neither did I,' Norton said, accepting the hand. He knew this was not the occasion to discuss his first encounter with Thanatos, eighteen years hence. 'Farewell, both.'

He turned the sand red and returned to his present. He landed on the street outside Luna's estate.

Satan reappeared, horns red-hot. 'How dare you – '

Norton lifted the Hourglass and turned the sand brown. Satan vanished.

He steadied the sand on green and turned to the front gate. All the Incarnations were there, and Luna herself. 'My stones told me to appear for this meeting, though I have pressing political business,' she said. 'Now I remember: I owe not only my life but my office to you. You helped me win my first election as a representative, and later my election as Senator. I am deeply in your debt.'

'And I in yours,' Norton said. 'Just do what you have to do when your crisis looms. We all must strive constantly to keep Satan at bay.'

'Yes, of course,' Thanatos agreed. 'But I wish we could reward you for your special effort – '

'There is no need,' Norton said, thinking of the bleakness he now had to return to, living his life opposite to them and the world, not even speaking of this matter as he moved into their past, lest that somehow change the course.

'*I* will attend to his reward,' Atropos declared, shifting to Clotho. 'Keep the sand green, Chronos, until we reach your mansion, so I won't forget.'

Norton looked at her. She had evidently prepared for this occasion, for she was ravishing. And she understood! He realized that there were, after all, compensations to his lonely office.

Author's Note

This is the second novel in a five-novel series. In the long Author's Note following the first novel, *On a Pale Horse*, I explained how, since the protagonist was Death, death and illness seemed to strike all around me while I was working on that novel, so that part of it was actually written in the hospital. You probably think I'm going to tell a similar story this time.

Correct. Except that, since this novel features Time, it was time that bedevilled me this time. I hesitate to conjecture what will bedevil me when I work on the next novel, *With a Tangled Skein*, in which Fate is the protagonist. But I expect it to be interesting, for Fate is a most intriguing and devious female. Stay tuned for the next Note . . .

I am a slow reader and a slow worker, and I do three drafts of each novel. Since I turn in about a third of a million words of fiction per year, that means about a million words of work per year, though only the first three hundred thousand are really challenging; the rest is mainly refining and polishing, in an effort to make this oft hellishly complex business of writing seem like the simple, relaxed flowing of prose. What I say in the finished draft is much the same as what I said in the first draft, but it comes across more eloquently. Polishing: a useful lesson for the hopeful writer. You say your tormented prose doesn't read as well as mine? Neither does mine, at first!

I get about six and a half decent working hours a day, after chores, meals, exercises, mail, and the sundry minutiae of mundane existence. That means I need to run a fairly tight ship and make my working time count – and I do. Other writers will tell you that it is difficult to know when a writer is working, for he may be reading a book or lying on a couch or staring glassy-eyed at a blank sheet of paper. No so with me; I confine my reading to off hours unless it is direct research, in which case I'm probably making notes on it. I have a couch in my study that I never lie on, and when I'm at my typewriter I'm typing without pause. I don't suffer from that dreadest of maladies, Writer's Block; as with stage fright, I realized early that I couldn't afford it, so I conquered it. I seem to be almost unique among the more creative writers in that respect. I understand some block up for a few hours at a time, and others for a few years or decades at a time. I view such writers as pseudo-professionals who are not really interested in working. If I am balked for a few minutes at a time, there is something wrong. So when I work, I *work*, and every hour counts. In that way I compensate for my slowness. I see myself, figuratively, as a locomotive, starting slow but proceeding along my limited track with heavy-duty reliability.

My time is precious. I work efficiently, no matter how far my imagination ranges. I write the first draft in pencil at about five hundred words per hour, though this is highly variable, depending on the nature of the material and the facility of my inspiration; this is the one time I might be observed doing something like staring at a blank page for a few seconds as the gears in my brain squeal and grind. A lost hour of time is a lost hour of work, and it hurts; my schedule is behind by that amount. I catch up by taking pencil and clipboard wherever I go so I can squeeze out a few more hundred words of text and thought. When I'm typing second or submission drafts on one novel, I'll start the pencil draft of the next, as I can't take my office machine around with me.

I'm not a fast typist, either, though I use the world's most efficient keyboard, the Dvorak Simplified, further modified for my needs; I may be the only writer with the sense to put the often-used quotation marks on the lower-case shift for added convenience. I am slow because my brain is always in gear, analysing, changing things, catching the sense of the material. Therefore I buzz along at about a thousand words an hour, every hour. I try to avoid typing in the chill of winter in my unheated study, so I'll concentrate on two first drafts then, and type both when the study warms. In the winter of 1982–83, I wrote the science fiction novel *Mercenary* and most of the fantasy *Hourglass*.

Most of? What happened – Writer's Block? Of course not! I ran out of time. Let me explain.

My correspondence has been picking up. This year I have been answering about fifty letters per month. Many can be handled by cards, but some require pages. 'Dear Mr Anthony: I love your Xanth books. When is the next coming out, and what is it about? Please send me your picture, a list of all your novels, your philosophy of life, and detailed advice on how to become a professional writer, and tell me how much money you make. PS, I am twelve years old.' That sort of thing. I answer seriously, but it is a challenge to keep up, and it cuts into my fiction-writing time. Twenty-five hours a month, just to answer my mail! My novels have been falling behind schedule. Time – I don't have enough of it.

Why not just stop answering fan letters? I understand many authors ignore their fan mail. I'm sure that simplifies their lives. I just can't do that. I feel that a serious letter – and when a twelve-year-old writes, it is quite serious to him – deserves a serious answer. There may be writers who don't really care about the quality of their fiction or of their personal relations; I *do* care. I do the best I can in whatever I am doing, whether it is a funny scene or a physical exercise or an answer to a fan. I admit to wondering sometimes why I bother, such as when I explain gently why I cannot undertake to become a regular correspondent and get a hurt, sarcastic, or abusive response. But such events are rare and outweighed by the letters of genuine appreciation and understanding, sometimes from the parents of children I have written to. I am trying to do my little bit of good in the world (that will do for part of my philosophy of life), and I have found that the letters I send are far more important to my fans that theirs are to me. No, I don't mean that to sound callous; it's just that I do receive hundreds of often-similar missives, while the fans on the other end may never have a more personal interaction with a writer they like. There is a current of desperation that runs through much of the mail I receive; that small personal touch my reply represents is vital. Some fans are lonely and some are ill; they write to me because they enjoy my fiction and perceive in me a person who cares, and in this they are not mistaken. But the time it takes, the time it takes! I am forced to perform triage on my mail: this letter must be answered promptly, though my paying work suffers; this one can wait; this other one does not have to be answered. At what point does my need to earn a living override the hurt feelings of a fan? If my mail continues to increase. I will not be able to answer even the first letter from some fans; this may have happened by the time this novel sees print. That will hurt; the cold equations always do. Sometimes I feel like the national budget: always a deficit. A deficit of time.

Then there are the extraordinary events that consume whole chunks of time. I don't mean they are amazing or unbelievable, just out of the ordinary. I address a class here, go to an autographing session there, submit to an interview, or participate in a convention elsewhere. I turn down the great majority of invitations; even so, there is something almost every month.

There are family events My daughters like to get me involved in their activities, and if there is one thing I place ahead of my writing, it is my family. Penny is learning how to drive now, and it would not be expedient to have my wife teach her; my wife can't even stand to have *me* drive when she's in the car. So Penny learns with me, much as she learned to ride the bicycle years ago, and I trust it is no serious affront to her if I remark on how nervous I can get when my fifteen-year-old daughter is at the wheel, demonstrating that *she's* not afraid of cornering at high velocity, that it is still possible to stall the motor four times when turning the car around, and managing to scrape the chassis against the road on a bump. Sometimes I think small trees quail when they see us coming, and quail are treed. But mainly it takes time, for I will not turn my child loose on the highway until I am reasonably certain she will survive the experience. A car is a powerful machine, a potential killer; she must learn the same respect for it that I have. I took my eyes off the road once, over a quarter century ago; next thing I knew, the car was in mid-air, and my only thought was whether I would ever regain consciousness after it struck the ground. As it happened, I survived the rollover with no more than a bruised shoulder, but I remain highly conscious of the hazards of carelessness.

There is land. My career as a writer has become increasingly profitable, but I have never been foolish with money. I seek to invest any surplus in something that is inflation-proof, and that is land. We can graze horses on land, and burn the deadwood from it in our stove, and grow new trees on it; and if a daughter should choose later in life to settle here, we have the land. We are buying all the acreage around us that we can and, while *Hourglass* was in progress, we bought the five-acre lot to our west and are now fencing it for pasture. The local railroad track on our east was taken up and the R.R. right of way put up for sale, so we started negotations for the purchase of some of that. They wanted an inordinate price. We pointed out that not only is this particular stretch inaccessible to anyone but us, the adjacent property owners; it is through the hill with such steep slopes that no vehicle can cross and no developer would build on it. Eventually we agreed on about half the original asking price. So that useless strip is on the way to becoming ours, and we expect to grow trees there and make it a refuge for local wildlife. But all this, however worthwhile, consumes – you guessed it! – time.

One trifling detail I may have neglected to mention about that useless gash on our east: it has a fictive identity, because I used it, in somewhat exaggerated form, in a series of novels. It is called the Gap Chasm of Xanth.

I'm not much for entertainment these days, because for me, writing is entertainment. But I do try to participate in things with my family. We're likely to watch television together; my daughters have learned to call my attention to the screen when a starlet in bursting bikini prances by. We'll go as a family to a movie; we went to *Tootsie*. Sometimes we can't all go, but we do what we can. I took my twelve-year-old daughter, Cheryl, to the Science Fiction Research Association annual meeting in Kansas, where she and I met the likes of Theodore Sturgeon, Fred Pohl, James Gunn, Jack Williamson, Harry Harrison, Lee Killough, and a host of academics. It was the first time I'd left the state to indulge in a formal science fiction gathering in sixteen years, and it seemed about time. I'm not keen on travelling; I have a lot of work to do at home, and travelling consumes great gobs of time. But I owed Cheryl an experience like this, complete with aeroplane ride, hotel stay, and her chance to meet the author of *The Stainless Steel Rat* series she enjoyed. It is not every child who gets the chance to meet a Real, Live Author, after all. Fine; we both enjoyed it, and she had a ball with the swimming pool and restaurant meals and even meeting a Piers Anthony fan her age, Mark Miller.

Then Cheryl spied the ping-pong – oops, I mean table tennis – tables and wanted to play. Now it happens that that game, by its misnomer ping-pong, was the one sport I was good at in my youth. I never went professional – I wasn't *that* good! – but I did play in scattered tournaments in college and the US Army. After I left the Army in 1959, I regretfully gave up ping – uh, table tennis. But now, with my daughter interested – well, to condense things somewhat, we now have a ping-tennis table at home, and all of us play, at varying levels of skill. But if there is one thing it takes to get in shape in table-pong, it is time. Sigh.

I discovered that there has been a revolution in the sport since my day. I used to use a light-cork-surfaced paddle – they now call them rackets or bats – but today cork is illegal, while sandwich rubber is in; that stuff didn't exist thirty years ago. No, it's not what they serve for lunch in cafeterias; sandwich rubber is a layered deal with sponge rubber inside, making the surface more bouncy and spinny. I was curious, so I started collecting paddles, questing for the Perfect Paddle. I shelled out sixty dollars for a championship-quality racket surfaced on one side with a designedly dead surface and on the other with a superlive surface called Tornado. (Tornado, as in spin.) The dead side makes spin drop dead so you aren't vulnerable to the superspin artists, while the Tornado is what those artists use to make you *need* the dead side. I discovered soon enough that I am predator, not prey; I had to use the live side, though in all candour I must say that none of this newfangled stuff matches the speed and effectiveness of an old-fashioned, two-dollar cork paddle. Maybe that's why cork was banned: too good, too cheap. I finally settled on a light, fast paddle with one live side and one superlive side, surfaced with the stuff the Chinese use to win world championships. No, having such a paddle does not make a person a world-class player, any more than having a good typewriter or a word processor makes a person a world-class writer. I *am* a world-class writer, but table tennis is just fun.

And while I was testing Tornado, as you may have guessed, a real, live tornado took aim at us, in the way such things do in my fantasy. Its aim was bad and it missed us by five miles and struck Inverness, Florida, instead, twisting off trees, destroying buildings, hurling a car six hundred feet and killing three people in it, and doing half a million dollars' worth of damage. It carried away the sign of the realtor who is handling our Gap Chasm purchase and damaged Cheryl's Middle School. Sigh – I really should have stayed with cork! But now that I have changed to the Chinese surface, the ill winds should have blown over.

Through all these distractions, I wrote and typed the novel. I had resolved to commence second-draft typing April first (no fooling!), because *Hourglass* was due at Del Rey June 1 and *Mercenary* at Avon August 1; at one month per draft, I could just make both deadlines. I prefer to run well ahead of deadlines, but now I was up against the wall, as it were.

There was one small complication: I had not yet finished writing the first draft of *Hourglass*. Between the correspondence, my daughter's driving, the land, and the table tennis, I had gotten behind. Well, no matter; I had eighty or ninety thousand words done. I started second-draft typing on schedule, trusting myself to write the remainder in spare time while the typing progressed.

Spare time? *What* spare time? Well, in the evenings I like to relax with inconsequentials such as supper, reading one of the squintillion publications we subscribe to, chatting with the girls, and watching TV. By cutting down on the reading and ignoring the TV, I could squeeze in some writing time. Unfortunately, I have another peculiarity: I get sleepy at night. Falling asleep while watching TV is harmless, but now I found myself trying to read and write with my eyes closed. I was coming up on the section of the novel involving relativity, for which I had to do some mind-stretching research, then integrate the material comprehensibly for the reader. So perhaps it is scarcely surprising that the writing was slow, and by April 16 I had typed ninety-eight thousand words and run out of the first draft – just as Norton's party came up against the giant termites, with the heavy intellectual material lurking just beyond. I was in as much trouble as Norton was! Do you have any idea what publishers do to authors who don't deliver on time? I'll give you a hint: I had already had a call from Del Rey Books, telling me to report with my family on June 3, 1983, to Dallas, where the American Booksellers Association was to have a convention. Yes, that's just two days after my delivery deadline, and yes, that's where President John Kennedy was shot twenty years before. I began to sweat. If I had no manuscript . . .

But hope was not yet quite gone. All I needed to do was take three days to buzz out the concluding six to eight thousand words of the first draft, another day for a brief Author's Note, then crank out the remaining second draft and be ready for the submission draft by the first of May. I mean, it was theoretically possible, wasn't it? I settled down to work – and discovered a few letters had accumulated. They do that when I am not on guard. All right, I'd take one afternoon to clear them out, then move on my text.

The first letter was to my agent, the man who sells my novels in New York. Beginning writers always want to know how to get a top agent and become an instant bestselling author. Forget it; an agent doesn't make you famous, he just gets better terms for you when you *are* famous. You have to get there on your own power. I sold eight novels before I took an agent; then my income commenced rising. This particular letter turned out to involve complex matters with four different publishers, plus a reorganization of the agency itself. One publisher had sent a statement of account that was so far off base that my wife and I were flabbergasted. It wasn't just that they were in error, to the author's disfavour by a healthy amount (it's *always* to the author's disfavour, for some obscure reason) – it was the way they had managed the error. Figuring it all out was like researching relativity, and I had to explain it to my agent in such a way that he could make it clear to the publisher, who naturally would not be eager to understand. That communication to my agent, with its multiple attachments, took me four hours to complete, and my afternoon was shot.

Okay, I'd do the other letters the next morning, 18 April, starting promptly at 9 A.M. But at 8:30 A.M. the phone rang; it was our building contractor. Oh, didn't I mention that? What with the table tennis and the boys my daughters fetched in to play Dungeons and Dragons and computer games, my wife decided we needed to expand our recreation space by enlarging and enclosing our porch, converting it to a heatable, coolable, silenceable playroom area. We had gotten an estimate – phew! who says inflation has been licked?! – and knew that work was to start in due course, after the property was surveyed (a red-tape requirement; of course it had been surveyed before, but now they wanted every cabin, pump, pole, and whatnot pinpointed, too). But this was so soon that we had not even signed the contract. Nevertheless, the crew was on its way to tear down our own porch, and we had to scramble to clear it: fifty-pound cans of horsefeed, chickenfeed, dogfood, an old trunk holding phonograph records dating from my college days, boxes of bric-a-brac, table tennis table, a heavy tool bench overloaded with ghod knows what, a refrigerator, and unclassified junk. I had to find a new shady location for my outdoor thermometer and humidity dial, used to keep track of daily highs and lows and conditions for my runs – I have run my three miles at temperatures as high as 102°F and as low as 39°F, and such extremes do affect my performance – and nowhere else was as good as the porch. These things could not be done carelessly, and we were still at it when the wrecking crew arrived. So while we were inside, signing the contract and forking over the $$$, they were bashing down the porch.

But that porch abutted our tightly fenced back yard, wherein lurked three of our dogs, Lucky, Tipsy, and Bubbles. Tipsy and Bubbles, spayed females, we had adopted from our neighbour's mongrel litter, which was about to be shipped off to a puppy mill; Bubbles was supposed to belong to the neighbour's boy, so he named her. We had brought her in with her sibling so the two would have warmth and comfort, as we could not bring them inside, where the indoor dogs would kill them, literally; though we were ready to return Bubbles when she was older, the boy had lost interest and she became ours. Tipsy was for Cheryl, and she may be an unusual dog. You know the rule about white on dogs? It's always on the tip of a dog's tail, even if nowhere else. Well, Tipsy has white on the tipsies of her pawsies, but none on the tipsy of her tailsy. Maybe she's unique in caninedom; I don't know. But mainly, that yard contained an earlier adoption, the male, Lucky. He had been a ten-pound waif, the prettiest and weakest of the litter of nine, so that he kept winding up (down?) on the bottom of the pile and yipping piteously. Pups play rough, especially when fed from one dish, and we were honestly afraid he wouldn't survive. He had taken to sleeping alone, under our car, to avoid getting chomped by the others. I was that way myself at that age in human terms; I have empathy. So we took him in, fed him, gave him good vet treatment – and soon he became a seventy-five-pound bundle of muscle who took no guff from strangers or his former littermates. I understand that, too. According to Carl Sagan on the *Cosmos* TV series, time and death are the secrets of evolution, and I'm sure it is so; I am quite interested in these concepts and have even been known to write novels about them. Sagan is a good man; he's my age. But the secrets of good living are not time and death, but care and love, even for the aggressive canine – or writer. Now we had to move our fence back before the porch came down, lest Lucky get at the workmen and take bites from unmentionable anatomy. So I got out with the post-hole digger and a roll of welded-wire fencing, working desperately. Just as the workmen reached the final wall, I completed the new fence. Robert Frost, in 'Mending Wall', discourses on whether good fences make good neighbours; in this particular case they do. But my writing day was gone.

Next morning the surveyors were at work; I put Lucky on the leash and took him for a walk in the pasture, and my wife did the same with Tipsy and Bubbles so the surveyors could enter the yard. I was a survey instructor in the Army, though probably in the intervening quarter century I have forgotten more than I ever knew about the subject. But I did understand why they had to run a traverse through the yard, though I could have done it by triangulation. Then we had to rush off, for I had to address the local Friends of the Library group, who were meeting in the City Hall. I don't charge for such things; I regard it as a public service. Libraries are well worth supporting, even though they aren't much on contemporary popular paperback fantasy. A local reporter was there, so he took notes, and next day he phoned me for an hour for an article. Finally, in the afternoon, I caught up on five more letters.

On the following day the man with the tractor arrived, and a huge truckload of fill-sand to buttress the new construction. I saw that truck and had a notion. We had this huge mudhole where the school bus turns around, just off the county-maintained road. That hole interferes with my three-mile run; I hate having to manoeuvre around that mire when my stopwatch is going, and sometimes get my foot gunked with mud. I doubt the cars enjoy it much, either. Could we subcontract for a load of lime rock? Yes, we could. So we paid for a twenty-ton load of it dumped in the puddle, and the tractor dozed it smooth. Beautiful! We had just done the neighbourhood a service, and maybe now the school bus wouldn't lose an axle in it. Three days later we had a five-and-a-half-inch drenchpour, and some unprintable drove his truck through while the lime rock was squishy, converting our delight to horrendous ruts that promptly solidified in place. We'll need another storm to soften them so we can undo the damage – and now we are in a drought. Such is fickle fate. Meanwhile, yet another writing day was gone, and the sand was trickling ominously through the Hourglass. I was getting nowhere! Writer's Block, where was now thy sting?

Naturally, once our old porch was gone, it took two weeks for the construction crew to begin work, while the refrigerator remained jammed next to the stove and the table tennis table next to the TV set, waiting for space to move back out, and the cans of animal feeds were squeezed in with our furniture storage. We tripped over boxes trying to get around one another and stubbed our toes on solidities that didn't used to be there. Such is the nature of progress.

But when I finally had time to write, I moved it right along, doing three and four thousand words a day. Then I typed it at six thousands words a day and got the novel finished by the end of April. Truly did T. S. Eliot say, in *The Waste Land*: 'April is the cruellest month.' But I had survived it.

On May first I started the submission typing – and got hit by another bundle of twenty letters, and appearances at a bookstore for autographing copies – hardly anyone showed up – and at a role-playing convention at the University of South Florida. I'm not much into role playing, but a number of my fans are, so I felt it behooved me to learn something about it. It was interesting; they gave me a beautiful stained-glass picture of Neysa the Unicorn and set up what I suspect is an unusual kind of panel. There were fifteen to twenty knowledgeable role players on the panel, and an audience of one: me. I got to ask anything I wanted to about the subject. It turns out that there are many types of such games, of which Dungeons and Dragons is one, with many shades of difficulty and experience. Some people like direct personal experience, such as racing in cars, while others prefer vicarious experience, such as reading fantasy novels; role playing falls in between, providing a more active experience than reading without the risks of real autoracing, warfare, or whatever. I discovered that these were my type of folk, with independent attitudes and wide-ranging interests, intelligent and motivated. I conclude that I'm more into role playing, in my writing, than I knew. But this, too, takes time. It didn't help that in May I also had to proofread the galleys for my novels *On a Pale Horse* and *Dragon on a Pedestal*; I'm a slow reader, proofreading is exacting, and my blood pressure rises as I encounter editorial changes in my prose. But I managed to complete everything in time.

I had one other interruption during this effort. My wife and I had to go for our six-month dental hygiene appointments. We take care of ourselves; I do eat carefully, exercise seriously, and keep up with the doctor, dentist, and oculist. But these things, too, take time, and it comes out of my working day. In this instance I took along a book to read and pencil and paper, so as to be able to use any slack time available. Sure enough, the hygienist was running half an hour late, so I read a little of Asimov's *Foundation's Edge,* then used it as backing for my pencilled notes. I noticed that others in the waiting room simply sat, some not even reading, merely waiting, as it were, in stasis. It is evident that others don't take time as seriously as I do; it doesn't really bother them to waste it. I am keenly aware that my duration in life is limited; am I unique in this? Even when I'm not writing, I am driven to make my time count. Call me a workaholic if you will, but to me, the indifference to the passage of time that most people evince seems like folly. To me, a life that is slack is a life being lived inefficiently. I don't like inefficiency.

I looked around the waiting room, listening to the interminable, innocuous sound piped in to soothe the animals. I noted the pictures on the walls and the Bibles placed there by the Gideons, right under the Winnie-the-Pooh cartoon mural. I am agnostic, not espousing any religion or pretending to know the actual will of God, but certainly there is much of value in the Bible, and I would read it rather than sit like a zombie doing nothing. I would read the Koran, too, or the *Bhagavad Gita,* or *Tao Te Ching,* the Chinese Way of Life. It is no bad thing to heed the significant thought of other ages and cultures, and to profit from their lessons. But no one was reading any of these here.

In my Note for *On a Pale Horse,* I concluded that we should live our lives in such a manner that we would not at the end be ashamed. Accepting this should we not also live our lives as efficiently as we can? Life is the greatest gift we know; what point is there in wasting any part of it? If we should not measure out our lives with coffee spoons, as in T. S. Eliot's *The Love Song of J. Alfred Prufrock* – when I was in the Army, we spoke of 'Private Prufrock' – we should also not similarly tune out in the lacunae of waiting rooms. This is our life; they are not making any more of it. And with this thought, written in a waiting room, I conclude.